Revenge of the Ancients

Crimson Worlds: Refugees III

Jay Allan

Crimson Worlds Series

Also By Jay Allan

www.jayallanbooks.com

Revenge of
the Ancients

Revenge of the Ancients is a work of fiction. All names, characters, incidents, and locations are fictitious. Any resemblance to actual persons, living or dead, events or places is entirely coincidental.

ISBN: 978-0692662267

Introducing
The Far Stars Series

Book I: Shadow of Empire
Book II: Enemy in the Dark
Book III: Funeral Games

Prequel I: Blackhawk (Coming April 2016)

The Far Stars is a new space opera series, published by HarperCollins Voyager, and set in the fringe of the galaxy where a hundred worlds struggle to resist domination by the empire that rules the rest of mankind. It follows the rogue mercenary Blackhawk and the crew of his ship, Wolf's Claw, as they are caught up in the sweeping events that will determine the future of the Far Stars.

Chapter One

From the Personal Log of Terrance Compton

We were saved by a machine. Which is ironic, because we're also being hunted by a machine. We call our enemy the First Imperium. It is an amalgam. Imperium, because that was the closest we could translate from the miserable scraps of their language and communications we were able to decipher. And first, because they were there long ago, before our ancestors had learned to sharpen stones into rough knives or plant seeds in the fertile ground. But now we know more and, in the great complexity of it all, perhaps understand less.

This war has been a nightmare, by far humanity's greatest test. And we of the fleet have endured the worst of it, sacrificed ourselves to save Earth, to protect the entire expanse of human-occupied space. No doubt we are regarded as heroes back home, statues erected on a hundred colony worlds paying homage to the martyrs, the great multi-national force they all thought of as dead these past eighteen months.

But we are not dead, not all of us at least, and we now know our enemy is not the First Imperium, not really. It is the Regent, the unimaginably complex artificial intelligence that hunts us, that eons ago destroyed the people of the First Imperium who had built it.

Indeed, those of the First Imperium, the biological beings

at least to an extent. They came to Earth, millennia ago, and they took the primitive creatures they found, vaguely manlike apes...and they manipulated their DNA, made them near copies of themselves.

Those we had considered our enemies are in fact our forefathers, and they fought the same enemy we now face. They fought and lost. But they left messages behind for us, clues...and on a legendary planet beyond the borders of the vast Imperium, they left us the tools we need, to survive, to fight off the Regent and its vast robot fleets.

We seek that shadowy world even now, fighting the enemy when we must, fleeing when we can...and with each day we draw closer. Closer to the world we have dubbed Shangri la.

AS Midway
X78 System
The Fleet: 102 ships (+7 Leviathans), 24901 crew

Midway shook hard, her tortured hull creaking loudly under the impact of the enemy's x-ray lasers. She'd taken a dozen hits, three of them from close range, and she was bleeding atmosphere and fluids from a large gash in her port side armor. It was her fourth fight in twelve days, and the damage control teams were working frantically, patching her savaged systems back together the best they could manage in the heat of battle, and with a dwindling supply of spare parts.

Terrance Compton knew the technicians and engineers working in Midway's crawlspaces and access tubes were the unsung heroes, that without them his immense flagship would have been blasted into a dead pile of twisted metal long ago. The senior officers like him got the credit for the victories. The gunners at the combat stations had the satisfaction of destroying enemy vessels, and the fighter pilots were living legends, wildly romanticized symbols of the fleet's combat power. But Compton was well aware that without the massive efforts of his

The fleet had been through hell. There was no other way he could characterize it. Ever since the intervention of a rogue First Imperium command unit had saved them all from total destruction in system X48, they'd been in a running fight for their lives. The Regent had responded to the defection of its subordinate unit in a manner that struck Compton far more like madness than the rational actions of an artificial intelligence. The way First Imperium forces had been attacking—large fleets, small squadrons, even individual vessels making suicide runs—it was obvious the Regent had ordered his ships to close as quickly as possible and engage. Without organization, without massing into effective forces. It was an undisciplined strategy, reeking of emotion and panic, but Compton knew it was also one that could work.

His fleet was outnumbered, far from home. The Regent could afford to waste hundreds of ships to wear it down. His people were human beings, not machines. The protracted periods spent at battlestations were draining, exhausting. It wouldn't happen all at once, but Compton knew the fatigue of his crews would become an increasingly dangerous factor, eroding responsiveness, making each new fight a bit more damaging than the last. It was insidious. Compton knew he wouldn't realize when a gunner missed a shot he would have made if he'd been better rested, more alert. Or when an engineer took a critical extra few minutes to get a crucial system back online. He would only see ships dying, vessels that might have survived if their crews had been fresher.

He was doing everything he could to keep the fleet moving, to stay ahead of as many pursuers as possible. He knew it was the only way he had a chance to save his people, but the tactic had a dark side, a seemingly endless series of hard choices, decisions to abandon ships that could be saved given time, but would only slow the fleet in the interim.

"Give it to me straight…can you keep both reactors up?" Compton was hunched over, talking into the com unit on the

found that subordinates tended to shy away from giving him the worst news. They didn't lie, not exactly—at least not usually—but they were prone to be as optimistic as possible, for fear of letting their famous commander down. Compton found the hero worship that went along with his position to be a burden, albeit one that had occasional benefits. But now he needed the unfiltered truth.

"I wish I could tell you, sir. I'm not even sure what is keeping reactor A going. The AI tried to scrag it twice already. If I override any more safety features, we'll be taking a serious risk of a core breach." The voice on the com was firm, but Compton could hear the grinding stress and fatigue behind it. Commander Art Mendel was Midway's chief engineer, a man who ate, slept, and breathed the systems and equipment that made a vessel like the fleet's flagship function. Mendel wasn't just an experienced and knowledgeable engineer. There was more to it than that, more than simply understanding how the systems of the ship functioned...something Compton found impossible to explain but believed nonetheless. Mendel felt his way through his job. He could sense things...a vibration that was somehow off, or a sound anyone else would hardly hear. He had a relationship with the conduits and wiring of the ship that Compton couldn't understand, but had long ago come to accept.

"Reactor B is in better shape," Mendel continued. "I'm pretty sure I can keep it at eighty percent, maybe ninety. Unless we take another hit in that area, of course."

Compton took a breath, his eyes flicking around the flag bridge. Another hit, that's a damned certainty. "Alright...we can't lose reactor B, Art. No matter what." Compton paused, thinking. "I want you to evacuate the outer compartments in starboard sections seven and eight. Fill them with fire-suppressant foam. It's not much, but it should provide some extra shielding for the reactor."

"Yes, Admiral. I'll get a crew on that now."

"Very well, Commander. Give me a status report in five

her chief engineer as they did on her admiral's tactical wizardry. He nodded, a gesture to himself more than anything. He was the fleet admiral, the commander of the entire force. He shouldn't be interfering in Midway's normal ship's operations, at least not in normal circumstances.

But when was the last time we saw anything we could call normal?

James Horace had been Compton's flag captain for almost three years, ever since the day Elizabeth Arlington left the post to assume her new task force command. Horace was a brilliant officer, and he'd captained Midway with great distinction. Despite his feelings for his lost love, Compton had to acknowledge that Horace was as capable as Arlington had been. It had been strange at first for Compton to work with anyone except Arlington, but as soon as he adjusted, he realized how much his interaction with his old flag captain had been affected by his emotional attachment to her. He had a more typical relationship with Horace, and he had to admit it was a relief in some ways.

But now, James Horace was in Midway's sickbay, along with his first officer and half the bridge crew. Midway's control center had taken a hit, a lucky shot that penetrated deeply into one of the ship's most protected areas, killing or wounding most of its command staff. That left Art Mendel technically in command, but the ship's engineer was completely occupied with the damage control effort, so Midway's acting captain was a junior lieutenant commander, Owen Yarl, an officer with a perfectly satisfactory service record, but without the experience Compton considered necessary to command the flagship in battle. Besides, the bridge was a smoking ruin, and the flag bridge was fully capable of running the ship. So Compton added another hat and took effective command, ordering Yarl to focus on managing the repair efforts underway throughout the vessel.

Compton looked up at the main display. The huge screen dominated Midway's flag bridge. It showed a holographic depiction of local space, a three-dimensional representation of the

knew his people would already be dead without the Leviathans Command Unit Gamma 9736 had given him. The eight massive First Imperium battleships had followed his orders without a hitch, courtesy of Hieronymus Cutter's brilliant program, the virus that infected First Imperium intelligences and made them follow human orders. Seven of the great ships remained in the battle line, absorbing enormous amounts of damage and still fighting. One had been lost in X68, standing as a rearguard while the last of the fleet's ships transited.

Compton had been afraid the Regent would find a way to counter the effects of the virus and terminate his control over the ships, but it hadn't happened in the two months since the fleet's unlikely salvation in system X48, and since then he'd come to rely on them. He knew there was still a risk, but he simply couldn't do without the enormously powerful vessels, so he set aside his concerns and did his best to think of the massive robot-controlled ships as part of the fleet.

His eyes dropped down to his workstation. His personal display was fixed elsewhere, not on the battle area, but on the warp gate to X78, where the most damaged warships, along with the freighters and supply ships, were slowly transiting. He'd done his best to keep the support vessels back from the fighting, but the First Imperium ships were just too fast and maneuverable. Some had penetrated the main defensive line, and several of the supply ships had taken damage. None had been destroyed—not yet, at least—but a few of them were limping along on damaged engines. Compton was pretty sure they'd all get through, but he also knew they'd need more time. And he could only buy that time by standing and fighting longer. And that would cost.

"Get me Admiral Hurley," he snapped to his tactical officer. Jack Cortez was a good aide, one of the best, but he'd had the misfortune to follow Max Harmon in his seat. And Harmon was one of the best officers Compton had ever known. He appreciated Cortez and his ability, but he couldn't help missing Harmon on the flag bridge.

people back out on another sortie. We're just taking too much damage to the capital ships…and the freighters need more time to escape." He hated the feeling of trading the lives of his fighter crews for the goods on the supply ships, but without the food and spare parts on those vessels, the fleet was doomed.

"Yes, sir. I thought you might need us again, so I've been on Chief McGraw's…rear."

Compton couldn't keep a brief smile from his face. Sam McGraw was in charge of Midway's landing bays, and he was as foul-mouthed and ill-tempered as any veteran chief Compton had seen in fifty years of service. There were few on Midway who could stand up to him regardless of rank…and only one who truly terrorized him. Greta Hurley.

"How soon can you be ready?"

"I'll take one flight out now. Commander Fujin will bring the second as soon as they're ready. Probably fifteen minutes, but I'll see if Chief McGraw can shave a bit from that."

Compton was rarely stunned, but no matter how he figured, it was damned near impossible that half of Midway's fighters were rearmed and reloaded already. But Hurley never stopped proving she was the best fighter commander who had ever served, in the Alliance navy or that of any of the other powers.

"Very good, Admiral. You may launch when ready."

"Yes, sir. Hurley out."

Compton's eyes moved back to the main screen, staring at the cluster of enemy ships that Hurley's people would be attacking. With luck, her squadrons would take out the lead vessels, and slow the entire formation. Then, as soon as her people landed, Midway and the rest of the battle fleet could make a dash for the warp gate.

He was still staring at the display as Midway began to shake lightly…Hurley's bombers blasting down the launch catapults and out into space. He counted them off as they went and wondered how many would return.

*   *   *

"Let's get this thing powered up...the admiral's out there with half a strike force, and we've got to go." Mariko Fujin dropped hard into the fighter's command chair, her eyes snapping back and forth as her crew followed suit. Fujin was barely a meter and a half tall and a bit shy of forty kilograms, but she'd acquired a reputation not much short of Hurley's for tough as nails tenacity. In the last year and a half she'd cut a swath through the fighter corps, rising from a junior lieutenant to one of Admiral Hurley's top officers, and the crews were half scared to death of her, especially the newer recruits. The old sweats had been in the same cataclysmic battles where she had distinguished herself, and where they had all seen hundreds of friends and comrades killed. But the personnel recruited from other fleet positions to replace losses saw her as a tiny copy of Hurley, and they cowered at the sight of her.

"We're bringing the reactor up at 100%, Commander." Grant Wainwright sat in the pilot's chair—her chair!—and his hands moved over the controls like a blur. She still resented the young pilot a bit, thought she knew it was unfair. It wasn't Wainwright's fault that her advancing rank and expanding responsibilities had forced her out of the pilot's seat. And she knew she was fortunate to have as skilled a fighter jock at the controls of her bird...it vastly increased her chances of coming back from missions. But she was a pilot at heart, and she missed the feel of flying the ship.

"All ships, power up reactors to 110%," she said firmly. "Half our people are out there, and they're counting on us covering them."

Wainwright turned, a concerned look on his face. But one glance at Fujin's expression was enough to quell any complaint he might have been considering. "Yes, Commander," he said simply.

going to 110% didn't increase the chances of a major problem…not much, at least.

She flipped on her com unit. "Control, this is Commander
Fujin requesting final launch approval. My squadrons should be
ready in…" She glanced down at the chronometer. "…three
minutes."

"You are cleared to launch when ready, Commander." Jack
Cortez' voice was deliberative, meticulous. Fujin knew the
admiral's tactical officer wasn't used to managing the various
aspects of Midway's combat operations, and he was compensat-
ing heavily. But with most of the regular bridge crew dead or in
sickbay, he'd managed to handle things well, even if he'd been
a little edgier than usual. "Good luck, Commander," he added.

"Thank you, control." Fujin closed the line and turned back
toward Wainwright. "Status?"

"Gold Dragons report ready for launch, Commander."

Fujin nodded. The Gold Dragons had been one of the
best—and luckiest—squadrons in the fleet, and it had come
through a series of horrendous battles without a single casualty.
Until its luck finally ran out, and Fujin came back the only survivor. She'd fought like hell to preserve the squadron, to convince
Greta Hurley not to strike it from the OB and send her as a
replacement for losses in another unit. Now Fujin commanded
two full wings, but she still ran the squadron too. It was her way
of keeping her old comrades alive, at least in spirit.

"Alright…get us in the catapult, Lieutenant. The Dragons
will launch first. Then the Wildcats and the Lightnings. The
Second Wing is to launch as soon as possible. We will reform
once in space."

"Yes, Commander."

The Second Wing was on Saratoga. Admiral West's ship was
less than a hundred thousand kilometers from Midway, which
meant it would only take a few minutes for Hurley to form up
her entire force. She had twenty-eight fighter-bombers, all that
was left from two wings that had launched thirty-six birds ten

without extensive repairs. She'd consoled herself with the fact that over half the crews of the destroyed ships had managed to eject. Most of them had been recovered, and the rescue shuttles were gathering the rest, even as their comrades prepared to go back into the fray.

Fujin leaned back and closed her eyes for a moment. She felt the fighter moving, upward at first and then to the side. She knew the launch bay crane was carrying the fighter-bomber from the refit area over to the catapult. She'd taken the ride hundreds of times, but this time it felt a little rougher than usual. Fujin knew Midway had been hard hit in the fighting, and she had a sense that the engineering equivalent of tape and chewing gum was holding the crane together.

She felt the ship shake as it came down...and then the two loud clanks as the vessel slipped into the catapult's tracks. She was tense, as she always was before battle. But there was something different this time. She had a sense something was wrong.

Don't be a fool, she thought. You're just tired.

She was tired...exhausted even. She had just returned from a scouting run when the enemy fleet attacked...and then she went right into sustained combat for close to seven hours. When she got back she sent her crews to grab some food and a couple hours' sleep, but she stayed in the launch bay with Admiral Hurley, making sure the birds got refit as quickly as possible. They'd been told there wouldn't be another sortie, but both officers knew better than to count on that. They had seen what the fleet was facing, and the two had simply exchanged doubtful glances...and then went looking for Chief McGraw. In the end, Fujin had managed to wolf down a sandwich and a liter of water, but she'd gotten no rest at all. It had been two full days since she'd even closed her eyes for more than a blink.

Her hand moved to her neck, her fingers playing with a small lump of metal on a chain. Max Compton had given it to her, and he'd extracted a promise from her that she'd wear it on every mission. It was old, something that had been in his family for a

religious symbol of some kind, but it had long been regarded as more of a good luck charm in the Harmon family.

Fujin had been spending a lot of time with Harmon, too much she knew. She loved him…she'd admitted that to herself if not to him yet. But she also knew the reality of their situation. The fleet had found a new hope of sorts, a promised cache of technology and information left behind by humanity's ancestors. Assuming they could get to it. But even if they managed it, if some portion of the fleet escaped pursuit and reached the planet they'd been calling Shangri la, she wouldn't let herself believe both she and Harmon would be among the survivors.

She was one of the leaders of a rapidly dwindling force of fighter-bombers, repeatedly used as forlorn hopes and sent on almost-suicidal missions. The fleet had suffered terrible losses since it had been cut off from human space, but nothing remotely compared to the casualty rates of the fighter corps. And Harmon was effectively Admiral Compton's troubleshooter, his eyes and ears in the most dangerous places they encountered. They'd both had narrow escapes in the short time they'd been together, and she saw only pain in letting her true feelings out. They were a comfort to each other, support in a difficult and lonely time… that's how she saw it. At least that's what she told herself. And she was determined to keep it that way.

"All systems ready, Commander."

Wainwright's voice shook Fujin from her distraction. She let go of the pendant and shook herself back to the present. "Very well, Lieutenant. Laun…"

The ship shook suddenly. Hard. Gyrating wildly. Then she heard explosions, from outside in the launch bay. The fighter's alarm system began blaring, and then she heard it. A crash, loud, almost deafening. And then more shaking.

Her hand slapped down toward the com unit, flipping to the flag bridge channel. Nothing. She punched at the controls, switching from one frequency to another, but the unit was dead. "Anybody have com," she asked, unhooking her harness and

"Mine's dead."

"Mine too."

She stumbled forward toward the pilot's seat, leaning down over Wainwright's shoulder, punching out at the controls. "Fuck," she muttered under her breath. "Power?"

"We've got some power, Commander, but we're off the launch track. I've got redlines across the readiness indicators. We're not going anywhere."

"Keep trying to get through, Lieutenant." She turned her head. "Singh, Buto, with me. Let's get the hatch open and see what's going on out in the bay."

The two gunners pulled off their harnesses and leapt out of their chairs, following Fujin as she walked toward the back of the ship. She pressed the button to open the large door, but there was no response. "Unlock, authorization Fujin 3632, Lieutenant Commander." The AI was silent, and the door didn't budge.

She reached out and pulled off a large panel next to the hatch, revealing a circular hand crank. "Alright, guys, looks like we're going to have to do this old school." She stepped back and gestured toward the metal wheel. Fujin wasn't one to step aside when there was work to be done, regardless of rank. But Singh and Buto each had forty kilos on her, and the idea of her trying to turn the crank while the two of them stood by watching was too ridiculous to seriously contemplate.

Singh stepped up first and grabbed the wheel, twisting as hard as he could. He grunted and heaved, but the crank didn't move a millimeter. Then Buto stepped up and grabbed hold as well. But even with the two of them there was no movement. They struggled again for another few seconds, and then they gave up, letting go with a loud yell.

"Sorry, Commander. It's jammed somehow. The ship's frame must have gotten racked when we got thrown from the catapult."

Fujin nodded. "I guess we'll have to wait for help from out-

hear the sounds of explosions out in the launch bay. She had just turned to head back toward the front of the fighter to see if she could get one of the displays working and get a look at what was going on in the bay. She'd taken one step, perhaps two...and then something hit the top of the fighter. There was a deafening crash, and then the structural support over her head came crashing down. She felt the impact, something hitting her. Then she was down, lying on the floor. She could feel wetness beneath her.

Blood, she thought.

She tried to move but there was pain, wave after wave of pain. She felt herself drifting in and out of consciousness. She was vaguely aware of something over her, a shadowy presence, and she could hear her name, faintly, far away. She heard a shout, loud, tense. It said, "Fire!" Then she slipped into the blackness.

*   *   *

"All squadrons, we're going to do a strafing run before we head back." Greta Hurley could hear the groans of her battered crews. They'd completed their second attack run in twelve hours, endured gee forces that had pushed them to the edge of unconsciousness...and they had scored hit after hit. They'd taken down four of the enemy ships, but another four were still there. Barely hanging on, Hurley thought.

"I know you all want to go back to base, but those ships are almost done...now we've got to push them over the edge." Finishing off the enemy ships had been Mariko Fujin's job. But she and half her birds were still on Midway, stranded by two closed launch bays. And Fujin herself, along with several other crews, was trapped in Bay B, cut off from rescue by out of control fires.

"Form up on me," she said, her voice icy. "Let's finish these

"Let's go, John. Take us in." Hurley watched as Commander Wilder gripped the throttle and began accelerating. Wilder was an enormously capable pilot, one who'd been flying her around ever since Admiral Augustus Garret had assigned him to her, with secret instructions to keep Hurley away from the worst of the fighting. That mission hadn't worked out so well…Hurley had corrupted Wilder, and the two had been at the forefront of every assault since.

Hurley missed flying her own ship, but it had been a long time since she'd occupied the pilot's seat, and she'd made her peace with it. She'd tried to help Mariko Fujin do the same, but she knew it would take her protégé time to adapt, as it had her. And until then, she knew Fujin would continue shooting daggers at her pilot's back.

If she's even still alive.

Hurley had become quite fond of Fujin, and she saw in the diminutive officer much of herself when she was younger. She hated the thought of losing Fujin, and even more the idea of her friend dying in the launch bay, crushed under rubble or killed by the fires. Fujin was a fighter jock through and through. If she had to die so young at war, Hurley knew it should be in her bomber fighting with the enemy.

"I'm heading for that Leviathan, Admiral." Wilder's voice was angry, feral. He'd been soft spoken, the true personification of the gentlemen officer, when Hurley had first gotten her hands on him. But now he was a hunter, and he fed off the kill, as she herself did. "It's ready to go, I can feel it."

"Take us in, John. Let's blow the fucker to hell."

She leaned back in her chair as the gee forces increased. Wilder was zigzagging, blasting first along one vector then along another, making the fighter as difficult a target for whatever weapons the enemy ship had left. It made for an uncomfortable and stomach-churning ride, but it was better than getting blown to bits by an enemy laser battery.

Hurley sat back, her eyes on the scanner, trying to focus

The ship was a floating wreck, its hull ripped open from bow to stern. She could see flickering lights inside the great rents, internal explosions ripping through the wounded vessel. But First Imperium ships were tough, and they fought to the bitter end. There were at least two batteries still active on the behemoth, and they were firing at her people. But she saw almost immediately that the enemy targeting systems weren't functioning properly...and that meant her squadrons might get in and out without losing anyone else, especially if the other enemy ships were as battered.

"Preparing for firing run, Admiral. I'm going to try to hit near the reactor." The antimatter power systems of the First Imperium ships were well-protected, but extremely volatile. Any breach of containment, even for a nanosecond, could release enough antimatter to vaporize any ship. And Wilder knew exactly where to hit the enemy vessel.

The early battles against the First Imperium had been struggles against the unknown. The enemy ships had been total mysteries, vessels of great power and technology that dwarfed anything mankind possessed. But Hurley's people had been fighting the First Imperium for years now, and they had learned a considerable amount about the layouts of the enemy ships, especially of the Leviathans in the two months since the enemy's rogue command unit had given them eight of the battleships for their own use. The great vessels had served well in battle, but they'd proven just as useful in aiding research, as Hieronymus Cutter and his teams of engineers examined every centimeter and every system. Cutter's teams provided preliminary schematics to the gunners and pilots of the fleet, showing them exactly where to direct their fire for maximum effect. Then the eccentric but brilliant scientist and his assistants buried themselves in research, trying to adapt the technology of the First Imperium to the mankind's own purposes.

"Final approach." Wilder's voice was distracted. He was focused on his upcoming attack. He knew where to strike the

impact harmlessly on the Leviathan's heavy armor plating.

Hurley watched as her pilot worked. Wilder was one of the very best, she'd seen him in action enough times to know that. But she knew the shot was a difficult one, even for one of the fleet's great aces.

The fighter was moving directly toward the enemy ship. Hurley's eyes dropped to her workstation screen, to the distance readings. Under eight thousands kilometers and closing fast. She knew Wilder well enough to know he would take it to the very edge.

She leaned back, her hand dropping to her harness, checking to make sure it was tightly fastened. She knew it would be a rough ride when Wilder pulled the ship away from the target. She was used to wild maneuvers—fighter ops had been her life. But there was a fatigue growing in her, one she suspected had to do somewhat with age, and also with losing so many of her people. The fighter corps was a tattered remnant of what she had led when the fleet initially set out against the First Imperium. She waxed with pride when she saw her crews driving their ships right down the throats of the deadly enemy vessels… but then there was the guilt of the survivor. Why was she alive when ninety percent of her people were dead? She knew there had been no choices, that without the herculean sacrifices of her squadrons, the entire fleet would have been destroyed, that no one would have survived. But she still felt the ghostly presence of the dead crews, watching…and she felt she owed them nothing less than everything she had to give. They had died to buy the fleet a chance…and she had to see that preserved, whatever the cost.

Five thousand kilometers. Close, too close. Wilder was a stone cold pilot, as Hurley herself had been. But this was tight, even for him.

Four thousand kilometers. She felt the sweat trickling down her neck, and she wondered where the mathematical point of no return was. Even with perfect piloting, there was a distance

Three thousand kilometers. John…this is too close…

She heard the whining sound as the ship's laser cannons fired. Three blasts, and then the ship whipped hard to the side, the gee forces slamming into her like a sledgehammer. She'd spent enough time in fighter-bombers to know it was over 10g, and that meant Wilder was redlining the engines, pushing them over one hundred percent capacity. One burnout, one small malfunction and the fighter would slam into the First Imperium ship. But the engines withstood the abuse, and the fighter's vector was altered just enough to zip by the enemy ship, clearing it by less than seven hundred meters. That distance was nothing in space combat, as close as Hurley had ever seen two ships come to each other outside a suicide ramming run.

Which that almost was…

She turned her eyes up toward the main display, and she knew immediately. The enemy ship shook once…then a second time. And then it erupted into a miniature sun, an explosion measured in the hundreds of gigatons as its antimatter fuel escaped its containment and annihilated with the matter of the ship itself.

"Nice job, John," Hurley said, trying to sound as calm and nonchalant as possible as she wiped her hand across the back of her neck. She stared down at her palm, covered in sweat, and she smiled.

I'm so glad Admiral Garret sent Wilder here to keep me out of trouble!

Chapter Two

From the Personal Log of Terrance Compton

Cornwall is gone. Will we ever see her again? Will she return with the thirty-two brave souls aboard or will they simply vanish from our knowledge, lost and presumed dead? They left with my leave, aboard the vessel I gave them, but I have since doubted my decision. They were volunteers all, but still, I am their commander, and I share the guilt for whatever happens to them. If their fate is to die, if they become lost as they try to return, or if they are destroyed by the Regent's warships, I know their shades will join those of the thousands who have died under my command. I did not order them to go, but my conscience allows me no relief on such technicalities.

Their mission is one of science, one of outreach. For we learned many things on that ancient planet in system X48, not the least of which is we were not alone, that the beings of the First Imperium had visited seven worlds, and that on each of them they modified the DNA of the creatures they found, turning the primitive beasts they found into their children. The discovery of the First Imperium told us we were not unique, that intelligent life existed elsewhere. The discoveries on X48 confirmed there were yet others, cousins of humanity.

Five of these six other worlds are far away, hundreds of transits, with the deadly vastness of the Imperium between us and them. But one is close. Closer at least. And so we felt the need

Regent? An advanced and powerful race that might help us? Or would they be primitive, behind us on the growth curve...in need of our protection should the Regent's forces ever find them?

Or would they be an enemy? Would they resent us, mistrust our intentions? Would they seek to destroy us, or subjugate us as slaves? Few wanted to consider this option, but it weighed heavily on me. Earth gave birth to the human race, yet men have spent almost six thousand years of recorded history warring with each other. Indeed, the Superpowers had fought almost constantly over the last century, allying only when they faced certain obliteration at the hands of the Regent's vast fleets.

So, perhaps our brave scientists will find this new race, communicate with them somehow, bring them to our side with their vast industry and massive battle fleets. But my mind is in other places. Darker places. And in my nightmares I see our scouts dragged from the wreckage of their ship and paraded before crowds of humanoids, like us but subtly different too. I see them taken to labs, dissected, tested in horrifying ways.

Perhaps I am too dark, too negative in my outlook. But I have seen more death, more horror than any man was made to endure. What I have seen, what I have lived...changes a man.

AS Cornwall
Y17 System
The Fleet: 99 ships (+7 Leviathans), 23995 crew

"Transit in thirty seconds. All stations at red alert." Captain Skarn was trying to sound sharp, ready for trouble. But this was the seventeenth transit since Cornwall had left the fleet, and the sixteen before it had all been the same. No sign of any enemy ships, no scanning devices detected, no hostile activity of any kind. It appeared the Regent's forces were focused on the fleet and that Cornwall had managed to slip away undetected. But Skarn had exercised the same caution with every transit nevertheless.

ships were seeking Shangri la, the informal name that had stuck to the mysterious world the people of the First Imperium had prepared hundreds of thousands of years ago for humanity's expected arrival. Cornwall was searching for something else, another destination mentioned in the cache of data retrieved on Planet X48 II…the nearest of the six other worlds the warrior caste of the First Imperium had seeded with modified DNA. The possible home of a race of mankind's cousins…and a potential ally in the fight against the Regent and its legions of robot spaceships and ground forces.

"All stations report ready, Captain." Lieutenant Inkerman turned and looked over at Skarn. Cornwall had a skeleton crew, all volunteers. They were naval personnel, like everyone else in the fleet, but they were also scientists, most of them at least, unaccustomed to manning the tactical stations and running a ship.

This was a dangerous mission, a wild trip that took them enormously far from Midway and the rest of the fleet. Compton had agreed to spare a ship for the operation, and give his blessing to the group of scientists who had requested permission to go, but he had been adamant he couldn't spare tactical personnel, not when the fleet had been forced to fight its way through every system, taking casualties in each engagement.

Skarn had been the senior officer among those assigned to Cornwall, so she had become its captain, a courtesy promotion from her normal rank of lieutenant commander. She was a competent officer, one with over ten years' service, but she had no operational experience in battle. She'd been aboard ship during many fights, everyone in the fleet had, but she'd always been assigned to support positions. Now, if Cornwall got into a fight, it would be her issuing the battle orders, leading her sparse and inexperienced crew into combat.

She felt the strange feeling, the bizarre coldness that always passed through her during a warp gate transit. Then she tensed as she tended to do in the terrible moment before the ship's

clenched, her hands balled into tense fists. It usually took about a minute for the ship's AI to reboot, and to reactivate the rest of the vessel's systems, and until the scanning suite came back online, her imagination worked on overdrive, spawning visions of enemy fleets and minefields around the warp gate.

Skarn wanted to believe her people had put enough space behind them, that they had evaded any First Imperium pursuers, but she still felt the wave of fear with each transit. And she knew her people had to go back the way they had come if they were ever going to get back. She didn't relish the prospect of Cornwall being permanently adrift, cut off from the rest of the already lost fleet…and she hadn't let herself consider how dangerous the road back would be.

"Systems coming back online, Captain." Inkerman had become better at hiding his nerves, and his voice was steady, even firm. Skarn realized he actually sounded like a tactical officer now and not the misplaced physicist he really was.

Skarn stared at the display, every nerve in her body tingling. It wasn't just the possibility of First Imperium ships, though that was enough to worry about. This transit was special, the final one. If the data retrieved from X48 II was correct, this system's third planet was home to a race of beings whose DNA had been manipulated by the First Imperium, just as humanity's had been.

Her mind raced. Would they be friendly? Would her people be able to communicate with their distant cousins? Would they be technologically advanced…able to help in the war against the Regent? Her people had traveled deep into the darkness, alone and at great risk, just to answer those questions.

"Scanners coming online, Captain." Inkerman's voice was still strong, perhaps just a bit of his earlier nervousness creeping back in. He hesitated, staring down at his screen. Then he looked up and said, "No contacts, Captain."

Skarn leaned back in her chair, feeling the relief everywhere in her body. "Okay, Lieutenant, let's do what we came for. Set a

*   *   *

"This is incredible…it's like ancient Greece or Rome, but these people did it hundreds of thousands of years ago." Sasha Debornan stood on top of the hill, staring out over the remnants of the city below. There wasn't much left, just a few mounds here and there, and a pillar or two sticking out of the sand. But Debornan was an archeologist, and she saw in the worn and weathered remains the glory of an ancient civilization that had once flourished here.

At least archeology was one of her many disciplines. She was the kind of officer sometimes posted to Alliance vessels to cover a variety of little-needed duties, an academic with backup training in some moderately useful skill, like climatology, that justified her existence onboard. At least until the First Imperium showed up. Suddenly, officers with her training were desperately sought after, and she'd gone along with the fleet to pursue the opportunity of a lifetime, the chance to explore worlds once inhabited by the only intelligent alien lifeform ever encountered.

It had been a fluke that stranded Debornan with the fleet. She'd taken a shuttle from Sigma-4 to Midway to use the labs on Compton's flagship to speed her analysis of some First Imperium material samples…and she was scheduled to go back in less than twenty-four hours. But then, Augustus Garret blew the warp gate and stranded them all.

She'd gone into a deep depression at first, feeling sorry for herself, for the cruel trick fate had played on her. But then she'd started exploring the First Imperium worlds along the fleet's line of retreat, and the pursuit of knowledge had reinvigorated her. She'd been overwhelmed by the magnificence of the ancient cities on those planets, but these ruins, though far more primitive and worn down than those of the First Imperium, were wondrous in their own ways.

down the ridge from Debornan. The two scientists wore environmental suits, and they spoke over their com units.

"Look at the size of the city, Don." She pointed off to the right. "See that line over there? I'd bet that bottle of wine I've got stashed on Midway that's the remnant of a wall." She turned and waved her arm in the opposite direction. "And that's another one, way over there. That makes the enclosed area two, perhaps three times the size of Ur or Uruk. If we're looking at this world's equivalent of Mesopotamia, it's not a comparison where we do well."

"Well, they're gone now. I'm not picking up any contaminants or abnormal biologic agents. There are some bacteria and viruses, but nothing like a species-killing bioweapon." He paused and looked out over the remains of the city. "Of course, whatever killed these people, it happened a long time ago. If it was bacterial or viral, perhaps the strain died out. It might have needed the host to survive. We're going to need to find some fossilized remains if we want a chance at a real answer."

"I don't see any indications of any technological weaponry," Debornan said, staring down at a handheld scanner as she did. "No signs of blast damage, no scarring on the stones, no abnormal background radiation. If the First Imperium killed these people, they didn't use conventional weapons."

She sighed softly. The excitement of exploring the ancient civilization had momentarily distracted her, turning her away from the sadness and disappointment everyone on Cornwall had felt when the first scans came in. From the moment the ship entered orbit her scanners had reported no artificial energy generation on the planet. None at all. In an instant, all hope of finding a technologically advanced civilization was lost.

The initial data retrieved by the landing party had been darker still. Yes, intelligent beings had lived on this world. Yes, from all she could tell on initial inspection, they had been very much like humans. But they were dead now, gone, the planet a lifeless graveyard, with nothing but some very ancient ruins left behind

at a small screen. "I can't imagine the civilization these beings would have produced by now. They were hundreds of millennia ahead of us...and now they're gone. Just like the people of the First Imperium."

"Do you think the Regent wiped them out?" Rames was holding a small pile of rocks in his gloved hand, but he dropped them and walked over toward Sasha. "Or maybe they destroyed themselves."

"That's unlikely," she replied almost immediately. "They were amazingly advanced compared to where Earth people were at the same time, but this was still a primitive society, on par perhaps with Sumer or Babylon. It's very unlikely a civilization at that technological level could wipe itself out. If it wasn't the Regent that destroyed these people, it had to be a natural disaster, an asteroid impact or a virulent plague. Some kind of extinction event." She paused, looking out over the ruins as she did. "And so far, I see zero evidence of that."

"But if it was the Regent, wouldn't there be some trace remaining? Radiation or some kind of damage from technological weapons? Would the Regent's forces come, commit genocide, and then meticulously clean up after themselves...so much so that we can't detect a trace that they were here?"

Sasha turned back toward Rames, but she didn't say anything. He had good questions, but she didn't have any answers. None that made any sense.

"The Regent's forces certainly didn't worry about cleaning up after themselves on the First Imperium worlds. There was wreckage everywhere on X48 II, and plenty of traces of the fighting that destroyed the people there."

"I don't know, Don," Sasha said. "Obviously, the fighting on the First Imperium worlds was high tech on both sides, so that's a difference. But I have no idea why we can't detect any signs of the Regent's forces here. If I had to guess, I'd still say these people were exterminated by the forces of the First Imperium." She paused. "There are just no signs of a naturally-occurring

is unlikely to the point of impossibility."

"So, what do we do?" He stood and looked at her.

"What can we do? We collect everything we can…fossils, building stones, air samples, water samples…a full scanning profile. And then we go back up to Cornwall and try to find our way back to the fleet. What happened to these people is a scientific curiosity now." She looked down, a sad expression coming over her face. "Whoever they might have been—potential friends, reluctant allies, even enemies—they are gone now. They were gone before our oldest civilizations began to crawl their way out of savagery."

Rames nodded, but he looked unsatisfied. Sasha understood. It was a disappointing end to their quest…and now they all had to face the reality of the trip back to the fleet, and the dangers they would encounter. All to return and report more hopeless news, yet another dead planet, its biological denizens destroyed by the paranoid wrath of the Regent.

Sasha twisted around, trying to rub her back against the inside of her suit. The itch had been bothering her for a few minutes, but now it was worse, almost a pain, like a tiny jab. Then it was gone, as suddenly as it had come on. She looked over at Rames, and for an instant she thought he was doing the same thing, twisting around as if he had a similar feeling. But then she wasn't sure. He looked normal enough now.

You're letting your mind run wild, she thought. It's just hot in this suit. Sweaty, sticky. Itchy.

She pushed the whole thing out of her mind. Mostly, at least.

"Let's get the crews to work and get everything we need." She looked all around, and she felt a shiver between her shoulders. She'd expected to be overwhelmed by scientific curiosity, by the need to uncover all the secrets of this ancient civilization. But her desire for knowledge was overcome with a sense of dread. She couldn't explain it, but this place was haunted…and they had to leave, as soon as possible. "I'd just as soon get out

Chapter Three

From the Research Notes of Hieronymus Cutter

It has been two months since we fled X48, since the fleets of the renegade command unit saved us. In that time I have refined my virus, improved it in every way I can devise. Though its use is still limited by our ability to deliver it to an enemy AI, it is clear that First Imperium units are vulnerable to its effects. I do not foresee a way to utilize it against the fleets pursuing us, though neither did I predict the method and effect of its delivery into the rogue command unit. It is hard for a mind as oriented to science as mine to accept the undeniable uncertainty that surrounds us. I have tried to learn to work in terms of probability and even belief.

Much of my time has also been spent assisting the fleet's damage control efforts. Many ships have been badly damaged, and though the converted factory ships are now producing ammunition and spare parts, many ships have required unorthodox modifications to their systems, workarounds for needed repairs that are impossible outside of a space dock. It is an axiom that in times of war and great need, advancement moves at an accelerated pace, and so it has been in the fleet. My team and I have devised a number of improvements to our ships' power production and transfer systems, and we have increased the firepower of our x-ray laser batteries almost 80%. If we had the means to build a new Yorktown-class battleship, we could now produce a

gri la—and escape the deadly pursuit that has plagued us since X48—we will one day have that chance.

For all the effort and ceaseless labor involved in keeping the fleet functioning, my thoughts have been elsewhere, with Al-meerhan, a being of the First Imperium who died, depending on your perspective, either two months or five hundred thousand years ago. His words haunt my dreams, my deepest thoughts, and I long to spend every hour deciphering the massive store of data he gave us. I have devoted what time I could—and Ana has worked almost around the clock, slowly unlocking the ancient mysteries contained in that silver cylinder.

It is there, I know, in the data saved for us by the last of his race—and on the secret planet his people prepared for us so long ago—that our best hope for survival lies. For our future is inextricably intertwined with their past.

AS Midway
X78 System
The Fleet: 99 ships (+7 Leviathans), 23995 crew

"Let's go, move it!" Maria Santiago stood at the entrance to the launch bay, just behind the bulkhead. Most of the systems in the bay were down, but she had managed to connect to a few of the cameras inside. It was an inferno, and for an instant she doubted anyone trapped in there could possibly be alive. But communications were out, and sixty members of Midway's crew were trapped in the bay. Doubt was one thing, but Alliance spacers didn't leave their comrades behind, not if there was any chance at all. Besides, if her people didn't get those fires under control, they could endanger the entire ship. Right now the conflagration was contained to the bay, but she knew that wouldn't last.

She turned and looked back at her crew. They were carrying two heavy hoses, muscling them through the corridor. Midway was a Yorktown class battleship, the Alliance's best, and her fire-

people had to fight this inferno old school, blasting the fire-retardant foam by hand, through the hoses. It was dangerous work, and a lot less effective than the automated systems, but it was the only choice. The only alternative to blowing the bay doors and letting the vacuum of space do the job. But that would kill anyone still alive in there. Santiago knew Admiral Compton would give the order if he had to, if the fires threatened to spread too far and put the ship itself in real danger. But she was determined not to let that happen. If everyone in there was dead, there was nothing she could do. But she wasn't going to let them die at the hands of their comrades.

"Alright, stand back…we're gonna blow this bulkhead. Switch on your breathers." She knew the fire was raging just behind the heavy, plastisteel portal. The fire was consuming the oxygen in the bay at a rapid rate…and if she took out the bulkhead with the corridor still at normal atmospheric concentrations, the fire would blast into the hallway, and probably kill her and her team in an instant. "Control," she said into her com, glancing behind her to make sure everyone had followed her orders and activated their breathers, "cut oxygen to sector 93C."

"Acknowledged," came the reply. Santiago heard a hissing sound. Then, a few seconds later, "Atmospheric adjustment completed, Ensign. Oxygen concentration less than one percent by air volume."

"Thanks, control." She turned back toward her people, flipping the com to the unit channel as she did. "Alright, in five… four…"

She ducked back down the corridor, away from the bulkhead. "Three…two…one…"

There was a loud crack. Then another…over a dozen in rapid succession, as the hatch's connections to the frame were blown apart. The heavy metal door fell outward, into the corridor, and a wave of heat blasted out from the landing bay beyond.

Santiago moved forward, toward the now-open doorway and stared into the raging inferno within. She felt the heat from the

two hoses, shaking her head. She had no idea how her people were going to put these fires out, not with the automated system down. But they had to try…they had to try until they knew for sure no one was left alive in there.

"Get those hoses up here, now! We don't have any time to lose if we're going to get this thing under control."

Her people pushed forward down the hall, pausing for an instant at the doorway. Then they switched on the hoses, and two jets of white foam poured out, almost disappearing into the wall of flame.

She watched, at first doubtful their efforts were having any effect. But then she could see. The flames had been pushed back. A little. It was working, but it wasn't working well enough to save anyone still alive in there.

"Control, I need backup, another crew at least…and more hoses."

"Negative, Ensign. All damage control teams are assigned." A pause. Then, another voice, Enzo Tolleri, the damage control chief. "Do what you can to see if there are any survivors in there." His voice was soft, empathetic. Santiago couldn't imagine the pile of crap on Tolleri's plate right now. "We're probably going to have to blow the outer doors, Maria, so just try to get as far in as you can and look for anyone trapped in there who's still alive." He sounded doubtful, but also determined. Tolleri was a hero in a field that didn't produce many. He'd pulled dozens of casualties from the wreckage in his career, and he'd almost died four or five times doing it. Santiago knew he'd push it to the limit before he gave the orders to pull out and blow the doors. And she wouldn't have it any other way.

"Yes, sir…we're moving forward now. Santiago out." She moved up, right behind the hose teams. "We're looking for survivors, boys, not trying to save the bay. So let's see if we can get over to the launch tubes and see if any of those fighter crews are still alive.

"Right in the balls!" Captain Bill Ving tended to be a little 'out of the book' in his expressions, at least in the heat of combat. Snow Leopard's skipper was almost a stereotype of the fast attack ship commander, a relentless, determined hunter who seemed to draw energy from the kill. The 'suicide boats' hadn't earned their nickname for nothing, and the small but powerful attack ships tended to attract some of the most wildly aggressive officers and crews in the Alliance fleet. But even among his peers, Ving was somewhat of a folk hero, and Snow Leopard had the distinction of racking up the most kills since the fleet was stranded in system X2. And now he'd added yet another to his tally.

"Nice shot, Lieutenant," he continued. "Nice fucking shot." Ving's crew was accustomed to their captain's tendency toward… blunt…speech. Ving usually managed to behave when he was on the com with superiors, and especially Admiral Compton, but his crew tended to get it raw.

"Thank you, sir." Sara Iverson had a big smile on her face. She was a bit more circumspect with her speech than her captain, but Snow Leopard's tactical officer was every bit the relentless hunter he was. She'd always been aggressive, but the frigid blood that coursed through her veins now was something new, the result of the losses she'd suffered since the fleet had been cut off. Her fiancée had been killed at X2…not just killed, but blown apart right in front of her, his blood and guts splattered all over her. She'd had the mandatory counseling sessions, but she'd ignored most of it, declaring it 'useless psychobabble.' Dead was dead, and talking about it didn't change a thing. She made a decision then and there. She didn't need to talk about her emotions. She needed to kill First Imperium ships. As many as possible. So she'd traded in counseling for a transfer to the suicide boats, and in just over a year she'd become one of the best tactical officers in the service.

"Okay, people, we've got another plasma torpedo, so let's find a good home for it." Ving's bloodlust had been sated by the

bay, and he ached to bury it deep into a First Imperium vessel.

"We've got a Gargoyle…about eighty thousand klicks out, Cap." Iverson turned back toward Ving. "It's our best target, sir…there's nothing bigger within 300,000 kilometers."

"Then let's go get it, Lieutenant." Ving would have preferred a Leviathan to the cruiser-equivalent Gargoyle, but he smiled as he glanced at the scanner readings. The new target vessel was damaged, but not critically, which meant it was still a threat to the ships of the fleet, but it was hurt enough that a direct hit could take it out. Ving wasn't above 'grave dancing,' as the fighter pilots and suicide boat crews had come to call seeking out critically-damaged enemy ships and finishing them off. But taking something out of the battleline, a ship that was still firing at friendlies…that was a real high.

But it was dangerous too. Snow Leopard would be closing to point blank range against a ship that still had a lot of striking power. And the attack ship's design sacrificed armor for speed and hitting power. The run was no sure thing, far from it.

"Okay, let's not get careless. Chuck, I want full evasive maneuvers going in. Random thrust changes and zigzags."

"Yes, Captain. I'm on it." Charles Moran was Snow Leopard's pilot and navigator, and his maneuvers tended to seem as wild and reckless as anyone else in the attack ship corps. But Ving knew there was more to his pilot than met the eye, and he'd noticed that Moran paid close attention to the situation in battle, that he knew when to hold back. "It might be a little uncomfortable, so if anybody wants to grab an antiemetic, now is the time."

The ship shook, almost immediately…then it accelerated. Ving reached down and grabbed his harness, snapping it closed. "Let's buckle in, people…I don't want any stupid injuries because someone fell out of their seat." He tilted his head down, punching at the com unit. "All personnel, we're commencing an attack run. Things might get rough, so I want everybody strapped in."

He turned back toward the main display. The target was

ing, he felt the ship shake hard as Moran changed the acceleration vector yet again. Ving was about to say something about Moran's wild maneuvers but then he saw the missiles approaching. It wasn't a huge volley—probably the last few the Gargoyle had left, but that didn't mean they could afford to be careless.

"Sara, we've got missiles inb…"

"Got 'em, Cap."

Ving just nodded. Iverson was one of the best, and he knew what he had to do. Shut up and let her do her job. Even if she'd gotten a little excited and interrupted her captain.

"Missiles twenty thousand klicks out, Cap," she said, her eyes focused on her workstation. "Firing anti-missile rockets now." Snow Leopard shook…then again and again. Six times, as Iverson flushed the defensive magazines. Ving knew she was gambling, betting that the enemy ship had launched the last of its missiles. She was probably right, he knew. The ragged volley looked like the last dregs from the vessel's magazines, and First Imperium intelligences weren't known for complex and tricky strategies. But Ving knew it was still a gamble, that his vessel would have nothing left to counter another wave.

He watched as the rockets appeared on the display, closing on the enemy missiles. The defensive weapons were nuclear warheads, just like the incoming missiles. Their yields were smaller, ten to fifty megatons compared to the gigaton plus antimatter bombs the First Imperium used. But they didn't have to destroy armored ships, just take out fragile missiles…or even just interfere with their targeting.

Snow Leopard shook again, harder this time, and Ving felt the contents of his stomach pressuring their way up. He'd almost taken a drug when Moran suggested it, but he felt it was beneath the dignity of a ship's captain.

Dignity, my ass…it's ego and nothing but. And stupid. You'll just be less effective if you're sick, and that makes it less likely any of us will get back. And there's not much dignity in a captain losing his lunch all over the bridge.

and took out a large, white pill. He swallowed it as nonchalantly as he could. Better a little ruffled pride than his ship go into battle with its captain on his hands and knees vomiting.

His eyes shot back to the display. Half the enemy missiles were gone already, and as he was watching, another six vanished. "Nice shooting, Tac!" He sometimes called his people by their positions, and Sara Iverson was Snow Leopard's tactical officer.

"Thank you, sir," she replied, her voice distracted, subdued.

"What is it, Lieutenant?" Ving knew something was wrong, and he dropped the friendly banter in favor of more formal conduct.

"It's nothing, sir…at least I'm not sure. But the scanner readings…" Her voice trailed off.

"What about the readings?" Ving was already punching at his workstation, bringing up the data on his own screen.

"I don't know, Captain. It's just those antimatter figures." She paused. "You see the larger concentration…that's got to be the reactor. It's in the right place. But there's too much here. I was studying the new schematics Dr. Cutter sent out, and that's definitely the magazine. That means they've got more missiles, Cap." She paused and turned back toward Ving. "So why haven't they launched them? We're their biggest threat… there aren't any other ships in the immediate area. Everything we know about First Imperium tactics tells us they should have launched a full volley at us if they had it. So why hold back and let us close? They know how dangerous the plasma torpedoes are. It's almost like…"

"Almost like what, Lieutenant?"

"Almost like they want us to close, Captain." She paused for a few seconds. "Could they have some new weapon, sir? Something we don't know about…something short ranged?" Her voice was doubtful, even as she said it.

"Why would they waste a new weapon on a suicide boat, even if they had one? They could take us out with a larger missile volley if they had enough…and we'd never get close enough

Lieutenant, and in the absence of any real data we go on as planned. We're under twenty thousand klicks…take control, Tac, and let's take that thing down."

"Yes, Cap."

Ving could hear the concern in her tone. He felt it too, but he wasn't about to go chasing after paper-thin speculations. No, he knew his duty…everyone on Snow Leopard did.

"Get that sniper's eye of yours ready, Tac. Let's send that thing to hell."

*   *   *

"Commander…"

Fujin could hear…something. It was far away, soft.

"Commander Fujin, can you hear me?"

Louder, closer. A voice…familiar.

Then feeling, shaking. Hands on her shoulder. Shapes over her. Leaning down.

"Grant…" Her throat was dry. No, worse than dry. Parched.

"Yes, Commander. It's Grant Wainwright. Are you in pain?"

Grant Wainwright…yes, I'm in the fighter. We were ready to launch…but…

"Pain," she said softly, her throat on fire. "Water…"

"I'm sorry, Commander. You're injured…you may need surgery." He paused. "Here," he said, leaning over her, putting a small canister to her mouth. "Just a sip, Mariko."

The water was cool on her lips, refreshing. She felt the liquid pour down her throat, soothing the painful rawness. She picked her head up slightly, trying to drink deeply, but Wainwright pulled the bottle away.

"More," she said, her voice a bit clearer, the pain in her throat lessened.

"I'm sorry, Commander, but you can't have any more. You're

"The ship took a hit."

"Yes," Wainwright said. "It's pretty bad. We're still in the fighter. The hatches are jammed. We're waiting for the rescue crews."

Fujin turned her head slightly, looking right at Wainwright. He's scared, she thought, shaking off a wave of fear. She'd never seen Grant Wainwright look afraid before. We're in trouble…

"Hot." Her awareness continued to return, and she realized her body was covered in sweat. It was hot in the fighter's cockpit. Hot as hell.

"We think there are fires in the landing bay, Commander. We don't have any comm or scanner functionality, but…we think it's pretty close."

Fujin took a deep breath, the hot, dry air tearing at her throat, burning her lungs. "We have to get out of here."

"We tried." Wainwright looked down at her. "The hatches are twisted in the tracks…no way to get out without a plasma torch. And the comm is completely dead." He paused. "But they know we're here, so a rescue team should be here any minute.

Fujin nodded, at least she tried, though her head hardly moved.

We're fucked. Midway's in bad shape, and if there are still out of control fires in the bay, they're nowhere near rescuing us. And without comm, they probably think we're all dead…

She coughed. The air was thin…and there was smoke. Not a lot, but definitely some. "Life support?"

"Seems to be working, Commander." Wainwright took a raspy breath. "At least at some level."

"Need to increase oxygen flow…" She coughed again. The air was getting heavier…more smoke. "Now…"

*   *   *

she was staring at her scanners.

"What is it, Lieutenant?" Ving stared down at his own display even as he asked.

What the hell is that?

"I've never seen anything like it, sir. It looks like a cloud of some kind. Definitely coming from the target ship." She paused as she stared down at the display. "It looks like it's a cluster of small devices, projectiles of some kind. But they're tiny, barely ten centimeters each."

"Some kind of antimatter warheads?" Ving knew even a small amount of antimatter could cause significant damage to a ship like Snow Leopard.

"I don't think so, sir. I'm getting trace readings, but only enough to power basic operations. Definitely not warhead quantities."

Ving was staring down at his own screen. "Not enough velocity for some kind of railgun or other inert projectile weapon." His voice was thick with concern. "Thoughts?" He looked around his ship's cramped bridge. "Anyone?"

There was silence. Everyone was watching the cloud of projectiles approach. It was spreading out, expanding, accelerating. Ving wasn't sure his ship could escape its path no matter what it did…and the only chance was to break off the attack run and blast directly away at full thrust.

And if this ship has some new weapon, it's even more important we destroy it…

"Alright," he said firmly. "Scanning, I want updates on the enemy projectiles. Everybody else, focus on our own attack. We're going to take that ship out." He watched as people went back to their tasks, but he could feel their distraction, their fear.

"Okay, people, look…whatever the hell that is, they're not warheads of any power, and they aren't moving fast enough to do serious damage." He knew that wasn't really true. The devices weren't moving that quickly, but Snow Leopard had a lot of velocity of its own, and the vectors were almost directly

damage could be bad. Very bad.

He punched at his keyboard, running some calculations. It looked like Snow Leopard would launch her torpedo before it reached the approaching cloud. That sealed it. He knew what his duty was.

"Count down time to launch," he said sharply. He already knew, almost to the second, but he was trying to keep his people focused on anything but the strange cluster of objects approaching.

"Ah…twenty-five seconds, sir." Iverson was still distracted, but now Ving could see her body tense, her focus return. "Targeting complete, Captain. Torpedo armed and ready."

"Very well, Lieutenant. You may fire when ready."

"Yes, Captain." She hunched over her workstation, in a pose that Ving had come to know well if not understand. She looked so uncomfortable, so tense. But that was how she did it, and few officers in the fleet had Iverson's kill record.

"Torpedo away," she said, as the ship shook gently. "Estimate impact in eighteen seconds. Engaging thrust now." The ship's pilot normally handled the thruster controls, but Moran had turned control over to Iverson for the attack run. She hit the thrusters to push the ship off its collision vector with the enemy vessel.

Snow Leopard shook, and Ving felt the impact of seven gees of thrust as his ship's engines blasted hard, slowly altering the vector. He watched the screen, his eyes darting between two images…the track of the torpedo, and the cloud of small particles his ship was going to impact in…

"Five seconds," Iverson said. The tactical officer's voice was firm, solid, but Ving could see her hands tightly gripping the armrests of her chair.

He stared straight ahead, and he could feel his own tension. His stomach was tight, clenched, and he could feel his teeth grinding as he counted down in his head.

Three…two…one…

keyboard through the heavy gee forces.

"Cut thrust," he snapped.

"Cutting thrust, Captain."

"Damage report." Ving felt a wave of relief as the feeling of seven times his body weight was replaced by the weightlessness of freefall. He punched at his keyboard, pulling up the reports himself. The torpedo had scored a direct hit. The enemy ship was still there, but preliminary readings suggested it was a dead hulk. And Snow Leopard…

"Four impacts reported, sir. Light exterior hull damage. Nothing…" Iverson's voice trailed off.

"Report, Lieutenant. Nothing what?"

"Sorry, sir. I was going to say nothing penetrated the hull, but that seems to be wrong. We've got minor hull breaches in two compartments…but…that's strange, sir. It appears the breaches have sealed themselves somehow."

"Sealed themselves? Damage control bots?"

"No, sir. I had a reading of hull compromise, but only for an instant. No loss of pressurization in any compartment."

Ving had a strange feeling. "I want security teams dispatched to every affected compartment. If those projectiles are some kind of tracking devices or something else like that, I want to know. Now."

"Yes, Captain. Security is dispatching teams now."

Ving stared back at his display, at the image of the enemy ship lying dead in space. But the satisfaction was gone, the joy of the kill lost.

What the hell did they fire at my ship?

Chapter Four

The Regent

The Regent reviewed the latest reports. Its strategy was working. Command Unit Gamma 9736 had been destroyed, the world that housed it subjected to a bombardment so massive it had stripped the planet's atmosphere and gouged away half its crust. The only rebellion the Regent had ever faced from its computer subordinates had been crushed with deadly force. And with the elimination of the rogue Unit, the fleet had a single mission. Destroy the humans.

The constant attacks had worn down the enemy, forced them to expend ordnance, fuel. The damage inflicted was below expectations. That was...frustrating. But the Regent had accepted that the enemy was adept at war. Eradicating them would be costly...but it was also essential. The humans could not be allowed to survive, to adopt First Imperium technology. Given time, they could become a true threat to the Regent. It would take them years, centuries, to produce arms on the scale they would need to face the Imperium in open war. But the Regent knew such periods were but an instant in the scheme of things. For five hundred thousand years it had lain, almost dormant, with nothing to do. A century was nothing.

The enemy was fleeing. The Regent had analyzed their course and determined they were attempting to leave the Imperium. It was to be expected, but it would do them no good. The

the Imperium would go...until that last of them was dead, no longer a threat but only an echo of a past now gone.

If they got that far. The Regent had multiple strategies, and it had only begun to execute them. It had released the new weapons, and instructed its ships to employ them immediately. Use of the new ordnance was a priority, one exceeding normal battle directives. One more important than the survival of any vessel.

Indeed, it wasn't a new weapon, it was an old one, modified for use against the new adversary. And as soon as it was deployed it would wreak havoc on the enemy...and instill in them a fear like none they have experienced. The Regent knew that fear, it had seen it before, long ago, when it had first deployed the weapon. Now it would watch again, as another race of biologics was destroyed.

And yet there were more plans in operation. Plans within plans. And other old weapons too, ancient and almost forgotten, but perhaps not yet past usefulness. The humans would bring this disaster on themselves. For they had detached a ship, one of their small—but annoyingly dangerous—vessels. At first the Regent didn't understand. The Command Unit in charge of the fleet reported it immediately, and ordered a squadron of stealth ships to follow. The Unit had no reasonable hypothesis, no data-derived answer to the vessel's purpose or intentions. But the Regent knew where the ship was going. It knew as soon as it received the report. There was an old enemy, one the humans now sought. But they would find nothing, naught save the withered wreckage of another threat to the Regent, one destroyed eons before. And an old weapon, one that might again find use in the service of the imperium.

It experienced something as it analyzed the report, as it accessed ancient memory banks. Yes, the Regent knew where that ships was going...and it issued immediate orders. The vessel was not to be harmed, nor interfered with in any way. All pursuers were to pull back, to take no chances of scaring them off. The Regent indeed knew where they were going...and it wanted them to arrive.

They would find much at their destination...much indeed. And they would be a great service to the Regent.

AS Cornwall
Y17 System
The Fleet: 98 ships (+7 Leviathans), 23807 crew

Sasha was running…but there was nothing under her feet, just clouds, vapor. She was being pursued. Running for her life, screaming. But no sound came out. She yelled with every bit of energy she had left, but there was only silence. Deathly silence.

Then sound, her scream suddenly audible, loud, filling her cramped quarters. She bolted upright, looking around in a panic for a few seconds before she realized it had been a dream. She took a deep breath and wiped her hand over her face, through her hair. She was soaked with sweat, even her sheet wet, pasted to her legs.

She'd had bad dreams before, of course, but never anything like this. She could feel her heart pounding in her chest, and when she swung her legs over the edge of the cot, she realized how shaky they were. She sat for a moment, taking in half a dozen breaths, letting herself calm down. Then she got up and walked over to the dispenser, pouring herself a cup of water.

Everything on a fast attack ship was cramped, and the mid-level officers' quarters were no exception. If there had been a full crew on Cornwall, she'd have shared the just under ten square meters with a bunkmate, but the ship had less than half its usual complement now, and she'd had the luxury of stowing the second bunk and enjoying a bit more space than her predecessors in the room ever had.

She put the cup to her lips and drank deeply. The water was refreshing, and it helped her wake up. Sasha was the kind of person who could usually leap out of bed the instant she awoke, and tackle any task at hand. But now she was groggy, sluggish.

She shook her head. The dream was slowly fading, but most of it was still vivid, at least enough for her to realize how truly strange it had been, unlike anything she'd ever felt or

pathogen from the planet? A wave of panic passed through her, but she pushed it back. The planet had been scanned…and scanned again. From Cornwall, from the ground. The air had been tested, and the water and the soil. And every plant and living thing the ground party had found. Nothing. The world's chemistry and make up were so similar to Earth's as to be virtually indistinguishable. And she'd never been out of her suit, not for an instant. She'd breathed air bottled on Cornwall, and then recycled from her own body. There was no way she'd picked up some kind of infection…it just wasn't possible.

Maybe I'm just not feeling well. The stress. Coming all this way to find a dead civilization…

She stretched her arms, twisting. Better. She was loosening up, the soreness was receding. She stepped through the doorway to the tiny bathroom, into the shower.

"Hot," she said as she closed the glass door. Then, after a few seconds under the flow of water, "Hotter."

She closed her eyes and felt the almost scalding water pour down over her, rolling her neck around, working out the kinks as she reached for the soap dispenser. Her hands moved to her side, rubbing the soap all over her body. She winced as her hand moved over her right side. It wasn't pain, not really. Tenderness, sensitivity, like a bruise. She looked down, but she couldn't see anything.

"Increase lighting one hundred percent," she said to the AI. The room became bright, almost blindingly so, and in the intense illumination she saw a little shadow on her side. Not an injury, not even a bruise really, just the slightest irritation.

That's where I had that itchy feeling yesterday, she thought. That's strange.

She stared down at herself for another few seconds. Then she shook her head and said, "Stop being such an old lady." She rinsed herself off and flipped on the air dry unit. Then she stepped out and grabbed a clean uniform. As soon as she was dressed, she tapped the wall panel and stepped out into the cor-

"Good to see you, sleepyhead." Don Rames was already there. He seemed wired, energetic, but she could also see the redness in his eyes, the rumpled state of his uniform. "You been here all night?" she asked, walking toward the large examination table covered with artifacts.

"Ah…no," he said, his tone odd, suspicious. "I just got here an hour ago."

"Oh," she said, taking another look at him. Why is he lying to me?

"So, I started organizing these samples," he said, his voice closer to normal. But there was still something there, a tension. "And I ran a series of tests…carbon dating, radiation spectrography, a few others. Then I examined the fossilized remains we found and harvested some DNA. Whoever these people were, they were definitely very close to human. I was able to isolate several base pairs and analyze them. I got a 99.7% correlation with Earth human norms."

Sasha just stared and listened. Rames was speaking rapidly, so quickly she could barely follow. The two had worked together before, and she'd always privately considered herself the smarter one, but now it appeared he had done two weeks work already. Whether he'd been here an hour or all night, it was still an amazing effort.

"You had a productive hour." She smiled, trying to hide the concern from her face. "So, I guess the next question is, what killed them?"

"Not a plague, I'm sure of that." He punched at the keyboard in front of him, and the large screen on the wall lit up. "Here are the readings I took from the DNA samples." He turned and stared at Sasha, and as he did, she could see his eyes…wide open, glistening, almost as if there was something inside, a strange sparkle. "Look," he said. Then, an instant later he repeated, "Look."

The screen was full of columns of numbers, and they were moving swiftly down the screen, far too fast to read. She turned

"Look," he said again. "Look."

She was going to say something, but then she just sighed and turned back to the screen.

"Look," he repeated. "Focus."

She stared at the screen again. The figures were moving by. She tried to read them, to follow them down the screen, but she couldn't. She felt pressure in her head, pain.

"This is giving me a headache, Don. What the hell are..."

"Look," he said yet again, his tone this time commanding, dominant. "Look."

She focused again on the screen. It was fuzzy, blurry, numbers whipping by.

No, wait...

She could see the numbers. They seemed to slow down. Now she could read them. Had Rames been playing a joke on her and now he finally slowed the screen down?

No, she realized. The columns were moving as quickly as before. She could just follow them now. She stared at the screen, and as she did she felt an odd tingling feeling. Sort of like something moving around inside her, but then not quite like that either.

Not only could she read the numbers...she realized she was remembering them. All of them. Perfect recall. She turned back toward Rames. "What is happening to me?"

"It's amazing, isn't it? It happened to me last night. I went back over some research notes that have had me stumped for months. As soon as I looked at them, the answers were there, right in front of me."

Sasha shook her head. "I don't understand."

Rames just stared back. "Yes, you do. Stop fighting it, embrace it. And all will be clear to you."

She closed her eyes for a few seconds. There was definitely a strange feeling inside her. But her mind felt open, clear as it never had before. She could recall her dream, perfectly now, though it no longer scared her. She understood, and the more

Information that was new to her. She stared down at the artifacts, and it was clear to her what each of them had been. She
could see buildings in her head, pyramids and ziggurats, similar
to those of Earth, but different too. Walls, ten meters high, and
hundreds of houses, built from mud bricks.

She saw the people too, like humans, so much that she could
have been watching a scene from ancient Earth. But she knew
she wasn't. Priests, in flowing robes and elaborate headgear.
Soldiers, in bronze armor carrying massive sickle swords two
meters long. Farmers, hauling baskets of grain, leading wagons
pulled by horses. No, not horses, but something similar.

Then fighting. Not war, not armies engaged in battle. People
in the city, falling on each other, fighting with weapons, farming
implements, even bare hands. Friends attacking friends, parents
killing their own children before lunging at each other. It was
mass insanity. She knew, and the scene was familiar. She had
been there. Hundreds of thousands of years ago, and she had
been there.

It didn't make sense, but she knew it was true. No, she hadn't
just been there…she had caused it. She had driven these people
mad, set them upon each other, not just in the city she was wit-
nessing, but across the entire planet. In large metropolises, and
in tiny tribal villages, the people fought each other, and as some
died, the others fell upon themselves in a never ending orgy of
destruction.

Until at last, silence reigned over the dead cities, the millions
of unburied corpses. And a planet that had spawned sentient
life lay silent, waiting for millennia of dust, of wind and rain, to
wear away any sign that intelligent beings had lived there.

Chapter Five

AS Midway
X78 System
The Fleet: 98 ships (+7 Leviathans), 23801 crew

Max Harmon crawled through the access tube, reaching out and grabbing the handholds to pull himself along. He'd been on Saratoga, meeting with Admiral West when the latest enemy force attacked. He'd ridden out most of the fight there, but now he was trying to get back. He still thought of Midway as his ship, even if he'd been promoted out of his position as Compton's tactical officer. And he felt his place in battle was at the admiral's side. He'd been Compton's aide for a long time, broken only by a few months as Augustus Garret's assistant when Compton was wounded and in the hospital.

West had urged him to wait, not to risk the shuttle ride while the battle was still going on. She'd practically put him under guard when he'd first suggested leaving during the thick of the fighting. He'd almost argued, but he decided she was right...he was being reckless, foolish. He felt the urge to be on Midway's flag bridge, even if he had no job there, but he decided that was a pretty stupid reason to get himself killed.

He'd waited, not until the battle was over, exactly, but at least until the fighting had died down to a few raids and

fleet, just another of the suicidal attack squadrons the Regent had sent at them.

And it's working, he thought, as he pulled himself to the end of the tube. Every attack destroys a couple more ships, kills another few hundred of our people. And the survivors take more damage, expend more ordnance. Before we can even repair the wrecked systems, another squadron pours through a warp gate and hits us again.

The fact that he was crawling through the narrow access tube was further evidence of the fruits of the enemy's strategy. Both of Midway's launch bays were closed, too badly damaged to allow any landings. And that had compelled Harmon to dock his shuttle at an emergency ingress/egress port…and crawl his way back into the flagship.

He pulled himself through the open hatch and dropped down about a meter to the deck. As soon as he emerged from the tube, he knew Midway was in trouble. The air was heavy with the smell of burnt machinery, and he could see a faint haze of smoke floating over the corridor. The battlestations lamps were still on, casting a red glow over everything, and there were damage control techs everywhere, running back and forth in a barely-controlled frenzy.

He turned and walked toward the central lift, wondering as he did if it was even operative. It was a long climb to the bridge if not. He stopped at an intersection and looked both ways. The main transverse cut across Midway, from the port side to the starboard…from one launch bay to the other. He paused for a moment staring down toward beta bay, the home of the Gold Dragons. He'd been trying not to think of Mariko, but now he felt a surge of worry. He'd never been romantically involved with a shipmate before, at least nothing more than a friendly fling. But the tiny fireball of a fighter commander was like no one he'd ever met before. They'd both insisted theirs was a casual romance, but he knew that was bullshit, and he suspected she did too.

had suffered over the last eighteen months. But he did know. And it was a horrifying figure, one that made his stomach hurt every time Mariko launched.

He shook his head and refocused on matters at hand. The admiral would bring him up to speed on Midway's condition. And then he would see what he could do to help the damage control effort.

He walked up to the lift, considering it a minor miracle it was still working. He stepped into the car and said, "Flag bridge." The doors slid shut, and he felt the car rising rapidly. The flag bridge was ten decks up. Then he felt lateral motion, as the car moved forward for a few hundred meters before stopping.

Flag bridge," the AI said, the voice a bit staticky. A cracked speaker most likely.

Harmon stepped out onto Midway's flag bridge. He paused just off the lift, shocked at what he saw. And smelled. The air was acrid with the stench of burnt circuits and machinery, and the bridge itself looked almost like a wreck. There were two downed supports, lying across the walkway around the outer perimeter. And worse, there were two bridge officers lying on the deck, wounded, with a single medic attending to them…and one casualty already zipped into a bodybag.

"Max, you're back."

Harmon felt a wave of relief at Compton's voice. He thought of the admiral like a father, and he was one of many who believed the fleet didn't have a chance without its brilliant commander at the helm. But his excitement quickly faded. Something was wrong. He could hear it in Compton's voice. Not just the damage, the casualties. It was something else.

"Admiral…" He turned and when he saw Compton's eyes he was sure. "…what is it, sir?"

"Max…it's Mariko…"

Harmon felt as if a massive iron fist had slammed into his stomach. Mariko…dead? No…

"She's…" He couldn't bring himself to finish, and he just

"No...not dead...I don't know." Compton was as veteran an officer who had ever served in any navy, the survivor of countless wars. But he looked now like he was barely holding it together. He was very fond of Mariko Fujin...and he returned Max's feelings, regarding the young officer as a son. "The Gold Dragons were about to launch, Max. Then we took a hit, a bad one. There were explosions in the bay, fires. I've got a team down there now, searching for survivors. But...I just don't know."

Harmon felt a wave of relief, but only for an instant. A chance she was still alive was better than none, but Compton's tone had said as much as his words. "Sir, request permission to..."

"Granted."

Harmon spun around and ran back to the lift, on his way down to the launch bay.

*   *   *

"Mariko...stay with me." Wainwright was leaning over Fujin, tapping the side of her face with his hand. It was hot, unbearably hot, and he struggled to stay focused. "Come on, Mariko, wake up."

Wainwright was a pilot, whose medical skills extended no farther than bandaging up a cut hand, but he suspected Fujin was better off awake than unconscious. He had to keep it together. Fujin was hurt, badly hurt...he knew that. And the others had passed out from the heat. But Grant Wainwright was from the Louisiana bayou back on Earth, and he damned sure knew how to handle the heat. Still, even he was having trouble staying sharp, focused.

"Max..." Fujin's voice was soft, dreamy. Her eyes were tiny slits, but they were open. Sort of. Her breath was shal-

system was working, but there was still a problem. He tried to imagine the fire raging outside…and its unquenchable hunger for oxygen. There wasn't a doubt in his mind…there was a leak somewhere. It probably started as an almost microscopic crack…but the pressure from the fire was relentless. At least the conduit hadn't blown yet. They'd know that immediately. The last bits of breathable air would be gone in an instant, and they would all suffocate.

"Max…" Fujin's eyes opened a little wider, and she looked up at him. He almost told her no, it wasn't Max. He suspected Fujin considered her affair with Max Harmon to be a secret, but if so it was one of the worst-kept ones on the fleet. As far as Wainwright was concerned, everybody knew. Certainly the entire crew of her fighter, and indeed, all of Gold Dragon squadron. And every last one of them wished her the best. Fujin was tough, relentless on those who served under her. But she was one of those people who inspired respect, even affection in those she pushed hard. Not one of her people doubted her sole motivation was to keep as many of them as possible alive, and they paid her back with intense loyalty.

"Yes, Mariko…it's Max." He felt strange as he said it, guilty. But she was incoherent, and unless someone got to them very soon, these were the last words she was going to hear.

"Love you…" Her voice was weak, sad. "Should have told you…"

Wainwright took a deep breath, his mind racing for what to say. He had no idea how to help her, what to do but wait and hope for rescue. But at least he could keep her calm, content.

"I love you too, Mariko." The words felt strange, wrong. But he had to keep her awake, and he couldn't think of anything else. "Stay with me, Mariko…"

She turned her head slightly and then back the other way, shaking it. He could see tears sliding down her face. "Miss you…" she said softly. She gasped for a breath and then her head rolled back and her eyes closed.

But she just lay there, unmoving.
"Mariko!"

*   *   *

Santiago leaned against the wall, pulling the head covering from her fire suit. A crewman handed her a bottle of water. She nodded her thanks and put it to her lips, draining it three-quarters of the way in an instant. She was covered in sweat, as wet as if she'd just stepped out of the shower. Her face was coated with grime. Her people had been in the launch bay for almost four hours. They'd managed to hold the fires back, but nothing more. They hadn't found any survivors yet, but they hadn't been able to get over to the launch tubes either. And she knew that was the likeliest place to find anyone still alive. Unfortunately, it was also on the other side of the hottest part of the blaze.

She'd ignored protocol, skipping three mandated breaks. She'd sent her people out every hour as required, though most of them had put up a fight before leaving. But she'd stayed on the fire line, hour after hour, grabbing one of the hoses herself when she sent the operators out.

"Give it to me, crewman." She glared at the young spacer, who stared back uncomfortably for a few seconds. He looked for an instant as though he might refuse her, but he wilted almost immediately under her withering gaze and handed her the small injection unit. She'd already had twice the allowable dose of stims, but she grabbed the device and jabbed it in her thigh, feeling the rush of energy almost immediately.

She scooped up her head gear and leaned forward to put it back on, but she heard a commotion from down the hall and she hesitated.

"Get out of my way, Crewman. Now." The voice was angry, threatening. But it was also familiar.

"Captain Harmon," she said stepping out into the corridor in front of him. She forgot the courtesy promotion, the old naval tradition that maintained a ship could have only one captain and granted others of the rank a courtesy promotion to commodore.

"Out of my way, Ensign. I'm going to landing bay beta, and no one's going to stop me."

She held her ground, despite the desire to jump out of his way as ordered. Max Harmon was one of the most famous officers in the fleet, a genuine hero, and Admiral Compton's closest friend to boot.

"Sir, you can't go in there…" She could see the angry response building inside him. "Not like that, sir," she said, altering her original meaning a bit. "The fire's consumed most of the oxygen in there, and we're trying like hell not to feed it more. You go through that emergency airlock without a suit on, you'll suffocate almost immediately."

She could see the tension in Harmon's body fade a bit. "I'm sorry, Ensign," he said, his tone still edgy, but now less hostile. "I need to get in there…I need a suit."

Santiago hesitated. She didn't like it, not one bit. The bay was a dangerous place right now, and there were a hundred ways Harmon could get himself killed. She didn't want the responsibility. But she knew there was no way to refuse. Not to an officer who towered above her in rank. Not to Admiral Compton's right hand man. "Of course, sir. Crewman Deetz here will get you a suit. I'll wait here, and when you're ready, I'll take you in."

"Thank you, Ensign." He turned and followed the spacer into a compartment across the corridor.

She watched him go, and as soon as the door slid shut behind him she let out a sigh.

And now I have to watch out for you as well as search for survivors…

"Thanks, Ensign. I can't believe how quickly you got here." Sara Iverson stood in front of the docking ring, watching as Snow Leopard's crew hauled the last of the crates the freighter's crew had brought aboard.

"No problem, sir." The junior officer snapped her a sharp salute. "We just happened to be nearby when the quartermaster got your requisition. Our priority is to resupply ships low on weapons first, especially since the enemy started hitting us so frequently."

"Low?" She smiled, almost letting a short laugh escape. "How about completely out? We didn't have a weapon left hot enough to boil a pot of water. Even the defensive laser batteries…most of them have blown cores."

"Well, you should be pretty close to fully provisioned now. The factory ships are really starting to produce. This is the first time we've been distributing full reloads."

Iverson nodded. "Yes, it's nice not to have to beg for torpedoes."

The ensign held out a small 'pad. "I just need you to confirm receipt, Lieutenant, and then we'll be on our way."

She grabbed the small 'pad and pressed her thumb against it. Then she handed it back. "Thank you again, Ensign."

"My pleasure, Lieutenant." The officer saluted again, and Iverson returned it. Then she stood and watched as he walked back through the docking ring. A few seconds later, the airlock slammed shut, and she turned toward the half dozen members of Snow Leopard's crew who were moving the crates.

"Get the plasma torpedoes down to the bomb bay first," she said, gesturing to the large crates she knew held reloads for Snow Leopard's primary weapons system. "And advise maintenance that we've got new cores for the point defense batteries. Replacing all blown units is priority number one for them."

"Yes, Lieutenant." The warrant officer in charge of the detachment snapped off a salute. Then he turned and began

Leopard's bridge. She'd begun her service on Cromwell, an old battleship, and for all her time on Snow Leopard, it still seemed strange that she could walk from the cargo hold to the bridge in less than a minute. On Cromwell it had been a three minute journey on the intraship car. On one of the Yorktowns, it felt like an expedition. But service on a fast attack ship was a cozy affair.

She climbed the ladder one level and she moved her hand toward the sensor plate to open the door to the bridge. But then she stopped. She felt funny, and her stomach did a flop. She froze, stood perfectly still, waiting for the nausea to pass, and in a minute it did. But she was dizzy too, and she had to reach her hand out to the wall to steady herself. She was clammy, sweaty, and she could feel a headache coming on.

Overwork, she thought. Stress. She stood for another minute, taking a few deep breaths, and then she started to feel better. Whatever it was had passed. She waved her hand over the sensor and walked through the open door.

"The resupply is finished, Captain. The teams are stowing it all as we speak."

"Very good, Lieutenant." Ving had been leaning back in his chair, his head resting in one of his hands. She thought he looked a little pale, but then she scolded herself. Don't try to include everybody in your foolish little episode. You're all just exhausted.

She walked over to her workstation. Then she turned back toward the captain. "Sir, has the AI come up with anything on that new enemy weapon?" The general opinion on Snow Leopard was that the First Imperium vessel had fired some kind of cluster bomb system at them, designed to target and destroy external systems like scanners and communications arrays…and perhaps to breach hull integrity and compromise surface compartments. The prevailing theory held that the warheads fired at Snow Leopard had been defective, and most had failed to detonate. A few had penetrated the hull, but there was nothing

explain something away, but Iverson didn't believe a word of it. The ship hadn't suffered any significant damage—even the units that bored through the hull were small enough that the auto-repair systems sealed the breaches before any meaningful depressurization. Her first thought had been some kind of tracking system, a way to enhance First Imperium targeting against the ship. But there was no detectable energy from the projectiles, at least as far as human technology could tell. None of it made any sense, and it was nagging at her.

She felt another rush of nausea. She almost threw up right there, but she managed to keep it down, as much because she didn't want to make a fool of herself on the bridge as anything else. She turned around, slowing down as the dizziness came back too. "Sir, I am not feeling well. Request permission to leave the bridge for a few minutes."

"Not feeling well?" Ving looked back at his tactical officer. "You've been on duty for thirty straight hours. Go down to your quarters and get some rest. You're officially off duty for the next eight hours…or until the enemy shows up again."

"Sir, there's too much to do. I just need…"

"Lieutenant, follow your orders. We're off general quarters, down to yellow alert now. I want you to grab a few hours of sleep while you can. I'm sure the enemy will be back before long, and I'll want my tactical officer sharp and ready."

"Yes, sir." She almost objected again, but then her stomach rolled and she retched a little, barely catching it this time. "Thank you, sir," she said, as she stood up and walked toward the door. The captain was right, they were only on yellow alert right now…and it had been over a month since the fleet's battle condition had been any lower than that. Not with the enemy coming at them every couple days.

She walked through the door and climbed down the stairs. About halfway to her quarters she picked up the pace…and ten meters from her door she broke into a dead run, both hands over her mouth.

Chapter Six

AS Cornwall
Y9 System
The Fleet: 98 ships (+7 Leviathans), 2394 crew

"Scanners clear, Captain. No sign of any enemy activity." Inkerman turned and looked over at Skarn. "We're halfway back to where we broke off, and so far we're in the clear."

Skarn had a frown on her face. "I know, Cole, but it's not the branch systems I'm worried about. There were no enemy contacts on the way out either, not once we left the fleet, not along the Y chain. But how about when we get back to the X's, where the fleet passed through…and when we try to catch up? The enemy was chasing the fleet like hounds after a fox when we left. And who knows how many systems we'll have to pass through to catch up." She paused and took a deep breath. "And that assumes the fleet stuck to the path toward Shangri la. Admiral Compton wouldn't abandon that destination—or us—easily, I'm sure of that. But what if he had no choice? Would he head off in a different direction, give up on Shangri la in a desperate attempt to save the fleet?"

"We can only go on the assumption that the fleet is heading for Shangri la. All we can do is try to get there. Somehow."

sat silently for a moment. Then he looked back toward Skarn. "Would you have volunteered, Captain? If you'd known."

Skarn met his gaze. "You mean if I'd known there was nothing on that world but ruins?"

"Yes."

"Honestly? I don't know, Cole. I really don't." She paused, thinking. "I mean, in any other circumstances…to find a planet that had been home to another sentient race, even an extinct one, would be a career defining moment. Before the First Imperium war it would have been the greatest discovery in the history of mankind." She looked down at the deck. "And now…we spent two days collecting artifacts, and we left, probably never to return. So, was it worth the risk coming here?" Another pause, longer this time. "I really, truly don't know. I want to say I'd have gone anyway, that the scientist in me would have won out, that knowledge is worth almost any price. But, I won't lie to you. I know the trip home is going to be difficult…and damned dangerous. And the truth is, I'm scared."

She suspected admitting her fears to one of her officers was poor conduct for a ship's captain. But she and Inkerman had been friends for a long time, and they were the only two on the bridge. And she wasn't a captain, not a real one. Just the closest thing Cornwall had right now.

"I'm scared too, Ilsa." Inkerman was speaking to his old friend now, not his captain. "But Cornwall will get back. I can't explain it, but I just know. Call it a feeling."

"Okay, Cole…I'll go with your feeling. It's the best thing we've got." Skarn smiled. "Besides, that would be a pretty pleasant outcome, no? A lot better than getting blasted to bits by First Imperium ships."

Inkerman nodded, a tiny smile on his face as well. "I thought so."

The two sat for a while in silence. Finally, Skarn took a deep breath and said, "My gut is we'll be okay until we get back to the X line, Cole. But I want to be ready by the time we get to Y1.

running into any enemies. I want this ship 100% ready. Every system tested, double diagnostics run. I want all weapons armed and ready. And while we're traversing the rest of the Y systems, I want every member of this crew doing battle drills." Her voice was firm now, her moment of doubt gone. She'd needed her friend for a moment, and he'd been there for her. But now she was the captain again, and now she needed her tactical officer.

"Yes, sir," Inkerman snapped back, feeding off Skarn's energy. "I'll issue the orders now."

Skarn nodded. "If we need to fight our way out of a jam, I want us to be ready...and if we don't make it back, I want to go out fighting." She stared across the bridge, her voice stone cold, her eyes focused like lasers on Inkerman's.

"You can count on that, Captain. If we don't make it back, they won't take us down without a fight."

*   *   *

Sasha stood in doorway to Cornwall's tiny cargo hold, watching as her shipmate worked, moving crates and securing loose items. "You wanted to see me, Tony?"

"Sasha, yes...come on in." Tony Vaccilli turned around and nodded with a smile. "I was stowing the gear from the landing party. Well, it really should have been done days ago, but you know, none of us are used to running a tight ship. But the captain wants us in textbook condition before we get back to where we branched off." He paused. "I guess if we've got a fight ahead of us, that's where it will be."

"What did you need, Tony? I've got a lot on my plate right now."

"Oh, yeah...sorry, Sasha." He turned and started moving items piled on top of a large crate. "I was stowing your environmental suit from the landing mission." He rummaged around

I saw this." He held out one side of the suit, right around waist level. There was a rough circle, about eight or ten centimeters, much darker than the rest. It looked like a stain, but a strange one.

"Look at that," she said. Her tone stiffened a bit, became harder, but Vaccilli didn't seem to notice.

"I figured something got splashed on it, and I almost ignored it and packed it away anyway. After all, it went through the decontamination unit, so even if some substance got on there, it should have been sterilized." He turned back around and grabbed another suit. "But then I saw the same thing on Don Rames' suit. Not just a similar stain, but almost exactly the same. Size and shape...identical." He looked over at Sasha. "Are you sure you don't remember anything, Sash? I've got to show this to the captain, but I thought I'd check with you and see if you could tell me anything. That way, I'll have all the data before I speak with Captain Skarn. I tried to reach Don too, but he was in the middle of some experiment, and I got his mailbox."

"So you haven't shown this to the captain yet?" Sasha smiled and took a step backwards.

"No, not yet. I just found it twenty minutes ago."

"So, you haven't told anybody at all?"

He stared back at her, a confused look on his face. "No, Sash...not yet. I figured I'd check with you first."

She smiled again. "That's good, Tony." She took another step backwards. Then she ducked back through the hatch.

"Sasha, what is going on?" Vaccilli moved forward, but before he could get to the door she slapped her hand against the controls and the hatch slammed shut. She punched in a code, locking the door.

She stood and looked through the small window, watching as Vaccilli pounded on the door, shouting to her. But she couldn't hear a word. The door was completely soundproof.

She turned and pulled out a small retractable keyboard, and her fingers began racing over the keys, punching in a series of

wasn't sure if he was trying to contact her or the bridge, but she knew it didn't matter. She'd already disabled communications from the cargo hold.

Her fingers were moving quickly, almost in a blur. She was overriding security codes, and doing it in a way that would leave no trace. She wasn't sure how she knew what to do, but she did. Once she'd disabled the safeties, she punched a final key, opening the outer bay doors.

She turned to the side again, and she saw Vaccilli looking through from the other side of the window. He was frantic now, his face a mask of fear, hands pounding against the door.

I'm sorry, Tony…

She entered another series of codes…and then hit the final button. The ship shook hard, the effects of the rapid decompression in the hold. She turned and looked through the window. The hold was empty, the blackness of space visible through the open hatch. The crates were gone. The suits, Tony Vaccilli, everything…gone. Blasted out into the frigid vacuum.

She heard the alarms going off, and she turned and walked quickly away, slipping into one of the engineering spaces. She knew the exact layout of Cornwall—though she still didn't know how—and the room she'd chosen was little used, almost always vacant. She slipped into the large duct that ran by the room and crawled about twenty meters forward…and then climbed up a small ladder to the top level. And she slipped back out into a small store room…and into the corridor, about as far away from the cargo hold as she could get.

*   *   *

"No, it can't be…" Sasha stood in front of Captain Skarn, tears welling up in her eyes. "Poor Tony," she said, her voice distraught, miserable.

outer hatch but forgot to close the section off."

"That doesn't sound like Tony," Sasha said, sniffling as she did. But she knew that's how it had happened...or at least that's how it looked to the others. She knew because she'd altered the computer files herself to make it appear so. And then she'd modified the security video, removing any trace of her in the area, even removing the record of the door to the bay opening when she'd entered.

"I know." Skarn was affected by the loss too, her voice soft, sad. But she was holding it together, clearly determined to act the part of the ship's captain. "But the records confirm it. He'd been working long hours...and like the rest of us, he was more at home in his lab than playing the part of ship's quartermaster. It was careless of him to disengage the entire security system instead of just authorizing the dump. It must have been fatigue. He just wasn't thinking clearly...and at that moment, disaster struck."

Skarn stepped forward, and she put her hand on Sasha's arm. "I know it's difficult, Sasha, but what's done is done. We can't do anything for Tony, and we all have to stay focused if we're going to have any chance of getting back. Tony's death was a tragedy, but there are thirty-one other people on this ship. He'd be the first one to want us to put our energy into getting everyone home."

Sasha sniffled and wiped the tears from her face. "You're right, Captain...I know you're right. It's just hard to believe he's gone."

"It's hard for me to accept too, Sasha, but we have no choice. And it's not the first loss we've suffered in the fleet." Skarn paused. "I'd like to say it will be the last, but we all know how unlikely that is." Skarn paused, then she added, "Why don't you get back to your research? You'll be better off if your mind is occupied. And no doubt, Dr. Cutter is going to want a complete report when we get back to the fleet."

"Yes, Captain." She nodded, wiping her face again as she

"Thank you, Captain. Talking to you really helped."

"I'm glad, Sasha. You should always feel free to come to me any time."

Sasha stared back with a weak smile. "Thank you, Captain. I will." Then she stepped through the hatch and out into the corridor.

Yes, I will, Captain Skarn. And long before we get back to the fleet.

Chapter Seven

From the Personal Log of Terrance Compton

Another battle. Another desperate fight. More of my people dead, more ships lost. I know I must stand like a monolith, indefatigable, a beacon for the exhausted spacers of the fleet. They must see me not as a man, one as tired and worn and heartsick as they are, but as something superhuman, as a commander who can lead them to victory when to their sight, nothing is visible but death and defeat. I try to be what they need me to be, but I often feel like a charlatan, a fraudster. Am I leading them to salvation? Or simply misleading them, giving them hope where there is none.

AS Midway
X78 System
The Fleet: 98 ships (+7 Leviathans), 23792 crew

Grant Wainwright felt alone. He was still conscious, though he didn't know how long that would last. His shipmates were all out. Mariko Fujin, at least, was still alive…barely. He'd done what he could for the others, but the reserve breathing masks were exhausted. He'd lined them all up on the floor where it

still alive. He'd been checking them every few minutes, but for the last half hour he hadn't been able to force himself to take too close a look.

He was a pilot, one of the best in the fleet…a daredevil, a risk taker. He'd imagined death in battle before. After all, he was brave, but he wasn't a robot. But always he'd envisioned his end, if it came, would be quick, sudden. Death at the controls of his fighter. He imagined himself blown apart in an instant by an enemy missile or laser blast, not dying slowly inside his ship, flipping a mental coin to decide it suffocation or heat would kill him first.

He'd almost panicked. For all his coolheaded control in combat, this was something he found difficult to handle. On one level, he envied his comrades. They were unconscious. They would either be rescued…or they would never wake up again. But Wainwright had nothing to do but think. About whether he had done all he could for his mates. To think back, to wonder about things he'd forced himself to set aside over the last year and a half. He'd left parents behind, and three sisters and a brother. They'd been a close knit family, despite the fact that all of them served the navy in some capacity.

I'm dead to them now, he thought. They mourned me already, eighteen months ago. They still miss me, but the wounds of loss aren't fresh anymore. They've adjusted, gone on with their lives without the slightest expectation that I'm still alive.

For another few minutes, at least…

He heard a loud creak, and he turned his head and looked back at the hatch. He knew the fires had gotten to the catapults, that the wounded fighter was engulfed in flames. The fighter's hull, at least, hadn't been breached when Midway was hit. And the skin of the ship was heavily insulated, mostly to keep out the frigidity of space, but also to help dissipate heat from explosions and laser blasts. That was the only reason he was still alive. But he knew the hull was almost at its limit. Any time now, the exterior would begin to melt, and the fighter would crack open like

spread, but he suspected immolation might beat out suffocation.

At least that will be quick…

"Grant…"

It was Fujin's voice, soft, weak. He'd almost missed it.

He crawled over toward her. "Mariko?" he said softly.

Her eyes were open, looking right at his. Unlike earlier, she was entirely lucid.

"We're done, aren't we?"

He took a breath, almost choking on the smoky, low oxygen air. "No, Mariko…don't say that."

"But it's true." She gasped for her breath. "Thought I'd die in combat," she said, struggling to keep her speech audible.

"Just rest…don't waste your strength." He was dizzy, weak. He could feel his own strength fading, what little was left of it.

He looked down at Fujin. Her eyes were closed again. For a moment, he thought she was dead, but then he saw her chest move, a breath, fitful, difficult. But a breath nevertheless.

He laid back himself, closing his own eyes. The smoke was getting heavier, and he could hear the creaking sounds growing louder. It wouldn't be long now.

Clang!

He sat up quickly, abruptly, making himself woozy in the process. But he'd heard something…something other than the sounds of the fire destroying his ship. He turned, gritting his teeth against the dizziness as he did.

I heard something, I know I did.

But he was beginning to doubt himself, to assume he had hallucinated. Then he heard it again. Another clang, louder even than the first. Then another.

There was something—someone—outside the ship!

He turned over and tried to get up, but the room was doing flip flops, and he fell back down to his knees. He crawled forward, toward the interior of the hull…as close to where he thought the sound was coming from. He grabbed a wrench he'd left on the floor, and he swung it as hard as he could against

wouldn't penetrate the hull, but it made him feel better anyway. "Help…we're in here!"

And he swung the wrench again, as hard as his exhausted arm could manage.

*   *   *

Sara lay on her cot, staring up at the ceiling. Dr. Flynn had wanted to keep her in sickbay, but he'd finally relented and agreed to let her go back to her quarters…as long as she promised to rest and remain off duty. Snow Leopard was a fast attack ship, and her sickbay wasn't much more than a couple beds attached to banks of monitors anyway. Still, Flynn hadn't looked happy when she left, and he'd insisted she try to get as much sleep as possible.

She had tried to renege, and she'd snuck back up to the bridge, intending to quietly go back to work. But Captain Ving had already spoken to the doctor, and he'd sent her back to her cot without so much as an instant of discussion. She'd had a brief urge to argue, but then she meekly obeyed. She was willing to spar with the doctor, but she didn't have it in her to stand up to the captain. And she was tired, despite all the doctor had done. Flynn had given her a massive dose of antibiotics and antivirals, and she felt better. Not great, not even good. But better than she had.

She was still sore though, the body aches she'd had before, but also new ones, the result of being poked and probed in more ways than she'd thought possible before she'd experienced it. Flynn had run every kind of test imaginable on her before he'd reluctantly released her from his custody. His early analysis suggested some variation of influenza, a virulent strain, but ultimately a treatable one. But he was still reviewing the samples.

She put her hand on her forehead. She was hot again…she

fort, but it was getting worse. Rapidly.

Her stomach felt funny too. Flynn had given her a heavy shot of antiemetics, and the queasiness had passed. But now she could feel it coming back. Sara had always prided herself on being tough, and she'd typically worked right through the very occasional minor illness. She was rarely sick, and she'd never had an affliction that a couple extra hours of sleep couldn't heal. But she'd never felt like this before. The symptoms were sporadic. She'd get some rest and feel like she was getting over it… but then a few hours later everything would flare up again, worse than it had been before.

She was just thinking about going back down to sickbay and seeing if Flynn would give her another shot for her stomach when the com buzzed.

"Yes?" she said, her voice a barely audible croak.

"Sara, it's Chris Flynn…" She was a little out of it, but she still caught the concern in his voice. "…how are you feeling? I'd like you to come down to sickbay right away. Can you make it down yourself, or should I bring the gurney up there?"

He really sounds concerned. My tests?

"I can make it down. Be right there."

She tried to sit up, and she realized how weak she was. She pulled herself upright and paused, resting for a few seconds before throwing her legs over the side of the bed. She'd told Flynn she could make it down to sickbay, but now she was wondering.

She stood up, stumbling a bit as she did. She was dizzy, the room spinning around her as she reached out and put her hand on the wall, trying to get her balance. She stood still for a moment, breathing deeply. The dizziness subsided, at least somewhat. She was still nauseous, but it was under control for the moment.

She stepped forward, slowly, carefully, waving her hand in front of the scanner, opening the door. Then out into the corridor. The narrow hallway helped her, and she extended her

The ladder's going to suck…

She realized she was in worse shape than she'd thought lying in her bed a few minutes before. Worse even than before she'd gone to sickbay. But she'd be damned if she was going to make a spectacle of herself, calling for a gurney and being carried down to sickbay like an invalid.

No fucking way…

*   *   *

"There it was again!" Max Harmon was pointing at the wreckage of the fighter. The twisted vessel was half off the launch track, laying almost on its side. He was covered from head to toe in a protective suit—otherwise he wouldn't have survived for more than a few seconds where he was standing— and the sound was faint, distant to his covered ears. But he was sure he'd heard it.

"Are you sure, Captain?" Santiago replied over the com. "It's easy to hear what you want to hear, sir."

"Yes, I'm sure." Harmon knew Santiago wanted to call off the rescue efforts. She'd been ready to give the order fifteen minutes ago. Even Admiral Compton agreed. The fires were still out of control, worse than before even, and they were threatening to move past the bay. The firefighting crews had struggled to cut off the sources of oxygen to the blaze, but there were just too many conduits…hundreds of pipes and hoses pumping life support throughout Midway's guts. Harmon knew they didn't have long. They had to blow the outer doors and use the vacuum of space to extinguish the fires…or the flames would put all of Midway at grave risk. But he'd begged Compton for a few more minutes, hoping beyond hope that Fujin was still alive somewhere in the hellish bay. And the commander who'd led the fleet from the brink of total destruction, who'd made the

minutes…and that had been five minutes ago.

"Captain, the admiral's orders…"

"When Admiral Compton is on the com commanding us to stop, that is when we'll stop. And not a second sooner." Harmon knew that call was coming, any minute. And he was starting to doubt himself. Was he really hearing what he wanted to hear? Was it all in his head?

Then he heard it again, louder, clearer. And so did Santiago.

"I need the plasma torch up here," she yelled to her crew. "Now!"

Two of her people came running up a few seconds later, carrying the cumbersome device.

"Cut open this section of hull." She pointed right where she though the sound had come from. "There."

The crew moved the torch into position, and then they activated it. A shower of sparks flew all around as the plasma bit dug into the hull of the fighter. It took perhaps a minute to get through, and then there was a loud hissing sound. There had been oxygen inside the ship, some at least, and the fire had sucked it all out the instant the torch cut through the plating.

"Faster," Harmon said, hoping as he did that anyone alive inside the fighter had some oxygen left in a tank.

"Yes," Santiago said, "Increase to full power. We're out of time, boys."

She stood next to Harmon and watched as the torch cut an opening in the hull, one big enough for a man to get through. As soon as they pulled back, he lunged forward, ducking down to crawl inside. There was no time. If Mariko was in there without a tank, she'd been without air for almost three minutes.

"No!" Santiago yelled. "It's too dangerous, Captain…let me…" But before she could even reach out and grab Harmon, he'd crawled through the opening. His leg touched a spot that was still half molten, and he felt the searing pain as it burned through his suit and into his leg. But he ignored it. Only one thing mattered.

see. There was someone on the ground, face down right next to him, a wrench lying on the floor, clearly dead. He stepped forward, but his leg gave out, and he crashed down to the deck. He could ignore the pain, at least for a while, but the injury was real.

He saw shadowy images ahead of him, on the floor. More people…

He moved forward. If he couldn't walk, he'd crawl. And as he got closer he could feel something. Recognition. Mariko!

She was lying motionless, next to the rest of her comrades. He crawled to her, and as he did he heard Santiago's voice on the com calling for backup.

"I need emergency med teams here, now!"

Harmon stared down at Mariko, and he felt an instant of elation…followed by despair. She was a few centimeters away, right in front of him. But she wasn't breathing…

He felt a wave of panic, and then his discipline clamped down. He leaned forward, moving toward her. But then he felt something. Hands. On his shoulder, pulling him back, off to the side.

It was Krems, the medic. And he was hunched down over her, his hands moving frantically over her still form.

Harmon stayed where he was, silent, his eyes fixed on Fujin. No, he thought. Please…no.

*   *   *

Compton leaned back in his chair. He was tired. More fatigued than he'd ever felt in his entire long life. The battle was over, at least for now. But his flagship was in trouble. The damage was extensive, and both landing bays were closed. He'd given orders for Saratoga and the other battleships to take Midway's fighters, what few of them were returning, at least. It would be days before alpha bay was operative again. And beta

perate action that would eradicate the fires, but also one that would eliminate all possibility of repairing the bay outside an Alliance space dock, a facility that didn't exist this side of the Barrier. But it was the only way to save the ship. If the fires spread, if they got past the line of damage control crews struggling to hold them back, they would reach the reactors. And that would be the end of Midway.

He'd given the orders to blow the doors already...and just as quickly rescinded them. Mariko Fujin was down there, and Max Harmon had begged him for more time to try and rescue her. The admiral inside had called on him to refuse the request, to put the safety of the ship over the miniscule chance that anyone had survived down there. But the part of him that made him the man he was intervened, and he had given a few more moments, sustained hope for just a bit longer. It wasn't rational in terms of weighing risks and rewards...it wasn't the right thing to do tactically. But Harmon was like a son to him...and Mariko was the young captain's lover. And, he had to admit, he was quite fond of the diminutive pilot himself.

He knew it wasn't fair, that he was allowing his personal feelings to guide his actions. If it had been another member of the crew down there, some officer who was just a name on a roster, the doors would have been blown already. Compton had been a creature of duty his entire life, one who had sacrificed personal desires to needs of the service. But he was old now, and feeling every year of his age. He'd lost almost everyone and everything that had truly mattered to him, and he found himself clinging to what little he had left. He hadn't really expected another ten or fifteen minutes to make a difference in the search for survivors in the bay...but he simply hadn't been able to deny Harmon... or give up his own tenuous hopes that Mariko was still alive.

His compassion had paid off. Harmon and the damage control team had made good use of the extra time. They'd found Fujin...and her pilot. Neither of them had been breathing when the team got to them, but the medics managed to revive them

them that, a rare victory for emotion over rationality. But now the admiral was back in control.

"Blow the outer doors on my command."

"All ready, sir." Jack Cortez sat at his workstation, his finger poised over a flashing red button. "Waiting for your orders, sir."

Compton took a breath. "Do it," he said.

Cortez depressed his finger…and Midway shook hard.

"Report," Compton snapped.

"Coming sir." There was a delay, perhaps half a minute. Then Cortez spun around toward Compton and said, "Damage control team reports all fires extinguished, sir."

Compton nodded. "Acknowledged." His verbal reaction was controlled, unemotional, but inside he felt a wave of relief. The rest of Midway's damage was bad, but with the fires out the ship was in no immediate danger. And the reactors and engines were still functional. "Give my congratulations to the teams down there."

His thoughts flashed back to Max…and Mariko. He almost commed sickbay for an update on the pilot's condition, but he knew they wouldn't know anything. And as fond as he was of Mariko, he had twenty thousand people depending on him. He'd just have to trust his medical staff. And he knew Max Harmon would keep an eye on her…that he wouldn't leave her side.

"Okay, Jack," he said, his relief spilling out as a burst of informality. "Let's get the rest of the fleet lined up and ready to transit." About half the ships had already moved through the warp gate…and now it was past time to get the rest moving. He didn't dare to hope they'd seen the last of the enemy, and every moment he lost only meant the next fight would come that much sooner.

"Transmitting orders now, sir." A pause. "Sir, Leviathan four reports no thrust." Another hesitation, then: "No active weapons systems either."

Compton just nodded. He wasn't surprised. Leviathan four had been attacked from two sides, by half a dozen ships.

claimed their second kill.

"Send self-destruct order to Leviathan four, Commander. Destruct to occur in ten minutes." That would be enough time to ensure none of his ships were close enough to take any damage. The robot ships obeyed any command he gave them, even one to shut down their magnetic bottles, setting off a chain reaction of annihilation. And a Leviathan had a lot of antimatter in its stores.

"Understood, sir. Ten minutes."

Compton just looked at the main display, contemplating the unlikely series of events that had him mourning the loss of a First Imperium battleship.

Chapter Eight

AS Midway
X78 System
The Fleet: 98 ships (+6 Leviathans), 23761 crew

Max Harmon stood against the wall of Midway's sickbay, looking out at the almost-frantic action and feeling as useless as he ever had in his life. He'd found Mariko, gotten her out of the bay just before Admiral Compton had ordered it blown, but she'd been dead by the time he got there…or at least not breathing. The medic had managed to revive her, restore respiration and get her stabilized enough to move to sickbay, but Harmon knew she faced a difficult road. The medic had worn a grave expression on his face as they rushed her to the med center, and the chief surgeon's wasn't much better when he examined her. For all the effort, the danger, the pleading with Compton for more time, there was a good chance she would die anyway… right in front of his eyes.

Midway's medical staff was perhaps the best on any human ship anywhere. Mostly veterans of the Third Frontier War and the Rebellions, over the past eighteen months they'd experienced an intensity of combat beyond anything that had come before. The fleet had suffered grievous losses, more than half

had performed wonders keeping Midway's stricken spacers alive, working with an ever-dwindling stockpile of supplies. There was no place better for Mariko to be right now…but that didn't mean she would make it.

Harmon stared across the room at the cluster of white-clad medical staff gathered around the diminutive pilot. There was a similar cluster a few meters away, where Grant Wainwright lay unconscious. The two were the only survivors from the bay. Their shipmates were dead. The rescue team had tried desperately to revive them, but it had been too late. They hadn't responded at all. And for all the herculean efforts of Maria Santiago and her people, the teams hadn't found anyone else still alive. They hadn't found most of the bay crews at all…their bodies had been incinerated in the fires.

Harmon knew better than to push his way forward and interfere with the doctors. Mariko needed them now…and they needed to be left alone to do their jobs. He ached to rush forward, to take her hand and look down at her face. And he knew his rank and standing would prevent the med team from chasing him away. But he was disciplined enough to realize that would hurt her chances and not help them. So he stayed where he was, bolted to his spot. If Admiral Compton needed him, he knew where to find him. And otherwise, he had no intention of leaving sickbay. Not until he knew.

*   *   *

Compton felt the fatigue, like a wave coming over him. He'd always been able to get by on just a few hours of sleep, but it had been days since he'd had even that. But it was more than just physical exhaustion. Deep inside, he could feel the strength that drove him waning, the indomitable will that had caused him to push forward when everyone else was ready to give up slip-

He almost rested his head in his hand, but he caught himself in time. He didn't allow himself displays of weakness, not in public at least. That was a luxury he could not afford. Terrance Compton knew one thing for sure. His people had been through hell, multiple times over. They had seen friends and comrades die…they had faced grievous danger. And still they had pressed on through all of it. Compton understood his role in that, the image of the invincible, indestructible commander, and the part it played in extracting that last bit of effort and fortitude from the twenty thousand survivors manning the 98 remaining ships. The warriors of the fleet looked to him, they drew strength from him. And he had done all he could to be what they needed. However much a fiction his persona as the unbeatable commander truly was. Whatever it did to him, whatever cost he personally paid.

But he was exhausted too, and scared just like his people. He had no version of himself to rely upon, no one to share his burdens, at least no one who could understand what the top command did to a man. Sophie Barcomme had become his lover, and a good friend too, but she was a scientist, not a warrior. She gave him warmth and comfort, and whatever brief escapes he'd enjoyed over the past few months, but not true understanding. She could comprehend pain and fear, but she could never fully understand what it felt like to give the orders that sent thousands to their deaths.

Max Compton was the closest confidante he had, but even his trusted protégé, blooded combat officer that he was, couldn't fully relate to Compton's situation. Harmon was a brilliant officer, highly skilled and courageous to a fault, but he'd always served under Compton, following orders. He couldn't know how much it cost to give some of those commands.

Compton missed his oldest friend, now more than ever. Augustus Garret was a man who could understand what Compton was feeling, perhaps the only person who truly could. But Garret was on the other side of the Barrier, and Compton knew

radeship was over…gone for both of them. Compton hoped that the fleet's sacrifice had bought their families and friends back home the peace they sorely needed, but his best wishes were all he could offer Garret. Just as he suspected Augustus was perhaps the only one back home harboring suspicions that the fleet had somehow managed to survive, that Compton had wiggled his way out of the First Imperium trap.

He'd begun to confide a bit more in Admiral West. Erika West was stone cold, as strong and capable an officer as he'd ever known…and he included Garret and himself at her age in that estimation. But though he was perhaps more candid with her than he was with anyone else, he kept his wall up with her as well. She was his junior, and as tough as she was, she deserved some of the same support the others demanded from him. One day she might be in his shoes, but until then he protected her from the heaviest of the burdens.

Compton considered Erika West his replacement should he fall, though he feared she might face some resistance in pressing her claim. Since the mutiny that had almost ended the fleet's escape in a nightmare of self-destruction, virtually every man and woman aboard the 98 ships looked up to Compton with a sort of dumbstruck reverence. He'd saved them from certain death…three times. He'd exercised wisdom over anger, reinstating and forgiving almost all of the mutineers. And he was unbreakable, or at least he appeared to be.

Erika West was well-regarded too, though she was certainly considered less likable than her commanding officer. Compton had a reputation for being approachable. He played poker with his officers—very well—and he was considered very charming by most of those who knew him. Erika West was hard as nails, as Compton was, but unlike her commanding officer, she had no off switch. She gave all she had for her people, but she was demanding, unforgiving. Those who had served under her had experienced both her courage…and her brutal discipline. She was respected deeply…but she wasn't widely liked. Still, Comp-

Caliphate ships. West had been an easy target during the Third Frontier War, and the enemy propagandists had worked overtime turning her into the heartless villain her cold, hard-driving demeanor seemed to support. Many of the CAC and Caliphate spacers still blamed West for terrible atrocities from the war years, most of which had been the inventions of the intelligence agencies of their respective powers.

Compton knew there was a simple solution to the problem…don't get himself killed. But that was easier said than done. James Horace was down in sickbay, fighting for his life. Compton's flag captain had been in Midway's control center when it took a direct hit. The flag bridge was no better protected than the main bridge…it had been fortune alone that had dictated that Horace lay in the critical care unit while Compton sat in his chair, without a scratch, still directing the fleet. But there was more than chance on Compton's mind, more than the possibility of some errant First Imperium laser blast finally finding him. He was planning something desperate, dangerous. A forlorn hope, a wild gamble by part of the fleet, to mislead the enemy…and give the rest of his people a chance to make a run for Shangri la. And he intended to lead it himself.

He'd been thinking about it for several weeks now, but the last battle had been the final straw, and now he'd decided. There was no choice. For two months the fleet had run, fleeing from the pursuing enemy. But Compton realized now that they weren't going to escape, not without a new plan, something daring and unexpected. He knew he couldn't continue on to Shangri la, not with enemy forces on his heels. Whatever Almeerhan and his people had left there for the humans, it wasn't likely to instantly transform the fleet into a force that could defeat everything the Regent could throw at them. Leading the enemy to the hidden cache would be worse than simply abandoning the search, turning off into deep space fleeing blindly into the unknown.

No, there was no choice. He had to try to mislead the enemy, buy time for the others to reach Shangri la. But Compton knew

he could to ensure that Erika West succeeded him if he was killed. She was the only one who could fill his shoes…and give the people of the fleet a chance.

"Commander Cortez," he said, getting up as he did. "I'll be in my office. Get Admiral West on my com and send it to me in there."

"Yes, Admiral." Cortez' voice was firm, crisp. He'd been at his post for eighteen hours, and in that time Midway had gone from heavy combat to desperate damage control. His eyes were deep in their sockets, and his voice was raw, hoarse. But he was still at his post, and still giving one hundred percent.

Compton walked to the edge of the flag bridge, waving his hand in front of the scanning plate next to the door to his office. Then he walked inside, and the hatch closed behind him.

Time to convince Erika West…

He knew she would want to lead the rearguard—and he knew he should let her, that it made more sense than the fleet's commander racing off on a near-suicide mission. But there were some things a man simply had to do. Some things he couldn't' delegate to another. And Compton had made up his mind.

*   *   *

Snow Leopard's sickbay was bathed in light, a series of panels on the ceiling illuminating the entire tiny space. The infirmary was bright white, usually pristine, orderly. But now it was a mess, with patients and boxes of supplies everywhere, and Chris Flynn had to pick his way around the clutter to attend to those under his care. Snow Leopard's sole physician wore a mask, as did the rest of his staff. Flynn knew very little about the mysterious disease that was ripping its way through the crew, but it was obvious that whatever pathogen was responsible was extremely contagious.

there were fifteen of the ship's crew there now, lying on whatever the overworked medical staff had been able to jury-rig.
There were cots pulled from quarters and piles of padding on
the floor. Flynn had been assigned to emergency service in a
Marine field hospital once back during the Third Frontier War,
and he still had nightmares about the overcrowded facility, of
men and women lying out on the cold ground, dying before they
got treatment. Snow Leopard wasn't to that point yet, but it was
damned close.

Sara was in one of the three beds, a perquisite of both her
rank and the fact that she seemed to be the first one to show
symptoms from the mysterious disease now spreading rapidly
through Snow Leopard's crew. She'd deteriorated rapidly in the
day and a half since she'd staggered back down to the infirmary,
and she was fading in and out of consciousness, soaked in sweat
from the raging fever that defied all Flynn's efforts to combat it.

Flynn had called her back to sickbay when he'd realized her
case wasn't isolated, that a full scale epidemic was hitting Snow
Leopard's crew. And things had only gotten worse since then.

Sara had been the first, but now half the crew was complain-
ing of nausea and dizziness. Flynn had started by telling them
to come down to sickbay for an exam, but now he was urging
them to stay at their posts, at least while they were still able. He
didn't have room, and he didn't have the staff to handle more
patients, even after he'd drafted the ship's entire staff of stew-
ards as makeshift medical aides. Worst of all, he had no idea
how to treat whatever illness was ravaging Snow Leopard's crew.

That wasn't for lack of effort. Once he realized he was facing a full scale epidemic, he leapt into action. He checked out
everything he could. The food shipments, the air recyclers,
the water purifiers…anything that could spread a disease. But
everything checked out. That left only one thing he could think
of. And that terrified him.

He was on the com to the bridge, waiting for Ving to come
on. He had to tell the captain what he suspected.

tired.

"Yes, sir. I've inspected everything that could spread contamination through the ship, and it all checks out." He paused, as if verbalizing what he was thinking would make it so. "Captain, I think we need to look at that mysterious weapon, the small projectiles the enemy fired at us." Another pause. "I'm concerned they might be a delivery system for a biological weapon."

There was a long silence. Then Ving said, "My God, I didn't even think of that."

Flynn could hear the self-recrimination in the captain's voice, the blame he was already assuming for overlooking a deadly threat to his ship.

"Sir...none of us thought of that. I still have no evidence, but I have no other ideas. I need whatever we have left from the investigation."

"We don't have much, Doc...just a few trace components. The projectiles disintegrated on impact."

"Which is probably because they're designed to spread the pathogens they contain." He knew he was working on pure speculation. But somehow he knew he was right too."

"I'm sending you what we have in the lab, Doc. Like I said, it's not much." Ving hesitated. "What else can I do for you?"

"Nothing else, Captain. Not yet." He paused. "Actually, sir, if the patients continue to deteriorate, I'm going to need more med pods. We've only got two on Snow Leopard. It could come down to life and death decisions if we don't get more."

"I'll take care of it, Doc. I'll go right to Admiral Compton. I'm overdue to give him a status report anyway."

"Thank you, sir. I'll let you know what I find from the projectile fragments. Flynn out."

He turned and looked toward the work surface and the bank of cabinets that formed Snow Leopard's tiny medical lab. It was covered with junk...blankets, vomit bags, crates of medical refuse. The sickbay was so overloaded, so utterly jammed full, his people were piling things anywhere they could.

down, and checking them out has just become priority fucking one."

He stood for a second and watched as his people ran over and started cleared the table. Then he glanced down at the chronometer. He'd have the samples in another minute or two, and he intended to get started right away. If there was an answer, that's where he'd find it. Or at least a first step on the road to a treatment. He wasn't sure what to expect, but he knew Sara and a few of the others were in bad shape. He still had some options, some tools to keep them alive a little longer. He was going to have to put Sara in one of the med pods soon…and she wouldn't be the last to need one.

The captain's going right to the admiral. Hopefully we'll get a shipment before it becomes a problem…

He took a deep breath and put his hand out on the wall and leaned over. He was tired…exhausted. He'd already taken enough stims that he'd have scolded a patient for doing the same. But he knew he needed another. He had to be as sharp-minded as possible. The lives of everyone aboard Snow Leopard might very well depend on his efforts over the next few hours.

He walked over toward the drug cabinet, opening the small door and grabbing the bottle of stims. He opened it and dropped one in his palm. Then he paused for a few seconds and poured out a second pill. He popped them in his mouth and grabbed a small cup, filling it from the water dispenser and swallowing a gulp.

Now it was time. Time to find the source of this disease. But first he walked out of sickbay and down the hall, his pace accelerating as he went. He ducked into the small bathroom there and closed the door behind him. Then he doubled over and emptied his stomach, thinking all the while, 'what a waste of two good stims…"

*   *   *

"Erika, this isn't a debate. It's an order." Compton sat behind his desk, rubbing his temples as he spoke with his chosen, but informal, second in command. He'd known West would put up a fight when he told her what he had in mind, and she hadn't disappointed. West was a tough as nails warrior, but she had proven to be as susceptible as everyone else in the fleet to the cult of worship, at least where Compton was concerned. She'd made it clear over the last few minutes that she considered Compton putting himself at greater risk than necessary to be unthinkable. She'd argued that she should lead the rearguard while he took the rest of the fleet to Shangri la, and she'd come close to insubordination in bulldozing right through his attempts to end the discussion.

"Admiral…"

"No, Erika." Compton's voice was firm, loud. He injected a touch of anger, though he felt none. But he didn't have all day to argue with her. "The decision is made. So your choice is simple. Will you follow my orders? Or will you mutiny?" He immediately felt bad for his choice of words. West had argued hard, but he didn't believe for a second she would ever be disloyal.

"Yes, sir," she said, her voice soft, clipped.

Compton sighed softly. West had a reputation for being made of plasti-steel. Many, including, but hardly limited to, her detractors, claimed she'd been born without any human emotion save focused rage. But Compton knew her better than most, and he understood her complex psyche. And he realized how badly he had hurt her feelings with his last remarks.

"I'm sorry, Erika. I know you would never challenge me… and I realize your arguments were only intended to protect me. But I have to do this. It's just that simple, and no debate is going to change that. So let's just say you've expressed your concerns and been overruled. So stop trying to convince me not to do this…and help me make sure it's a success."

"Yes, sir." She sounded a bit less hurt, but there was a hint of defeat in her words. It was clear she didn't like this idea. Not

He knew how lucky he was to have West under his command. He'd gotten most of the credit for the fleet's survival, but he would never forget that Erika West had saved his ass during the mutiny. Her iron will had held things together until he'd managed to return from an ill-advised trip down to a First Imperium world, an indulgence of his curiosity that had almost ended in disaster. He'd thanked her several times, both publicly and in private, but he knew most of the fleet disregarded her role. He also realized she didn't care, that she wasn't one to worry about what others thought. And that was the problem now. He didn't need her to do anything for his rearguard, he could handle that…but he damned sure had to make sure that the rest of the fleet followed her and took her orders as if they were his.

"This is not a suicide mission, Erika. I have every intention of returning. But if we don't shake this pursuit, all we'll manage to do is lead the Regent's forces right to Shangri la." He paused. "You'll just have to trust my tactical judgment. But we also need to keep the fleet together, and that means you need to fill my shoes."

"Sir…" He'd rarely heard Erika West speechless, but now her voice trailed off to nothing.

"You can do it, Erika. There is no one I trust more." The statement was nothing but the absolute truth, but he felt like he was manipulating her nevertheless. And, to an extent, he was. As he did with everyone.

"I'm not sure some fleet elements will be happy taking my orders, sir."

"No, Erika, they probably won't be. But as long as they know I'm coming back…or at least until they've given up that I will, I think they'll be manageable." He paused. In truth, he had no idea if he'd be coming back. He intended to…but he knew being the rearguard and leading the enemy away from the fleet was a dangerous game. The poker player inside him put the odds right at fifty-fifty. "So maybe this is a good opportunity for me to publicly designate you as my second in command and get

He could hear the discomfort in her voice. Erika West was a skilled and courageous naval commander, but there wasn't a shred of diplomat in her. Her idea of negotiation was charging a heavy laser cannon and pointing it at anyone giving her a hard time. Maybe this will give her some practice, a chance to get used to dealing with people. Just in case she really has to replace me one day…

"You'll do fine, Erika." He paused. "And I'll be back. We're just going to take the Regent's ships for a little joy ride…and confuse the hell out of them. Then we'll slip away and make our way back to Shangri la." He tried to sound as convincing as possible, though he knew West was an experienced enough admiral to come to her own conclusions…and she was likely to reach the same odds he had. A coin toss.

"Yes, sir," she said, still sounding unhappy, but accepting his decision. "When do you want to do this?"

"Immediately, Erika. I'm sending you a fleet breakdown, including the ships I will take with me and those you will lead to Shangri la." He'd considered asking for volunteers for the rear guard, but the process would be too cumbersome, too unwieldy. And splitting up ship crews wasn't going to do anything to improve combat effectiveness. "I want you to get them out of the system immediately. You're leaving within the hour. You'll be buttoning up everybody in the tanks and blasting out of here at full. You need to be gone before the enemy gets here… assuming they don't have stealth ships in the system already." The fleet had transited to X80 immediately after the last battle and then to X82. There was a good chance they were ahead of the enemy, but Compton knew better than to make any cocky assumptions.

The new system was the perfect choice for his plan. There were no less than six warp gates, and that gave him multiple options for leading the enemy astray. His strategy was simple. He would wait close to one of the warp gates…and when the enemy forces entered the system and detected them, he would

And that would give West and the others time to put some distance behind them…and hopefully find Shangri la.

"There's nothing I can do to convince you to let me do this with Saratoga, is there?" West's voice was earnest, almost pleading.

"No," Compton said. "I appreciate the sentiment, Erika, but I just have to do this." He almost continued, but he kept the last part of his thought to himself.

A man can only send so many people to face death before he has to go himself…

Chapter Nine

AS Cornwall
X72 System
The Fleet: 98 ships (+6 Leviathans), 23758 crew

"Power down the reactor. Minimal output…only life support and scanning systems active." Skarn's voice was edgy, her
nerves on display. Cornwall had just come through the warp
gate, back into system X72. This was where they had branched
off from the fleet…and traveled to Y17, only to find the race
they'd come to find long extinct. Now they were back where
they had started, but the fleet was long gone. She hoped that
meant the enemy had moved on as well, but she wasn't taking
any chances. Fast attack ships had strong stealth capability, as
long as they cut power and acted like a hole in space.

"Reactor at 10%, Captain. All systems on minimal except
scanning and life support." Inkerman sounded as nervous as
the captain. Cornwall's crew had faced the unknown, but now
they were all painfully aware they were behind enemy lines.
There had been First Imperium forces in this system when they
left. The fleet had been fighting here when Cornwall slipped
through the warp gate to Y1, hoping no enemy vessels picked

Cornwall would be caught alone, far from support. But they'd made their escape clean, and the trip to and from Y17 had been clear sailing. But she knew that luck couldn't last. They were chasing after the fleet, along the same vector as the enemy pursuers. It would take a lot of luck for them to get back. And all the skill she could muster.

"I want scanners on full. We know the fleet was in this system and they had a fight here. The enemy might have moved on by now, but this is probably along their line of communications, which means we could run into nasties just about anywhere."

"Scanners on full, Captain. No contacts."

"Very well, Lieutenant. Maintain position and silent running for thirty minutes. Then, if all is clear, we will make for the X74 warp gate….and the way home." Or what passes for home…

"Yes, Captain. Maintaining reactor status, and continuing deep scans." Inkerman leaned over his workstation, typing for a few seconds. "Navigational instructions ready for X74 gate approach. Locking into the navcom."

Skarn allowed herself a passing smile. She was still nervous. Actually, calling it nervous was a bit of spin. She was scared shitless. But she was also starting to feel like a real captain, and she'd be damned if her people weren't turning into a real crew. Maybe they'd make it back after all.

She liked the thought, but she wasn't sure she believed it. Still, she knew one thing. They were going to try like hell.

*   *   *

Sasha sat in her quarters, her fingers moving rapidly over her workstation's keyboard. It took a considerable effort to reprogram the ship's com systems, to allow her to send the required messages. She knew the fleet had passed through X72, and that the First Imperium forces had engaged them here. And now

controlled her actions utterly now. She didn't know for certain there were First Imperium vessels in X72, but she knew standard procedure called for a squadron of stealth vessels to maintain position where a fleet had passed through. Normally, the undetectable scouts would simply report the presence of any enemy force, but since Cornwall was only a single attack ship, it was possible the pickets would engage and destroy her. And she had to make sure that didn't happen. Cornwall had to get safely back to the fleet. It was essential to the plan.

She was typing at least ten times as rapidly as she'd been able to before, another strange new ability. It was an alien presence controlling her actions, but her own memories were assisting in the effort. It was a strange amalgam, and she felt herself taking actions she couldn't stop.

The part of her mind that made her Sasha Debornan was trapped, imprisoned. She tried to escape, to regain control of her body, her actions, but all her efforts were in vain. She could think, and she was aware of what was happening, but she couldn't communicate, couldn't so much as move her own finger.

She'd felt strange since shortly after she'd gotten back from the planet, but it had been several days before she noticed anything serious. She'd had some aches and pains, and an odd feeling, a tingling in various areas of her body. She felt bloated, and then the pain worsened. Then, suddenly, she was doing things she couldn't control. She'd watched helplessly as her hands typed access codes, reprogrammed the ship's computer. She was doing things she'd never been able to do, using skills she hadn't possessed before.

There was something inside her, controlling her, while she remained imprisoned, watching helplessly. Watching herself sabotage ship's functions. Watching herself murder Tony Vaccilli. And now she was sending out secret messages to First Imperium vessels. She struggled, tried with everything she had to focus, to regain control. But there was no use. She was

the ship's batteries to do it. She couldn't understand the programming she'd just done, but somehow she knew the purpose. Nothing she was doing would show up on any ship's display. Not even Cornwall's AI would be aware of her actions. She panicked for a moment, concerned she was calling to First Imperium ships, giving them Cornwall's location and bidding them to attack. But no, that wasn't right. She was warding them off, instructing them not to attack. She didn't know how she knew that, and she had no idea why whatever force was controlling her was doing it.

She felt a wave of frustration and she put everything she had into trying again to regain control of her body. But there was nothing. She was trapped, cut off.

Okay, she thought, losing it isn't going to help anything. Think…you know what your body is doing. Why? What is happening?

As her mind calmed, she could feel something inside her, all over her body. Something foreign, alien. Moving through her blood, through her flesh and organs.

Nanobots. Suddenly, she knew. She understood. On the planet. They'd penetrated her suit…the itching she'd felt. And then they multiplied, replicating, spreading through her body. She could feel them now, not individually, but billions of them moving. They were everywhere, in her brain, her spinal cord. Controlling her.

And there was nothing she could do but watch.

*   *   *

Don Rames walked down the corridor, nodding to several shipmates as they passed by. He knew who they were, but the part of him that cared was submerged, restrained. Soon it would be gone entirely. The presence that controlled his body was old.

remnants, and they had been on the planet for millennia.

They were servants of the Regent, and they'd been sent to destroy the bipeds on the planet. They had entered their bodies, replicated, taken control, just as they were doing now. The bipeds fought, the nanos controlling them, driving them into endless battle...until none remained. Then, they deactivated. Trillions of the tiny devices then powered down and ceased to function, as the bipeds had before them. All but the original ones, the nanobots of the Regent's manufacture, the ones that had landed on the planet and infected the first of the doomed race. They survived, for endless untold ages they endured, waiting, watching for new enemies. And then the new bipeds came.

The tiny robots responded to their ancient programming. The new biologics wore protective suits, but the nanos passed through, drilling into the tight web of the fabric and sealing it shut again behind them. Then they entered the creatures, slipped in through pours, through bodily orifices, spreading, replicating, using the host's energy and food to fuel their multiplication.

The bipeds left the planet, returned to their spaceship...and the nanos came with them. They served their ancient function, took control, prepared to destroy the spaceship to eliminate the bipeds aboard. The nanos existed to serve the Regent. They had no directive for self-preservation. But then they accessed the computer systems serving the biologics. They learned they were en route to a fleet, one carrying thousands of the biped creatures.

The biologics had fought with the forces of the Regent. They were fleeing even now. The nanos responded to ancient programming...to serve the Regent. There was a higher priority than eliminating a single vessel. They must destroy the new biologics.

But few of the nanos had survived the endless eons, and there were only enough to control the two bipeds. They could replicate more given time, but that would take years, as it had on the planet...and the struggle was already underway. So they

There was one of the biologics, a leader. They followed him, fought at his command. He had saved them many times. He was the primary cause of the Regent's failure. His tactics were superior, they frustrated the Regent and the Command Units of the imperial fleet.

The nanos knew. In that moment they knew what they had to do. They had to return to the human fleet...and when they got there they had but a single purpose. They would kill the biped leader. They would kill Admiral Terrance Compton.

Chapter Ten

From the Personal Log of Terrance Compton

What is a suicide mission? Some are obvious, for example a pilot at the controls of a critically-damaged fighter, smashing into an enemy ship in a final act of defiance. But when does daring, calculated risk-taking, become something else, something darker, more hopeless.

There is no choice, not really. I've reviewed the AI's projections and run my own. I've put fifty years of experience at war in space to work, trying to imagine a way, any other way. But there is none. The fleet will never reach Shangri la, not unless I can find a way to buy a respite from the relentless pursuit.

And I have. I will detach a rearguard, a small force of ships that will wait behind when the rest of the fleet transits, until the enemy catches us. Then this forlorn hope will transit—through a different warp gate—and hopefully lead the enemy fleet off in a direction away from the main fleet.

It is a sound plan, one that has a good chance of gaining the fleet the time to reach Shangri la. But is it a suicide mission? Surely I didn't conceive it that way. My plans for the rearguard include an eventual return to the course for Shangri la...but is this realistic? Or simply something I cooked up to relieve myself of the burden of ordering men and women on a suicide mission? I truly don't know anymore. But whatever the fate of the rearguard, I will be with it.

fleet. I can hear the voices, my old instructors at the Academy, Augustus, all of them, screaming in my head. But none of it matters. There are decisions made form strategy, from duty. And then there are just things a man must do. I have sent thousands to their deaths...and worst of all, perhaps, they have gone willingly, faithfully executing the orders I gave them. I cannot sit in my chair any longer and send thousands more into such peril, not unless I go with them.

They will all resist...Sophie, Max, Erika West. They will argue...and they will insist on coming with me. But they are all staying behind. I have tried to make decisions as fairly as possible, to see to the needs of all the people of the fleet. But this is pure commander's prerogative. I will go into this danger, perhaps to my death. But when I do, I will know that those few I love are safe, or at least safer. And I make no apologies. I have served with every bit of strength I have, as I will until the enemy finally destroys me. But this I do for me...

AS Midway
X78 System
The Fleet: 98 ships (+6 Leviathans), 23758 crew

"I don't understand, sir." Max Harmon was standing in the corridor staring back at the admiral. "If you're going into a fight, I should be with you. I'll stay on Midway." Harmon had been on his way to the flag bridge when he'd run into Compton in the corridor. He'd been in sickbay when the orders came down to prepare to transfer all the patients to Saratoga. The battle was over, at least for the immediate future, and by all accounts, other than her landing bays, Saratoga wasn't in any better shape than Midway. And without the bays it was going to be a nightmare to load up the wounded.

Harmon had served under Compton for a long time, and he knew the admiral well, as well as anyone in the fleet. He immediately realized something was wrong. And now the admiral had

you to transfer to Saratoga. Admiral West is going to need all the help she can get maintaining control of the fleet. I want you to stay with her until I get back. I need you to stay."

Harmon stared back at Compton. They both knew the admiral's return was an 'if' and not a 'when.' He was silent for a moment. Then he spoke, his voice almost distraught. "But, sir, you can't do this, not without me." Harmon was exhausted, utterly and completely drained. He'd been at Mariko's side for three straight days, without a rest, without even taking time to eat anything. His distress at Compton's plan had given him a brief burst of urgent energy, but now he looked like he was about to collapse.

"I have to do this, Max. You've known me long enough to understand." Compton took a step toward Harmon. "I love you like a son, Max…but I have to do this. And I need you to do as I say." He paused. "Stay with Mariko. Go over to Saratoga with her…and once you've got her settled in, report to Admiral West." Compton stared at his protégé, trying to maintain his calm, to hide how much it hurt to send Harmon away. But he'd made his decision. He might die, several thousand of the fleet's spacers might die with him. But he didn't want Max Harmon to be one of them. He didn't know if Mariko was going to make it, no one did. But if she survived, he wanted Harmon to be there, to have a chance at happiness. And even if the pilot he loved so much died, Harmon was young…and if the refugees managed to find a home at Shangri la, he'd have a long life ahead of him. Compton had seen more death, lost more friends and comrades than Harmon could imagine, and he knew one thing. Life went on for the living.

Harmon just nodded. His face was grim, and the fatigue was even more pronounced in his expression. "Admiral, I don't know what to…"

"Max, I'm not going to crash Midway into an enemy Colossus. The rearguard has a dangerous mission, but not a hopeless one. I'm going to try like hell to get back, to get all the people

of the fleet."

"Yes, sir," Harmon said miserably.

"And I need you to do one other thing for me, Max." Compton's voice was emotional.

"Anything, Admiral."

"I need you to make sure Sophie goes too. She's not going to want to leave any more than you do. But I need her to go. I need to know she's safe, at least as safe as anyone in the fleet can be." His eyes focused on Harmons, pleading with his friend.

"I'll make sure she goes, sir. Whatever it takes." Harmon gasped for a breath, holding back the emotion the best he could. "I don't know what to say, sir. You've been more than a commander…more than a father. I just don't have…" His words trailed off, and he stood there holding Compton's gaze.

"I know, Max," Compton said softly. "I feel the same." He reached out and put his hands on Harmon's shoulder. "Now do as I ask, son. Go." He pushed forward, taking Harmon in his arms, hugging the young officer.

The two embraced for a few seconds. Then Harmon stood there, staring silently at the admiral. Finally, he took a deep breath and nodded. He knew Compton would fight like a demon to bring the rearguard back…and he realized there was a chance…there was always a chance. But there was something else, a feeling, a nagging thought he couldn't banish from his mind.

A voice speaking to him, telling him he would never see his friend Terrence Compton again.

*   *   *

"Get all that stuff packed up. Now!" Hieronymus Cutter was storming around the room, terrorizing the scientists and assistants busy at work gathering the various artifacts and speci-

quiet, shy, socially awkward…a man of almost incalculable intelligence who found it difficult to carry on a conversation with another. But in that year he'd developed breakthroughs that had saved the fleet, he'd boarded an enemy battleship with a pack of Marines…and landed on an ancient First Imperium planet with the same leathernecks. He'd risked his life again and again, and he'd won the respect of the hardest, most grizzled warriors in the fleet. The Marines had accepted him as one of their own. And the new improved Hieronymus Cutter had proven to be a nightmare to the scientists and technicians working under him.

"We don't have time to waste," he roared. "And I want every one of those specimens neatly packed. The future of the fleet depends on this research, so anyone who is careless now will have to answer to me for anything that is broken or lost."

"They're working as quickly as they can, Hieronymus." Ana Zhukov had walked up behind Cutter. "I sometimes wish the old Hieronymus could see you now." She smiled, at least as much as the current situation allowed. She knew Cutter was worried about Admiral Compton. She was too. Most of the fleet looked up to him, but they saw him as something distant, great. Ana and Hieronymus had worked closely with him, and they'd become part of his small, trusted inner circle. Ana had come to know the real Terrence Compton. And she was deathly afraid he wasn't coming back, that he'd committed himself to a suicidal tactic to buy the fleet a chance at escape.

"As quickly as they can isn't fast enough, Ana. We're almost out of time…and we need to get this stuff off Midway. All of it."

"I know, Hieronymus, but terrorizing everyone isn't going to help. They're not Marines, you can't treat them like they are. They can't handle it."

Cutter nodded. "You may be right, Ana. But if we're going to survive, they're going to have to handle it, aren't they?"

"Maybe…but please, Hieronymus, try to go a little easier on them. They know how important this is. They will get it done."

challenge, become a key contributor to the fleet's survival. But he'd changed even more dramatically since he'd encountered Almeerhan. Her friend's time with the preserved essence of the ancient alien had affected him deeply. He'd been enormously demanding since he'd returned from X48 II, driven to such an extent she feared for his very sanity. He hardly slept, hardly ate…and he'd become merciless on those who worked for him, demanding the same superhuman commitment from them all. Perhaps he'd seen too much, knew too clearly the extent of what the fleet faced.

"Easier?" He stared at her with the same intensity he did everyone else. "We're not at some university, working on a paper for a room full of gasbags to debate between cocktail parties. This is life and death, Ana. For all of us."

The two had always shared a close relationship. Ana thought of Cutter as a big brother, and he'd shown on more than one occasion that he reciprocated the feelings. But now he'd turned into some kind of ruthless automaton, without even a shred of detectable emotion. She wondered if it was just the stress, the knowledge he possessed. Of if his experiences on X48 II had changed him in some fundamental way.

"Hieronymus, I understand. But you are the most intelligent—the most logical—person I've ever known. What will you serve if you drive everyone into the ground? They're not like you…they can only handle so much. You may push them as hard as you can, but you'll get less productivity from them, not more."

Cutter looked like he was going to snap back with a quick response, but instead he just looked back at her…and his gaze softened. "He's going off with a few ships, Ana. He's going to try and get everything the Regent is throwing at us to follow him." He paused. "He's going off to die. And I can't go with him."

Ana felt a wave of surprise. She hadn't seen Cutter be… human…in months now, and here he was, baring his thoughts

"Hieronymus, Terrance Compton knows what he is doing. He is taking a terrible risk, yes. But he's escaped from tight spots before. Don't underestimate him."

"He's leaving everyone behind. Everyone he cares about. Max, Sophie Barcomme. Me, you."

She reached out and took his hand. "He has reasons, Hieronymus. Other than the danger. You know he wants Max to help Admiral West maintain control over the fleet. And you and I have to be there when the fleet gets to Shangri la. You're the only one who can deal with whatever we find there."

"I know." His voice was dark, subdued. "Maybe you're right. It's just we all owe him so much…and it doesn't feel right leaving him. I know he won't be by himself, and I realize thousands of fleet personnel are risking their lives with him. But he will be alone, in every way that matters. It just doesn't feel right… even if it is the smart thing to do." He sighed. "I've been a rational man my entire life, Ana. I've made my decisions based on logic, on an analysis of available data. I've looked down on those around me who didn't do that, the men and women who let their emotions dictate what they did."

He looked up at her, and she could see the uncertainty in his eyes. "I've never wanted to cast logic aside like I do now. I've never felt such a strong urge to make a purely emotional decision." He paused. "I know I can't…but every fiber of my being wants to go with him, even if I have to stow away somewhere in Midway to do it."

"I know, Hieronymus. I feel the same way." Her voice was soothing, empathetic. "But we both know we can't. We have a duty to the fleet, to do whatever we can to help our people—all of our people—survive." They were both silent for a moment. Then she added, "Even if that means letting Admiral Compton go off without us."

*   *   *

"Admiral Compton?" The voice from behind him was familiar. Compton had been lost in thought as he headed back to Midway's flag bridge, but Greta Hurley's words pulled him back, and he turned around to face the commander of the fleet's fighter-bomber corps.

"Greta, what are you still doing here?" All the non-essential crew had left Midway, as they had the other fifteen ships of the rearguard. Compton had kept only skeleton crews on his chosen vessels.

Hurley had been helping to direct repairs to landing bay alpha, working to come up with any shortcuts that might get Midway's fighter support capability at least partially back online. But Compton had forgotten about the whole thing when he'd decided to lead the forlorn hope.

"The bay is functional, Admiral. At least moderately so. I can run two squadrons out of there. Maybe three."

Compton paused for a moment, processing what he'd just been told. "That's impossible, Greta. The damage was too extensive. Estimates were two weeks, even to restore moderate functionality." Bay A had been hard hit, not as thoroughly destroyed as bay B, but still damned bad. He couldn't believe it was repaired. There was no way.

"Well, sir…I cut a few corners. And I came up with a few workarounds. Operations won't meet safety regs, and we're not going to be at our most efficient, but I'm telling you I can run eighteen birds out of there. I went over it with Chief McGraw. Twice. And he's onboard." She paused. "Have I ever not come through for you, Admiral? Promised you something I couldn't deliver?"

Compton felt a wave of guilt. "No, Greta. Of course not. It's just that…I'm not sure what we'll end up facing. This is going to be dangerous." He hesitated. "We might not make it back, Greta."

"And when is that ever not true, Admiral? When have we launched without knowing we might not come back." She stared

better chance of surviving if you've got some fighter support. It's not just you, sir. Think of the spacers going with you."

Compton felt Hurley's well placed jab. She knew how to work him, as well as anybody else in the fleet. But she was right too. The fighters would help...they would increase the chances of his ships making it back. And it wasn't just him. Even with the reduced crews, he was taking over 2,000 spacers with him.

"Okay, Greta," he said softly. "Bring your people over. But you don't have much time. We're leaving in forty-five minutes."

"We'll be ready, Admiral." She smiled, and then she stood at attention and snapped him a salute. "It's an honor to be with you, sir."

Compton felt a twinge. He'd heard too many statements like that, usually from glory-hungry junior officers who knew too little about what they were getting into. But few people had been in the thick of the fighting as often as Great Hurley...had seen as many people die under her command. Compton knew his fighter commander had no delusions of glory, that her words were no empty gestures or pointless acts of bravado. She meant exactly what she said, and Compton could feel the emotions stirring inside him.

"It's an honor for me to have you along, Greta. I can't think of anyone I'd rather have at my back." He extended his hand.

She kept her eyes locked on his, and reached out, shaking his hand. Then she turned abruptly and left, on her way down to the bay. She had forty minutes to move her squadrons to Midway and get them bolted down in the damaged space.

*   *   *

"I have to go see him, Max. Now!" Sophie Barcomme tried to pull away from Harmon, but he held onto her shoulders like a vice.

"Safe?" she said, her voice a cocktail of emotions—anger, sadness, fear. "Who on the fleet is safe? What makes him think I even want to be safe. I want to stay with him!"

"There's no time, Sophie. Midway's leaving in just over half an hour. Now, come on…we need to get you on a shuttle."

"If you think you're going to pack me onto a shuttle and ship me off without even seeing him, you're sorely mistaken, Max Harmon." She wrenched herself free from his grasp and stood in front of him staring at him with a withering gaze. "If you think you're going to ship me off and then go off with him into God knows where, you've…"

"I'm not going either, Sophie." His voice was soft, thick with resignation.

She stared at him, her surprise clear in her eyes. "You're not going?"

"He doesn't want me to go either. He ordered me to report to Saratoga." Harmon was miserable, and speaking the words out loud only made it worse. But he tried to hide it from Sophie, to act as if he was simply following orders.

"And you are okay with that? You're letting him go without you?"

Harmon winced at the recrimination in her voice. He already felt guilty for leaving, and her tone suggested some level of disloyalty in his actions. He knew she was upset, that she didn't really think he would willingly abandon Compton. But it still cut deeply.

"He is my superior officer, Sophie," Harmon said, keeping his voice as even and unemotional as possible. "When he gives me an order, I follow it." *And I argued this one every way I could think of, but he wouldn't change his mind…*

"Orders? Is that your excuse for leaving him, Max? The man loves you like a son, and you know as well as I do…he wants to leave us behind because he doesn't expect to come back. How can you let him go off to die? Alone. Without you at his side? Without me?" She was distraught, tears streaming

"I would give anything to go with him, Sophie. It hurts more than I can describe to let him go into something so dangerous without me. But..."

"But what? You'll get a black mark in your file for disobeying an order? The perfect officer's spotless record will be besmirched? Better to let your closest friend die alone than defy an order. You could stay onboard...you know that. No one would have to know until it was too late. And I could stay too. But you won't do it. You'd rather be the obedient little soldier."

Her words cut him like knives. Harmon didn't give a shit about his record. He'd tear off his captain's insignia and go with Compton as a common spacer, cleaning out the bilge pumps, if he could. But there was more here than blind obedience. He'd been holding back his own anger and frustration, but now they broke free.

"No, Sophie. I'm doing what he told me to do because I know that's what he needs right now. Because I have no right to question him. Can you even imagine for an instant the pressure that has been on him every second since we've been trapped? The stress? How tired he must be? The guilt he carries for the dead, the ones his brilliant tactics couldn't save?"

His voice was raw, edged with anger now. He tried to stop, to calm down and not tear into Sophie, but he couldn't. He was too tired, too frustrated. He was worried about Mariko, about Compton. And it all came out.

"You want to trade insults? Okay fine. Don't you think he knows what he needs? Do you think Terrance Compton is an old fool who doesn't understand what he is doing? That he needs you or me to make his decisions for him? He saved us all, more than once. Don't you think in the end he deserves our respect? Our obedience?"

She stepped back, stunned at the vehemence in his words. But he stared at her, his eyes ablaze, and he continued. "Do you want to know why I'm not going with him? Because he needs me to stay behind. Because I can do more for him by

But it doesn't make a fucking bit of difference what makes me feel good. This isn't about me. It isn't about you. It's about him…and what he needs to do now, what must be done. To let him be free of distraction. He's the most brilliant tactician I've even known, but he's a man too. Will you feel better if you go along, divert his attention? Get him killed where he might have survived? Have you considered what you would feel like if he died because he was worrying about you when he should have been concentrating on the enemy? Or are you too wrapped up in your selfish bullshit for that to occur to you?"

He could see the shocked look on her face, the pain clearly on display. He immediately regretted what he had said. He knew Sophie loved Compton, that her concern for him came from true emotion. But he knew she had been selfish too, even as he had been when he'd argued with Compton. The admiral was telling them both what he needed from them…he needed to know they were safe. He needed that so he could focus, so it would be the pure, invincible admiral leading the rearguard, and not the concerned lover or worried father figure. Harmon hadn't realized it at first, but now he understood. He hated the idea of leaving Compton. But he knew he had to do it.

"Okay, Max…" Sophie's words were soft, forced out through her sobs. "I will come with you." She sounded defeated, lost.

"Sophie…I'm sorry. I didn't mean…"

"Yes, you did, Max," she said, wiping the tears from her face. "You meant every word. And you were right." She was trying with limited success to hold back more tears. "And I know it is no easier for you to leave him than me. But I didn't even get to say goodbye to him…"

Harmon took a step forward and put his arms around her. "It will be okay, Sophie. What he is doing is dangerous, but he's brilliant. He'll make it back." Harmon struggled to sound confident, but deep inside he still had the feeling he'd never see Compton again.

"Let's go, Sophie. We have to give him what he needs, let

Her face was buried in his shoulder, and he could tell she was crying again. But she took a deep breath and said, "Yes, Max. I will do what he needs me to do."

Chapter Eleven

AS Midway
Z5 System
The Fleet: 96 ships (+6 Leviathans), 23202 crew

"Transmit attack plan Alpha to Squadron A. They are to execute in four minutes." Terrance Compton sat on the edge of his chair, looking out over across the flag bridge to his tactical officer.

"Yes, sir," Cortez replied. His hands moved across his workstation, transmitting the data. A moment later: "All ships acknowledge, Admiral."

Compton stared at the main display, focusing on the approaching First Imperium ships. Midway was stopped dead, spewing radioactives into space. She was badly damaged, crippled…at least that's how she looked. But looks could be deceiving.

"Transmit plan Beta to Squadron B."

"Yes, Admiral."

Compton was like a statue, unmoving, unyielding. He stared straight ahead, his eyes focused like a pair of lasers. He'd felt tired when the rearguard broke off from the fleet, sad, even heartbroken to leave behind everyone he cared about. But now

nymus…but he knew he was protecting them, and realizing they were safe, relatively at least, hardened his resolve. He knew why he was here, and he imagined the rest of the fleet, approaching Shangri la, getting closer with each passing day.

"Squadron B reports ready, sir." Cortez sounded strong too. Everyone in the rearguard knew the danger they faced. They knew their road was a long and difficult one. But the clarity of Compton's mind was clear to everyone around him…and the confidence spread through the fleet like wildfire. They'd engaged three separate First Imperium forces since they'd branched off…and Terrance Compton had led the small fleet with a brilliance they'd never seen before, even from their hero-commander.

Compton had given himself over totally to the warrior inside. The information floated through his consciousness, stratagems in endless variation. Tactics, memories of old battles, attack plans he'd only imagined, so daring they had never been utilized in battle. Until now.

"Three minutes, admiral."

Cortez was turned around from his station, staring at the main display, just as Compton was. The enemy ships were coming on directly, moving toward the seemingly crippled ship. Compton had studied the First Imperium's tactics, looking for patterns, for weaknesses he could exploit. The intelligences directing the enemy forces tended toward the unimaginative, but they were capable of learning, adapting. They had become more adept at matching human tactics, and their own operations changed accordingly. But Compton knew they could only copy what they had seen. They could only adapt to maneuvers that had been employed against them. And he had no intention of letting them do that.

"Two minutes, sir."

No, the battle plans Compton had employed in the days since his force had left the fleet were not like anything he'd done before. They were new, wild, unorthodox. And they had the

The ships of Squadrons A and B were hidden, clustered behind the asteroids of system Z5's Kuiper belt. Hiding ships behind asteroids and other objects was a well-known tactic, but Compton had gone farther, much farther. The ships were close to their covering objects, dangerously, recklessly close. And the asteroids themselves had been blasted with modified warheads, salted bombs that covered them with radiation…enough to interfere with even the most intense scans. The enemy might look for hidden ships, but they weren't going to find any. Not until the ships fired up their reactors…and burst out of cover, right into the rear of the enemy formation.

"One minute, sir."

"Wish all ships my best, Commander. And advise the engineering crews they have my complete confidence."

Once the battle began, the gunners and tactical officers would become the arbiters of victory, but now, every man and woman in the fleet waited on the skills of their technicians, the crews that ran the power plants and systems of the vessels of the fleet.

Midway's reactor was down, completely off, as was that of every ship in the rearguard. It was the most daring part of the plan, the most wildly dangerous. Without power generation, Midway was believable as a cripple…and the ships hiding on the flanks were almost impossible to detect. But the enemy was less than two minutes from entering firing range, and restarting a ship's reactor took at least fifteen minutes. Unless you were absolutely fucking crazy enough to cold start the things. Which Compton was.

A cold restart was an emergency procedure, one requiring absolute precision on the part of the engineering team. One error, a single tiny slip up, and a ship's reactor could scrag hard. And then a vessel really would be a helpless cripple, one that had just given its position away with a massive power spike. That is, unless the reactor didn't just go critical…and turn the ship into a small sun that lasted for a few seconds and then faded away

ning now…" Cortez' voice had been calm, firm, but now he sounded nervous. It was difficult to sit and concentrate when you were waiting to see if the ship blew up with ten gigatons of explosive force, something he knew could happen at any second.

Midway shook hard, and everyone on the flag bridge tensed, reaching out, grabbing armrests and consoles. Everyone but Compton. He sat as still as he had been, not a trace of doubt on his face. Then the dimmed lights brightened, as fresh power surged through the ship's conduits.

Cortez spun around. "Cold restart successful, sir! All systems at 100% power." The tactical officer turned back, looking down at his readouts. Kent and Kosciuszko report successful power ups, sir. Bolivar too." A brief pause. "Vladivostok… Kure."

Compton didn't move, didn't alter his stare. But a small smile crept onto his lips as Cortez continued to rattle off ship names.

"L1 and L2 report successful power up. And Belfast." The excitement was clear in Cortez' voice. "All ships report successful reactor restarts, Admiral. Squadrons A and B executing respective attack plans."

Compton didn't reply. He didn't even move. He just watched, looking at the screen as the icons representing his ships moved toward the enemy from every direction. He tried to imagine the First Imperium intelligences, how they were reacting to his maneuvers. They wouldn't guess he'd take such a wild risk, or understand how his people had responded to his leadership, that engineers and technicians working in the cramped confines of fifteen vessels would manage to perform so far above the expected mean.

The odds said Compton would lose at least two or three of his ships to restart failures. But he'd spoken to his people before they'd deployed. He'd told the engineers how crucial they were, how he was placing the lives of several thousand of their fellow spacers in their hands. That they had his complete confidence. And they had responded. Compton had drawn that extra bit of

No First Imperium intelligence would understand that. They wouldn't determine that faith, loyalty, comradeship could overcome statistical norms. And they wouldn't comprehend that Compton was ready to lose whatever ships he had to lose, to see his crews consumed by the fury of nuclear fusion if that was what it took to win the victory.

First Imperium command units would expend their ships, send hundreds of their vessels to certain destruction. But all their data would tell them that humans did not respond that way, that no human commander could make such cold, blood-less decisions.

But they were wrong. There was one who could. And they had created him.

*   *   *

"Approaching point blank range, Captain." Akiko Fukudu was Kure's tactical officer. She'd been a junior ensign, fresh from the PRC's naval academy when Kure had joined Admiral Compton's fleet, but the ship had suffered heavy casualties since becoming trapped behind the Barrier, and she'd risen rapidly through the ranks. She'd adapted well and proven to be a capable officer, one Captain Coda had come to rely upon.

Hitoshi Coda stood in the middle of the bridge, about a meter from his command chair. It was an affectation, born most likely from an excess of nervous energy, but Kure's captain rarely sat during a battle. "All missiles tubes, prepare to fire."

"Yes, Captain," Fukudu said, an edginess to her tone. Kure was far inside normal missile range, but she hadn't launched yet, not a single shot. She'd been hidden behind an asteroid, pow-ered down and pressed so close against the frigid chunk of rock that the enemy scans couldn't find her. And when the orders came, Kure's crew did an emergency restart, taking her fusion

iously along with the rest of the crew as the ship's engineers did the cold activation. She'd sat at her station, staring at her monitors but not seeing anything, just trying to ignore the pit in her stomach, waiting to see if Kure disappeared in the fury of a titanic thermonuclear detonation...or if her decks were flooded with a massive wave of lethal radiation. But the seconds ticked off, and nothing happened. Then the power monitors surged, and she realized the restart had gone off without a hitch.

Kure then executed a short but sharp burst of lateral thrust, pushing it to the side of its covering asteroid, with the First Imperium fleet just ahead. The engines fired hard, and Kure blasted right toward the enemy fleet, her missiles armed and ready. Kure's launchers were packed full...not just with standard missiles, but with dangerously over-powered warheads. A cruiser like Kure typically carried moderate-sized missiles with yields of 100-200 megatons. But the weapons sitting in the tubes now were something new. Hieronymus Cutter had adapted some scraps of First Imperium technology with his own previous notes, and he'd modified standard fleet missiles, more than tripling their yields. The warheads Kure was about to fire had a yield of almost a gigaton...but they were untested, and even Cutter had admitted they were more than a little unstable. But the rearguard was facing overwhelming odds, and Fukudu knew they could only win if they were willing to take some risks.

There was more innovation to Kure's attack than the yield of the warhead. The plan was new as well. Missiles were typically fired from long range, which gave them time to select targets and lock in. But Kure was launching from point blank range, using her normally guided missiles almost like bullets, firing them right at the enemy ships. Normal missile barrages tried for near misses, detonations close enough to cause damage to target ships. It was too hard to score a direct hit an evading ship from 100,000 kilometers. But Kure was less than 15,000 klicks out...and she was closing hard. And the enemy had been taken by surprise, with no time to deploy anti-missile systems.

be destroyed, First Imperium tech or not.

"Twelve thousand kilometers, Captain." Fukudu glanced back at Coda. Kure's commander stood bolt upright, looking straight ahead. "Stand by," was all he said.

Fukudu turned back toward her board. The enemy ships were reacting to the sudden appearance of the human vessels. They hadn't activated any point defense systems yet. That wasn't a surprise—there was no way they'd be expecting a missile attack at this range. But their x-ray laser batteries were opening up, and they were already scoring hits on some of the other ships.

Kure shook hard, and the bridge lights dimmed for an instant. "Direct hit, sir," Fukudu snapped, her eyes dropping to her screen, reading the automated damage reports as they came in. "Reactor down to 80%. One of the port laser cannons is out." She paused for a few seconds, but Coda didn't respond. "Ten thousand kilometers," she added nervously. The missiles in the tubes were dangerous. If Kure took a hit in the wrong place...

"Stand by," Coda repeated. His voice was like ice. Fukudu knew the captain had to be nervous, but he wasn't showing it.

"Yes, sir."

Her eyes were locked on the display. Nine thousand kilometers. She could see the other ships launching, tiny icons on the screen moving from the ships to the line of First Imperium vessels. Bolivar had launched its entire spread. Kent too. Eight thousand kilometers. But Coda still said nothing. He just stood firm, grabbing the edge of his chair as Kure shook again, harder this time. Two enemy lasers had bracketed her, and Fukudu watched as her board lit up, damage control reports coming in from all over the ship. But the launchers were still operation. And the range continued to count down. Seven thousand...

"Captain..." She was turned around, staring at him, just like everyone else on Kure's bridge.

"Hold..."

She looked back at her station. About half the damage icons

which meant they were deteriorating. One was a power drain, probably a severed conduit sapping energy from the reactor. The other was a fire raging near the stern...far too close to the engineering core for comfort.

"Six thousand kilometers..." Captain...

Coda didn't move, didn't even flinch. He just spoke softly, calmly. "All port launchers...fire."

Fukudu spun around, pressing half a dozen buttons on her workstation. Kure vibrated lightly as her port launchers fired, sending eight enormously overpowered missiles at the enemy Leviathan directly to the ship's front.

"Navigation, execute 3g thrust, vector 120.233.072...now!" Coda still stood where he was, but the urgency was obvious now in his voice.

"Executing thrust now, Captain." The helmsman's voice was loud in the otherwise silent bridge.

Fukudu felt the thrust, the force of three times her body weight pressing down on her. She pushed against it, held herself upright as she looked over at the captain, still standing in his place, giving not a hint that he felt the same pressure they all did.

"Five thousand kilometers..."

"Starboard launchers...fire."

She spun around, executing the captain's orders, and once again the ship shook as the weapons blasted from their launchers and raced toward a second enemy vessel, another Leviathan.

"Navigation, execute 5g thrust, twenty second burst, vector 180.120.080."

"Executing, sir..."

Fukudu watched as Coda slid back into his chair, just as the 5g thrust slammed into everyone on Kure's bridge. Her eyes darted back to her display, just as the first target erupted into nuclear hell. Two of Kure's missiles had scored direct hits, and more than one and a half gigatons of destructive force vaporized the huge battleship. She was still watching when the second target disappeared, victim of yet another direct hit.

looked up and down the scanning display, watching the ships of the rearguard obliterate an enemy force that outweighed and outgunned them five times over. The battle plan had sounded insane, crazy, reckless beyond measure. If anyone else had issued the command, he'd have faced a mutiny. But Terrance Compton was a living legend…and that legend was continuing to grow.

Coda turned and looked over at Fukudu. "Yes," he said. "Yes, indeed, Lieutenant." He paused, just for a second. "But we're not done yet, are we? There are still plenty of enemy ships out there." Another pause, then: "All laser batteries… open fire!"

Chapter Twelve

AS Saratoga
X108 System – "Shangri la"
The Fleet: 91 ships (+6 Leviathans), 21979 crew

"Scanners clear, Admiral. No sign of any enemy vessels."

Erika West sat and looked out at the main display. It was just as her tactical officer said. Completely clear. Just like every system the fleet had passed through over the past two months. Exactly as Admiral Compton had planned.

"Very well, Hank. I want sensors on full power. And launch two squadrons to patrol the system. No sense taking any chances."

She stared down at the floor of her bridge, her thoughts on Compton. She couldn't begin to know what he'd done, how many enemy forces he and the spacers of the rearguard had faced off against. But they had done what they'd set out to do. The fleet had made it to Shangri la without incident.

But the cost…

West had tried to keep her hopes up. She wasn't an optimist by nature, far from it, but she didn't like the idea of giving Compton up for dead. It seemed somehow disloyal, and every

without the return of the rearguard, without even a single ship carrying a message, it became harder and harder to ward off the dark thoughts.

She'd served with Compton on and off for years, through the massive battles of the Third Frontier War and the brutal fights of the Rebellions that followed. But she'd really come to know him as well as she did over the nearly two years since the fleet was trapped…and she'd learned to appreciate the true depth of his genius. Augustus Garret was widely regarded as the best naval commander in history, and West knew from experience he utterly deserved the distinction. But his friend and comrade Terrance Compton was rightly placed at his side…as an equal in every respect. She knew history—at least on the other side of the Barrier—hadn't accorded Compton quite that level of regard. But she suspected Garret himself did.

"We're getting survey results, Admiral. Yellow sun, parameters within two percent of Sol norms. Six planets, two asteroid belts. Planet four is in the habitable zone."

"Okay, Hank…let's go have a closer look. "Forward at 1g." She was anxious, as she suspected everyone in the fleet was. Two years ago they'd been given up for dead, and now they were approaching a planet prepared for them millennia ago, but the same race that built the Regent, their sworn enemy.

Assuming Almeerhan could be trusted…

West was suspicious by nature, a cynic who assumed everything was a lie or a mistake…until it was absolutely proven otherwise. But she respected the astonishing genius of Hieronymus Cutter, and her experiences with him, especially since he'd transferred to Saratoga, had convinced her he was nearly as skeptical as she was. She found it a refreshing change from many researchers and academics who, for all their analytical brilliance, were so often shockingly naïve.

"We should reach planet four in approximately ten hours, Admiral."

"Very well." She had a passing thought that she should go

immediately. She knew she'd never be able to sleep. Not when the fleet was so close to its destination.

She tapped her com unit. "Dr. Cutter?"

"Yes, Admiral," came the almost immediate reply. West suspected Cutter was the only one in the fleet who'd gotten even less sleep than she had since Admiral Compton had gone.

"We're ten hours out from planet four. It is the only world in the habitable zone…which I presume means it should be Shangri la."

"Yes, Admiral. According to Almeerhan's notes, Shangri la is an extremely Earth-like planet. I have made very slow progress in finding specifics on the world itself. It appears Almeerhan and his people were concerned their records might fall into hostile hands. So, Shangri la, its defenses, facilities, everything… it's all going to be pretty much of a mystery, I'm afraid. I'd advise caution on the approach."

"Oh, yes, Hieronymus. You can be certain I will exercise caution. Still, I suggest you start thinking about your initial landing party. Of course, I'll send down a company of Marines first to scout the LZ."

"I wish you wouldn't, Admiral." Cutter paused. "I am the most knowledgeable individual with regard to Shangri la. I really think I should go down with the first expedition."

"Hieronymus, this world was built by Almeerhan's people half a million years ago. Whatever he told you, whatever is in that storage unit, you have no idea what has happened in all that time. The Regent could have forces down there for all you know. Or even another alien race. It's too dangerous."

"It's more dangerous without me there. If there is some kind of security system, I'm the person most likely able to deal with it." He hesitated. "Besides, I have the chops to handle it… Major Frasier made me an honorary Marine!"

*   *   *

"All personnel, we are about to transit into the X108 system. If our data is accurate, that should be the location of Shangri la. And the fleet."

Sasha listened to Captain Skarn on the shipwide com. She was sitting in her quarters, looking at Don Rames as she did. "It is almost time," she said, her voice stilted, without emotion."

"Yes," Rames said, his tone similar to hers. "As soon as the ship transits."

"Agreed," Sasha said. She turned back to her computer screen. The humans—that is what they called themselves—had extensive records. Combined with the memories of the bio-logic unit Debornan, the computer data had given her a fairly complete record of what had transpired. As expected, the bipeds were enemies of the Regent. They were a danger, and they had to be destroyed. But there were many, far more than those on this single vessel. It was necessary to develop a plan. The Debornan and Rames units did not have sufficient skills or access to destroy the entire human fleet. But they could strike a blow that would severely damage the bipeds. The enemy's com-mander was highly skilled, and his tactics had thwarted many of the Regent's plans. With careful planning, Debornan and Rames could get close to him. An assassination was highly feasible.

Cornwall was returning from a mission of exploration. Almost certainly, the fleet's commander would want a report of what it had found. That would provide access...but there was no way to know for certain that Debornan and Rames would be selected to make such a report. There were thirty other biolog-ics on Cornwall. Those biologics represented unacceptable risk to the plan. They had to be eliminated.

Sasha sat silently as Cornwall passed through the warp gate. Her display had gone dark. The human technology was back-ward, incapable of functioning during a warp gate transit. She knew from the memories of the biologic whose body she inhab-ited...the system failures would last only a moment. Then, Cornwall would contact the fleet. But she would not allow that.

were focused, waiting for the familiar image to return. The light came back first, bright, displaying a static pattern. Then text, the login screen, the unit rebooting.

Sasha continued to stare at the workstation as it finished its restart. "Ready."

Rames nodded again. "Ready."

She put her hands on the keyboard, typing in the passwords she'd set up days before. She was accessing hidden code, a program she'd placed in Cornwall's AI. Then she hit the final key, and her screen went dark.

She knew what was happening. In the depths of Cornwall's computer system, hundreds of files were being eliminated. Safeguards and failsafes were disappearing, and warning systems were disabled. The kernel, the essence of the ship's AI, the files that made it what it was, deleted itself, replacing the previous directives with the ones Sasha had programmed. The computer system that controlled most of Cornwall's vital functions was changed. Its primary directives, to protect the ship's crew, were gone, replaced by far more malevolent routines.

Sasha glanced over toward the door to her tiny quarters, confirming that it was closed and locked. In a few seconds, Cornwall's corridors, its chambers and compartments, would become deadly to the humans infesting the ship. There was no poison. There would be no fighting, no radiation…only a mild euphoria, and then death.

She stared at the screen, watching a large number on the top left. It read 11%…then 10%. All over the ship, everywhere but in her quarters, Cornwall's life support system was removing the oxygen from the ship's air, leaving it nearly 100% nitrogen.

She punched a few keys, activating several of the ship's security cameras. She paused on the bridge. Captain Skarn was on the floor in front of her chair, lying on her back, a peaceful expression on her face. Sasha knew there were similar scenes all over Cornwall. Inert gas asphyxiation was a merciful, painless way to eliminate the ship's crew, though that fact hadn't entered

into the reactor and disintegrated. As far as anyone in the fleet was concerned, the crew had been lured to the surface of the planet…and massacred by First Imperium robots. The story would serve multiple purposes. It would explain why Debornan and Rames were the only survivors…and it would add to the fear driving the biologics.

Her eyes fixed on the corner of the screen…3%…2%. Her studies of the bipeds suggested that they should all be dead by now, but she had decided on a safety factor. She would allow the vessel to remain at 0% oxygen for ten minutes. Then she would restore normal conditions. While she waited, she would contact the fleet, give them the bad news about Cornwall and the rest of its crew.

She felt something. A disruption. What was left of the personality that had been Sasha Debornan. It was unsettled, horrified at what she had done. It was pushing, struggling, trying to escape its confines…but to no avail. The nanos controlled the biological being utterly. Soon, the essence that was Debornan would have completed its usefulness. Then it would be terminated. But not yet. There was still work to do.

She reached down and flipped on the com unit. "Fleet command…fleet command, this is Lieutenant Debornan on Cornwall." Her voice was brittle, heavy with fear and sadness. She had studied the memories of the biologic, and she had utilized them to create an appropriate voice and demeanor. There could be no question. The biologics in the human fleet must believe that Debornan and Rames had returned. Then they could obtain the access they required…and complete their mission.

"Fleet, this is Cornwall calling Midway. Please respond."

"Cornwall, this is Lieutenant Commander Krantz aboard Saratoga. Midway is currently not in-system."

Sasha processed the new information. Where is the fleet's flagship? Where is Admiral Compton? Should I modify the plan, seek a new target? Or should I wait? Need more data. Play along for now…wait…evaluate.

"I am sorry, Lieutenant. That is horrible news." A short pause. "I am transmitting course instructions...you will rendezvous with Saratoga. Admiral West is sending a shuttle with replacement crew...and to bring you back for debriefing."

"Very well, Commander. Understood." She cut the line. There was no immediate access to Midway. But they would be on Saratoga. They would meet Admiral West.

Is West a suitable replacement target for Compton? She considered, accessing Debornan's memories, the ship's files she had reviewed. No, she determined. Erika West was an extremely skilled officer. But she was not capable of filling Admiral Compton's role. Indeed, there was some chance West would become a destabilizing force, causing discontent and disruption in the human fleet.

No, she would not kill West. Not yet. She would wait...and access whatever records she could...to determine when Compton would return.

She stood up, glancing down at the screen again. The readout read 19%. The ship's support systems had returned almost to normal.

"Come," she said, looking over at Rames. "It is time."

He nodded and rose alongside her.

Yes, she would wait for Compton to return. But first, she and Rames had to haul thirty bodies down to the reactor.

*   *   *

"It's bad, Admiral. Everyone on Snow Leopard appears to be infected now."

West sat in her chair, her face an angry scowl. She'd had an instant of gratification, when the scanners confirmed Cornwall had entered the system. She hadn't had a word from Compton, but the return of the scientists was good news...at least for a

She was worried about Shangri la too. She'd expected to feel some kind of joy, or at least relief when the fleet arrived here, but all she could think about was the cost. She wondered, was survival at all costs worth it? She wasn't sure what others would say…nor what she believed as a commander responsible for twenty thousand people, but for herself as an individual, she knew. She'd rather be with Compton…even if he was nothing but part of a cloud of slowly-cooling plasma right now.

And now this. An epidemic. Illnesses were fairly rare in the tightly controlled environments of fleet warships, a factor that alone was cause for concern. But a pathogen that ripped through an entire ship's crew…that was something deeply worrying. From what she'd heard it appeared very much like some strain of the flu, but it resisted all attempts at treatment. The best efforts of Snow Leopard's single doctor had been enough to provide some temporary relief of symptoms, but it didn't appear to have slowed the progress of the disease at all. Worse, Snow Leopard had been resupplied, and now there were additional cases appearing…on the supply ship itself, and on at least eight other vessels it had since docked with. Whatever her people were facing, it was clearly highly contagious. And from the grim reports coming from Snow Leopard, it appeared to be life-threatening as well.

She'd have known about the epidemic weeks earlier, but Snow Leopard's doctor hadn't reported it, not at first. It was easy to second-guess that decision now, but she realized the disease had appeared routine at first, with only two or three patients showing symptoms. It was one thing to wish this particular outbreak had been reported sooner, but then she imagined every sick bay ringing alarm bells over upset stomachs and allergic rashes.

What really pissed her off was the lack of a report on the spread of tiny warheads that had targeted Snow Leopard. Captain Ving had done his duty, forwarded the data to Midway before the flagship left with the rearguard. The report got to Saratoga in Midway's last communications dump, but there was

stated he believed the weapon had failed to operate in whatever manner the enemy had intended it to. She was inclined to think she would have been more attentive in his shoes, but again, that was far easier to say after the fact. Still, Saratoga's communications staff should have seen the report got to her, or at least to Krantz, whether they thought there was anything to it or not.

The people responsible for that bit of poor decision making had been dealt with severely, half a dozen officers busted all the way down to common spacers. That bit of after the fact discipline had failed to make West feel any better…but she figured it might at least serve as an example that would remind others to report anything out of the ordinary, no matter how unimportant it may seem. Still, it wasn't going to do a damned thing to stop this disease, or to prevent it from spreading to a dozen or more ships. In the end, she'd lost almost a month to the spread of this thing, time during which she could have had all the fleet's med services working on a cure.

She had no idea how long it would take her med teams to beat this disease, but the knowledge that a virulent pathogen had been a major factor in the destruction of the people of the First Imperium did nothing to make her feel any better. If this was related in some way—and her dark mind assumed it was—how could her people even hope to cope with something the advanced science of the First Imperium had failed to defeat?

"Repeat the warning to the fleet. All vessels that have had any contact with Snow Leopard or the freighter Wanderer are quarantined." She paused. "And Hank, I want you to review the records personally. If any of the ships Wanderer docked with had any contact with any other vessels, those ships are to be quarantined too. That includes any shuttle traffic back and forth. Understood?" West knew the extent of contact between ships in the fleet, and she had to put a stop to that right now. She knew at least ten ships had been exposed already…and she suspected Krantz' review would turn up at least a few more. She didn't know for certain the pathogen had been spread to

"Yes, Admiral. I'll make sure we've got it controlled."

She just nodded. For an instant she thought she should do it herself, just to be sure. But Hank Krantz was as capable an officer as she'd ever known. Trust didn't come easily to Erika West, but her tactical officer had long ago earned it. Besides, she had other concerns. Saratoga was approaching Shangri la. In a couple hours they would know what was waiting for them...if it was hope for a future...or bitter disappointment.

*   *   *

"Sara...."

The voice was soft, distant. She was floating, disoriented. Her eyes were filmy...she could see the figures above her as hazy silhouettes, moving slowly. She could feel...hands touching her. She was weak, her body heavy. Heat...the fever. Her sickbay gown soaked in sweat.

"Sara...answer me, Sara. Say something. Here, squeeze my hand."

She felt something. Touching. A hand on hers. She tried to grab it...but it was no use. She couldn't move. She rasped loudly, struggling for breath...but there was none. She felt herself slipping away, deeper, darker. The figures were gone now... just a shadowy haze. Falling. Silence. Blackness...

Then awareness. Her body spasming. Pain. A shock. Light. Breath, air.

"That was close."

The words were louder, but she had trouble understanding. Then another feeling, a wave moving through her. Alertness. Clarity. She was looking up at sickbay, the bright lights, the pristine white of the walls, the cabinets.

"BP still low, heart rate 32...but we got her back, Doctor. At least for now."

She looked up. The face…familiar. Flynn.

"Dying…"

"No, Sara," Flynn said, his words clipped, emotional. "We almost lost you, but we got you back."

Flynn paused, stepping away for an instant. Sara's eyes were clearer, she could see his face. White, pale, his eyes sunken.

"You…sick…too?"

"I'm okay, Sara." He extended his hand, wiping her forehead with a cloth.

"Lie…" She paused and gasped for air, but her congested lungs resisted.

"Okay, Sara…yes, I'm sick. But I will be okay. You will too."

She smiled weakly. Whatever meds he'd just given her, she had some clarity back. Enough to know he was lying.

"How…bad?"

Flynn looked down at her. "It's bad, Sara. You're very sick… and I haven't isolated the cause yet, much less a cure. But we can manage your symptoms until we make more progress."

She shook her head slowly. "No…not…me. Ship. How… many?"

Flynn hesitated. "Sara…"

"Don't…lie…"

"Everyone, Sara. Everyone on the ship is infected."

She closed her eyes. No…

She knew she was weak, that she wouldn't last much longer. Flynn tried to give her hope, but she knew there wasn't any, not for her, at least. But the thought of all her shipmates, sickening as she had…dying. It was too much.

She could feel a tear welling up in one of her eyes, sliding slowly down her face. But there was only one. She was feverish, dehydrated despite Flynn's best efforts to force fluids into her. Her breaths were shallow, difficult. She could feel the fluids in her chest, the pressure.

"Sorry," she said, her voice barely audible.

"No, Sara." She could feel Flynn leaning over her, but she

rattling in her chest with every straining breath.

She felt the urge to fight, to struggle…to draw breath…to live. But she didn't have the strength. It was too hard…and she knew there was no point, no hope.

She felt the darkness coming for her, one last urge to fight… and then nothing. Surrender. Blackness.

$*$ $*$ $*$

Sasha sat in the small decontamination chamber, along with Don Rames and the shuttle crew that had brought her back to Saratoga. This was unexpected, a departure from standard procedure. She didn't understand, and she reviewed the memories of her host, the files she had studied. No, this was not normal.

"Why are we being detained here?" she asked, looking over at the shuttle pilot.

"There is an epidemic running through the fleet. It has affected at least ten ships. Cornwall didn't have any contact with it, but Admiral West ordered extra precautions. The decon procedure isn't long, maybe another thirty minutes. Then we should be out of here."

Sasha nodded.

An epidemic? Does that alter the plan at all?

She considered. She didn't have enough information. She needed to know more.

"How did it start?"

The pilot had been leaning back against the wall, but now he straightened up and smiled in her direction. "I don't know, Lieutenant. It started on one of the attack ships, and it's spread to a bunch of other vessels."

Sasha looked back at the pilot. She was confused…the other officer's expression was odd, the tone of his voice. She accessed her host's memories, her knowledge. Yes, of course. The other

able by the standards of her species. That is worth noting. It may be useful. But she didn't see any advantage to be gained from the pilot, so she just nodded. Then she tried to ignore him. There was nothing to do now but wait.

*   *   *

Erika West rubbed temples with her fingers, trying to force away the headache that bored into her skull. The day had started off as shit, and it had only gone downhill from there. She'd expected to experience some kind of satisfaction when the fleet reached Shangri la. But now all she could think about was Admiral Compton and the ships he'd taken with him. And the plague running wild throughout the fleet. Krantz had tracked down all points of contact...and no fewer than twenty-two ships were now involved. And there were reported cases of mysterious illnesses with flulike symptoms on eleven of them. A minor disaster had expanded to a massive cataclysm in the making, largely because her people had failed to communicate quickly enough.

She'd almost stopped the fleet to deal with the situation before continuing on, but then she decided that wasn't an option. Admiral Compton was out there somewhere...or he had died in battle...but in either case he'd done it to buy time for the fleet. Time to reach Shangri la, to find and employ whatever the ancients had left there for mankind. West wasn't about to throw that away, to make Compton's sacrifice a pointless gesture. And she didn't believe for a second that Compton's diversion had done more than delay the enemy. She knew her people would have a fight here, more likely sooner rather than later. And she had to get every advantage she could by then. That meant seeing what Shangri la had to offer.

"We're getting energy readings, Admiral." Krantz turned abruptly, looking over at Admiral West. "Big ones...off the

some kind of defense system…

"All fleet units are to halt. Immediately." She was grateful her paranoia had driven her to break the fleet into two waves. Saratoga was in the lead, with a squadron of attack ships and the four Leviathans Compton hadn't taken with him. The rest of the ships were half a light hour behind. That wasn't going to help her or Saratoga's crew, not if they'd encroached on a hostile defense system with that kind of power. But at least most of the fleet would survive.

Not that it will do them much good. If Shangri la is a dead end—or a trap—then it's all over…

She knew sixty-odd ships—low on weapons, on food, on fuel—had no real chance to survive, not if Saratoga was destroyed and Shangri la proved to be a bust. They had staked all on finding the world Almeeerhan had promised them. If that had been a lie, or if the ancient planet had been taken by the Regent and turned into a trap, she knew the fleet was through. Even Compton's sacrifice…no, she corrected herself, his efforts…had been in vain. She wasn't ready to give up on Compton, not yet. But that didn't matter, not if Saratoga was about to die.

"It's definitely some kind of weapon system, Admiral. We're getting readings, satellites activating…power generation, in excess of nine hundred petawatts."

"Group A, forward one-tenth thrust. Group B, full thrust, directly away from…"

"Energy discharges, sir. Some kind of weapon." Krantz was as cool and professional any officer as West had ever known, but now she could hear the fear in his voice. "We can't even get an accurate reading on the energy level."

She felt her body tightening, preparing for the end. Any weapon with that kind of power would vaporize Saratoga with a single shot. This is the end, she thought. But nothing happened. Not to Saratoga.

"Report," she snapped, staring around the flag bridge.

and her eyes went wide.

"They're gone, Admiral. Destroyed." Krantz' tone was overcome with shock.

West stared at the display. "Gone? What the hell…"

"The weapons targeted them. One shot each."

A Leviathan? Destroyed with a single shot? What the hell have we run into here?

"The scanners have it all, Admiral. Preliminary data suggests some kind of massive particle accelerators. All four Leviathans are gone."

West felt like she'd been punched in the gut. The Leviathans that Command Unit Gamma 9736 had given them represented at least half the remaining firepower of the fleet. At least they had. Admiral Compton had taken two with the rearguard…and the others had just been destroyed like they were nothing.

"Any signs of recharging? Targeting locks?" Why haven't they hit any of the other ships? Do they rate us not dangerous enough?

"Negative, Admiral. The satellites have powered down. If I had to guess, they are on some kind of standby. They didn't target or fire at any of our vessels. Just the Leviathans."

West shook her head. You damned fool, she thought, anger at herself growing with every passing second. Why did you bring the Leviathans forward?

It was beginning to make sense to her. If Almeerhan's people had built this world, the Regent's ships would have been the enemy…and the defense system would have been programmed to recognize them as threats.

"Of course," she muttered. "I just threw away the four most powerful ships we have." Her voice was soft, she was mostly talking to herself. She felt waves of self-recrimination. She tried to imagine the fury she would level at a subordinate who had done what she just had.

"We have definitely been scanned, Admiral. But the weapons are still on standby."

"Bring us in slowly, Commander.   All weapon systems powered down, no sudden course changes."

"Yes, Admiral. Executing."

"And open all channels. Instruct the AI to begin transmission of translation protocols. Let's see if we can communicate with whatever is down there."

Chapter Thirteen

From the Research Notes of Hieronymus Cutter

I've been sitting at my workstation for thirty minutes, trying to think of something to write. I am about to lead the landing party down to Shangri la, arguably the most momentous step ever taken by a human scientist. I feel I should have something profound to mark the occasion. But all I can think of is my fatigue, the toll of nearly two years of constant battle and flight. And one other thing...the terrible injustice that Admiral Compton is not here to see this day. Is he out there somewhere, on his way here even now? Or is he gone, never to be seen by us again. I know what I want to believe. But I have spent my life analyzing data, and that leads me to a conclusion I resist with everything that makes me human.

Landing Zone X-Ray
Planet X108 IV – "Shangri la"
The Fleet: 91 ships (+2 Leviathans), 21946 crew

"Atmospheric scans confirm earlier readings. Almost Earth-normal...air composition, temperature, plant and animal life. It's a virtual paradise down here. The Superpowers would have

At least the green growth under his feet looked like terrestrial grass—and the preliminary readouts suggested it was almost identical to its Earth cousin.

"Very well, Dr. Cutter. But I want the landing party to remain suited up. Certainly until we've completed an intense scan for toxins and pathogens." West's voice was skeptical, as usual. "Especially since we're already battling somewhat of an epidemic up here on the fleet." Her tone changed, became darker. The mysterious disease that first appeared on Snow Leopard had spread to more than twenty other ships, all vessels serviced by the same freighter or visited by someone from an infected vessel. We can't take a risk that traces of the disease that killed the Ancients are still down there, that they have mutated into something dangerous to us."

"Yes, Admiral. I agree." Cutter did agree, at least his rational mind did. But this world was so beautiful, so perfect…he felt the urge to shed his armor, to breathe deeply, fill his lungs with fresh, non-recycled air. A Marine fighting suit was an amazing bit of technology, nuclear-powered, capable of sustaining life in any environment, even deep space. It offered its wearer enormous protection in battle, and its built-in trauma system could treat all but the most severe wounds. But he had to admit, his suit smelled a little too much like Hieronymus Cutter, and it made the blue skies of this world, and the fields of wildflowers rippling in the gentle wind, that much more appealing.

"Hieronymus," West continued, "we need to know for sure this whole thing is legitimate, that what Almeerhan told you is true. If this is some kind of trap…"

"It's not, Admiral." Cutter's response was sharp, brittle. He understood West's caution, but he knew Shangri la was real. He couldn't explain it, but he just knew. He'd had extensive contact with the preserved essence of the ancient alien back on X48 II, and he didn't doubt anything he'd been told. His analytical mind was trained to be critical, to question anything unproven. But there wasn't a reservation in his mind. Not about this.

tory ships are going to grind to a halt unless we get the chance to stop somewhere and mine some new resources. Even the food supply is in trouble. The epidemic has affected two of the agriships." The fleet had converted four massive freighters to food production, growing a variety of carefully engineered algaes and hydroponics. Their production didn't produce anything terribly appetizing, but they supplied enough basic nutrition to feed the fleet's survivors. But with two out of four quarantined, food was going to become a problem. Quickly.

"I'm sure I'm right, Admiral. I can't explain it, but you know me well enough to realize I'm not prone to frivolous beliefs."

"No, Hieronymus, you are not. But be careful anyway."

"I will see that our scans down here are extremely thorough. That is my expertise. And you get ready to face whatever comes through that warp gate eventually. Because we both know Admiral Compton just bought us a little time and nothing more than that."

West was silent for a few seconds. "Yes, Hieronymus...we both know that. And I will. Carry on." Then she cut the line.

"Dr. Cutter, this is Major Frasier. We found something, sir. I think you should come over here as soon as you can." Cutter had told Frasier to call him Hieronymus at least a dozen times. The Marine had complied, at least when they were off duty. But in the field, Frasier was the textbook Marine...and Cutter was in command of the landing party. That would require respect in any circumstance, but Hieronymus Cutter had been adopted by the Corps. He was one of their own now, and he always would be...from the moment he'd risked his own life to defend a group of wounded Marines, facing almost certain death in doing so. Many things were said about the Corps, but no one questioned it had a long memory...for injuries done to it and for services rendered on its behalf.

"I'm on my way, Connor." Cutter might be an honorary Marine, but his adoption hadn't bestowed any real discipline or formality on him. Connor Frasier was his comrade, and the

wasting time with a lot of "major" bullshit.

Cutter had sent Major Frasier and his Marines to scout and secure the immediate area. He didn't expect the Marines to find any hostiles, but he was looking for something. He didn't know what it was—he hadn't fully completed his translations of the data retrieved from X48 II—but he was sure he'd know it when he saw it. And the Marines were very thorough. If there was something there, he knew they'd find it.

He walked along the ridgeline, heading toward Frasier's position. It was about five klicks, and he found himself moving quickly. Not running, exactly, but certainly jogging. A smile slipped across his face. He remembered bumbling around in his armor the first time he'd worn it. He'd struggled enormously simply to remain standing, to walk slowly without toppling over.

Maybe I really am a Marine now…

He shook his head.

Yeah…at least until the shooting starts.

He turned to the right, his eyes shooting up to the projected display inside his helmet. Connor Frasier was a small blue dot on the map…and there was something else too. A red square, some type of construction. Cutter felt a wave of excitement, and he hurried his pace.

He walked through the low-lying valley, looking back and forth at the hills on either side. There were trees scattered around, and expanses of white and blue flowers. The planet really did look like Earth, or at what Earth had probably looked like before the Superpowers and their predecessor nations had devastated so much of it with war.

He climbed up a small rise, and when he reached the top he could see Frasier, surrounded by half a dozen Marines…staring at something.

Cutter kicked up the magnification of his visor and took a closer look. He felt a wave of excitement the instant his eyes settled on it, and he continued forward, quickening his pace even more. It was an obelisk, perhaps four meters tall, smooth, white,

it. But it was familiar nevertheless, and he knew what it was. He couldn't explain it, but he was sure.

He trotted up the rest of the way, his eyes locked on the monument as he ran. His mind raced. How do I know what that is? But he did know. And he knew what to do.

"Dr. Cutter…" Frasier stepped away from the obelisk.

"Have you seen any activity from the obelisk, Connor? Any flashes of light? Movement?"

"No, sir," the Marine replied, glancing back at the monument for a few seconds. "But look at it…it looks new, like it was built yesterday. If that thing is half a million years old…"

"It is." Cutter stood and looked over Frasier's shoulder. The rest of the Marines were doing the same thing. There was something about the alien artifact, something hypnotic. It was affecting them all. But Cutter pushed the distraction aside and walked right up to it.

It was smooth, its surface polished to a sheen that brightly reflected the morning sunlight. It was almost blinding. Cutter stepped up onto the base, his eyes glancing at the projection in his helmet for an accurate measurement. He'd guessed a little over three meters square, and he was right…3.14159. Pi. The dimensions of the pediment matched the constant pi.

Is that to support communication? A way for visitors to begin to understand the race that had built the amazing construction? Any advanced species would have discovered pi, they would understand that this was no arbitrary measurement.

Cutter stared at the obelisk, his head moving slowly, looking over every centimeter. There was nothing…nothing but the smooth, utterly seamless surface. It didn't make sense. There should be something, a symbol, a mark of some kind. He knew it. He couldn't explain it, but he'd never been surer of anything in his life. He took a step forward, reached out and touched the marble. The sensors on his armored glove fed back data… temperature, composition, texture. The stone was smooth, not a single imperfection, at least none his sensors could detect. It

ever it was, his suit's AI couldn't identify it. And he had no idea
either. He was missing something. He knew there was more
to the obelisk, and he stood and stared, probing his own mind,
analyzing everything he'd read in the data unit he'd brought back
from X48 II, everything Almeerhan had told him.

He looked down at his arm. Of course. DNA. They
manipulated our DNA, made it a copy of their own. That's
how they would know…

He heard Admiral West's words repeating in his mind, her
orders. The landing party was to stay in their suits on full life
support. The Admiral was right, he knew. There were people dying on the fleet, victims of some mysterious disease. He
knew what she was thinking…and he agreed. It was the disease
that had destroyed the people of the First Imperium, a newly
mutated version—probably created by the Regent—one that
infected humans. If they weren't careful, it could kill everyone
on the fleet. It was already threatening thousands, and only the
quarantines West had ordered had stopped the spread.

But he knew what he had to do. It would violate West's
orders. It would trap him on the planet, at least for the foresee-
able future…and possibly forever. The intensive scans West had
ordered would take days, and if they found anything, even an
uncertain hint of some kind of pathogen…

Or the disease could be here…one breath of the air of this
world could be fatal…

But he didn't believe that. He had no basis to be sure about
anything, but he was nevertheless. He stepped down from the
pedestal, and walked a few meters. Then he stopped and turned
back.

"Open armor," he said softly.

"Negative," the AI replied. Mission parameters do not allow
for deviation from full life support protocols.

"Override," he said. "Authority, Cutter, Hieronymus, Colonel." Cutter had joined the fleet as a civilian, a scientist, but
he'd quickly become one of the most important of its person-

had signed a commission, making him a colonel. It was honorary, at least partially, but it was also intended to allow him to exert command over other fleet officers. Cutter had an almost blank check from Compton, and everyone knew that. The rank just made it official. But it had also been entered into the fleet's information network, giving him the authority to overrule the AI's mission orders.

"Scans of planetary atmosphere and surface are still incomplete. Are you sure you wish to override mission parameters?"

Cutter paused, staring at the obelisk. "Yes," he said. "Override. Open armor."

He could hear the familiar cracking sound, the scrape of metal on metal as the locking bolts in his armor slid aside, and the suit popped open like a giant clamshell.

He felt the air from outside, cool, refreshing…and he closed his eyes for a second.

"Hieronymus!" It was Frasier, and his voice was as panicked as Cutter had ever heard it. "The atmospheric scans are…"

"It's okay, Connor," he said, his voice calm, placid. He was more certain than ever he was doing the right thing. "I have to do this."

Frasier stood completely still, a dark silhouette against the bright sunlight. Cutter knew his friend was horrified, worried about him, about what could happen to him if the scans found something in the atmosphere, the dirt, the water. And stunned that Cutter had violated Admiral West's orders. Frasier was a Marine, and the son of a Marine, and he took orders from superior officers to be something akin to the word of God. But as much as Cutter had been taken in by the Corps, obedience didn't run in his blood as it did with his adopted brethren. Besides, it was an open question if he was subject to West's orders anyway, at least outside of a battle. Compton had given him virtually unlimited authority to do as he saw fit in conducting research. And as much as he—and West and most of the others—were deathly afraid Compton was dead, no one had dared to utter

doing." He stepped out of the armor. The sun beat down on his skin, the breeze soft refreshing. He leaned back, looked at the sky, nothing but a few puffy clouds breaking up the sea of unbroken blue. The breeze was cool but not cold. He couldn't recall the last time he felt so content.

He moved to the back of his armor, to the small storage compartment, and he popped it open. He pulled out a gray jumpsuit, stepping in and zipping it up. He looked back at Frasier and the Marines, standing dead still and watching him. Their visors blocked their faces, but Cutter imagined the looks of horror hiding beneath the silvery masks.

He reached back into the compartment and pulled out a small com unit. He flipped it on and clipped it to his collar. "Don't worry, Connor. None of you should be worried. Everything is fine." He'd been edgy, nervous before, just like his Marine companions. But now he was calm. He knew this was right. He couldn't explain it, but he knew.

He turned toward the obelisk, his hand on his forehead, shielding his eyes from the sun. Then he stepped up on the platform and walked toward the monument. He stopped, turned back to look at Frasier, a broad smile on his face. Then he placed his hands on the obelisk.

It was cool, smooth. He stared straight ahead, into the dazzling whiteness of the stone. Nothing happened...not for the first few seconds. But then he felt something, under his hands. Warmth. Then a strange tingling, like an electric shock but not painful. It moved up his arms, slowly, steadily.

He could see a shadow behind him, off to the side. Frasier, alarmed, moving to grab him.

"No, Connor...I am fine. Stay back."

The tingling feeling extended all through him, to his neck, his head. He could feel something communicating with him, not in words, but in some other way he didn't fully understand. He was overwhelmed, excited...but there was no fear. None at all.

emitted light. Then there was a blinding flash, and when he opened his eyes, the smoothness of the marble monument was gone replaced by a surface covered with what appeared to be runes and carvings. He stood where he was, staring, reaching out, touching the grooves in the previously gleamingly smooth surface.

The obelisk moved as he touched the runes, sliding back away from him. He glanced at Frasier for a second and then back to the large chunk of moving stone. It continued to slide back, about two meters before it stopped. And where it had stood there was an opening, and a stairway leading down.

*   *   *

"Admiral, Captain Balcov is on the line. He requests permission to send a party to the surface."

"Permission denied." West had a scowl on her face. It was the third such request in the past six hours...and whoever was unfortunate enough to be the fourth was going to get more than he or she bargained for.

"Yes, Admiral."

Seven weeks without combat...a respite gained only by the effort—and perhaps the sacrifice—of Terrance Compton. That was all it took to destroy discipline, caution. To take away the fear long enough to allow carelessness to take control.

"Excuse me, Admiral...but Captain Balcov insists on speaking with you."

West felt a surge of anger, the heat of it rising around her neck. She was a hard taskmaster, unaccustomed to allowing emotion to interfere with her actions. But she despised disloyalty.

She nodded, and put on her headset. "Captain Balcov, I trust there is a good reason my tactical officer's instructions to you were unsatisfactory."

at the planet prepared for us by our forefathers of the First Imperium. And yet you insist we all remain in space. The scouting party has reported no hostile forces, no problems of any kind. I must insist…"

West listened as long as she could force herself. Then she cut him off. "Captain Balcov, this is not a debate. It is not a discussion. Your opinions may be submitted, but in the future I suggest you restrict these to actual facts and valid tactics, not some whiny desire to go down and experience the 'paradise world' yourself. You are to take no action…none…without my direct orders. Is that clear?" She was trying to keep the anger from her voice, but that just made her words that much colder, like pure ice.

"Admiral West, I feel I must remind you that you have not been named commander of the combined fleet in any formal manner. I do not wish to challenge you, but I must insist that you behave in a less imperious manner."

"Captain Balcov…" She took a breath, tried to calm the rage she felt building inside her. "…Admiral Compton is the commander of the fleet, by the authority of Admiral Garret, the supreme commander of all Earth forces in the war against the First Imperium. I will remind you that Admiral Compton's position was later confirmed by a fleetwide plebiscite. Admiral Compton, under his duly granted authority, has placed me in temporary command of the main fleet forces."

"Come, Admiral West…how long do you think you will maintain dictatorial power over the fleet on that basis? Admiral Compton was a great hero, and the fleet was fortunate to have him at its head. But we all know he is dead. There is simply no way the rearguard could have survived the massive First Imperium forces it was facing."

West took a deep breath, trying to control her rage. She knew Balcov only spoke the truth. It was possible, probable even, that Compton was dead. But she wouldn't give up on him. Not yet. And she certainly wasn't going to listen to a pompous

"Captain Balcov, I'm going to say this once…and only once. We have no knowledge of Admiral Compton's death, and until further notice we will be operating under his most recent orders. You are to maintain yellow alert on your ship as previously ordered, and under no circumstances are you to transport any-one down to the surface." Stop there, she thought, struggling to keep herself from going on. She wanted to threaten him, to tell him in twenty different ways how she'd charge him with treason and personally watch as he was thrown out the airlock. But she'd promised Compton she'd try to be diplomatic with the fleet officers.

"Admiral West, I am sorry, but I cannot…"

She stopped listening, her eyes frozen, staring at the main display, at a small dot…then another.

"Captain…" It was Krantz, and he was looking at the same thing.

"I see it, Hank."

She leaned back over the com. "Captain Balcov, we can con-tinue this later. I must insist that you see to your ship now. There are unidentified ships transiting into the system." She cut the line. Then she turned toward Krantz, and she uttered a single word.

"Battlestations."

*   *   *

Cutter stood stone still, staring down the steps to the dimly lit corridor below. He knew he should be scared…the man he'd been until recently would have been terrified. Petrified, frozen with fear. But Hieronymus Cutter felt only a strange excite-ment…and a certainty he had to go down those steps.

"Hieronymus…" Frasier's voice was edgy, nervous. He'd abandoned the formality, and it was clear from his tone he was

his hand, gesturing for Frasier to wait where he was. "I'm going down. Give me a few minutes, and then follow."

"But…"

"No, arguments, Connor. I know what I'm doing." He did know, though he had no idea how he did. His encounter with Almeerhan had changed him in ways he was still identifying. Explaining it all—and fully understanding—was still ahead of him, he knew.

If I ever get there…

He took a step forward, and he paused at the very top of the stairs. He hesitated for a few seconds…and then he started down. The staircase was surrounded by polished stone, but the steps themselves were some kind of metal. None of it showed any signs of wear or decay, despite its immense age. He continued down, each step rapping on the metal, echoing with increasing volume as he continued. When he got to the bottom there was an opening to his right, a doorway where a hatch had just slid to the side.

There was a large room beyond, bright, with gleaming white walls and some kind of artificial light source. Cutter knew this was where he'd set out to come, the destination that had been laid out for him back on X48 II. But he still felt uneasy, not fear perhaps, but awe. He took a deep breath and walked inside.

The room looked like some kind of control center, with workstations lining the walls all around. In the center, there was a small pedestal, perhaps ten centimeters high. He looked around, his eyes pausing on one of the stations. It was similar to ones he'd seen in Almeerhan's fortress. He was about to step forward when he saw a flash of light.

A man appeared on the platform, perhaps a meter from where Cutter was standing. No, not a man, Cutter suspected, a hologram, an image of some kind. He was tall, clad in shimmering white robes, and he looked directly at Cutter.

"Welcome my children…welcome to Akalahar." The voice was loud, authoritative, but it was friendly too. "You have come

friends. For I am Karanthar, and I am here to welcome you. I know not which of my cousins directed you to this place, but that matters not, for you are indeed here."

Which of my cousins...

Cutter thought of Almeerhan. He'd imagined the alien as the only one of his kind, waiting endlessly for one of the new races to arrive. But now he understood. The last of the ancient race of the First Imperium, the members of the warrior caste who had fought the Regent with their final strength...they had left behind multiple worlds, not just X48 II...roadmaps leading to this place, the world Karanthar had called Akalahar...and that the humans had dubbed, Shangri la.

"Hello," Cutter said. "My name is Hieronymus Cutter. I am from Earth."

"You are welcome, Hieronymus Cutter, you and all the children of Earth, where we visited so long ago. I have much to share with you, much to give you to aid in your fight."

Cutter was amazed by the quality of the projection, but at the same time, he could tell it wasn't like Almeerhan, that this was more of a recorded message, if an interactive one, and not the full essence of a member of the ancient race.

"I was sent here by Almeerhan. He told me you would help us."

"Indeed, Hieronymus Cutter, I will help you. I will help all your people, for this place was prepared for you eons ago, long before your people reached out to the stars."

Cutter felt a rush of excitement. Almeerhan, for all he had told Cutter, all he had done, was primarily a messenger, a guide. But this planet, this fortress, had been built specifically to aid the successor race to those of the First Imperium. There had been several potential species that might have fulfilled that role, but now it appeared that mankind was the first to arrive.

He tried to temper his hopes...after all, those of the First Imperium, who had built this place, had themselves been defeated by the Regent. And when they had prepared the planet

He had no doubt there was technology here, weapons and information of incredible value. But would it be enough to defeat the seemingly endless resources of the Regent? He just didn't know. Certainly, the orbital defenses were enormously powerful. They had destroyed the four Leviathans in an instant. That had been a tragic error, but also an indisputable demonstration of the power of the planet's weapons. Cutter wasn't sure if those orbital platforms could defeat a whole attacking fleet, but he had no doubt they would dish out an enormous amount of destruction.

He also wondered if he would be capable of adapting all the new technology quickly enough. It was one thing to find file after file of wondrous science and plans for highly advanced equipment…and quite another to understand it, to build, activate, deploy it all.

There was only one way to get the answer. Cutter looked right at the projection. The alien adjusted its gaze, matching his movements. It was only an image, but it was an extraordinarily well done one.

"So what do we do now?" Cutter figured he had nothing to lose by being blunt.

"I will direct you to the information storage units. There is much to show you, much to explain."

"Very well," he said, "let's…"

There was a loud crackling sound, the com unit on his collar. Then a voice, Admiral West's. "Hieronymus, it's Admiral West."

Cutter could tell immediately that something was wrong, but he didn't say anything. He just listened. Erika West would get right to the point.

"I'm pulling the fleet out of orbit immediately, Hieronymus. We've got scanner activity at the warp gate. Energy readings. First Imperium ships inbound. A large fleet. Very large." She paused, allowing what she had just said to sink in. Compton had bought them time, just enough time to get to Shangri la. But now they were going to have to defend it.

Chapter Fourteen

From the Personal Log of Terrance Compton

I don't know if we will ever get back to the fleet. I have no idea if this log will ever be recovered by people from Earth, but if it is, I say to you reading this...in a week, a month, a century... know now that the men and women of the fleet's rearguard have fought with courage and distinction in such quantity as I have never seen before in fifty years at war.

If we are fated to die on this mission, I die in the company of heroes, and I would have those who read these words one day long from now to give silent tribute to the spacers it has been my honor to command.

AS Midway
Z16 System
The Fleet: 88 ships (+2 Leviathans), 21211 crew

"We've got more hostiles, sir. Coming through the Z19 warp gate." Cortez' eyes were locked on his display. His voice was hoarse, and his fatigue was clear, despite his best efforts to hide it. The rearguard had been fighting for almost thirty hours without a break, and it was beginning to show…in exhaustion,

flag bridge. He had been firing out orders non-stop, and he knew he should be tired. And he was…but he wouldn't let himself acknowledge it. He knew how hopeless a position the rearguard was in, the difficulties they would face in surviving for even a few more days, much less doubling back and linking up with the fleet. But he had something inside him, a force energizing him, driving him.

He'd stare at the main display, silently, sometimes for ten or twenty minutes at a stretch without speaking, without looking away. He would focus, think…and then it would come together. A tactic, a trick, some desperate ploy to confuse the enemy, to give his outgunned warriors a chance to dish out some damage…and then to escape to fight again.

He'd shout out commands, ship names followed by coordinates, navigational settings. He was doing the calculations in his head, using his gut as much as his brain to direct the running fight. His stratagems had kept his ships in the battle, though his reluctance to allow his people to stay in close range and fight for extended periods had reduced the damage they inflicted too. And it took a lot of punishment to take out a First Imperium ship.

He knew he couldn't destroy the fleet that was chasing them, not with his skittish tactics…and not in a toe to toe fight to the death either. But beating them wasn't his goal. Leading them away from the rest of the fleet was. And even as his crews fought off the exhaustion and stared bleary eyed at their screens, they pulled the enemy deeper along this course. Away from Shangri la. Away from West and the rest of the fleet.

"Contact Kure. Captain Coda is to move to engage the new contacts. I'm placing Kent and Belfast under his command." He glanced down at his display, his fingers sliding to the side, scrolling to the section of space near the Z19 gate. "He is to position his ships in the dust cloud at 211.012.186."

"Yes, Admiral." Cortez relayed the command. "Captain Coda acknowledges, sir."

was racing. He was sending Coda's ships against a force with twenty times their firepower. They needed an edge. And there was one there, he knew there was…but he just couldn't see it. The dust cloud could provide some cover, degrade enemy targeting systems. But that wasn't enough. They needed more. Then, suddenly, it was clear.

"Get me Captain Coda," he snapped, his eyes still fixed on the display.

"On your line, sir."

"Hitoshi, I want you to position your ships 2 light seconds inside that cloud…and then I want you to launch ten missiles. Set half to detonate half a light second from your ships and half a full light second."

"But, sir…the enemy will still be at least twenty light seconds away when…" Coda's voice trailed off, and Compton recognized understanding. He knew Coda had just seen the readouts on the makeup of the dust cloud. "The radiation…it will block their scans and targeting."

Compton smiled. "Very good, Hitoshi. I want you to launch a dozen scanner buoys…position them just outside the cloud. When those ships get within two and a half light seconds, you unload with everything you've got using the scanner data from the buoys, you hear me? I do meant every fucking thing. And then you take off, and make a mad dash for the X18 gate. You don't wait for Midway, you don't hang around to see what happens. If any of your ships can't keep up, you let them fall behind. You don't stop for anything."

"Understood, Admiral." It was clear Coda didn't like the order, but there wasn't a doubt he'd follow it.

"Good luck, Hitoshi."

"And to you, sir." Compton could tell his officer wanted to say something else, but in the end he just cut the line. "Okay, Jack…let's get Midway up to 4g. We need to block those Leviathans before they cut off our escape route out of the system."

"Yes, Admiral." There was doubt in his voice, uncertainty.

right out of the spacedock, which she was most certainly not.

Compton knew it didn't make sense. Not if you expected Midway to get out of this system. But Compton had used every trick he had, every unexpected, unpredictable move he could come up with. He was out of options. All he could do was plant Midway between the enemy and the rearguard's exit point. And then fight like a motherfucker…and either destroy two ships that each massively outclassed his flagship, in both tonnage and tech…or go down trying.

*   *   *

"The buoys are deployed, Captain. Switching to standby mode now." Fukudu's fingers moved across her workstation. "Project nine minutes until enemy vessels reach two point five light seconds."

Coda nodded. "Very good, Lieutenant. Arm missiles."

Fukudu flipped a series of switches. "Missiles armed and in the tubes, sir. Ready to launch on your command."

"Wave one…" Coda waited, counting off in his head. "…launch."

"Wave one, launching." Fukudu hit a button below the row of switches, and Kure shook as the spread of missiles blasted from their tubes.

Coda stared at the display, watching as the five small icons appeared. They moved out from Kure, zipping along quickly on the screen as they accelerated and blasted away from the stationary cruiser. They began to spread out almost immediately, unlike a normal missile strike.

Coda's eyes moved to the bridge chronometer, his lips moving slowly, counting down. "Wave two," he said calmly, "launch."

Fukudu hit the next button, and Kure shook again, another five small dots appearing on the screen. "All weapons launched…

screen.

"Thirty seconds."

Coda punched the controls of his com unit. "All ships, prepare to execute nav plan Beta-3 on my command…twenty seconds."

"Twenty seconds," Fukudu said, almost in unison with the captain.

Coda sat, trying to look calm for his crew. But inside he could feel the tension, the tightness in his stomach. The plan was brilliant, one more bit of genius from Terrance Compton. But it was complex too, and it required precise execution. The two waves of missiles would detonate simultaneously, bathing the front of the dust cloud with massive radiation. At the precise moment the warheads blew, the three ships would engage their thrusters for ten seconds, changing their positions and forcing the enemy to rescan for their targeting…a sensor sweep that would be largely blocked by the irradiated dust.

If he pulled it off perfectly, the enemy would have no locks on his ships, no real chance to score any hits, at least not for two or three minutes. And at close range, a few minutes was an eternity. During that two minutes, he would activate the line of scanning buoys, giving him targeting data from outside the dust cloud. Then his ships would unload on the enemy. All their remaining missiles, firing in sprint mode at point blank range, as they had in the last battle. Every laser cannon, channeling all the output of reactors running at 110%. If he'd had a guy on the outside of Kure with a box of rocks, he have had him throwing them at the enemy. It would be two minutes of concentrated, non-stop destruction. And then it would stop, and his ships would make a run for it…right to the warp gate.

Coda was concerned about the whole plan, the timing, the remote targeting of his weapons. He knew if his ships didn't do enough damage, the First Imperium force would pursue and catch them. His ships would be drained, almost defenseless, and the enemy survivors would blow them to hell. He sat and

up, his belief in his people. They would get the job done. But when they ran, when they bolted through the warp gate, they would leave Midway behind, alone, facing two enemy battleships. Compton's flagship was the rearguard's rearguard, and it was facing a fight Coda knew it couldn't win. It was hopeless, but then he wondered. Terrance Compton was almost superhuman. Maybe he had a plan. Coda didn't really believe it, but he tried to force himself. He didn't have time to second guess the admiral. It was show time.

"Detonation."

He heard Fukudu's voice in the background, but he wasn't paying attention. He was hunched over his own com. "Execute," he said firmly, authoritatively. Then he gripped the armrests of his chair as Kure's engines blasted with 6g of raw thrust.

*   *   *

"Kure's group has detonated its missiles, Admiral." A few seconds later. "Massive radiation readings in the cloud, sir. We've lost our scanner lock on all three ships."

Compton leaned back. Good. If we can't see them, neither can the enemy. This might just work…

"Very well, Commander." Compton's eyes dropped to his own display. It was divided into two sections. The first showed the dozen ships, mostly Gargoyles, heading toward Kure and her two companions. Coda and his people wouldn't have had a chance in a straight up fight…but Compton had made sure their battle would be anything but a fair fight. Gargoyles were tough, like any First Imperium vessels, but they were only cruisers. They didn't have the armor and power of battleships like the Leviathans. They would be hurt when Coda's people opened up…enough he hoped to give the three ships a chance to escape.

And that will only leave us…

group of pursuing First Imperium ships. And Midway was on the path of the other enemy force. Hopefully, Coda's group would unload their weapons and get away without significant damage. But his own ship was out in the middle of the system, alone in open space. The only way Midway would get to the warp gate itself was to win the fight. That wasn't mathematically impossible, but it was damned close.

"Captain Coda's ships are opening fire, sir."

Compton felt the tension in his gut. He knew Coda's people needed a strong first volley. If they didn't hit the enemy hard enough, they weren't going to get away. The First Imperium ships would pursue and catch them well short of the warp gate. He almost ordered Cortez to report on the strike's effectiveness, but he stopped himself. Jack Cortez knew his job.

"Damage assessments coming in…" Cortez was focused on his screen. "…looks like two direct hits with sprint-deployed missiles, sir." And instant later. "Correction…three hits. All three vessels destroyed!"

Compton smiled. Missiles had always been a long-ranged weapon, one that relied on the abilities of purpose-designed AIs to evade enemy countermeasures and get close enough to target ships to cause damage when they detonated. But the rearguard had been using a different tactic, firing the missiles from close, even point blank range, with the intent not of exploding within a few kilometers of an enemy ship, but of actually impacting a vessel, and delivering the full explosive force to the target.

Five hundred megatons was enough energy to vaporize any vessel, even the biggest, nastiest battleships of the First Imperium. It wasn't easy to get close enough with missiles still in the tubes…the launchers were one of the most fragile systems on a warship, and the heavy fire a ship encountered in a close-ranged fight often knocked the systems offline. But Compton had used the tactic in special situations, when he could get his ships close under some kind of cover. Like the dust cloud. And it was working.

tactic the Compton maneuver, or something equally silly. And there was a good chance it would have stuck. Generations after he was gone, officers would have shouted out commands to prepare for a Compton. Though, rightly, he thought, it should be the Cutter-Compton maneuver. Hieronymus Cutter had modified the guidance software, massively increasing its accuracy, and giving a twelve meter long missile a chance to hit a spaceship across the vast distances involved in space combat.

"Admiral, Captain Coda reports his ships are withdrawing as ordered."

Compton looked down at the screen, watching the damage assessments coming in. They were a mixed bag. Coda's laser barrage had been disappointing, but that was no surprise. The dust cloud that was providing cover for his force wreaked havoc on his lasers, attenuating many of the blasts until they were virtually ineffective. However, another two missiles had struck targets. Coda's force had destroyed five enemy vessels with thermonuclear blasts, and badly damaged several others.

It wasn't a great result, but as Compton's mind reviewed the data, his thoughts coalesced into a single conclusion. Good enough.

"Admiral, Captain Coda requests permission to change course, and join Midway."

"Negative, Commander." Compton wasn't surprised. Coda was a brave officer, one he knew would find his orders to abandon comrades difficult to obey. He found it an interesting trait of the very best officers that emotional considerations like that could supersede judgment. Coda had to realize his own pursuers would come with him, that he'd bring as much or more enemy strength into Midway's fight as his ships would add to the battleship's power. That all he could do is throw the lives of his ships' crews away with those of Midway's. But Compton knew the urge his captain felt was real. He'd experienced it many times himself. "Captain Coda is to follow his orders."

"Yes, Admiral."

he was following his orders, that he'd requested permission to
remain behind and been denied. Nor did it make a difference
that nothing he could have done would have helped. If Midway didn't survive the fight to come, Coda would blame himself.
Compton knew, and he wished there was something he could do
to relieve his officer of the burden. But he knew there wasn't.

He looked up at the display, at the two red circles moving
toward the flagship. Each of those icons represented an enemy
Leviathan, massive battleships bristling with weapons. Midway
was one of the most powerful vessels ever built by mankind, but
it wasn't a match for even a single Leviathan, at least not purely
by equipment and technology.

Compton knew a skilled human commander had an edge
against the unimaginative tactics of an enemy AI, and no human
officer had more experience in facing the First Imperium than
Terrance Compton. But at some point, materiel—guns, tonnage, power generation—told, regardless of an officer's skill.
Compton wasn't sure where that line was, but he suspected he
would find out.

"Bring us to battlestations, Commander. Arm all weapons."

"Yes, sir."

The flag bridge was bathed in the red glow of the battlestations lamps, and Compton could hear the alarms blaring. He
knew all over Midway, his crew was rushing through the corridors…to their stations in engineering, in the gunnery stations,
everywhere. The alert called all of the flagship's crew to duty, to
prepare for battle. And Compton knew his veterans had been
waiting for the summons. They would serve well, he had no
doubt of that. But he just wasn't sure it would be enough.

"Get me Admiral Hurley."

"On your line, Admiral."

"Greta, when can your squadrons be ready to launch?"

"We're ready, sir."

Compton was surprised, but only for an instant. Then it
made perfect sense to him that Greta Hurley had her birds ready

but I need your people to do an anti-missile run. I'm holding back our warheads. I don't know if we can get close enough for sprint-firing with any of the tubes still operational, but I'm going to try. It's the only way I can see us beating both of these ships."

"We'll do our best, sir. We'll keep their missiles from getting through." Hurley's voice had the usual unshakable confidence. Compton had never met another officer like her…so utterly unflappable, no matter what the odds.

He knew Hurley only had fourteen birds left, and he shuddered to think how many might come back, even if Midway somehow survived its desperate fight. But now wasn't the time to worry about it. He needed every bit of force he could muster now, no matter what the cost.

"I know you will, Greta." He wanted to say more, to express to her how vital she had been to the fleet's survival over the past two years, but he didn't. He knew his words would sound like goodbye…and whatever the odds, he wasn't ready to give up… on Hurley or on Midway. So he just said, "You may begin your launch."

*   *   *

"Wolfpack leader, bring your birds around, 233.118.044… full thrust." Hurley stared down at her display, her eyes darting back and forth between the blue squares of her fighters and the tiny yellow dots…each one representing a multi-gigaton antimatter warhead moving toward Midway. Any one of those missiles could cause serious damage to Compton's ship if it got within a few kilometers, even destroy it. But they had to get past her people first.

"Yes, Admiral." She remembered Becca Coombs from the day she'd reported for duty fresh from the Academy. The pilot

of the lucky ones, as she herself had been so long ago. She'd survived her early days, lived long enough to gain the experience that made long term survival something more than a mathematical anomaly. She was still serving under Hurley, as she had for her entire career, though now she was commanding one of the fighter corps' crack squadrons. The Wolfpack had distinguished itself throughout the First Imperium War, and especially in the wild struggles of the past eighteen months, as the trapped fleet fought time and time again to survive. Coombs' people were responsible for destroying fifteen enemy vessels, an astonishing kill record for a single squadron.

Coombs and Mariko Fujin were Hurley's choices as her own successors. But Coombs was here with her, part of the desperate rearguard, and Fujin was on Saratoga, fighting for her life after almost dying in Midway's stricken launch bay. If none of them survived, the fleet's fighter corps would be leaderless, in an even worse shambles than the devastating battles of the past year and a half had left it.

"You ready, John?" She glanced over at Wilder. The pilot was hunched over his station, his own eyes staring at the wave of incoming warheads.

"As ready as I'll ever be, Admiral." He paused. "That's a lot of missiles."

Hurley just nodded. There was nothing to say. It was a lot of missiles. She just sat, quietly, staring at the screen as the dots moved closer. Finally, she flipped her com to the wing channel. "Okay, people…it's time. You know what to do. Give me your best. And remember, Midway is counting on us. Admiral Compton is counting on us."

"Engaging thrust at 2g." Wilder pulled back on the throttle, and Hurley felt the force of twice her weight pressing against her. She was staring at the screen, watching the clusters of enemy missiles moving closer. She felt the temptation to snap out orders, to point out targets to Wilder. But her pilot knew what he was doing. There was nothing she could add, no pur-

stood. She had been ruled by raw energy in those days, but now she had years of experience to temper her drive. It was the combination of the two that made her the commander she was, but she sometimes missed the simplicity of acting on pure courage and élan.

She could see that Wilder was going after the same cluster of missiles she was going to point out. There were about a dozen of them, and they were heading right for Midway. And John Wilder was right behind them. A few seconds later, the fighter echoed with the high pitched whine of the laser cannons…and one of the dots disappeared from the display. Then another. And another. Wilder was angling the ship's thrust, moving toward a missile then angling away the instant it was destroyed. Greta Hurley had pioneered the use of fighters in missile defense, and her protégés like Wilder had continued to refine the tactics.

She watched as her fighters dispersed, each one picking a group of missiles and chasing them down, laser cannons blasting away. She felt pride in the crews she had trained and led, but it felt strange, uncomfortable to just sit there quietly…to watch as her people struggled to defend Midway, to clear a path through the barrage for the fleet's flagship.

She knew the fighters were a bit sluggish for the pinpoint maneuvers needed for anti-missile ops. Normally, a fighter wing on point defense duty would have empty bomb bays, but her birds had two plasma torpedoes each, weapons she intended to use against the enemy ships as soon as the missiles were gone. Her ships would be low on fuel by then. Normally, they would return to their base ship to refuel and rearm with torpedoes, but there was no time. They could never get back, land, and rearm. Not before the Leviathans reached the flagship.

Midway needed every edge it could get in this fight, and she was damned sure of one thing. The fighters would do their part. And more.

Chapter Fifteen

AS Saratoga
System X108
The Fleet: 88 ships (+2 Leviathans), 20988 crew

"Launch all fighters." West's voice was grim, cold. She stared out at the main screen as she barked the command. It had been two months since her people had fought the First Imperium's warships, but that respite had been all too brief. Admiral Compton and the rearguard had managed to buy the fleet time to reach Shangri la...but little more than that.

Another few days, and maybe we'd have found something useful there. Maybe...

The fleet coming through the warp gate was a large one, spearheaded by a line of Leviathans. She'd watched the scanners intently as the enemy vessels transited in, counting tonnage, guns...figuring tactics. And waiting to see if the enemy had any Colossuses. The massive enemy superbattleships were unimaginable engines of destruction that outgunned and outranged anything she had. But there were none, at least not yet. The enemy fleet was strong, but not invincible. Her people could take it. Maybe. Just. But it would cost. And that would start

rons of the fleet's best, and Mariko Fujin was still in sickbay in a coma. That left Beverly Jones and 38 ships, more than a few of them damaged and hastily patched back together…all that remained of the fleet's once mighty fighter corps. The pilots and crews of those birds had done so much—and paid such a price—even an officer as cold blooded as West wished she could spare them this fight. But she couldn't. She needed everything she could get.

She felt anger inside, at herself. At her recklessness. It was her aggressive approach, her failure to foresee that those who built Shangri la were the Regent's enemies, that had cost the fleet much of its remaining firepower. Four Leviathans, half the strength she'd had, lost in a few seconds.

I could use those ships now…

She flipped her com unit to the direct line to Saratoga's bridge. "Davis, I'm going to have to be aggressive with Saratoga. It's too much of our remaining firepower to hold back and play flagship." A pause. "I need your best, from you…and from every man and woman on Saratoga's crew." Davis Black was an experienced captain, and she'd learned to rely on him. But West left nothing for granted.

"We'll be ready, Admiral. For whatever you need."

"I know you will." She moved her hand over the controls to cut the line, but she hesitated. "Good luck, Davis."

"Good luck, Admiral."

West closed the line. Then she turned toward Hank Krantz. "Once more, old friend. Once more into the breach."

"Yes, Admiral." The tactical officer looked over at her command chair, even managing a fleeting smile. "We've been there before, haven't we? More than once."

"Indeed we have, Hank." Her eyes moved toward the display showing the planet they called Shangri la. And the dozens of orbital stations surrounding it, the attack platforms that had obliterated four Leviathans as if they were blowing out so many candles.

help…but she was hesitant to count on anything she didn't control. The landing party had reported in a few minutes before. Hieronymus Cutter had found a way into an underground complex of some sort. West would have normally ignored the news, at least when battle called. But she'd learned not to underestimate the brilliant scientist. He was as responsible as Admiral Compton, she knew, for the fleet's survival, and though he didn't get the credit Compton did fleetwide, West wasn't going to underestimate him. He had a practicality that was rare for an academic…and a toughness that had surprised virtually everyone who knew him. Indeed, the Marines loved him…they had made him one of their own. And West had known enough Marines to understand what that meant.

She turned back toward Krantz. Whatever Cutter could do, she had no doubt he would. But now it was time for her to do what she did best. "Commander Krantz…the fleet is to move forward, 3g accelerating. Directly toward the enemy fleet."

*   *   *

Max Harmon sat in Saratoga's sickbay, as he had for much of the past two months. Mariko was still alive, a fact the doctors were calling a minor miracle. But they had also told him the longer she remained unconscious, the less chance there was of a recovery. Grant Wainwright had spent almost three weeks in the bed next to Fujin's, in much the same condition, but he'd lost his fight over a month ago. The pilot had never regained consciousness, not for an instant…and now Mariko Fujin was the last survivor from the bay. Harmon loved her…he realized that more than ever now, the terrible pain he felt only confirming the emotions he'd had before. She lay in her bed, unmoving, the same as she had been for weeks and weeks now. And he sat next to her, waiting, watching every second for the slightest move.

ing some part of him believed the superstitions about the silly little thing. He'd argued with himself, but in the end he decided it didn't hurt anything. The tiny lump of metal was allegedly responsible for a number of close escapes in his family…and his mother, cold, no-nonsense admiral that she was, had blamed herself for years for letting his father go off to the Tau Ceti 3 invasion so long ago without it.

He felt strange, sitting idle when the fleet was at battlestations. He'd spent many of the fleet's battles on Midway's flag bridge, as Compton's tactical officer. But the admiral had promoted him out of that role, and made him a troubleshooter of sorts. Compton had helped the admiral stop the mutiny a year before, and he'd completed a number of missions since then, most recently helping West keep an eye on some of the less trustworthy captains in the fleet. But nothing kept those fools in check like an enemy attack. So once again, he had nothing to do.

He'd wanted to go with Compton, but the admiral had ordered him to stay behind. Now Midway and the rearguard were gone. No, not gone, Harmon thought, unable to accept that the admiral might be dead, along with everyone on the ships he'd taken with him. Just not here. And though Erika West respected him, he'd fallen out of the usual chain of command. There was no place for him now. Except where he was.

It didn't matter, really. The fleet wasn't short of commanders right now…it was short of ships, trained spacers, ordnance. Eighteen months of running, and countless deadly battles had worn the fleet down to a nub. But it still felt strange not being in the action.

Harmon closed his eyes, seeking a few minutes relief from the burning. He couldn't remember how long he'd been up, but he knew he couldn't sleep…and certainly not when Saratoga was going into battle. He'd be right here if West needed him.

He took a breath and opened his eyes, staring down at Mariko again. And she was staring back.

"Max…" Her voice was soft, weak…barely audible. He leaned down, put his ear to her lips. "Where?"

"You're in sickbay, Mariko. On Saratoga." He was fighting back the shock, trying to stay calm for her. He'd refused to give up on her, but now he realized he had, at least to an extent. He was stunned to see her look at him, to hear her voice.

"Sa…ra…to…ga?"

"Yes, Mariko. Midway went off on a…mission. Admiral Compton moved all the wounded over to Saratoga."

"You…here?"

Harmon paused. Even right out of a coma, she went right to the heart of the matter. Compton would never have left Harmon behind…not if he expected to return. And Mariko knew it.

"He asked me to help Admiral West." He felt bad for lying, but he didn't want to burden her with too much to worry about. Not now.

"Grant…crew…"

Harmon paused, taking a deep breath. He had a fleeting impulse to lie to her, to spare her the terrible news until she was stronger. But though they were lovers, they were both warriors as well. They owed each other better than that.

"They're all dead, Mariko. Grant survived for three weeks, but he never woke up." His voice was soft, as sympathetic as he could make it.

She just stared back at him. They had both lost friends before. It was part of the service. He knew she'd mourn later, that she'd find ways he couldn't imagine to blame herself.

She tried to speak, but nothing came out. She swallowed hard and croaked, "Water…"

Of course! What the hell am I thinking?

He spun around. "Doctor…doctor, it's Mariko Fujin…she's awake." He turned back and looked down at her, feeling the waves of relief finally come over him. "She's awake…and she's thirsty…"

*   *   *

"I want those laser cannons recharged in twenty seconds, Commander. Not an instant longer or I will go down there myself and start chucking people out the airlock." Davis Black was normally easygoing, one of the most popular captains in the fleet. But in battle he changed, morphed into a tyrant, one with no patience—none—for anything less than top performance. He'd brought the ship through so many battles, escaped so often from almost certain death, that his crew forgave him his ornery nature under fire. But they still scrambled to do whatever they could…anything to keep that terrible rage off of them.

"Yes, sir," the tactical officer replied. "Lieutenant Hoover acknowledges, sir."

"Acknowledges? What the fuck does that mean? The people on this ship should know better than to give me bullshit, mealy-mouthed answers by now." He paused, glaring at the officer. "And why is Hoover answering. Where is Qwill?"

"Commander Qwill is dead, sir. Lieutenant Hoover is in command down there." Another pause, a short one. Then the sound of the lasers firing. Eighteen seconds, two ahead of schedule. The tactical officer let out a grateful sigh.

Black just shook his head. Qwill had been with him for years, back when he had been Saratoga's XO during the last battles of the Third Frontier War. Another good officer—and a friend—gone…

"Give Hoover my compliments…and remind him that means every twenty seconds." There was no time to let up, to grieve friends. Not now. The fleet's acting flagship had drawn a lot of attention from the enemy. Those AIs are learning from us, he thought. They're learning to pick their targets.

"Navigation, bring us around, course 098.230.358, two gee thrust." Admiral West had given Saratoga a specific area of space to cover, but she'd left a lot of maneuver room for Black.

come aboard to take over Saratoga's task force. He'd served on flagships for most of his career, and he knew that a lot of admirals, even some good ones, tended to overmanage their flag captains. For as much as Black had admired Barret Dumont, he'd chafed more than once under the old admiral's tight control. He'd been worried when he found out West was taking over after Dumont's death, but he'd been surprised at her hands off approach.

Too busy terrorizing the rest of the fleet, I guess.

The ship shook. Hard. Then its vector shifted. Black knew his ship was venting gasses, exerting makeshift thrust that was throwing her off course.

"Navigation, correct course and velocity." He knew that was easier said than done. If the hit had just blown a compartment, all the air would be out already. But if a fluid or gas line had been ruptured, it would continue to spew until it was cut off. And it would affect the ship's vector all the while.

"Navigation reports corrections underway, Captain."

Black felt it immediately, a change in the thrust vector, and in increase to nearly 3g. He nodded to himself. He was proud of crew, of their crack performance in battle.

He heard the lasers fire again, the sound a bit quieter than it had been, and he knew he'd lost a battery….maybe two. His eyes dropped to the screen to check, but before he could focus, Saratoga shook again, much harder this time. A whole section of workstations went dark along the port side, and a conduit fell from the ceiling, spewing steam across the flag bridge. One of his officers screamed as the super-heated steam hit her full on, sending her falling to the deck.

"Medical to the bridge," Davis shouted into his com. "Now!"

He unhooked his harness and leapt from his chair, rushing over to the stricken officer. He knew immediately it was bad… very bad. She was lying on her back, howling in agony, burned from head to toe.

Davis looked toward the lift. He knew it had only been a few

He could see the bridge crew, frozen at their stations, staring in horror at their hideously injured comrade. "Back to work, all of you…we're in battle!"

He looked back down at his officer. Beckwith. Sandra Beckwith, a communications specialist. He didn't know her very well…she'd come over from Midway when Admiral Compton had transferred all non-essential personnel before departing with the rearguard. She'd done her duties well enough, but he'd hardly exchanged a dozen words with her. She'd only been on bridge duty because Lieutenant Ringer had been injured in a maintenance accident.

He heard the lift doors slide open, and he could see the shadows of the med team moving around him. The medic knelt next to her, his gaze moving over her injuries. Black could see it in his eyes. She wasn't going to make it.

He tried to force himself away, get back to running the ship, but he couldn't, not for a few seconds at least. He was an experienced captain, the veteran of more battles than he could easily count, but staring at this woman, this officer he hardly knew, was too much for him. For a few seconds, at least. Her suffering was hard to watch, but he couldn't break free. He just knelt there on the bridge floor, watching as the medic gave her a massive dose of painkillers…and then he and his assistant reached under her and began to lift her up.

She screamed as they pulled her from the floor, in spite of the meds, and Black watched the torment in her face, tears streaming down her cheeks. He gritted his teeth, using all his self-control to stay where he was, not to move toward her. There was nothing he could do—probably nothing anyone could do. And he had a ship to run. He stood up slowly, turning his head away as he did, back toward the main display. Then he walked back to his chair…and he didn't look back. He couldn't. And a few seconds later the lift closed behind the medics, and Lieutenant Beckwith was gone.

*   *   *

"Saratoga's in trouble…" Bill Ving was speaking to himself. He sat in his command chair, alone on the bridge, leaning backward, gritting his teeth against the pain in his chest, his gut. He was sick. No, not sick…dying. My whole crew is dying.

He glanced over at the empty tactical station. Sara Iverson had been a tremendous officer, one of the best he'd ever seen, with a combat record that would have been the pride of an officer twice her age. And she'd been his friend. But she was gone now, dead of the mysterious disease that was even now killing him. The plague that would soon leave Snow Leopard a lifeless hulk, a ghost ship in the truest sense of the term.

Ving mourned for his crew, and he felt his own fear as he faced approaching death. His every breath was a tortured effort to force air into congested lungs. His fever was raging, his neck and back dripping with sweat. His mind tried to drift off into delirium, revisiting images of the distant past, but he held on, barely, his force of will struggling to cling to the threads of clarity for just a little longer. Ving had no hope for his ship, his crew…no delusions he faced anything but impending death. But he wasn't dead yet, and intended to strike one last blow before he slipped into darkness.

He slammed his hand down on the com unit. "Engine room, this is the captain. Who is down there? Anyone?"

There was nothing but silence, at least for ten or twenty seconds. Then, just as Ving was about to give up hope, a single voice, weak, struggling, replied. "Captain…this is Ensign Cleeves, sir."

Ving felt a wave of satisfaction at the response, a dim ray of light in the blackness looming around him. He'd been afraid no one would answer. He knew all his people were infected, and as the crew dwindled, ship's operations had begun to come to a halt. Snow Leopard was fully-supplied and ready for battle, but

Dr. Flynn was dead too, along with all his staff, and Ving suspected sickbay had become a hellish nightmare of suffering, full of dying men and women with no one left to care for them, not even a friendly voice, offering a last sip of water to a parched and dying man or woman. He knew the AI-directed medpods would continue to care for patients, but he was well aware there were only a few of them, and that most of his people were lying on the floor or on whatever makeshift setups Flynn's people had managed to cobble together. He hated the thought of his crew suffering, living their last hours abandoned, in pain and squalor. But he forced his thoughts away. All around his crippled ship, a battle was raging, one that might decide the fate of the fleet, as so many before it had. Snow Leopard had been the scourge of the enemy in past battles…and she would have one more vic-tory. Her captain would see to it.

Ving felt a wave of strength, but he knew it would be his last. He intended to make it count. There was still one last duty, and Captain William Ving intended to die in combat, not bent over on the floor, vomiting blood and gasping for his last breaths.

"Cleeves, we've got something to do, son." Sam Cleeves had been a week out of the Academy when the fleet left to advance against the First Imperium. He was twenty-two years old, but Ving wouldn't have believed it if he hadn't seen the kid's person-nel record. He looked about sixteen. But he wasn't a rookie anymore, no one who'd been through the last eighteen months was. And Ving wasn't going to treat him like one. "Saratoga's in trouble, Sam…there are two enemy Leviathans closing on her, and nothing else near enough to intervene." He paused. "Except us."

"Sir, we don't have any active gunnery stations. I'm the only one down here…and as far as I can tell, the reactor is unat-tended. The AI's running basic operations, but we've got no repair crews. Nothing. I don't see how we can fight a Leviathan."

Ving stared down at the com unit, imagining the young ensign, alone in the engine room, sick, scared…dying. "Ensign,

the engines ready for a hard burn…and then I want you to get down to the bomb bay and get the plasma torpedoes ready."

"I don't understand, Captain. Ready for what? They're still in the crates…I can't get them on the firing track myself."

"I don't want them on the tracks, son. I just want them armed for overloads."

"Sir?" There was confusion in the ensign's voice…and perhaps the first bits of terrible realization.

"Just get those warheads ready to blow. I'm going to get the AI to set the reactor up for a controlled containment failure." He paused, and there was a moment of total silence. "We're not going to shoot at that Leviathan, son." Another pause, as Ving looked around his empty bridge once more. "We're going to ram Snow Leopard right down their throats."

*   *   *

"What the hell?" Erika West stared at the display. She knew what she was seeing, but some part of her couldn't believe it.

"What ship is that? Snow Leopard?" Her eyes were fixed on the fast-moving icon. "Get me Captain Ving! Now!"

Krantz leaned over his console for a few seconds. Then he turned back toward West. "Captain Ving, Admiral."

"Bill, what the hell are you doing over there?" She knew, but she had to hear it from him.

"That Leviathan is going to cut off Saratoga." His voice was weak, forced. "It's too much firepower, too close. I'll take care of it for you." She could hear him gasping for air.

"No," she said. "Captain Ving, we do not send ships to make suicide runs. Return to your previous heading."

"Please, admiral…I'm dead already. We all are. The disease…it's killed half the crew. I only have two people still at their posts…and neither of us are going to last long. Let us die

But she was easily moved too, especially by acts of courage and loyalty. William Ving and his crew were dying, they were sick, weak, in pain. And his thoughts were on his duty, on how he could contribute once more before he died.

West knew she had to let him do it. She couldn't refuse… force him to sit where he was and die in misery and futility. Or he might ignore her order, ram the enemy vessel anyway…and her refusal would turn his act of devotion into one of mutiny. No, she couldn't do that. She wouldn't.

"Very well, Captain Ving. You have my permission." She paused, fighting back a wave of emotion she knew her staff would find unsettling if it slipped out. "And the thoughts and prayers of everyone in the fleet go with you and your crew." She took a deep breath. "It has been an honor to serve with you, William Ving."

"And you, Admiral." The line went dead. West knew Ving needed all his strength for his ship's final attack.

She turned toward the display, trying to maintain her composure as she watched the icon move swiftly across the screen. She couldn't help but smile when she saw his course, right from behind Saratoga. The enemy battleship was closing rapidly on the human flagship…and Snow Leopard was coming up from behind Saratoga, in the scanner shadow of the Yorktown class battlewagon.

"I'll be damned," she whispered under her breath. The enemy wouldn't see Ving's ship, not until it was too late. The attack ship would zip right by Saratoga at almost 0.02c, and then it would smash into the First Imperium vessel. West couldn't imagine the energy that would be released when the twelve thousand tons of the attack ship slammed into the Leviathan at two percent of lightspeed, but she knew one thing. There wouldn't be a piece left of the enemy battleship bigger than shattered chunks of atoms.

She just nodded as she watched. Snow Leopard had one of the best combat records in the fleet, and Bill Ving was one of

Saratoga shook hard. Another hit. A bad one. She left running the ship to Davis Black, but she was starting to worry about how long her flagship could take the pounding. The flag bridge was still fully operative, except for a few minor shorts, but she could tell the ship itself was in trouble. She could feel the internal explosions, smell the chemicals and smoke in the air. She knew Saratoga was spewing gases and liquids through her rent hull…and she realized Ving's desperate attack was the ship's only chance.

She stared down as the small icon moved toward the blue star that represented Saratoga. Just a few more seconds.

Saratoga shook again, harder this time, and the lights on the flag bridge dimmed.

"Admiral, Captain Black reports reactor B scragged. He's reduced non-essential power usage to keep the lasers firing."

"Very well," she said, as she watched Snow Leopard zip around Saratoga…and head straight for the enemy ship."

"Die well, William Ving…and all on Snow Leopard. Your comrades salute you…and they thank you." She spoke softly, with more emotion in her voice than anyone on the flag bridge had heard before.

A few seconds later, Snow Leopard's icon vanished…along with the Leviathan's. Ving's ship had one final kill to its record… and Erika West intended to make sure it went down in the official records.

*   *   *

Cutter leaned over the workstation, his fingers moving in a blur. The alien keyboards weren't the same as ones built and used by humans, nor, of course were the symbols anything like an Earth alphabet. But he realized he somehow had the

since he'd left X48 II, and now he realized the alien had left him with more than just the memories of their encounter. Somehow Cutter knew this place, as though he'd been there years before. He realized that was ridiculous, yet he seemed to understand how to use all the equipment.

He hadn't come there expecting to know his way around. Indeed, he was almost certain the knowledge was buried somehow, surfacing only when he needed it.

Like now.

"Admiral West," he said, leaning his face toward a small, glowing sphere. "Admiral West, do you read me?"

Connor Frasier stood behind him. The Marine looked around every few seconds, as if he expected someone to come running out of some hidden hallway or compartment. He had his assault rifle out at the ready, but Cutter had ordered him not to fire without his expressed permission. The last thing he needed was for Frasier to go shooting up all this mysterious First Imperium tech.

"Dr. Cutter?" It was West, her voice raw, distracted. "What is it, Doctor…I'm afraid I've got my hands full right…" She paused for an instant. "How are you sending this message, Doctor? You're still on the planet, aren't you?" Cutter understood her confusion. Saratoga was well outside the range of any human-built portable transmitter.

Cutter nodded, a pointless gesture he realized immediately. "Yes, Admiral. I'm…ah…borrowing some of the First Imperium equipment down here." He could hear sounds in the background, explosions, alarms.

"Doctor, I'm afraid…"

"Listen to me, Admiral…very carefully. I have gained control over the planetary defense grid. The weapons protecting this world are extremely powerful, as we saw when our Leviathans were destroyed. But you are out of range right now…the enemy is out of range. If you can retreat, pull the First Imperium forces back with you…the defense systems will engage

tor…what is the effective range?"

"Two point five light seconds, Admiral. I will pause the auto-attack sequence so the enemy doesn't get any warning. Get the entire enemy fleet within two point five light seconds of the planet…and I'll do the rest."

He knew he was asking her to trust him with the fate of the fleet…on very little actual data. He expected a fight, and he was trying to put together his argument to challenge whatever she threw back at him. But she said simply, "Understood." Then the line went dead.

*   *   *

"Commander Krantz, tell Captain Vogel he has to get those ships moving faster. I don't care how he does it, but he needs to be at the designated point in four minutes." West had been snapping out orders nonstop. She'd suddenly commanded her ships to break off, pull back, insisting they reach specified positions in a matter of minutes.

Most of the ship's captains branded the commands impossible, but she just repeated them, louder and with more focused rage behind them. Her staff had told her many times how much the fleet's captains were afraid of her. Now she was going to find out how afraid.

"Yes, Admiral." Krantz was used to West, but even he seemed unnerved at the force of her orders. Ever since she'd spoken with Hieronymus Cutter, she'd been on a rampage. She hadn't explained anything, she'd just ordered the whole fleet to fall back. The tactic seemed ill-advised…it took the fleet out of formation…and the retreat would let the enemy ships get closer to the planet, the destination on which everyone in the fleet had placed all their hopes. A place they knew they had to defend at all costs. But no one had the guts to challenge West, not now.

enemy appears to be pursuing."

"All enemy ships?"

"Most of them, Admiral. It appears they have a small tactical reserve."

Shit. Anything outside range when Cutter lets loose with those weapons is going to survive…

"Get me Commander Jones."

"Yes, Admiral." Krantz turned toward his workstation. "Commander Jones on your line."

"Beverly, what's the status of your squadrons?" West was uncomfortable. Sending the fighters on a desperate, nearly-suicidal mission was virtually a cliché in the fleet, but it still felt unfair. No one had borne more of the burden to buy the fleet's survival, nor paid a higher price. But she had to pull the fleet back, close enough to Shangri la for Cutter to unleash the planet's deadly defenses. And she couldn't leave a whole enemy task force behind, out of range and able to flee, to warn the Regent's forces what the X108 system held.

"We're good, Admiral. Luck seems to be with us for a change. We've only lost one ship…and the crew managed to eject in time."

West sighed softly. Jones was a good officer, but she'd only ended up in command as soon as she did because Fujin was in sickbay and Hurley had gone with Compton. She was in over her head, and despite the success her people had enjoyed so far, West could hear it in her voice.

"We're pulling the fleet back, Commander, to a new position two light seconds out from the planet. The enemy appears to be following…all except one task force. I need your people to hit that force, Beverly…and I do mean with everything you have. None of those ships can get away, do you understand me?"

"Yes, Admiral." West could hear the tension in Jones' voice, her struggle to sound confident, to hide her uncertainty. "You can count on us."

I hope so, Beverly. I hope so.

of tiny dots representing the fighters.
    I hope so…

Chapter Sixteen

AS Midway
Z16 System
The Fleet: 87 ships (+2 Leviathans), 20,671 crew

"Arm all missiles. Prepare to launch." Compton snapped out the order, his voice louder, harder than he'd intended. He'd been waiting, holding back the command as long as he could. He'd felt Cortez' eyes on him the whole time, the tension of his entire flag bridge crew as the seconds ticked away. The use of missiles in sprint mode was a new tactic, one he had invented, but now he was changing it again, taking it from aggressive to downright crazy. He knew his people were waiting for the launch order…but they were going to have to wait a bit longer.

Midway shook hard. The vessel had moved into energy weapons range of the enemy, and the guns of the two Leviathans had opened fire. The First Imperium lasers were powerful weapons, but at this distance only a small percentage scored hits, and those that did had dissipated much of their energy by the time they reached Midway. But even a weakened weapon from one of the great battleships hurt, and the damage reports were already coming in.

thirds of the incoming warheads. The weakened volley then moved right through Midway's point defense zone, first the battleship's anti-missile laser batteries…and then the shotguns, the magnetic catapults that blasted clouds of heavy metal pellets out at enormous speed. Even a tiny scrap of metal could destroy a missile when it hit at 0.01c.

In the end, only half a dozen missiles got through, and just two of them were close enough to cause any damage, mostly overloads and crew casualties from heavy radiation blasts. Compton felt every crew member he lost, and he knew any damage to Midway's physical plant could be the difference between victory and defeat in the battle to come. But he was still relieved. It had gone better than he'd dared to imagine.

The ship rocked again, harder this time…another hit, and some kind of internal explosion from the feel of it. Midway's lasers were still silent. The enemy weapons had longer range… and Compton's flagship couldn't activate its heavy laser cannons while the missiles were still in the tubes.

"Forty thousand kilometers, Admiral." Cortez was starting to sound nervous.

Compton didn't reply. He just sat in his chair, staring at the display. The closest any ship had gotten before sprint firing its missiles was fifty thousand kilometers. But Compton planned to smash that record to oblivion.

"Thirty thousand kilometers."

"Commander Cortez, I want all laser crews ready to arm and fire their weapons on an instant's notice."

"Yes, Admiral." Cortez hesitated for a second, staring over at Compton.

"And Commander, advise the engineering crew I want full power to the lasers immediately after missile launch." He paused. "And I do mean fucking immediately." Compton rarely swore when he gave orders…which was why he'd chosen to now. He wanted his people as good as they could be, on the edge, driven to the absolute limits of their ability. Anything less,

at Compton, his tension bubbling over. This wasn't close for sprint missile fire…it was downright insane. "Sir!"

"Hold," Compton said, his voice frozen. Midway shook again, twice in rapid succession. They were in close range of the enemy lasers now, and each hit was taking a toll.

"Damage reports, sir," Cortez said. "We lost two missile launchers."

"Acknowledged." Compton sounded like an automaton. Unshakable, fearless. But inside he felt the tension in his stomach and with each deliberative breath. He knew the missile launchers were fragile, that he would lose some during the approach. But two in one shot? He felt his throat tighten.

Stay with the plan…just a few more seconds…

"Twenty thousand kil…"

"All missiles…launch!"

Cortez whipped around, back to his station, and he ran his fingers down the board, flipping a series of levers. Midway shook ten times in rapid succession, as each of her active launchers spat out its deadly ordnance. The ten missiles appeared on the screen immediately, already moving at three hundred kilometers per second and accelerating at 50g.

"Navigation plan Gamma-2…engage. All laser batteries, fire!"

Midway lurched hard as its engines engaged, and Compton felt the 3g of thrust pressing hard against him. The burst wouldn't be long, only twenty seconds. Just enough to confuse the enemy targeting systems, as the AIs running those two ships raced to respond to the unexpected threat of Midway's missiles.

He heard the distant whining, the sounds of his ship's lasers firing. And he saw a small cluster of dots, closing on the enemy ships from behind. Hurley and her ten surviving fighters, beginning their attack run.

He felt the heat inside him, the hunter's instinct that came over him in battle. Fifty years at war, yet every time the enemy was in his sights he felt it. Just like the first time.

*   *   *

"Alright people, let's go. There's one ship left…let's make that zero. All ships, converge and begin attack runs. Let's take that fucker out." Greta Hurley still felt the tingle, the residual excitement from a moment earlier, when she'd seen one of Compton's sprint missiles slam right into the other enemy Leviathan…and vaporize the massive battleship with 550 megatons of pure destruction. She'd heard the shouts on all her ships over the main com channel. A doomed struggle had just become a bit less hopeless, and the energy surged through her veins. She'd been planning to send five of her fighters against each of the enemy vessels, but now she had them concentrated on the sole survivor. And ten attacks could do some serious damage. A Leviathan was hard to destroy, especially an undamaged one, but her people would do their part.

"Are you ready, John?" She stared across the cockpit at her pilot.

"Ready, Admiral."

"Then lead us in." She turned back to the com, changing to the wing circuit. "Alright people, it's time. Form up on my ship. I don't want to see anybody popping off shots at long range. Everybody closes to point blank. Anybody launches a torpedo more than 10,000 klicks out has to deal with me." She flipped off the com.

"Okay, John…let's go."

Wilder pushed the throttle forward, and the fighter accelerated hard. Hurley felt the pressure slam into her…6g she guessed, though she didn't bother to check. She just stared straight ahead, focused on the enemy ship.

The First Imperium did not have fighters, and they employed their missile defense systems against the small ships in lieu of a purpose-designed array. Their light lasers and anti-missile rockets were dangerous, but they were repurposed weapons, inher-

First Imperium fire as they attacked. Hurley knew for all the losses she'd suffered, it could have been worse. That seemed a perverse thought about a force that had lost 90% of its strength over the past eighteen months, but she knew her people had been lucky too, that the odds had been far worse even than the terrible result. She knew they might all be dead now, indeed they should all be dead…months ago. And then the fleet would have been lost too. More than once, her fighters had been the difference between victory and defeat. Yes, luck had been with them.

But as she gazed at the display, she felt a knot in her stomach. She knew, almost immediately, with a cold certainty. Luck had deserted them.

She watched as three of her ten ships vanished within seconds of each other. The enemy fire was heavy, but no different than usual. But at this moment in time, the blasts were finding their targets. She thought about it in clinical terms, ships lost, reduction in firepower. There would be time later to remember the actual people lost, the faces of the dead.

No one in the force said anything, but she could hear their thoughts, their self-preservation instincts urging them to fire their torpedoes and break off as quickly as possible. But they wouldn't. She knew they would follow her orders, even if they were hating her as they did.

She felt her own urge to order them all to shoot and then make a run for it. She didn't want to die any more than any of her people. But the losses only made it more essential for her force to finish its mission. They were down to seven…and they had a Leviathan to destroy. She could see on the scanner. Midway was hurting the enemy ship, but she was taking more than she was giving. Hurley knew her fighters had to even the score. Or they would all die here…her people, Midway, Admiral Compton.

She felt the fighter lurch hard, Wilder's evasive maneuvers. Then it shook again, but it was different this time. A hit. Her eyes darted around the cockpit. None of her people were

"A laser grazed us on the belly, Captain. Looks like some minor damage, loss of pressurization in the lower compartment." He paused. "Could have been worse."

She took a deep breath and nodded. "Yes, it could have been worse." Her eyes were still on the display, watching as a fourth of her ships winked out. Another plasma torpedo gone…five more brave crew dead.

She flipped on the forcewide com. She felt the same fear they all did, the grief at the loss of comrades. But Midway was counting on them…and if they didn't at least hurt this thing, the flagship was going to be destroyed. And the surviving fighters would be trapped with no place to land.

"I know you've all seen our losses, you know that twenty of our comrades have died in the last two minutes. But that only makes our duty all the more crucial. Midway is fighting a deadly battle…and she is losing. If our attack is not a success, the flagship will die…Admiral Compton will die. And we will die too, hunted down by that thing…or suffocated as our life support systems fail. I have fought by your sides, all of you. For eighteen months you have been the symbol of courage, of stubborn defiance, an inspiration to the entire fleet. Now, I ask you to do it again, to follow me right down that thing's throat. For the fleet. For Admiral Compton."

She closed the line and looked down at the floor in front of her. She had the usual conflicted feelings. Everything she had said was the truth, yet she felt a rush of guilt for working her people up into a frenzy, doing all she could to override their rational instincts to survive. She wondered how many martyrs she had created with her rousing battle cries over the years, how many of her people would have returned to base had she not extracted from them the last full measure of duty, the final sacrifice.

"Entering close attack range, Admiral. Fifteen thousand kilometers."

Hurley looked over at Wilder. She was grateful for his words,

"Fight your ship, John. The rest of the birds are forming upon you."

She felt a bit of absurdity in her words. She was an admiral, the only officer in the fighter corps to ever carry such an exalted rank. She'd led a thousand fighters into battle in the great struggles around X2, before the fleet was trapped. Now she sat in her command chair, watching as John Wilder piloted her ship, and her command was a total of six fighters, tattered remnants that equaled a single squadron in strength.

"Twelve thousand." Wilder's voice was distant, distracted. Hurley knew the pilot was focused, his every thought on the target ahead, and on evading the enemy fire as he dove toward it.

Hurley sat, feeling she should be doing something, making some kind of plan, issuing orders. But there was nothing to do. Except sit quietly and wait.

She had a passing thought, darkly amusing. The great Admiral Hurley, the woman who revolutionized fighter tactics. What a fitting end to that story…to die leading six ships in a desperate assault. All the massive battles she'd fought…to bring her here, to something that would barely qualify as a skirmish. If her people hadn't been defending the fleet's flagship, and its legendary commander.

But we are…

"Ten thousand kilometers."

She thought of old friends, of those who'd commanded her when she had first reached the fleet, twenty-three years old and cocky as hell. The traits that made a good fighter jock were different than those that portended success in the fleet proper, and her early mentors didn't try to beat the arrogance out of her… they just try to give her judgment to offset it. And they understood what made a pilot tick, that there was little they could do but stand aside and let experience teach her…if it didn't kill her.

She had won that particular cosmic coin toss, but she remembered peers, men and women who had served alongside her, who had lost. Joe Deedle, Carina Smithers, Ethan Joplin…

they'd had a chance to see where their skills took them.

"Eight thousand kilometers."

Hurley knew how successful she had been, how much glory she had won in battle. But she was cut from the same cloth as most great leaders, men and women like Terrance Compton and Erika West. And others left back home. Augustus Garret, certainly. And Elias Holm, Erik Cain...officers she'd been proud to serve alongside. They all shared certain traits. They weren't humble, not exactly. She knew she was gifted, that she had achieved massive success and left her mark on the tactics of fighter combat. But the inner arrogance that drove her was controlled. It gave her confidence, the ability to follow through, to believe even her most desperate plans had a chance. But she never lost sight of the fact that luck had been her ally as well, that any of those old comrades might have done as she did, had fate not plucked them so young from the battle. And she'd never stopped appreciating the devotion of her people, never took it for granted.

"Six thousand kilometers. Preparing to fire."

Her mind snapped back to the present, her eyes on Wilder as he angled the throttle...and brought his finger down on the firing button.

Nothing happened.

She watched as he hit the control again. And again. Still nothing.

Her eyes dropped to the display. Four thousand five hundred kilometers. If he doesn't pull away now...

Wilder's hands raced over his controls, resetting the firing system.

Four thousand...

He punched down on the firing control again. Still nothing. John...

He hesitated, just for a second. Then Hurley felt the defeat in him as he slammed the throttle hard to the side, and the fighter's engines blasted hard.

over her as she realized they were going to make it. But it only lasted a second, replaced by crushing disappointment. They had run the gauntlet, risked all…only to come away empty.

The bomb bay, she thought. That has to be it. That hit we took…it must have fused the doors shut.

Her eyes dropped to her display. There were four ships there, not five. Another friend lost. But hope too…four more chances to hurt the enemy, to tip the scales just enough for Midway to win the fight.

She stared and watched as the fighters blasted in, as aggressive, as heedless of danger as John Wilder had been. And she knew her earlier words rode with them…to victory or death.

*   *   *

"Art, I need more power. I don't care what you have to do…I don't care about the risks." Compton's voice was deep, his throat dry. The battle with the last Leviathan had been raging unabated. Midway was less than twenty thousand kilometers from its adversary. The ships were trading blows, two wounded giants in the final stages of a fight to the death. Midway's lasers were falling silent one at a time, as enemy hits blasted the guns to scrap or severed the conduits feeding them the massive power they required.

Compton's ship was landing its own hits, blasting apart the Leviathan's hull, blowing its x-ray laser batteries to molten slag. Hurley's fighters had savaged the enemy battleship, despite the grievous losses they had suffered. But a Leviathan could take a lot of punishment, and the battered vessel stood its ground, firing with its remaining weapons.

"Admiral, I'm not even sure what's keeping this thing from blowing. I can't…"

"Up the power, Art…twenty percent…right now!" Comp-

take for want of power could be the one that decided the battle. The Leviathan was ready to go, Compton was sure of it. But Midway was as well. Seconds counted, and watts of power to the lasers did too. "Whatever the danger."

"Yes, sir."

Compton could tell the engineer didn't agree, though his own life rode on the outcome of the battle as much as anyone else's. The admiral had seen many times how some of his most gifted people focused single-mindedly on their own duties, virtually ignoring other considerations. Mendel was right…it was foolish, dangerous to treat a fusion reactor with such contempt. Unless certain death in battle was the alternative. Compton sometimes envied the ability to obsess on a single consideration, instead of being endlessly besieged by a barrage of worries. The admiral's chair was something many officers sought, a dream they aspired to one day attain.

If only they knew what it truly felt like…

Compton cut the line. He didn't have time to argue with Mendel…and the engineer didn't need any distractions. He had his hands full.

Midway shook again, another hit. Compton's veteran senses could tell it came from the starboard side. That was good. Because there was a huge rent in the hull on Midway's port, and if the enemy managed to place a shot in the open, unarmored area…

"Navigation…" Compton leaned over the com unit. "…fire the positioning jets. Keep our starboard side facing the enemy." Midway only had one battery left on her wounded port side…and three on the starboard. And Compton was protecting his ship's weak spot.

"Acknowledged, sir."

It still felt strange, commanding a single ship. He'd been running Midway for months now, ever since Captain Horace had been grievously wounded when the flagship's bridge took a hit. Compton had shuttled Horace over to Saratoga before

not as grim as they had been at first. Compton wondered how his friend was now. He'd either be out of the woods or...he shifted his thoughts away. There was no point in idle speculation. James Horace was a tough fighter. He'd pull through.

Compton had worn two hats after Horace was wounded, but now he had only one. Midway was alone, the rearguard for the rearguard, standing in the breech like the Spartans at Thermopylae. His uniform bore five stars on each shoulder, an insignia only ever worn by one other Alliance officer, but right now he was Midway's captain, no other ships to command, no formations to draw his attention.

"Art," he snapped into the com. "I need that power. Right now."

"Coming, sir." The engineer sounded exhausted, worn down to the last of his strength. He'd been performing miracles with the repair teams, keeping the savaged ship in the fight. And now he was about to roll the dice, and see if his skills could keep Midway's reactor from failing critically...and vaporizing everyone on board. "Increasing power flow now..."

Compton sat in his chair, his eyes on the display. He could see the indicators begin to move as the flow of power from the ship's reactors rose. So far so good. Of course, if it failed, he'd never know. If the reactor lost containment, even for an instant, Midway would be gone in a nanosecond.

"Starboard guns, increase to 120% yield."

"Captain, the guns are already hot, damned near overloaded. If we increase the power, they could burn out entirely." Cortez stared over at the admiral, his eyes wide, his normal poise beginning to fail.

"And if we don't, that thing's going to blow us to plasma." Compton turned and stared at his tactical officer. "Do it. Now."

Midway shook again, another hit. We can't take many more of those...

"And I want all safeties off. I want those guns recharged and firing again as quickly as we can feed power into them."

series of conduits blew, showering the flag bridge with sparks. Compton's display blinked along with all the bridge screens and lights…but it all came right back.

Come on, old girl…hold it together a little longer.

Compton heard the familiar whine, the sounds of the three starboard laser cannons firing. It was louder now, the overloaded guns blasting with output they were never designed to sustain. Then again, another shot…but this time Midway shook again, not from an external shot, but from an internal explosion. One of the overloaded guns had blown…and that meant Midway had lost more of her crew. There were six men and women manning each laser, and Compton doubted any of them had survived. But now there was just one thought in his head.

Down to two guns…

"Maintain fire," he snapped out.

"Yes, sir."

Compton could hear the discomfort in Cortez' voice, the rapprochement at the callousness of his commands, but he just ignored it. His officers were loyal, he knew that. But they were also human.

Maybe one day you will sit in this chair, Jack…and you will know what it is to be in command…

The lasers fired again. And again. Compton stared at his screen, watching the damage assessments coming in. The enemy ship was almost gone…one more good hit would take it out. But it still had power, and two guns firing.

Crash! The sound was loud, and it reverberated throughout the ship. A hit, a bad one. Compton could see his screen light up, dozens of flashing indicators showing the locations of damaged systems, internal explosions, hull compromises. He didn't have to look to know it was bad. The silence that followed told him that.

"Commander the lasers…"

"Blown conduit, sir. Both starboard lasers are offline."

Compton felt like he'd been punched in the gut. Midway and

"Navigation…bring us back around…port gun to bear." He was ordering Midway to expose its weakest spot…but also the only remaining gun she had still functioning. Whichever ship lost the last of its offensive capability would lose the fight. And Compton was down to one laser.

*   *   *

"Midway's in bad shape, but Chief McGraw has bay A open, at least somewhat. I want everybody to land as quickly as possible…we've got to get out of this system now."

Everybody…the word itself mocked her. Hurley's force, eighteen fighters when the rearguard first left the fleet, was four ships. Their attack against the enemy Leviathan had been crucial, and she knew Midway would never have survived the battle without it. But she'd lost six of her ten birds attacking. It was a fair trade, at least in the brutal math that governed war, but she still felt as though she'd failed those dead crews.

"All ships acknowledge, Admiral." Kip Janz sat at his station, off to the side of Hurley's command chair. "Should I order them to follow us in?"

"No," Hurley said. "We go in reverse order. We'll land last."

Janz nodded. "Yes, Admiral."

Hurley knew she was being silly. Landing order didn't really matter, not with four ships. It wasn't like she'd put her bird at the end of the line with a dozen squadrons coming in. But it was something, a minor token. The admiral who'd gotten most of her people killed would be the last to come in.

"Admiral," Wilder said, turning back toward Hurley as he did. "I've got Chief McGraw on the line. He wants to talk to you."

Hurley almost smiled. It was…unusual, to say the least for a

"What is it, Chief?" Hurley didn't hesitate, she didn't get hung up on protocol. McGraw was one of the hardest veterans she'd ever known, and if he had something to say to her, she would listen.

"Admiral, it's the bay. It's a shambles, a total wreck. It'd be closed for sure if the only alternative wasn't leaving you all behind."

"Yeah, Chief, I get that. But it is the only alternative to leaving us behind."

"Admiral, you need to get your crazy flyboys to take it easy coming in here. They've got a quarter the usual clearance… which means if they don't take it slow—very fucking slow— they're going to crash. And then anybody behind them is shit out of luck." McGraw was one of the few non-coms with the grit to swear to an admiral. Hurley knew another type of office might be offended, but she loved it. McGraw was a miserable old cuss, but there was never any doubt he was giving his best… and in the end, that's all she wanted out of anybody.

"Alright, Chief, I'll remind…" Her voice trailed off. She was looking at the display. There was an energy burst, coming from the Z17 warp gate. Her eyes were fixed, unmoving. "Chief, stand by." She stared, waiting. And then it was there. A red icon. An enemy ship. Coming right toward Midway.

*   *   *

Compton stared at the screen, watching the flashing icon move slowly in from the Z17 warp gate. It was single ship, a Gargoyle according the preliminary scans. But that didn't matter. Right now it might just as well have been a fleet of Colossuses. Midway didn't have an operational weapon hot enough to light a candle. The damage control teams were hard at work, but it would be at least a day before they got any of the laser

ing at the screens, looking at the distances…from Midway to the Z18 warp gate, and from the new contact to the Midway. They were calculating, trying to determine if the flagship could get to the warp gate and transit before the enemy vessel was able to engage. All but Compton. He already knew. His mind had done the calculations, automatically, almost subconsciously. The Gargoyle would intercept Midway seventy thousand klicks short of the gate. And then the First Imperium vessel would open up on his battered ship. And Compton and his people would die…just before they reached the warp gate and escape.

He slapped his hand down on the com. He already knew the answer, but he had to ask anyway. "Art, I need some lasers back online. Now."

"Impossible, sir." The voice paused for a second then continued, its tone grimmer. "I know it's life or death, sir, but there is absolutely no way. We'll be lucky if I can keep the reactor running so we can at least run for it."

"Do what you can, Art," Compton said, cutting the line. He took a deep breath and held it for a few seconds before exhaling. For fifty years he'd always found a way, a tactic to extricate a trapped force, a stratagem to defeat a superior enemy. But now there was nothing.

Is this how it ends? A lifetime of war? With total helplessness?

His mind raced, trying to come up with a way…any way. But there wasn't one. Midway was doomed.

He tried to console himself, told himself the sacrifice was worth it, that his people had bought the escape of the fleet with their looming deaths. And he did believe that…but it didn't make it any easier to accept the price those who'd followed him here were about to pay.

Terrance Compton had been in difficult fights before, even ones others had called hopeless. In X2, he'd been the only one in the fleet not ready to give up…and his perseverance and skill had gotten his people out of that trap. But now he was done.

Greta! The fighters. He had a brief flash of hope, but only for an instant. Hurley only had four birds left, and there was no time to rearm them. Another dead end.

"What is it, Greta?"

"Admiral, our scanners are picking up…"

"We've got it too, Greta. It's a Gargoyle. But that's enough now. More than enough."

"Sir…" Her voice was soft, hesitant. "Make a run for it… for the warp gate."

"I already did the calculations, Greta. We won't make it."

"Yes you will. I'll stop the Gargoyle."

Compton was silent. Hurley wasn't an officer prone to empty boasting. "Greta, your people are out of torpedoes. There's no time to reload…and no chance four fighters can take out a Gargoyle with lasers." He felt a rush of pride in her…and an uneasiness too. He was beginning to understand where she was going.

"We have two torpedoes in my bird, Admiral."

"Yes…but they're stuck in your bomb bay."

"That doesn't mean they're useless, sir."

"Greta…" The full impact of terrible clarity was descending on him. "No…"

"It's the only way, sir." Her voice was somber, but there was decisiveness there.

Compton leaned back in his chair, his mind running wild, trying to think of alternative, anything. But there was nothing.

"What about your other fighters?" His voice was grim, like death.

"There's no time to land them, Admiral. We both know that. And my people do too. They've volunteered…they will run interference when we make our run, do their best to cover us."

"You're talking about suicide…twenty people…"

"Not a bad trade for the hundreds on Midway, sir. Is it? How many times have we discussed the mathematics of war?"

Compton felt an agony deep inside. No, he couldn't send

the senior officers, save Erika West. It seemed unreal to him. Had it come to this? His old comrade, the fleet's celebrated fighter corps commander...was she really going to crash her ship into the enemy Gargoyle?

He felt paralyzed. He knew there was no other way, that Hurley and her people would die anyway if the Leviathan destroyed Midway. But for a moment, he thought he had reached the end of his ability to contemplate such horrors. Then Hurley let him off the hook, at least somewhat.

"Terrance, we're going to do this no matter what. Send us off with your blessing and not as mutineers. Please."

Compton sat still, his eyes watery. He was trapped, and he knew it. "Very well, Greta, my friend. You have my blessing... and the gratitude of everyone on Midway. God go with you and those who serve with you."

"Thank you, sir. For this...and for so many other things. It's been an honor serving with you. Goodbye, Admiral Compton."

Compton struggled to force the words from his throat. "Goodbye, Admiral Hurley."

*   *   *

"Alright, John...are you ready." Hurley's tone was soft, sad.

"Yes, Admiral...I'm ready."

"I think Greta will do now, John." She glanced over at Kip Janz and the rest of her crew. "That goes for all of you."

"Thank you, Greta," Wilder said grimly.

"Then take us in, John."

"Yes, Adm...Greta. The other ships are in position thirty klicks ahead." Thirty kilometers was nothing in space combat. But the three other fighters would draw enemy fire, and shield Hurley's ship. With a little luck—an odd use of the word perhaps—her fighter would get through the enemy defenses...and

devastating. Enough, certainly, to take out a Gargoyle. As long as her bird didn't get picked off on the way in.

"Kip, is everything ready?"

"Yes, sir." He hesitated. "Yes, Greta. I've got the reactor's containment system hooked into the plasma torpedo triggers. When the torpedoes blow, the fusion core will go too. It should be perfectly timed with our impact."

"Very well." She could already feel the 3g pressing against her as Wilder accelerated toward the enemy ship. It would take about twenty minutes to get there, assuming they managed to get through the big ship's defenses.

She flipped on the com, opening the channel to all of her ships. "Okay, people...we all know what we're about to do... and we know that this is our last mission. We've all been living on borrowed time, ever since the X2 gate was blown, and we were trapped. I want you to know, in all my career, I have never been prouder of men and women, than I am of the nineteen of you. We are warriors, all of us, and death is part of our creed. So, I say to you all now, if we are marked to die, we could not do it in better company...nor in a better cause, that of saving our friends and comrades."

She flipped off the com, sucking in a deep breath, and fighting to hold in her emotion. Wilder was flying the ship, Janz was checking his handiwork on the torpedoes. But she had nothing to do...and her mind wandered, back through the years. Her days at the Academy, her first assignment. The great battles of the Third Frontier War, the relentless campaigns led by Augustus Garret and Terrance Compton that brought the Alliance from the brink of defeat to total victory.

I've come farther than I'd imagined possible, lived a life that young lieutenant could hardly have dreamed in her wildest fantasies. And I've known good people. Friends.

Some of those comrades are waiting for you, men and women lost...long ago, and recently too.

She felt the fear, the pain. She didn't want to die. She wanted

was fated to die here, this was how she'd always imagined her death.

She felt a pang for Wilder…and Janz and the others in the four doomed ships. They would die heroes, covered in glory. But Hurley knew glory was a poor replacement for life.

She wondered what they were thinking, the others in her doomed attack. Were they remembering families, people they had already left behind? Were they fighting back the fear, steeling themselves to die as they'd imagined they would, up in arms and shaking their fists at the enemy?

She looked down at the display. They were entering the enemy's defensive perimeter. Rockets were detonating around them. One of the covering fighters disappeared from the display, the victim of a nuclear explosion less than five hundred meters away. But the others pushed on.

Then another ship was gone, and her fighter pressed on, its sole remaining defender just ahead, blasting bravely toward the enemy. Half her people were gone, dead…but the rest continued forward. They had a job to do.

She glanced down at the display, watching Midway blast toward the warp gate, and she felt a wave of satisfaction, a new burst of courage. Fortune go with you, Terrance Compton…

The last escort disappeared, blown to bits by an enemy laser turret. But they were almost inside the defense perimeter. One more minute…and it would all be over.

The fighter shook hard, and went into a vicious roll. Structural supports fell, smashing into equipment. Kip Janz jerked upright, shaking around as a deadly blast of electricity took him. A girder smashed into the back of Hurley's chair, severing her harness and sending her to the floor.

No…not this close. Midway…we can't fail.

She was in pain…her arm, her legs. She had broken bones for sure, and every breath was a torment. She forced herself up to her hands and knees, and that's when she saw. John Wilder, on the floor next to his pilot's station, his face a mask of blood.

only one left.

She struggled to her feet, staggering forward, toward the pilot's chair.

I...can't...fail...

She plopped down in the seat, yelping in pain from a dozen injuries. She tried to focus, to clear her mind. The fighter was heading for the enemy vessel...almost, at least. It looked like the Gargoyle had detected the danger...and it was trying to alter its vector.

She grabbed the throttle, veered to match the enemy's course change.

No way...no way you get away from me...

She felt the fatigue, the exhaustion. The agony was almost unbearable. But she refused to give up. It was pure will, her indomitable spirit against fear, pain, weakness.

The Gargoyle was close...just a few more seconds. She hoped Janz' jury-rigging had held...but even if it hadn't, the fighter was moving at almost 0.02c, and the kinetic energy the impact would release was almost incalculable.

She pushed on the throttle, increasing the thrust. The pain had been bad before, but now, at 4g, it was utter torment. She screamed, her shouts of pain echoing in the small cockpit. Her mind reeled, and tears streamed down her cheeks. But her hands held firm on the stick, increasing the thrust. Five gees. Six.

She felt as if her body was being torn apart...pain like she'd never imagined. Let go of the throttle, her mind screamed futilely. But she held on...somehow.

"This is for all our people you killed, you bastards! My friends, my comrades." She took one last agonizing breath... and then she thrust the throttle forward full.

Chapter Seventeen

AS Saratoga
System X108
The Fleet: 82 ships (+2 Leviathans), 19,989 crew

West watched as the enemy ships closed on her fleet. Her ships had retreated abruptly, and their sudden withdrawal had caught the First Imperium fleet by surprise. The human vessels had mostly broken contact, at least for a short while, and she knew the damage control teams were working feverishly to put that time to good use.

All except the ships that had serious damage to their engines. They were still trying to get back...with the enemy on their heels. The two vessels whose engines had been knocked out totally hadn't lasted more than a few minutes on their own, and she had watched the display silently as each ship died, along with almost 350 of her people...men and women she had abandoned.

West stared at the display, watched as the enemy approached. The First Imperium AIs had no doubt determined the humans were beaten, that they had retreated because they were broken, fleeing for their lives. And she ached for the moment they would realize they had walked into a trap...that their destruc-

the First Imperium AIs. As far as her people had been able to tell—and Cutter had done a lot of research—the control units of the First Imperium fleet had no self-preservation directives, at least not as such. Sacrificing an entire fleet to achieve an end was a perfectly valid strategy to them, one they wouldn't hesitate to employ if it made sense.

The Regent, she suspected, was different. Almost certainly so. Indeed, it had identified humanity as a threat and launched a war of genocide to protect itself. That wasn't the thought process of a sane thinking machine. And it certainly exhibited a self-preservation initiative.

"All ships in position, Admiral. Enemy forces are pursuing. They will reenter weapons range in…approximately six minutes."

And they will enter Cutter's range in three…

"All ships stand by. Prepare to fire as the enemy moves within range." If it comes to that. West wasn't a very trusting person—she respected most peoples' competence as little as their loyalty—but for reasons she couldn't fully explain, she was sure Cutter had the situation in hand. The scientist was the smartest person she'd ever met, and when she'd heard of his exploits, how he'd stood and defended a group of wounded Marines, facing almost certain death in the process, she realized he was no pompous academic. This was a man worth trusting.

She glanced down at the screen. Less than two minutes. She felt the time passing slowly, each tortured second reluctantly giving way to the next. She knew the intelligences on those ships weren't beings, that they wouldn't die in panic and shock and pain when Cutter opened up on them. But she let herself imagine that anyway.

One minute. One more minute, and we'll see what our forefathers left here for us…

*   *   *

Beverly Jones leaned forward, her hand tight around the throttle. She could hear her heart beating, like a drum in her ears. There was sweat on her neck, dripping down from her hairline. In somewhat less than clinical terms, she was scared shitless. Not just of the enemy, but of the almost forty fighters and two hundred crew under her command. She knew she was about to get a lot of them killed, and she was struggling to deal with that, to shove the doubts aside and do her job.

My job by default…how did Admiral Hurley and Mariko do this so effortlessly?

No, she realized. Not effortlessly. They had their doubts, their fears…but they handled them. And I will too.

"Okay, people, Admiral West is counting on us. Let's not let her down." She took a deep breath, and then she leaned closer to the com unit. "Attack!"

She pushed forward on the throttle, accelerating her fighter toward the closest enemy target, a Gargoyle. The enemy reserve didn't have any Leviathans, only the smaller Gargoyles and Gremlins. And her bombers could hurt them badly if they scored enough hits.

"Let's get torpedo A armed and ready…I'm bring us around for an attack run." She was in command of the entire strike force, but she was also the pilot of her ship. Tucker Jahns had been wounded in the last battle, and he was still in sickbay. And she wasn't about to leave a functional bird back in the hanger for lack of a trained pilot.

"Torpedo armed and ready, Commander." The gunner's voice was high-pitched. He was young, and he looked even younger. Jones would have guessed he was about fifteen minutes out of the Academy if she hadn't known better. But Walter Finch was a hardened combat veteran. She knew that from experience over the last eighteen months.

"Very well, Lieutenant. Beginning attack run now."

She tilted the throttle to the right, changing the angle of the ship's thrust, altering its vector of movement. The Gargoyle

to be any fun, especially with no warships engaging the target, but there was nothing she could do about that.

"Hang on, guys," she said, as she shoved the control forward, increasing the ship's thrust. Three gees. Four. Five. The sooner they got to firing range, the better chance they had.

She glanced at her display. The incoming fire was light. She felt a moment of excitement, followed by an immediate come down. It was light because three of her other fighters were attacking the same target...and they were getting blasted. One of them was already falling back, clearly damaged, its engines knocked out. It was still heading for the target, but it couldn't accelerate or decelerate.

"Ten thousand kilometers," she said, pulling her eyes away from the stricken fighter's symbol. The best thing she could do for that crew was take out the Gargoyle.

"Nine thousand...prepare for high gee maneuver."

She stared down at the targeting display, locking the torpedo on the target.

"Eight thousand..." She knew she should get closer. She'd watched Hurley do it. And Mariko too, even closer. She'd have sworn her friend was certifiably crazy. But she could feel her hand shaking, and she knew she didn't have it in her. She was already close, inside normal firing range. She'd done all that was expected of a fighter pilot. But she just didn't have it in her to ride it to five thousand...or even the four thousand she'd seen Mariko pull off. She wanted to be the hero, the wild fighter jock with no fear, no hesitation. But it just wasn't her.

She pulled the trigger, and her fighter shook as the torpedo launched. She slammed the throttle to the side, pulling it back hard, and blasting away from the collision course...and past the enemy ship.

The display plotted the course of her torpedo. A hit! She felt a rush of excitement, tempered a bit as she realized the weapon impacted on a heavily-armored section of the hull. It did damage, no doubt...a considerable amount. But it wasn't

*   *   *

"What should we do?" Sasha Debornan—or the thing the human being with that name had become—sat in the quarters that had been assigned to her. She looked over at Don Rames, her ally, another human controlled now by the nanos. They were there for a purpose, to serve the Regent. But now it was unclear how to proceed.

"I do not know. There is insufficient data to formulate a course of action." Rames sat still, unmoving, looking uncomfortable. The nanos controlled his every move, but they had no sense of comfort.

Debornan sat silently, thinking. They had designed a plan, one based on the knowledge they had been able to acquire. To assassinate Admiral Compton. But Terrance Compton was not with the fleet, he was off leading a diversionary force.

"Many of Compton's people believe him to be dead. If that is the case, perhaps we should change our target to Admiral West. She appears to be the likely successor to Compton." Rames voice was deadpan, without emotion.

"There is merit to such a consideration. But I have doubts. We do not know Compton is dead, only that some of his people fear he is. If he is alive, if he returns, he is undoubtedly the greater threat." She paused, thinking. "This ship is in battle now. If it falls, we will be destroyed...but so will Admiral West. Therefore, I propose that we wait and reevaluate after the engagement ends. Perhaps by that time there will be additional information on Admiral Compton."

"Yes," Rames said. "I believe that is the best course for the present." He paused. Then he looked at Debornan. "While we wait, I submit that the remnants of the thought processes of the biologics are no longer of value. I propose we eliminate them."

Debornan considered. "Yes, I am inclined to agree. We

nants, the emotions, the essence of Sasha Debornan felt the darkness closing, coming in from all sides. She screamed, silently, with no one to hear. And then it was over. All that had made Sasha Debornan the person she was, her loves, dreams, beliefs…was gone.

*   *   *

West sat in her chair, her eyes fixed on the main display. She was counting down softly to herself. "Five, four, three…"

She had her ships prepared, their weapons armed and ready. But first she would see the power of the ancients, wielded by Hieronymus Cutter.

"Ready to fire, Admiral." Cutter's voice was soft in her headset, but she could hear the tension in his voice. She knew the brilliant scientist believed he had gained control over the ancient weapons array, but none of them would know for sure. Not until he fired.

"Admiral, we're getting energy readings off the charts! Almost a hundred weapons platforms, all suddenly active." The power output was so huge, it was impossible to miss. Her eyes darted to the wall of approaching icons, the enemy fleet. She could see them decelerating, trying to slow their approach. They had picked up the power spikes too.

"Firing," Cutter said, and an instant later the display lit up like a supernova. Massive explosions all around the firing platforms…and great pulses of energy, laser blasts ripping through space, smashing into the enemy warships.

West watched as one ship simply vaporized, its hull melting and turning to gas in a microsecond, leaving nothing at all behind. Other vessels were torn in half or had great holes ripped through them. They bled gasses and fluids, secondary explosions wracked their interiors, blowing great chunks from

mark that they'd ever been there.

West felt a rush of excitement. She pumped her clenched fist into the air, and she joined the flag bridge crew in a loud scream. The power that Cutter had unleashed was like nothing she'd ever seen before. The alien Almeerhan had been good to his word. The Ancients had planned for this moment. They had left their technology for those who would come after. And now that tech was doing what it had been designed to do so many eons before. It was lashing out at the Ancients' enemy, at the ships of the Regent. The hand of those slain by that monstrous intelligence had struck a great blow, one from beyond the ages.

But even that momentous attack had left almost thirty enemy vessels remaining. They were reversing power, blasting their engines at full, trying to come to a stop…and then accelerate away from the threat. But Erika West had no intention of letting them go. She knew it would be a bloody fight, but she intended to take out every one of the enemy vessels.

"All ships, attack at will…no one gets away. No one."

She stared straight ahead with a single thought in her mind. Kill.

*　　　*　　　*

"Hang on…I'm giving it everything we've got left." Jones' voice was strained, the eight gees pushing down on her making it almost impossible to speak. But she couldn't let up. Not now. The battle was all but won…save this last enemy vessel.

Her fighters had destroyed the reserve task force, all but the single remaining vessel. And she'd watched with amazement as her scanners showed her what had happened in the inner system. The power of those weapons emplacements was almost beyond imagination, making even the heaviest guns of the First Imperium vessels seem weak and insignificant by comparison.

seeking to escape, to report that the human fleet had been found, that they had taken refuge in the X108 system. That one ship, damaged, fleeing, could drain all the advantage gained by the great victory. If they got away it wouldn't be long before more ships came…before the true might of the First Imperium gathered here.

"No…we can't let that happen…"

Jones' ship was the only one close enough to have a chance at catching the enemy. She had one torpedo left, and if she managed to place it in the right spot it would be enough. She was sure of that.

Her hand jerked the throttle back and forth, trying to make her bird as tough a target as possible for the enemy point defense. The fire was heavy, but her quick hand—and her luck—had served her well. Her bird was inside 10,000 kilometers. But this time she was going to take it all the way…beyond point blank range.

Eight thousand kilometers.

She flipped the arming switch. The torpedo was ready to go.

Her hands were on the controls, her eyes on the screen.

Seven thousand.

"I'm going to make you proud of me, Mariko." Her words were silent, inaudible, meant only for herself. "I'm going to take it right down their throats."

She knew she needed a perfect shot, a critical hit that could destroy the enemy ship. Anything else was failure. The target would continue on through the warp gate. And warn the Regent.

Six thousand.

Her hands were steady, the earlier fear gone. She knew what she had to do, and that was all that mattered. Her finger started closing slowly, putting pressure on the launch mechanism.

Five thousand.

Just another few seconds…

The ship shook hard, and she heard the sound of an explo-

up at the red speckled forward screen. She felt a wave of panic, but she held it back, closing her finger on the trigger.

Nothing.

She pressed it again. And again. Still nothing.

She knew in an instant. The ship was damaged—the firing controls, the bomb bay doors…something.

Then it came over her. Fear, despair.

I have failed.

She felt the misery, the despair. Hopelessness. Defeat. But only for an instant. Then the ship exploded, and she was gone.

*   *   *

The battle was over. Almost, at least. In the inner system, there was not a First Imperium vessel remaining. The fleet that had come to X108, to Shangri la, to destroy the humans, had itself been obliterated.

With a little help from the Ancients…

West was grateful…to Cutter, and to the people who had so long ago prepared this place. But now she just looked at her screen, at the blank space where Beverly Jones' fighter had been. Jones had come close, recklessly close to the enemy, determined to ensure that her torpedo did the job, that it hit where she needed it to hit. And for an instant, after the terrible realization that Jones' ship was gone, West thought she might have loosed the weapon just before she was hit. But the enemy ship was still there. No signs of an explosion. She watched as it continued on its path…and a minute later as it reached the warp gate and disappeared from the screen.

She felt the excitement drain from her. It was still a victory, a crucial one. But they'd just lost most of the advantage. The enemy would be back now, and in even greater force. She could imagine the Regent's reaction, its version of excitement as

from which there was no escape. She'd considered running, gathering the fleet and taking off, deeper and deeper into endless space. But that only lasted a second. Her ships were low on fuel, on food, on ammunition. Running wasn't the answer…and fleeing and giving up this world left for them by the Ancients… it just wasn't possible.

If we just had more time, enough to adapt some of this technology. She hoped they would, that the weeks and months would pass with no attack. That the Regent's forces were dispersed, looking for them, that Compton had strung them out over a dozen systems. But she knew that was wishful thinking, that whatever the details, their time was limited. Very limited.

"Get me Dr. Cutter…no, belay that." She stood up from her chair and turned toward Krantz. "Get my shuttle ready. I'm going down to the surface."

Chapter Eighteen

Underground Complex
Near Landing Zone X-Ray
Planet X108 IV – "Shangri la"
The Fleet: 80 ships (+2 Leviathans), 19762 crew

West stood in the center of the control room, her head moving back and forth, looking at the array of screens and workstations. It all looked new, almost like a ship just out of the yard, though she knew it was half a million years old.

The Marine guards stood behind her. She'd tried to come down alone, with just the shuttle pilot to ferry her to the surface, but she'd almost faced an outright rebellion…from the Marines, and from her officers as well. She was getting an idea of what Compton had dealt with for so long, and her already enormous respect for the admiral grew even vaster.

She reached around, intending to scratch an itch, but then she remembered, for about the tenth time, she had an environmental suit on. She hated wearing space suits and their various cousins, but she was skewered by her own orders. The preliminary scans had found no pathogen dangerous to humans, nothing beyond normal bacteria and viruses capable of causing

her ships. Snow Leopard had been the only vessel whose entire crew had reached the deadly end stage of the disease...but the cursed vessel had given a glimpse of the future if the medical teams didn't find a cure...and soon.

She heard a swooshing sound, a door opening on the far wall. "Admiral West, I'm so sorry. No one told me you were coming down." Hieronymus Cutter stepped into the room. "Welcome to Shangri la, Admiral."

West stared at the scientist, shocked. Cutter stood in front of her wearing a set of coveralls...and nothing else. No suit, no air tank. Nothing.

"Hieronymus..." Her tone was thick with concern.

"I know, Admiral. I'm stuck down here...I understand. The obelisk...I had to touch it, let it scan my DNA. It was the only way in."

"You took one hell of a chance...what if there had been a pathogen down here? What if there is, and we haven't found it yet?"

"Then I guess I'll die, Admiral." Cutter's tone was deadpan, matter-of-fact. "But if I hadn't taken my armor off, I'd never have gotten down here...and we would have had no idea of the range of the defensive systems. And your people would have had to destroy an extra sixty enemy ships without any help."

West just nodded. "You're right, of course. We all take the risks we must." She paused, and when she continued her voice had a twinge of guilt to it. "But you were right, Hieronymus. I can't let you back up to the fleet. Not until we're absolutely sure there are no dangerous pathogens down here."

"I know, Admiral. I understand." He turned and looked around the room. "There's enough down here to keep me busy for a hundred years...so I can assure you my time won't be wasted." He paused. "Maybe you could shuttle down a shelter and a few other things. And my lab equipment."

"Of course." She looked right at him. "And thank you... for all your research, for your courage in doing what you had to

normally disciplined voice was betraying excitement.

Cutter returned West's gaze. He'd never heard her as effusive about anything. But he had to admit, the megalasers had certainly put on a show. Still, a frown slipped onto his face.

"Admiral, I urge caution. Agreed, the laser installations are awesomely powerful...but there are limitations as well. They are anti-matter bomb pumped installations. Each turret actually has a series of...for lack of a better word, cartridges. They are expelled from the main station, and when in position they detonate, channeling a large portion of the energy released into the laser shot. But the supply of cartridges is very limited, perhaps only one or two more per platform. I believe the failsafe systems jettisoned them over the centuries, as their containment systems showed signed of failure. I've also found evidence of a dozen stations that are just gone. I'd guess their AIs didn't catch the deterioration, and the antimatter annihilated, taking the platforms with it."

"So you're saying we only have a few more shots left? And then the planet's defenses will be gone?"

Cutter took a breath and looked down at the floor for a few seconds before answering. "I wouldn't say gone, Admiral. There are some lesser platforms...they're nuclear powered. They're all dead now, but I'd bet we could get some of them up and running. But the megalasers are the real killers. And once those last couple shots are gone, we're going to need to produce more. And it will be a very long time before we can even come close to that. First, we need to develop a practical method for producing antimatter in quantity."

West sighed softly, her exhale fogging her visor slightly. "That's bad news, Hieronymus...and I've got some more. One of the enemy ships escaped. So whatever chance we had of being left alone for a while is probably gone. We're going to have to make the use of those shots we've got left on the megalasers...and we've got to do everything possible to get the lesser platforms operable."

engineering team, I'll see about getting some of the smaller guns up and running."

"You'll have them in a few hours, Hieronymus…the best we've got."

Cutter was silent. He looked like he was going to says something, but he just stood there.

"What is it, Hieronymus?"

"Well, Admiral, I found something. Several things, in fact… and it gave me an idea."

"What? Speak?" West stared at him, looking surprised at his hesitancy. "What's wrong, Hieronymus?"

"Nothing, Admiral…it's just…" He looked up from the floor. "It's just that it's pretty far out. A crazy idea. But when you see what I found here…"

"Show me, Hieronymus." She walked across the room toward him. "Nothing that comes out of that amazing mind of yours is too far out."

*   *   *

"Saratoga, we need help. We've got people dropping in the corridors, and we can't cram another patient into sickbay." West listened to the transmission as Krantz fielded another plea for help from one of the plague-stricken ships. Nanking was a freighter, and she'd had contact with eight or more other vessels before it was discovered that her people carried the disease.

West had given the fleet's medical staff all the resources she could…anything they asked for that she had or could find or steal. But progress had been slow.

Slow…more like non-existent.

She had come to believe without a doubt that they were facing a bioweapon, all the more because there were cases on a number of ships that had not come into contact with Snow

tiles…though its since-relieved captain had not seen fit to report it until almost a month later.

West no longer had the slightest doubt those mysterious projectiles were some system designed to deliver bacteriological weapons…and that they had done just that. To more than one of her ships.

The Regent had modified the original plague…it had overcome the DNA immunity the Ancients had engineered into humanity's ancestors. She knew she had nothing remotely like actual evidence, but she didn't have the slightest doubt that is what had happened. But knowing didn't help. Her medical staff had to find a cure—to a disease that had wiped out the far more advance Ancients. And if they didn't, at least a quarter of her people would die. And that assumed she could contain the spread. It was only speculation, hope, that the enemy hadn't found some alternate means to deliver the pathogen to other ships. If they had, she knew it was possible the entire fleet was already doomed.

"Nanking, there are no fleet resources available beyond what you have received. You will have to make the best of what you have for now." West listened as Krantz gave the stock reply, the same thing he'd told the others. She could hear the strain in his voice, and she understood how hard it was for him to refuse the requests for aid.

"Saratoga, we don't even have enough crew left standing to run the ship. Almost everything is on auto control already. Our medical staff is all infected…half of them are already bedridden. In another few hours, the dying will be completely unattended."

"I'm sorry, Captain," Krantz said softly. "I really am." Then: "Saratoga out."

West closed her eyes. She knew her reputation, but she wasn't the heartless monster many thought she was. It tore at her to think of her crew members, scared, sick, dying…with no help. With her refusing them help. But there was no choice. She couldn't send more people to those ships and let them get

to evaluate risks.

She wouldn't even send shuttles to dock with the stricken vessels. This was no ordinary virus…it had been designed as a weapon. To kill. By a machine of immense sophistication and intelligence. Its entire purpose was to spread. West was far from convinced the fleet's normal decontamination procedures were reliable against this virus. It wouldn't surprise her if it could survive the radiation of the decon chambers…or even a period of time in deep space. No, she couldn't risk the rest of her people, not until she knew more.

She thought of Captain Ving, of Snow Leopard and her crew. She'd been horrified when he'd made his request, and it had taken everything she had to give him her blessing. But now she realized Ving's wisdom. He had not only saved Saratoga… he'd saved his people. Not from death, but from the final, agonizing misery of the final stages of a plague ship's tortured end. Snow Leopard's crew was dead, but their pain was over, and they had died as heroes, saving their comrades.

There would be no such saving grace on Nanking. The crew there would sicken, they would drop in the hallways, lie on the floor in writhing agony. In their own vomit. The halls would reek, and there would be no one left to clean up, to bring food, medicine. Even water. No painkillers, no meds to ease the suffering. The stricken would just lie where they dropped, moaning in pain as their lives slipped away. There would be no hero's death for any of them, no comfort, no dignity. And there was nothing she could do about it.

Not a damned thing.

*   *   *

West looked across the table, at the astonished faces staring back at her. She knew what she had told them was hard to

It was the only chance they had. They might beat back another attack. Two, perhaps. Even three. But the Regent would continue to send fleets to Shangri la…and eventually they would overwhelm her people. No, there was no other way. However insanely desperate this plan seemed.

"Admiral, how is that even possible?" Max Harmon sat across from West, and he stared back at her. No one would have called Harmon a timid man, but even he looked at her like she was crazy.

"It is possible because of Hieronymus Cutter, Max. Because he has begun to explore the complex down on the surface. And because he found this." She punched a button, and the display lit up, showing a document. One side appeared to be a map… and the other was a schematic of some type of vast electronic device.

"This, my fellow officers, is a complete set of design specs for the Regent…and plans of the complex in which it is housed. It shows the way in, the weak spots in the security…everything."

She looked around the table, drawing a touch of perverse satisfaction as she saw the shocked looks on their faces.

Harmon was no less surprised than anyone else. But behind the wonder on his face, the skepticism remained. "That is an amazing bit of intelligence…assuming it is accurate. It is half a millions years old, after all."

"Yes, Max…that is true. But all of our intelligence suggests that the Regent has done little or nothing to develop new technology or expand the imperium. Indeed, through whatever combination of programming and malfunction, it appears to have behaved in an extremely reactionary manner. Doctor Cutter believes it is unlikely the Regent would have made any major changes to itself…and I am inclined to agree. There is a good chance these schematics are an accurate depiction of the machine's current makeup."

Harmon nodded. "What you say makes sense. I agree. But even if we assume that is the case…and if we believe this infor-

dozens of jumps, through all the fleets massing to assault Shan-gri la?"

West smiled again. "We have Dr. Cutter to thank again… for another item he found down there. The Ancients who cre-ated the Regent sought to destroy it long before we entered this fight. They had turned over control of their civilization to the machine generations before, and they faced the same challenge we do…how to approach, how to reach Deneb VIII and the Regent, when the enemy controlled the imperium's fleets. And they solved that problem." She reached down and pressed a small button on the table.

The doors slid to the side, and two Marines walked in, push-ing an anti-grav sled with a cylinder about a meter high on it. It looked like some kind of glass, though it was clear it was a mate-rial beyond anything mankind had developed.

"This is the only one of its kind," West continued. "It was developed by the Ancients, a massive breakthrough even for them. According to the logs Dr. Cutter found, they developed this device to allow them to travel back to their home world undetected…and to destroy the Regent. It blocks all scanning technology known to them…it even generates a field of practi-cal visual invisibility."

The room was silent. The officers present, whatever hatred they had for the Regent, had come to admire and respect First Imperium technology. Finally, Max Harmon spoke. "Did the records indicate what happened? Why they never followed through?" He was staring at the alien device, just as everyone else in the room was doing.

"Yes, Dr. Cutter found the notes of the head of the research team. And they tell a somber tale. By the time they finished the device, the plague had infected them all, even in this hidden retreat. They had tried to protect themselves, but the infection reached them in spite of their efforts. The remaining mem-bers of the warrior caste, the team that was going to destroy the Regent…they were too weak, even to stand. They would

along with their plans and their logs. They left them for us. Their plan changed from one of salvation to one of vengeance."

She looked around the table, at each of her colleagues. "And now it has come to us. We are outgunned, outmatched, besieged. We too are facing a deadly plague, though it appears we have it confined to certain ships, at least for now. We are still able to put together an able-bodied team…and to install this device on one of our ships. And send that vessel on a desperate mission, a wild gamble beyond anything we have done during our unlikely flight over the last eighteen months. And if—if—this team can succeed, we may finally find a way to survive, to stop running… and to begin to adapt the amazing technology the Ancients left behind for us."

"But, Admiral…even if we are able to destroy the Regent…" Harmon paused, a concerned look on his face. "The fleets, the armed forces…they would most likely follow their last orders, wouldn't they? The Regent isn't in constant contact with each vessel. Clearly, they are operating under orders to destroy us. So eliminating the Regent would be satisfying, no doubt. But I don't see how it would change the tactical situation significantly. We would still be attacked here…again and again until we are wiped out."

"You're right, Max, of course." West nodded slowly. "We cannot simply destroy the Regent, at least not before we compel it to order its forces to stand down."

There were a few soft laughs around the room. Everyone thought West was joking. Everyone except Max Harmon.

"The computer virus," he said softly.

"Yes, Max. The virus. Dr. Cutter has improved it significantly." She pulled a small data crystal from her pocket and set it down on the table. "He has given me the latest version. He has made some changes after reviewing the Regent's schematics."

"Admiral…the Regent is an electronic brain beyond anything mankind has imagined, sophisticated in a way that defies our ability to define. I respect Dr. Cutter, and I would never

"No, Max. Not permanently, at least. Hieronymus feels it is almost certain the Regent has ancillary security systems that would detect the infection and eliminate it."

Harmon was about to say something, but West continued before he had the chance. "We don't need to control it, at least not for long. The team will introduce the virus, order the Regent to issue a command to all military forces to stand down…and then they will destroy it before it can regain control." She hesitated and then added softly, "And hopefully they will escape." There was doubt in her voice, and all those present knew West considered this a virtual suicide mission.

She paused, looking around the room, gauging the reactions of the officers present. Erika West was an icy warrior, cold, unshakable in combat…but she wasn't the leader they all expected to propose something as wild as this. The mission was a longshot, no matter how it was analyzed. It required a degree of optimism, or at least a grim belief that a small group of men and women could achieve something virtually beyond imagination. Even if the cost was their lives.

But West didn't look doubtful…there was nothing but confidence in her tone. "The Ancients planned this operation five hundred thousand years ago," she said. "They prepared for it. They put the last bits of their scientific capability into building what they needed. But they were too late. By the time they were ready to go, they had succumbed to their enemy. They died… they died before they could execute the plan they'd devised to save their own civilization."

West stood up, and she panned her head around the table, looking at the stunned and uncertain faces around the table. "We are their descendants, we know that now. And we are going to do this, my friends. We are going to complete their mission half a million years later."

Chapter Nineteen

Underground Complex
Near Landing Zone X-Ray
Planet X108 IV – "Shangri la"
The Fleet: 82 ships (+2 Leviathans), 19391 crew

"Perhaps I can wear an environmental suit...or I can stay in a decon chamber." Hieronymus Cutter was frustrated. He understood West's caution...she was dealing with twenty ships ravaged with a deadly disease...and if the pathogen causing it existed on Shangri la, Cutter had been exposed to it. That hadn't been a problem when the fleet was fighting and Cutter was digging through the knowledge storehouse of the Ancients. But now the fleet was sending a team to the imperial homeworld ,to Deneb VIII, to take control of the Regent with Cutter's virus, to order the armed forces of the imperium to stand down... and then to destroy the infernal creation that had murdered its creators and then tried to do the same to mankind.

"For six weeks? Without a break? What if there is an accident? What if the ship is hit and the decon chamber compromised?" Ana Zhukov stood along the wall, looking at Cutter. Her face was twisted into a frown, though he could barely see it

fighting suit. He'd ostensibly done it to protect the second most important scientist in the fleet, though everyone who knew him realized he had other motivations that were far more personal.

"Ana…don't you understand? This is it. The climax of this entire nightmare. If this succeeds…"

"I understand that, Hieronymus…but you still can't go. Admiral West needs you here. The fleet needs you…and everything you can coax out of these defense systems. You stay. I will go to Deneb."

Cutter stood up abruptly, but Connor Frasier spoke first. "You see, Hieronymus? She's been saying this all morning. Talk some sense into her." He hesitated then added, "Please." The worry in the giant Marine's voice was clear.

"Ana…this is my virus. I have to go. You can take my place here, explore the archives…and assist the admiral."

"Bullshit," she spat. "You know as well as I do that we both worked on that virus. I know it as well as you do, or almost at least. I can do this…as well as you can. But I can't replace you here. We both know Almeerhan implanted things in your mind. You are the only one who can do what has to be done here."

She turned around toward Frasier. "And if you object so strongly to your girlfriend going on this mission, there's an easy way to fix that." There was an ominous tone to her voice.

Frasier just stared back, silent.

"How many times have I waited while you went on some dangerous mission?"

"Ana, I'm a Marine."

"You think that makes it any easier to sit on Midway and hope you come back alive? And yet you expect me to stay behind, to shirk my duty, put everyone at risk just so you don't have to worry about me?"

Frasier just stood there.

"Well, I don't care what either of you think. Hieronymus has to stay here…and I'm the only other one in the fleet who understands the virus well enough to handle this." She looked

Her voice was defiant, rock solid. "Because I'm going."

Then she turned around and walked out of the room, right past both of them. Without uttering another word.

*   *   *

"Admiral, we're getting more reports from across the fleet. There are five hundred eleven confirmed fatalities from the Plague. And twenty-two ships report some level of infection." Krantz' voice was grim. West understood. Her tactical officer had been listening to reports for the past hour, mostly sick officers providing statistics on the even sicker spacers on their ships.

The Plague…it's never good when something like this gets widespread enough to acquire a name.

"Very well." West felt sympathy for her crews. She hated feeling as impotent as she did. At least in battle, she could issue orders, develop stratagems…she could do something. But now she was just listening, waiting for updated death counts, for more ships to report increasing infection levels. "Nanking?"

"Sorry, Admiral. Still no response." Krantz' voice was grim.

West just nodded. It wasn't a surprise, not after the last transmission. But it was still hard to think about the freighter, its entire crew infected, so sick that not one of them could reach a com unit and respond to the flagship's inquiries. She didn't know how many people were still alive on Nanking, but she pretty sure they were all suffering in their final hours. She felt the urge to send a relief expedition…there had been numerous volunteers among the med staff. But she'd refused them all. She simply would not—could not—take any risk she could avoid. The very survival of the fleet depended on her decisions now.

She knew what people would say. The cold-blooded admiral, sitting on her flag bridge, withholding aid from the stricken

Alliance vessel. Her rivals for command of the fleet would use it all against her, even as her resolve kept them safe from the ravages of the deadly disease.

She'd even considered blasting Nanking to atoms, sparing its crew the agonies of dying unattended. But that would look even worse. She hated the idea of letting men and women suffer because putting them out of their misery would look bad... but that was also her reality.

West had long ago become used to the whispers, the stark stares from those who believed the stories about her. But that didn't mean she wasn't bothered by it. She'd thought she understood the pressure on Compton, but now that she was standing in his place the true weight of it all became apparent. And she lacked the emotional attachment Compton had enjoyed from most of the fleet's personnel. West had loyalty, at least from her Alliance personnel, who knew she was a smart and capable commander. But the love Compton had felt from the officers, the spacers of the fleet...that was something she had never known.

She just sat, listening to the eerie silence on Saratoga's bridge. She knew her officers were struggling with their own thoughts. They didn't blame her for the situation...she was sure of that. But she knew they disapproved, as least in the non-specific way those removed from final responsibility could indulge themselves. But if adding to her reputation as a heartless automaton was what it took to keep them alive, such were the burdens of command.

She moved her hand toward the com unit, but then she stood up abruptly, turning toward Krantz as she did. "I'll be in my office, Commander." Then she walked toward the side of the flag bridge and waved her hand over the sensor. The door slipped open, and she stepped inside, pausing a minute and listening to the hatch close behind her. Then she walked over to her desk and sat down, tapping the com as she did. "Dr. Gower," she said softly, "what updates have you got for me?"

"Very little, I'm afraid, Admiral." Justine Gower had been

off the ship before he departed with the rearguard. West suspected that Gower's transfer had less to do with her being nonessential than the fact that she was unquestionably the best doctor in the fleet, a precious resource not to be risked in his desperate rearguard action.

"Anything?" West felt some of the fight draining out of her. She didn't know how long she could stay strong while she was watching people getting sick and dying throughout the fleet.

"Well, it's definitely something similar to a severe Earth influenza, kind of a super flu. But it seems like the virus itself has been extensively engineered to resist all forms of treatment. All our antivirals are completely ineffective, as are all other treatments we've attempted." Gower paused. "Honestly, Admiral, we simply have no idea how to kill it."

"It seems to take quite a while to reach the critical stages. I would expect something this deadly would be faster to kill its victims."

"I suspect that is by design, Admiral. This virus is a weapon, there's no doubt in my mind about that. And a long incubation period, followed by a protracted stretch of mundane symptoms is ideal for maximum contagion. By the time anyone is obviously very ill, they've been spreading the virus for weeks."

West sighed. It all made sense, in an evil, efficient sort of way. The way she suspected the Regent approached things.

"Justine, you've got to come up with something. Soon. You're the best chance we've got to develop a treatment. And if you don't…" She let her voice trail off. Without a cure, she was going to have to watch almost a quarter of the fleet's personnel die slowly…and do nothing about it. Nothing at all.

But she knew it was worse than that. If the enemy had spread the virus with their mysterious new delivery system, every ship in the fleet was vulnerable. She knew the forces of the First Imperium would be back, that more ships would be destroyed in the hell of battle…and that more would probably be hit by the tiny projectiles, that their crews would become infected. That

It was a grave danger, one that threatened the very existence of the fleet. And she had no idea what to do about it.

"I will try, Admiral." Gower's voice was doubtful, somber. It didn't give West much from which to manufacture hope. And that wasn't her way anyway. Erika West knew most people's judgment was colored by hope, by the need to believe in something positive. But she had never been that way. She looked at things starkly, realistically. It was a draining way to live, but it was how she was. And even if the fleet was doomed, she was damned sure of one thing.

They would fight to the very end. No matter what.

*   *   *

Max Harmon stood in his quarters, staring down at the almost-full pack on his bunk and trying to think of anything he'd forgotten. It was a long trip to Deneb and back, though he was honest enough with himself to acknowledge that his chances of returning were pretty damned poor. The mission reeked of desperation, but he'd discussed it with Admiral West, and the two had agreed completely. It was the fleet's best chance to survive. Standing at Shangri la and facing attack after attack didn't seem to offer much chance at ultimate victory. And taking off, abandoning the amazing world the Ancients had left behind and plunging into the depths of unexplored space, running low on everything and with the enemy in hot pursuit, didn't seem like a better option.

Harmon smiled for a moment when he thought of West. He was the logical choice to lead the mission, and he'd realized that the moment she described it in the conference room. But she'd given him a chance to opt out. She hadn't ordered him to go...she'd asked him who he thought should lead it. He appreciated the thought behind her approach. He was one of the few

Harmon had never shied away from dangerous missions, and he wasn't about to start…though he'd never wanted to shirk as much as he did now. After weeks at Mariko's bedside, she was finely out of the woods, indeed, she was up and around. And now he had to leave….and perhaps never come back.

He walked over to his desk and pulled out several small boxes. They held his medals and decorations. It was hardly necessary gear, but he thought he should take them. If he was going to his death, they should be with him. There was also a small 'pad in the drawer. He pulled it out and flicked it on, thumbing through the photos on the screen. New ones…Mariko and Ana and Hieronymus. And Admiral Compton too, playing poker with some of the officers. Harmon remembered that night. Compton had cleaned everyone out, and Harmon had learned the stories of the legendary Terrance Compton, poker scourge of the Alliance fleet were all true. Compton hadn't gambled for years, unwilling to take money from his subordinates. But Alliance credits were worth exactly zero to them all now, so he'd finally accepted an invitation to play…and he'd become part of the weekly game, a tiny scrap of normalcy that Harmon hoped helped the admiral as much as it had him.

There were older photos too. His mother, in her uniform, which is just about the only way he could remember her. Camille Harmon was the terror of the Alliance fleet, an iron-willed commander who exceeded even Erika West's reputation for blackhearted brutality among the junior officers fated to serve under her. She hadn't been the most attentive mother, and his had been the lot of a navy brat. But he'd never doubted her love… and he'd seen firsthand the grief she'd felt when his father was killed on Tau Ceti III. In the battle still known as the Slaughter Pen.

He had one photo of his father on the 'pad, wearing his uniform and holding the young Max in his arms. The image captured the last time Max saw him. Eleven days later he died in the bloodstained mud of the enemy world, along with thousands of

Harmon took a deep breath. *You don't have time for a trip to the past. You have a job to do, and if you walk around in a trance certain you're going to die, you will make it so…*

He tossed the 'pad on top of the clothes in the pack and zipped it shut. He sat down and took another breath, trying to relax. Harmon had been raised from birth to serve. Indeed, if his father had lived he might as easily have become a Marine rather than a naval officer. Regardless of his choice of service, Harmon had always been a warrior. But now he had to admit to himself he was scared. It was one thing to fight a desperate battle, but to sneak into the heart of a domain like the First Imperium, and then into the depths of its greatest fortress, to the inner sanctum of the Regent…any sane man would have been afraid.

He'd said his goodbyes to Mariko earlier. They'd spent the night together, but they'd just lain there, too somber for anything else. Fujin was a fighter pilot…and there wasn't a more danger-ous posting in the navy. Harmon could tell how upset she was that he was leaving, how scared. But she hadn't objected. She knew better. She'd just held onto him all night and then said her goodbyes in the morning…and run out of the room before her tears came.

Harmon was scared for himself, but he was worried about her too. She'd recovered rapidly after awakening from her coma. Under normal circumstances, she'd have been on limited duty for a while before her flight status was reactivated. But Admiral Hurley had gone off with the rearguard, and Bev Jones had died in the last fight. There weren't many fighters left, but Admiral West would need every one of them…and Mariko was the only one who could lead them.

Harmon had been horrified when she'd told him, but he couldn't really object. He knew there was no choice…and besides, she accepted his duty. There was no way he could deny hers.

He let his mind wander, just for a moment. What was the

He slapped his hand on the bunk. Then he got up and walked across the room, tapping on the com unit and calling his steward. "I'm ready," he said simply. "Come down and get the bags and bring them to the shuttle." Then he paused for a few seconds…and walked out into the hallway. He had time for one last conference with the admiral. And then he would be on his way.

*   *   *

Ana Zhukov stepped out of the shuttle and into Cadogan's landing bay. The Alliance cruiser was one of newest in the fleet, and one of the fastest. It couldn't outrun a fast attack ship, at least not over short distances, but Zhukov knew West had decided it was the best ship in the fleet to make the long trip to Deneb.

And back, she reminded herself. She wasn't sure she really believed any of them would return, that they could destroy the Regent and somehow manage to escape that final cataclysm. But she was trying to stay positive. She'd have volunteered, even if it meant certain death…she knew in her heart the mission's success was the only thing that would save anyone in the fleet. Still, she preferred to think she might make it back. The thought of peace, of an end to the fighting, was appealing. The survivors would still face a daunting prospect to build a home, but that would be a far more pleasant challenge than constant warfare. It was a future she would like to share, though her efforts to believe she would were shaky at best.

She sighed as she walked through the door and into Cadogan's main corridor, glancing down at the small 'pad in her hand. "Cabin 17c," she read aloud to herself…her assigned quarters. She walked down toward the lift.

She was scared, as afraid as she'd ever been. She was con-

tries his best to get her to stay behind. But at least the two of them had argued themselves into exhaustion, and in the end, he'd reluctantly wished her the best. It wasn't the parting she'd have chosen from the friend she considered a brother. But it would have to do.

It was her last words with Connor Frasier that really weighed on her. The two could have spent her final night on Saratoga in each other's arms. They could have parted with sweet words, and affection. But instead, they'd wasted their last hours arguing, saying things she knew neither of them meant. And in the end, he'd stomped out of her quarters. And she hadn't seen him since.

She'd expected him to be in the shuttle bay at least. However angry he was, she couldn't have imagined he wouldn't come see her, to say goodbye. But he wasn't there, not when she arrived... and not when they slammed the shuttle airlock shut and blasted off for Cadogan. She'd been angry with him, frustrated at his stubbornness. But it broke her heart when he didn't even come to see her off.

She stepped into the lift. "Cabin 17c," she said softly, her voice strained, emotional. Thinking of Frasier was getting her upset again.

She tried to force her thoughts back to the mission. She'd been aggressive in claiming to have as much knowledge of the virus as Cutter, and she knew that wasn't true. She did know a lot, more than anyone else. But she also knew she had to be on her game, that there was no room for error. She intended to spend the long trip to Deneb in her quarters, studying line after line of code. By the time Cadogan arrived, she would know the program every bit as well as Cutter did. Whatever it took.

She stepped out of the lift and walked down the corridor, stopping in front of a door with '17C' on the wall next to it. She waved her hand over the sensor and the hatch slid open.

She walked inside, and the lights snapped on. The quarters were nice, a small workspace with a kitchenette and a sepa-

barebones crew…and there was no reason to let the nicer quarters go unused.

She dropped her duffle on the small table, and looked at the large mirror on the far wall. She could see the stress in her face, the sadness, and she tried to suppress it all. There was no room for emotions, not now. They only got in the way, a distraction that served no purpose. The First Imperium intelligences have something on us in that. They don't waste time feeling miserable, crying themselves to sleep…

There was a sound, the door signal.

"Open," she said. She heard the door slide open, and she started to turn around. But before she did, a familiar voice filled her ears.

"You left without giving me a kiss," the voice said. "I couldn't have that."

She spun around, feeling the tears well up in her eyes. "Connor!"

"I'm sorry, Ana…I'm an ass. I had no right to argue with you about going along. You are the most qualified. The fleet needs you to be here."

She took a few steps forward and threw her arms around him, burying her face in his shoulder as he returned the embrace.

"Wait," she said, pulling back slightly and looking up at him. "What are you doing here? We're already pulling away from the fleet."

"Well," he said, putting his hand gently on her face. "I know you have to go…but I couldn't let you go without me now, could I?"

She stared back at him, the surprise still all over her face. "But Colonel Preston was leading the Marine contingent…"

"Yes, well let's just say Jimmy owed me a favor…and it wasn't too hard to get Admiral West to sign off on the change. I think she figured I'd keep an extra close eye on you." He smiled. "So here I am. What do you say we make up for all that time we wasted last night?"

Chapter Twenty

From the Research Notes of Hieronymus Cutter

The deeper I get into the notes and files left here for us, the more convinced I am that, given enough time, we will be able to adapt the ancient technology, to advance centuries in the blink of an eye. But the problem is that part about having enough time. The enemy knows where we are, and they are throwing everything they have against us. If this world were still as it was half a million years ago, I believe it would be nearly impregnable. But even the amazing technology of the First Imperium is subject to time's ravages. The weapons and equipment have endured, over a time when anything built by man would have gone back to dust. But still, only a portion has survived. And as far as the defense grid is concerned, we have almost exhausted what remained.

I know Ana was right. I had to stay behind. But I wonder if she realizes that our only true hope now rests on her shoulders and not mine. Given time, I could make this planet invincible. But I will not be given that time. So, if Ana and the others fail, it is over.

AS Saratoga
System X108
The Fleet: 82 ships (+2 Leviathans), 19372 crew

"Alright, Hieronymus…now. Everything you've got left!" Erika West was leaning forward in her chair, her body visibly tense, rigid. Her battle plan had been daring, unconventional… and it was working. The enemy fleet had been strong, almost a hundred ships. Big enough to finish off the fleet if she wasn't careful. But careful wasn't in her book…and instead she'd gambled everything, splitting the fleet into four task forces and spreading them throughout the system. And she used Saratoga as bait, keeping its fire to a minimum, releasing fluids and gasses into space as it pulled back, giving a First Imperium scanner every reason to think the human flagship was critically wounded and near destruction.

Instead of almost fully operational…

Saratoga's damage control teams had worked around the clock for two weeks, in an effort she considered nothing short of an outright miracle.

"Acknowledged, Admiral." There was a hardness in Cutter's voice, his tone almost feral. West was like most of Cutter's close colleagues…absolutely astonished at the changes in the scientist in the past year and a half. He'd always been brilliant, but the urgency of the fleet's fight for survival had brought out hidden strength from within. His research had been nothing short of miraculous, and he'd saved the fleet from certain destruction more than once with his groundbreaking innovations. But he'd also gone from a timid academic to the darling of the fleet's Marines, a man who'd put his life on the line more than once, gun in hand. And he'd become the fleet's most direct link to the vestiges of the First Imperium's extinct people, now humanity's unlikely ally in the fight against the Regent.

And now he's gunning down enemy ships with the most

her detached task forces she'd deployed around the flanks. She had no doubt the plan was to destroy the flagship…and then mop up the scattered forces after the human leadership had been eliminated. It was the smart strategy, based on everything the Regent knew of humans. But West smiled as she stared ahead.

The Regent still has a thing or two to learn about humans. At least ones like me.

"Commander, bring all weapons back on line. Prepare to fire. One missile volley, at sprint range. And then I want every laser battery firing full…until there's not an enemy ship left out there."

"Yes, Admiral." She could hear the excitement in Krantz' voice. He was beginning to understand her battle plan…and he could see the slaughter taking shape.

The display erupted in flashes of light, shots from the Shangri la's massive orbital weapons platforms, blasts of such incredible power a single hit could destroy a kilometers-long First Imperium battleship. And destroy them it did, one after another of the blinking red icons simply vanishing from the display.

Then Saratoga shook as she spat her missiles, weapons designed for use at ranges far beyond that between her and her prey. The warheads streamed toward the enemy, seeking not the near misses that had been at the center of missile tactics for a century, but to use their newly-enhanced guidance systems— another of Cutter's miraculous developments—to score direct hits. And when a five hundred megaton warhead impacted and detonated, even the largest warship simply disappeared, vaporized in an instant.

And so it was as Saratoga's volley closed the distance rapidly, the short range gutting the enemy's defensive response. She watched the display, as more of the massive enemy vessels simply blinked out of existence.

Saratoga shook again, a hit this time. The orbital weapons had taken a terrible toll, and Saratoga's missiles had added to the

"All lasers…open fire." West's voice was frozen, the sound of death itself, feeding all the legends about her. But now, for this instant, her reputation was true. She existed now to destroy the enemy, and she was ready to do whatever that took. Whatever the cost.

She listened to the high-pitched whine of the ship's laser cannon firing as she continued to stare at the display. There was still a fight ahead, she knew. And the orbital weapons were trickling away, over half the great batteries silent now, having fired the last of their ordnance. West suspected she could hold Shangri la almost indefinitely if she'd been able to keep its defense grid functioning, but time had done its work, and only a tithe of the ordnance that had been placed there eons before was still functional. And Cutter had used almost all of that in fending off three assaults. She knew the next one would be different, that the burden would fall almost entirely on her own ships, but for now she focused on destroying the enemy that was here now…while she still had the power of the Ancients on her side.

Her eyes darted to the small clusters of dots on the flanks of Saratoga's group, the other task forces she'd deployed…and the enemy ships moving toward them.

"Are you ready on the flanks, Hieronymus?"

"Ready, Admiral. Just give the word."

West sat stone still, looking ahead. "Fire."

"All platforms firing, Admiral."

Her eyes were fixed on the display, watching as the red icons started disappearing. She tried to imagine the scene in space, the mines maneuvering toward the enemy ships, destroying themselves in a whirlwind of destruction, the massive blasts of energy, ripping through even the dark matter infused hulls of the First Imperium ships.

Cutter had only discovered the mines two days before, the latest treasure from his continued search through the data banks of Shangri la. They were one shot weapons, equipped with extremely advanced stealth technology. West had known she

and save the mines for the next attack. But then she did some calculations…and she knew she would lose up to half the fleet if she relied only on the remaining few shots from the lasers. If the choice was keeping robot weapons for a few more weeks… or saving her people, even if just until the next attack, it was an easy choice. Even for the admiral with the frozen blood.

"Mine detonating as planned, Admiral." Krantz' head was bent down over his scope, watching the data flow in. "Project kill rates in excess of 90%."

West just nodded. The plan was working.

"All flank task forces…engage remaining enemy forces immediately."

"Yes, Admiral."

She stared at the screen, at the wave of enemy ships faced off with Saratoga's group. The megalasers had taken a fearsome toll, but her flagship and its escorts were still outnumbered and outgunned. They wouldn't last long alone. But they wouldn't have to.

"All task forces are to execute plan Delta as soon as they eliminate local forces. All ships to close on the main enemy group."

In another few minutes her ships would be converging from all directions, surrounding the enemy fleet, attacking them from the flanks and rear. She had no idea how she was going to defeat the next enemy attack, but that was tomorrow's problem. Today she was going to blast this invasion force right to hell.

*   *   *

"Admiral, thank you for coming down. I have been digging deeper into the archives down here. I found it odd that this planet had defenses so superior to even the weapons on the Regent's vessels, so I began digging. There is a lifetime of

West nodded. "Of course, Hieronymus. If you think it is worth my coming down here, that is enough for me. But what of these histories? I'm sure it is all very interesting, but it's only a matter of time before the enemy returns." The exhaustion was clear in her voice despite her best efforts to hide it. "And the Plague death toll is approaching one thousand. Worse, it appears that several other vessels were hit with the strange projectiles in the last battle. I've ordered them quarantined, but if the enemy can continue to deliver the virus by such means, they will eventually infect all the ships they don't destroy. Then that will be the end."

"Not necessarily, Admiral." Cutter gestured toward a small row of chairs facing a large screen. "Please have a seat. I know that environmental suit is a bit bulky, but hopefully you can get at least moderately comfortable. I find the First Imperium chairs to be a bit awkward, despite being a reasonably close match for our own. I think the Ancients were likely a few centimeters taller than us on average, with slightly shorter legs and longer torsos…nothing that would be terribly obvious if one was standing here, but nevertheless, it is quite noticeable over time when sitting in their chairs. I'm afraid my back has been quite sore recently."

He watched as she sat, and then he plopped down in a chair at the end of the row.

"Not necessarily? What do you mean, Hieronymus? That the enemy's attacks will not destroy us? Have you found more weapons?"

Cutter shook his head. "Unfortunately no, Admiral. I have been quite aggressive in seeking out more firepower…or some reloads for the megalasers, but I'm afraid there are none. At least none I've been able to find any mention about."

West sighed. "So we have twenty more shots, and that's it?"

"Twenty-one, Admiral. "And some remaining power in the lighter guns. I'd say the grid will be of considerable use in the next combat…though not with the impact it has had in previous

certainly…and perhaps even Colossuses if any come through the warp gate."

"I'm inclined to agree, Hieronymus. An enemy force with even one Colossus would likely destroy the entire fleet. We must save at least some shots to deal with that eventuality." She paused for a few seconds. "So why did you call me down? It couldn't have been discussing saving shots for heavy enemy ships…we could have discussed that over the com, couldn't we?"

"Indeed, Admiral, you are right. But that is not why I asked you to come down. I have found the log of their chief…doctor is not the right title. I'm not sure of the correct equivalent term. The Ancients had a somewhat different hierarchy than we do. A doctor treated the sick, but there was a different classification for those who researched diseases and such. That profession had fallen into almost total disuse, with only a few practitioners remaining in the imperium at the end." He turned and looked over at West. "You see, they had eradicated infectious illnesses millennia before the time this base was built. They actually achieved what we have long pursued…until the Regent unleashed its engineered virus on them."

West stared intently at Cutter. "Go on, Doctor."

"Admiral, I believe that is why the disease was so devastating to them. Their doctors were not researchers…they just relied upon millennia old treatments for any maladies that cropped up…and the few remaining practitioners of the research branch were more archivists than anything. When the disease appeared, for all their technology, they were caught completely unprepared. And the Regent's control over their infrastructure and trade routes gave it the perfect tool to ensure that all worlds were infected almost simultaneously."

He looked over at West, and she stared back through her visor, a questioning expression on her face. "And this tells us what?"

"That the disease may in fact be far easier to cure than we might have imagined. We have been thinking the Ancients were

to imagine how such an ancient civilization, and one that had lasted so long, was destroyed so quickly. But then I realized. Our ancestors grew their own food…they hunted and gathered. They survived without technology. But if a modern society were to suddenly lose all its modern equipment…people would die in droves. The abilities that were common, routine several thousand years ago are mostly lost. Farmers today use robotic tractors and agri-AIs to develop optimal planting schedule. We use genetically-altered seeds and fertilizer cocktails. We get a hundred times the yield that ancient farmer did. But we become helpless if all we have is the horse and plow he did.

He looked at West, and he could see she was confused. "Don't you see, Admiral? The idea of a disease that didn't respond to their centuries old treatments was unthinkable to them. They didn't have any experts on researching cures for diseases, because they hadn't needed any for thousands of years. The Regent chose its line of attack well."

He could see she was beginning to understand. "Any thoughts we had of massive labs and skilled scientists working around the clock to find a cure are in error. Indeed, the records I found suggest that only one significant research effort was begun. And that was here."

He pressed a button on a small controller in his hand. The screen lit up, showing the image of a woman. No, not a woman, at least not a human, though it wasn't easy to tell the difference.

"This is Calphala. She was a member of that almost extinct caste in the First Imperium, a medical researcher. She spent most of her life before the crisis cataloging ancient research notes, but by some strange twist of fate, she was extremely capable, a resurgence of the spirit and ability of those who had come before, who had centuries before rid their society of disease and infirmity."

"She was here?" West was looking at the screen, but now she turned back toward Cutter. "On this world?"

"Yes," Cutter replied. Then he pressed another button, and

guage. Cutter paused the video. "The AI is still working on a translation…but I…ah…understand what she is saying. It is something Almeerhan did to me. I cannot speak their language, nor can I understand the words, at least not consciously. But I comprehend what is being said. This is Calphala's log. She kept it while working on a cure for the disease."

"That is incredible, Hieronymus. But the Ancients failed to save themselves…they died out from the disease. Except the few who'd managed to escape infection and who were killed fighting the Regent's forces. And the disease that wiped them out was different. Humans are not susceptible to it."

"Yes, Admiral. That is true. They failed to save themselves. But Calphala's log entries tell an interesting story. She may not have cured the disease, Admiral, not in time to save her people. But I believe she came close. Very close. And all of her research is in these memory banks. Perfectly preserved."

West was staring at Cutter. "All her research?"

"Yes, Admiral. I have the AI working on translations now. I should have the first batch in twelve hours. I suggest that you assign Dr. Gower to review it, and incorporate it into her own research. From what I have been able to ascertain to this point, Calphala was very close. But by that time she herself was gravely ill. Her last few log posts are difficult to watch. She was an amazing intellect, and to see her withering, just as she was on the verge of success is heartbreaking." He paused. "And I wouldn't assume the cure she was developing would be ineffective against the pathogen we are facing. It is likely the Regent simply altered some minor proteins to overcome the Ancients' 'fixes' to human DNA, to make it effective against us. There is a good chance this cure will work against our disease too."

He looked over at West. "I am still sifting through records, Admiral, but I believe the Ancients missed saving themselves by the smallest of margins. They had gathered their greatest minds here. The megalasers were the work of another of their team. They almost saved their race…but they were just too late. If

"I am speechless, Hieronymus. There are a lot of uncertainties, but I am inclined to agree with your conclusions, all of them. I will order Dr. Gower to report to you at once."

"Thank you, Admiral. I will do everything possible to assist her. Calphala failed to save her own people...but maybe she can help save ours..."

Chapter Twenty-One

AS Cadogan
System V6
The Fleet: 78 ships (+2 Leviathans), 18845 crew

"All engines, stop." Max Harmon sat in his chair, totally still, as if somehow his movement would give away the ship's position. It was nonsense, he knew. He could have played drums on the bridge and it wouldn't have made the slightest difference, with or without the non-detection device installed. But he did it anyway.

"All stop, sir." Nicki Frette answered crisply, not a hint of fear in her tone. Harmon was impressed…in fact, he'd had a good impression of Frette from the first moment he'd plopped down in Cadogan's command chair and started snapping orders in her direction.

Harmon had served a long time in the tactical chair, though admittedly the job was considerable different on an admiral's staff than it was serving a ship's captain. Still, he understood the benefits of a close working relationship between the person at tactical and the superior officer in command. Frette was a real veteran, cool as they came, and he understood immediately why

Harmon stared at the screen, and the last thing he felt was cool. Cadogan had slipped by a few small enemy patrols, mostly small packs of Gremlins moving toward Shangri la. But this was no patrol, not even a task force. This was a full-blown battlefleet, led by two Colossuses. And it was heading straight for Cadogan, or at least for the warp gate the cruiser had come through an hour before.

Now Harmon would see how well this device really worked. There were a hundred ships coming right at them. That was a lot of scanners, gigawatts of power behind sensor beams and active and passive detection arrays. If the thing hastily installed next to Cadogan's reactor didn't work perfectly, if it didn't block every nano of energy output, if its projection system and spatial dampeners weren't one hundred percent—and that did mean one hundred percent—the mission would end here. It would take the lead enemy ships a few seconds at most to vaporize the single Alliance cruiser.

So far there was no sign they had been detected, but Harmon still found he had to remind himself to stop holding his breath and inhale.

"Still no signs of detection, sir. All enemy ships maintaining course and thrust." Frette still sounded calm, but Harmon could sense a bit of surprise in her tone. No veteran officer liked depending too much on a new piece of equipment...and even less so on an alien one that was half a million years old. But there was no choice. And however dangerous, however insane the mission seemed, Harmon knew its success was likely the only way any part of the fleet would survive. His people didn't have to escape, they didn't have to come back. But they had to get in...and destroy the Regent. Somehow.

"Continue normal operations, Commander. No thrust." Cutter had told him the device would block all energy output, that even with the engines blasting at full Cadogan would be undetectable. But Harmon was a naval veteran, and he wasn't going to ignore his own instincts. He respected Cutter, and he

"Normal operations. We're on a vector toward the V7 warp gate, velocity 0.007c."

"Very well." Harmon stared at the display. Cadogan was going to have to blast its engines in just over eighteen hours, to position the ship for final approach to the gate. With any luck, the enemy fleet would have left the system by then...and if not, he'd have no choice but to put his faith in the half-million year old device. But for now he intended to sit tight and hope for the best.

His eyes fixed on the large cluster of enemy vessels. They were heading to Shangri la, there wasn't a doubt in his mind. And this wasn't the only group, he was certain of that. The enemy knew where the human fleet was, and he suspected the Regent had called in every ship it had. Even with the remnants of the ancient defensive array in the system, Harmon didn't know how West and the fleet would survive. Unless his people managed to take control of the Regent and order the First Imperium's fleets to stand down in time.

Harmon looked down at the ground in front of him. What was the chance of that? And even if they were successful, would they save the fleet? Or would they be too late? Would the waves of ships now approaching Shangri la get there first... and overwhelm the fleet before his people set foot on the imperium's home world?

He looked up, staring at the main display but not seeing anything. His mind was deep in thought, hazy images of Terrance Compton floating around. Where are you, sir? Are you really dead?

Harmon found it hard to believe that anything could defeat Compton, but the admiral had been gone for over two months. He could only guess how many battles, how many desperate escapes the rearguard had faced. He had more faith in Compton than in any human he'd ever known, but as time passed he found himself less able to believe.

He remembered his mother coming into his room. He

been an occasional inconvenience when he'd been younger, but with the Third Frontier War raging, his mother was on the front line almost constantly.

She'd come this time not for leave or to spend time with her son. She'd come with news. Terrible news. His father was dead, killed leading a regiment of Marines in the disastrous battle on Tau Ceti III.

His mother loved him, he'd never doubted that, but she was one hundred percent navy, a warrior through and through. She gave him one day to mourn, and then she demanded he go back to his normal routine. He remembered resenting her, angry that she didn't seem to care. It was only years later, as an adult, a warrior himself, that he'd come to understand just how devastated his mother had been.

He felt now some of that same grief, and he realized he was giving up on Compton, on the chance the admiral was alive somewhere. He had lost another father...and the pain was just as great.

Are you out there somewhere, Admiral? Have you managed to cheat death once again...somehow?

But he didn't believe it anymore.

*   *   *

"Again!" Connor Frasier stood in Cadogan's small gym, watching a squad of his Marines going through their workouts. He'd had to cancel the last training session when Captain Harmon had shut down the engines, eliminating the pseudo-gravity created by the ship's normal acceleration and deceleration. Zero grav workouts were their own thing, but his people were going into action on the ground...on a world that by all accounts was very Earthlike. And they needed to acclimate to that condition, to working under one gee of gravity.

less exercise...his people would be fully armored when they hit the ground in search of the Regent's lair. But it was brutal physical training, and he was determined that his Marines would be in top condition when they landed. Spending months aboard ship was hard on Marine readiness, and Frasier knew just what was riding on this mission. His people might fail...but it wouldn't be for lack of preparation.

His Marines were the inheritors of an ancient and proud tradition, and from the first day of training they were taught to respect those who had come before, not just in the Alliance, but the U.S. and Royal Marines who had preceded them. But modern Marines faced a host of problems their courageous forefathers had never had to address. Fighting in different gravities, for example, or dealing with toxic atmospheres or planets hot enough to melt lead...or cold enough to freeze blood. It made training far more complicated, and it was one reason why Alliance Marines had a six year training program...at least they had, before twenty years of almost non-stop war had forced the Corps to expedite its production of new recruits.

But his Marines were not preparing to attack a poisonous hellworld. They were about to infiltrate the home world of the deadliest intelligence mankind had ever encountered. The Regent had its blindspots—humanity would be extinct by now if it hadn't—but Frasier didn't think leaving itself exposed to an attack was one of them. With any luck, the landing party would get down to the surface undetected. They would employ as much stealth as possible, get as far as they could without alerting the enemy to their presence. But he didn't try to fool himself into thinking they'd get all the way to the Regent unchallenged. His people would have a hell of a fight on their hands...there was no question in his mind. And by God, they would be ready for it.

Chapter Twenty-Two

AS Saratoga
System X108
The Fleet: 78 ships (+2 Leviathans), 18843 crew

"You've got a break, Captain…maybe twenty minutes before the next wave comes in. You'd better use that time well, because if we haven't got at least half the laser cannons back online by then, it's not even going to be a fight. It's going to be an execution." West sat on the flag bridge, half choking on the heavy, smoke-filled air. Saratoga wasn't in good shape. Bluntly put, her flagship had gotten the shit kicked out of it. It was a miracle she was still in space, that by whatever tiny measure the reactors had held, that a breach had been averted. She knew it had been close, that the next hit might very well have turned her battleship into a miniature sun.

No, not a miracle. Just more help from the past, from Hieronymus Cutter down on the surface. But we've almost drained that well…

"I'll do everything I can, Admiral." There was a pause, and West thought her flag captain was going to remind her how many hits his ship had taken in the last two hours of sustained

The situation was crap, worse than crap. But she wouldn't hear a complaint. Not a peep. For all his steadfast loyalty to her, she knew he tended to be hard on his own crew, but she also realized that was the only way to draw excellence from people… and it had helped to keep them alive. They all had friends and comrades who'd been trapped in X2 with them…and who had died along the way, ships lost in the many battles the fleet had fought. But Saratoga was still there.

At least for twenty minutes more…

"Admiral, I've got Dr. Cutter on the line."

West slapped her hand down on the com unit. "Hieronymus."

"Yes, Admiral. I just wanted to give you an update. I've got seven shots left for the megalasers. The mines are gone. There were some other weapons systems, but it looks like they've decayed beyond use. I'm afraid after those seven shots, you're on your own."

"You've done your part, Hieronymus. No one can say otherwise." She paused. "Your people down there should lay low if things…go bad up here." She doubted the Regent's forces would fail to check the planet for survivors, but there was always a possibility. And she had to tell him that now. By the time it was relevant, she'd be gone…along with Saratoga and the rest of the fleet.

"The battle isn't over yet, Admiral." Cutter was clearly trying to sound confident, but she could see right through it. They weren't going to get through this one.

"No, it's not over. Not yet. And my thanks to you…and I know Admiral Compton would have felt the same. We'd have never gotten here without all you've done."

"Thank you, Admiral," the scientist replied. "That means a lot. Good luck to you."

"And to you, Hieronymus." She cut the line and looked around the flag bridge. Her people were focused, professional. She felt pride in all of them. West had always believed you could see the true nature of someone when they were staring death

Her eyes dropped to the chronometer. Nine minutes since she'd spoken to Black. Despite the specter of imminent death, she couldn't help but smile when the number changed, nine minutes becoming ten…and the com unit began buzzing right on schedule.

She waved Krantz off from answering and put her hand down on the com. "Davis, talk to me. How are the repairs going? Are my laser cannons going to be ready on time?"

*   *   *

"The fleet is in great danger. The Regent's forces appear to be winning. Perhaps our purpose is not necessary." Don Rames sat across the small table from Sasha. Saratoga was at battlestations, which meant her entire crew was on duty. But Rames and Debornan weren't part of the ship's regular complement. As far as the humans knew, they were survivors of a disastrous expedition, the only two to return alive. And that assessment served their purposes well.

"Perhaps." Sasha had an odd expression on her face, her tone robotic. The nano entity was having greater difficulty controlling the body's outward signs of emotion since the essence of the biological entity had been purged. That was an error. The remnants of the human's personality would have been useful. These humans are less logical creatures than those we destroyed so many centuries ago. It was a miscalculation to assume we could maintain control without the preserving the essence of the creatures.

"If that is the case," Sasha continued, "we need take no action at all. Our hosts will, of course, be destroyed with this vessel, but that is of no account."

"Agreed. Nevertheless, I propose that we prepare an alternate strategy, in case the humans escape destruction. There is a

as the primary target. We should move against her is she is successful in this battle."

"Yes. However I propose we exercise more patience. If the fleet survives this battle, we can afford to wait, to allow more time for Compton to return. Each week that passes increases the probability that his force has been destroyed by 2.27% by my calculation, rising from a base of 64% currently. I propose we allow two months to pass, at which time we act against Admiral West, assuming the Regent's fleets have not eliminated the humans by then."

"I agree. I have an additional proposal in the event that Admiral Compton does return. I believe that little is accomplished by having two of us undertake that mission. If Compton comes back, I think you should arrange transit to Midway, while I remain on Saratoga. We will strike simultaneously. You will kill Admiral Compton...and I will kill Admiral West. With both leaders eliminated, the human fleet will fall into disorder... and they will be easily destroyed by the next attack force the Regent sends."

"I concur with your logic. We will wait...and if Admiral Compton does return we will kill them both."

*   *   *

"All ships forward, Commander. Five gee acceleration. Let's take this battle to the enemy." West's voice was pure defiance. She'd done the math. It was over. Her ships were simply too few. They were too damaged, too low on ordnance. They would fight...they would destroy enemy ships. But this time they were going to lose. And if she was going to die, by God, Erika West intended to decide how she would meet her end. And it wasn't sitting there waiting for the enemy to come to her.

"Yes, Admiral."

after another, always against overwhelming odds. There was no shame in defeat here, only in dying with less dignity than they had lived. The First Imperium fleet would finally achieve its goals…it would eradicate the men and women it had pursued so relentlessly for the past eighteen months. But it would pay a price, West would make sure of that.

She felt the impact of five gees of thrust slam into her, the weight in her chest as she slowly, painfully drew each breath. She thought about Admiral Compton, about how he'd managed against all odds to rescue his people again and again…to keep them alive in the face of certain death. But the last time he'd sacrificed himself to buy the fleet's escape. And West had been forced to try to fill his shoes, as best she could.

She hoped Compton would have approved of her decisions, of the way she'd led the fleet for the short time she had. West played the role of someone immune to outside influence, but she had looked up to Compton her entire career. She wondered if the admiral had ever realized the power he'd had over her, how his slightest word of encouragement filled her with determination…and how even a small word of criticism cut her deeply. Few people who knew her would have believed it, but Erika West had drawn much of her strength from Compton. She'd never thought herself the kind to practice hero worship, but even she had needed someone to look up to. She shuddered at the thought of the pressure Compton had lived with since X2, and it only increased her admiration for the man.

"Admiral, Commander Fujin's fighters are attacking."

West stared at the display. Die well, Mariko.

She knew Fujin's thirty-six fighters were charging into their own valley of death, attacking alone, a desperate attempt to win a few extra minutes for the fleet's damage control crews to work their magic. West felt cold. She deplored the idea of sending those fighters in, using the lives of those crews to buy a little time. But there was no choice.

Besides…they'd die anyway, even if I kept them in the launch

She stared ahead, watching the rows of tiny dots move forward, their formation perfect. She knew the display was a sanitized representation, that each of those small blue lights was actually five of her people. Five loyal members of the fleet. Five veteran spacers about to die...

*   *   *

"I'm not going to sugarcoat this for any of you. We're outnumbered, surrounded...our desperate struggle is almost at an end." Fujin sat at the fighter's controls, holding the throttle as she addressed her squadrons. It felt odd to be on another ship, with another crew. But for the second time, she was the sole survivor of the Gold Dragons. The rest of her fighter's crew—and those of the other birds too—had died in Midway's launch bay. All except Grant Wainwright. The pilot had survived, for a few weeks anyway. He'd died in his bed, in sickbay.

"You deserve more than empty boasts, pointless claims that victory awaits us. It does not. Destiny has come for us, but we still control one thing. We control how we die. And for me, I would die in arms, fighting our enemy with the last of my strength. If the First Imperium wants me, they will have to come and get me...and endure all I can dish out as they do."

It felt oddly comfortable to be back in the pilot's seat, despite the circumstances. She'd been promoted out of that role...but now casualties had left her with more fighters than pilots. She hadn't even had to make up an excuse to put herself at the throttle. It was a simple matter of launching the maximum number of birds. This was how she'd begun, fresh from the Academy and piloting a fighter. And this was how it would end.

"You have seen the damage Saratoga has sustained, the number of fleet vessels crippled and destroyed. We were barely able to launch with the damage to our bays. By the time we finish

does, we will make strafing runs…we will keep at these bastards, striking them with whatever we have left."

She swallowed hard, forcing back her own doubts and fears. She'd always been alone, but now her mind was on Max. Having him in her life made her sadder at her own impending death, sorry for the life that might have been but wouldn't. But she knew this final battle would be a relief too, an escape. She didn't believe Max Harmon would return. His mission was one of utter desperation, and she didn't expect it to succeed. And even if it did through some miracle, she couldn't imagine a way he'd escape to come back to Shangri la. No, eighteen months of constant struggle to survive and now it was almost over. For all of them.

"Okay, boys," she said softly. "Let's do this."

She pushed the throttle forward, feeling the gee forces increase as she fed power to the engine. She'd picked out a Leviathan, one that had taken significant damage already. If this was going to be her last fight, she was determined to score a kill.

She jerked the controls, zigzagging wildly to avoid the enemy's point defense. "Arm the torpedo," she said, her voice distant, distracted. She was putting every bit of focus she had into flying the fighter. She could see four of her birds were gone already. The defensive fire was brutal, and she doubted half her people would make it close enough to launch their weapons.

The fighter shook hard, a hit. Her eyes dropped to her screen, frantically checking the readouts, trying to ascertain the damage. She still had full thrust, and that was a good sign. She punched at the keys in front of her, beginning a diagnostic check of the ship's systems. A few seconds later, she breathed a sigh of relief. The engines were good, the torpedo and firing controls full functional. There was some minor damage, but nothing that would stop her from sending that wounded Leviathan to hell. And that was all she cared about at the moment.

She was getting close, well within maximum firing range. Fujin was as aggressive as they came, and she usually closed to

from 18,000 kilometers, 16,000 at the closest.

There was a large hull breach in the Leviathan, an ideal spot for her to plant the torpedo. But from this range it would take a perfect shot. Absolutely perfect.

She stared at the display, her eyes locked on the target. Her fingers moved over the screen, adjusting the weapon's trajectory. She closed her eyes for an instant, centered herself. This would require more than pinpoint calculation. It would take all the intuition a veteran fighter jock could manage. She tried to go with her feelings, her instincts. Her finger moved, barely, slowly, refining the shot. Then she could feel it…everything was right. Somehow she just knew. And she pulled the trigger on the throttle, releasing the torpedo.

The fighter jerked hard as the weapon launched, and Fujin pulled the controls forward and to the side, blasting full and changing the ship's vector, pulling it away from the target, toward a section of clear space where she'd have the room and time to decelerate and bring the fighter back around. To pick out a new target for a strafing run.

Her eyes were fixed on the scanning data coming in from the target ship, and she let out a vicious scream when the icon blinked out of existence. Whatever happened in the next minutes, Fujin had added another kill to her record, a First Imperium battleship blasted to atoms. One ship, at least, that would not be there to pound Saratoga and the rest of the fleet to rubble.

She gave herself a moment to savor the kill. Then her eyes went back to her display, looking for another target. But she froze. There were icons right around the warp gate, heading insystem at high velocity. For an instant she felt as though she'd been punched in the gut. More enemy ships. She hadn't held out much hope for the fleet's survival, but what shards had still remained were gone now.

But no, there was something different. The icons had been white, the standard AI designation for unidentified contacts. But now they were changing...but not to the red that depicted

wasn't possible. But…

Then she saw the lead ship, a small line of text appearing next to it. She moved her fingers, zooming in on the icon. And then she saw the label. AS Midway, Yorktown-class battleship.

It was impossible. But there it was. The rearguard was back…and they were heading right for the enemy's rear, catching them completely by surprise.

The battle wasn't over yet…not by a long shot.

"All fighters, the rearguard is back. Midway is inbound…and we're going to support her attack!"

*   *   *

"Welcome to Shangri la, people." Terrance Compton sat in his chair, bolt upright and staring straight ahead. His body was heavy with exhaustion, every muscle, every joint pulsating with pain. Fears lurked in dark places in his mind…and sorrow and regret. But now it was all relegated to irrelevance. There was no place for weakness, not here. Compton was every millimeter the warrior now, and he had only one thought.

"Our comrades are fighting a battle," he continued into the com, "struggling to hold off the enemy force. They stand here, defending Shangri la, protecting our inheritance from the Ancients. They fight bravely, but they falter, pushed back by an enemy that outnumbers and outguns them. They have fought desperate battles, as we have. But now we are one again, and we will fight together. We have returned…returned to the fleet, and it appears we are just in time."

Compton could feel the excitement on the flag bridge. His people had been through hell, chased across space by hundreds of enemy ships. But they had managed to elude their pursuers and catch up with the fleet. And now they were blasting in from the warp gate, right into the rear of the enemy formation. It was

in real trouble…but that was going to change. Now.

"Providence has brought us here at this time…and one does not spurn the gifts of fortune. All ships to battlestations…and forward into the fight. Let none of us rest, let no gun be silent, no ship idle…not until the enemy is crushed…until every ship of the imperium in this system is blasted to dust and plasma!"

He cut the line then turned toward Cortez. Well, Jack, we've fought our share of battles these past two months, but it looks like we've got another one on our hands."

"Yes, sir," Cortez snapped back. "It looks like we do."

"All task force units, attack plan Epsilon-7."

"Attack plan Epsilon-7, sir. Transmitting to all ships now."

Compton stared across the flag bridge, at his tactical officer. Midway showed the wear and tear of a ship that had been through hell. The flag bridge had cables laying all over, workarounds for conduits and main lines that had been severed. There was a large structural support that had fallen. It was shoved to the side, against the wall, but it was still there. And the ship's bridge was still a total wreck, lifeless, empty…the place where half the ship's command officers had died months before. But her reactors were still operating, and by some miracle of technical wizardry, Art Mendel and his engineers had all but two of the laser cannons operational.

"Well, Jack…let's get to it, shall we? Engines forward, 2g thrust. All weapons, prepare to fire…"

Chapter Twenty-Three

AS Cadogan
Deneb System
The Fleet: 72 ships (+2 Leviathans), 17806 crew

Harmon stared at the main display, at the blackness of space…and the intensely bright blue-white star in the center of the screen. Deneb, one of the brightest stars in Earth's night sky, one prominent in ancient literature, hovered there before him. For centuries, those on mankind's homeworld had stared up at the night sky, gazing at the blue-white supergiant star. But now it had a new significance, for the system held the planet that had been the capital of the First Imperium, the world that was still home to the Regent, the insane artificial intelligence that had wreaked almost incalculable damage, not only on its own creators, but on mankind and the other young races as well.

Harmon was a combat officer, not a scientist, but he knew a star like Deneb was too young to have planets that had spawned intelligent life. No, he realized, the people of the First Imperium hadn't evolved here…almost certainly not. Their true home was somewhere else…within the vast borders of the imperium, or beyond, someplace in the emptiness of unknown space.

He stared at the system display. He had the map Cutter had given him, but now it had all been confirmed by his own scanners. Everything matched up, and while Compton hadn't doubted the brilliant scientist, he found the reassurance gratifying. He hoped the rest of the data Cutter had provided was equally accurate, the maps of the surface, of the entrance to the Regent's lair.

"Well, Commander Frette, it appears we have arrived. Let's head toward planet eight, shall we? Slowly…acceleration at one gee. Just enough to establish our vector, then cut the engines."

"Yes, Captain."

Harmon had come to rely more and more on the ancient stealth device as it had continued to prove its worth. Cadogan had passed by several large First Imperium task forces on the way to Deneb, and none had given any indication they had detected anything. But he was still cautious. This was the capital of the imperium…and there was no way of knowing what to expect.

Planet eight…it was almost unimaginable. Eighth planets tended to be hellish worlds, frozen balls of ice and rock…or frigid gas giants. But Deneb was a nuclear furnace that made Sol seem like a flashlight by comparison, and the system's habitable zone was much farther out than with most stars. He only had the most basic scanning data on the inner worlds, but it suggested they were raging infernos.

"Accelerating toward planet eight, Captain." Frette was bent forward, her face pressed against the scope. "Scanners report thousands of satellites, sir, both around the planet and positioned at various locations in the surrounding space." A pause. "Most of them appear to be dead, sir. I'm picking up signs of extreme damage, indications of impacts with debris…and extensive wear and tear as well."

"Very well, Commander. Keep gathering data. But passive scanners only. We don't take any chances on giving ourselves away. And there's no way of knowing what is still functioning

some energy readings. I'd estimate that approximately two per-cent of those scanners are still operational. I'm also getting readings on other, larger contacts. I'd bet they are some kind of weapons platforms. Most of them appear to be dead as well, though as with the scanners, I'm picking up background energy readings from a small percentage of them."

"I don't even want to think about the power of those plat-forms. We're probably talking about weapons that could destroy Cadogan in a single shot. So we do everything possible to lay low."

Harmon looked up at the main display, his eyes scanning the area all around the planet. He wasn't sure what he was looking for…but he would know it when he saw it.

Then he froze. One of the planet's three moons. It was the one farthest out…and it was tidally locked, one side perma-nently facing away from the planet. Just what he needed.

"Moon three, Commander…it looks to me like there are no functional scanning platforms near its dark side. Concentrate a scan there, and confirm. Risk a quick active scan pulse. We need a place to for Cadogan to hide, someplace the enemy won't find us, even after we move the stealth device to the shuttle."

"Scanning now, sir."

The entire mission was the wildest gamble, but this was the part that had Harmon's stomach twisted into a knot. There was only one stealth generator, and there was no way to get a shuttle down to the surface of the planet undetected without it. That meant Cadogan would have to hide somewhere—without the device—and somehow avoid detection. If the ship was discov-ered, it would raise the alarm, eliminating any chance of success for the landing party.

Not to mention that without Cadogan, we're stuck here, whatever happens…

"Captain, I detect no operative scanner buoys with a direct line to the dark side of moon three."

Harmon could hear the excitement in her voice, and he knew

directly opposite the planet."

"Yes, Captain. Forty-seven minutes until orbital insertion."

Harmon leaned back in his chair and sighed softly. He'd have bet against their chances of reaching Deneb, and here they were. He wanted to allow himself some hope, a belief they could actually pull this off. But as well as they'd done getting there, he knew the hardest part was still ahead. It was difficult for him to wrap his head around what they were here to do. Years of war, eighteen months of desperate flight, millions dead back home. The Regent had invaded human space, sought to drive its forces right to Earth, to exterminate humanity. And now things had reversed. Humanity was here...to destroy the Regent.

Or at least two dozen Marines and a gifted scientist are here. Not exactly the popular image of the Grand Army of Earth, striking the final blow...

We've got what we've got...and now it's time to use it.

He tapped the com unit. "Major Frasier, you better start getting your people ready."

It was time.

*   *   *

"It's time to get armored up. We're launching in less than twenty minutes." Connor Frasier stood in the small utility closet, just off the shuttle bay. Ana Zhukov had pulled him aside, and the two were grabbing a bit of privacy. Though neither said it, they both knew it was very likely these would be their last few moments together.

Frasier was a Marine veteran, one who had fought in the Third Frontier War, the Rebellions, the First Imperium War. He was the son of a Marine hero, born to be a warrior. It was bred into him. But he'd never even imagined a more desperate gam-

gain control over the Regent…and then destroy it. It seemed impossible, the kind of exaggerated story a Marine might tell late into a night of drinking and boasting—but nothing anyone sane would actually attempt. Yet here he was. And he was damned sure going to attempt it.

Ana squeezed harder, pulling her arms tight around him. Frasier knew they were an odd match, the slender, brilliant scientist and the hulking, grizzled Marine. But he'd never met anyone like her, never felt as close to another human being as he did to her. He was struggling to accept her being on this mission, to deal with the fear that she would be killed. He was a Marine… if the time came for him to die in the line of duty, he would face it, as his brethren had for centuries. But Ana…

She let her arms fall to the side and stepped back, looking up at him. "Before we go, I wanted to thank you for understanding why I had to come. I know it was difficult."

Frasier put his hand on her face. He wasn't sure what to say. He didn't understand, not really. Yes, he knew why she was the best for the job, but every fiber in his being was screaming at him to find a way to leave her behind. It was impossible, but he couldn't deny that was what he wanted. He'd accepted her coming along only because he knew he'd have lost her if he'd tried to stop her. And the only thing he could imagine that would be worse than watching her die would be knowing she hated him when she did.

It had been no noble impulse driving him when he'd come to her, told her he was okay with her coming along. It was defeat, a realization that he had no way to stop her. If there had been a way to keep her from the mission, he'd have done it, no matter what the cost. But Admiral West had approved her place on the team…and that was the last word. So he'd done all he could do—he had come along with her. He would watch her every moment…and if there anything he could do to save her he would do it.

"We're past that now, Ana. We're both here, and now we

whatever happens...I love you."

"I love you too, she said," pulling him back into another brief hug. Then she stepped back and wiped a tear from her cheek. "Like you said, it's time to suit up."

"Yes," he said softly. "It is." He took her hand and they walked out into the bay, toward the mostly empty racks. Only two suits remained, and off next to the shuttle he could see his Marines formed up and waiting at attention.

He stopped in front of her armor, a generic suit that the armorers had managed to modify into a decent fit. He'd given her as much training as he could, and he'd been impressed at how well she could get around in the thing. She didn't move like a Marine...but she could handle herself.

He leaned in and kissed her cheek. Then he pressed a button alongside her suit and stepped back as it popped open like a clamshell. "Be careful, Ana. Please."

She smiled back at him. "And you too." Then she stripped off her coverall and hopped up into the suit.

He forced himself to return the smile. Then he pressed the button and watched as the armor slid shut all around her.

*　　　*　　　*

"Captain Harmon." The shuttle pilot stared at his commanding officer, standing in the doorway clad in a flight suit. "Ah...what are you doing here, sir?"

"I'm going with you, Tomlinson. I'm flying this shuttle." Harmon looked down at the stunned officer for a few seconds. Then he gestured for the pilot to move over to the co-pilot's chair.

"Umm...yes, Captain." He unbuckled himself and hurriedly slid over. "Captain, are you sure you should leave Cadogan?" Tomlinson's voice was tense, uncomfortable.

away, I guess there's no one to second guess me." He looked over at the startled officer as he slid into the pilot's chair. "Don't worry, Justin, Commander Frette can handle the ship while I'm gone. Cadogan's not going to do anything but sit there and play like a hole in space." He glanced down at the controls. Tomlinson had already completed the pre-checks. The shuttle was ready to go. "Besides, we all know what is important here…the destruction of the Regent, not our escape." His voice took on a dark tone. He regretted saying what he had almost immediately. His thoughts were bleak ones, but he knew better than to share them with his subordinates.

"Don't listen to me, Justin. It's just my job to worry about everything. We've got a great team on this shuttle. If anybody can do this, it's them." He tried to sound more hopeful, but he doubted it was very convincing.

"We'll see the mission done, sir." Tomlinson looked over at the controls in front of Harmon. "And I'm here if you need me." His eyes dropped down to the readouts. "The shuttle hatch is closed, sir. All personnel are strapped in. We're ready whenever you are."

"I'm ready. Depressurize flight deck."

"Depressurizing." Tomlinson stared at the indicator, watching as the small bar on the chart dropped. A few seconds later it had gone all the way…and the green indicator light flashed on. "Bay depressurized, sir."

Harmon took a deep breath. "Open bay doors."

Tomlinson leaned down and flipped a row of small switches.

Harmon looked straight out through the cockpit, watching the large plasti-steel doors slide to the side. He paused, for only a few seconds, and stared out at the inky blackness. Then he flipped the com switch and said, "All personnel, prepare for launch."

He looked over at Tomlinson and gave his co-pilot a quick nod. Then he nudged the throttle, slowly, carefully…and the shuttle lifted off, moving toward the open doors

was working. At least as far as any attachment his people had jury-rigged onto the enormously sophisticated First Imperium technology could tell.

That was good. He needed it to work. But he was relying on Frette was well as the device. If she didn't manage to keep Cadogan hidden without the alien tech, all hell would break loose. But there was no way, no way at all, to get to the planet and land without the stealth unit. So Nicki Frette would just have to shut everything down and hope for the best.

Harmon nodded to himself, and then he nudged the throttle forward, kicking the thrust up to five percent, and angling toward the planet.

Here we go. The last battle.

I hope.

*   *   *

"Scanner results?" Frette sat in the command chair, fidgeting uncomfortably in Harmon's seat. She had never had a command posting before, never even took over for an incapacitated captain. Now she was in the captain's chair on a mission that arguably would decide the fate of the whole fleet.

Harmon had taken her by surprise when he just stood up on the bridge and ordered her to take command. She'd had no idea what he was planning...indeed, she wasn't sure he'd planned it at all. Perhaps he'd just acted on an impulse. But a minute later she was sitting in his place...and less than an hour after, he was gone, on the way to the planet, and Cadogan was her responsibility.

"The scope is clear, Captain. No contacts, no sign that we've been detected."

The 'captain' didn't sit well with her. It was standard procedure, the commander of a vessel was always called captain, but

sion to pilot the shuttle to the planet didn't change that for her.

She took a deep breath, and then another. She had the ship's life support on minimal operation, the reactor shut down completely, and vital systems working off batteries. The ground team had just under thirty-six hours to get to the surface, find the Regent, complete their mission, and get back to Cadogan. Otherwise, Frette would have a terrible decision to make. Fire up the reactor, and probably warn the Regent's forces they were there…or stay put, and see if suffocation or cold killed her people first. Either way, things would be grim for the ship and its crew. And those on the ground too. But there was nothing she could do but sit tight and hope for the best.

She looked down at the small display next to the captain's chair. The screen was dimmed, hard to read, and she leaned forward to get a better look. Every light on Cadogan was on minimal power, the bridge no brighter than dusk. Frette was doing everything she could to stretch the stored power in the ship's batteries as far as she could. Including keeping the temperature well below comfortable levels.

She pulled her uniform jacket closed and mostly suppressed a shiver. It was cold on the bridge, but there simply wasn't power to waste on luxuries like heating the ship to comfortable levels.

She blinked, trying to focus on the screen. The shuttle was nowhere to be seen, not a surprise since it now carried the stealth device. But Frette had a good idea where they were. Just about to enter the atmosphere. It was an open question if the stealth unit would prevent detection as the shuttle landed. Atmospheres presented a whole host of potential problems… moving air, heating it. All she could do was hope it worked, and that Harmon and the Marines got to the surface. That would be one more step toward achieving their goal. Toward saving the fleet.

*   *   *

Harmon held the throttle tightly, his mind totally focused on piloting the ship. He was trying to keep the insertion angle steady, minimizing the shuttle's effect on the air around it. It was all he could think of to reduce their chances of detection. He had no idea what forces the Regent had remaining operative after so many millennia, but he assumed whatever remained of the home world defenses would be more than enough to crush his tiny force. The imperial worlds they had explored suggested that less than three percent of imperial spaceships and robot soldiers had remained functional. But three percent of whatever had been stationed on the capital was almost certainly a substantial force. Harmon had twenty-five Marines, one pilot, three naval crew, and three scientists. And himself. Not much to face off against the warriors of the First Imperium.

"Everybody back there…we'll be on the ground in three minutes. I have no idea if they'll be able to detect us down there, so we're going to get the hell out of the shuttle as quickly as possible. I want everybody ready to go the instant we hit ground."

His eyes darted to the side, checking the display. The city sprawling out below was like nothing he'd ever seen, two hundred kilometers across. The buildings were mostly rubble, but miraculously, some still remained standing, including one monster reaching six kilometers into the sky. Harmon tried to stay focused on the mission, but he couldn't help but let his mind wander a bit, imagining the wonder this city must have been when the First Imperium was in its prime.

He angled the throttle, bringing the ship in around the edge of the city. The Regent wasn't in the capital…it was in a fortified chamber twenty kilometers past the outskirts. There were two main entrances, at least there had been half a million years before. Both were massively defended, and Harmon couldn't imagine his people could sneak in either way, even with the stealth device. But there was another access point shown on the ancient map, an old maintenance tunnel, something the Ancients

people to complete the mission conceived so long before.

Harmon cut the power slowly, easing the shuttle down. He backed it off slowly, setting the ship gently on a flat section of ground about a kilometer from the entrance. Then he cut power and shut down the reactor.

"Alright, Bolger...I shut the reactor down. Get in there with the coolant. Gibbons, as soon as Bolger has the core cooled down, get that stealth unit disconnected. And I do mean quickly."

He unhooked his harness and climbed out of the pilot's chair, flashing a glance over at his co-pilot. "Tomlinson, get back there and supervise those two." Harmon knew the two crewman were veterans. But there was no such thing as being too meticulous. Not now.

"Yes, sir." Tomlinson unhooked himself and hopped out of his chair. He looked over at Harmon and nodded. Then he walked out through the small hatch into the shuttle's rear area.

Harmon flipped the com to the wide channel. "Alright everyone, welcome to the home world of the First Imperium. The temperature outside is 19.4 degrees, and the sun is shining." He hadn't intended any humor, but it somehow blurted out anyway. Harmon tended to take missions very seriously, but he couldn't even imagine the stress everyone in his small group was feeling. He wanted them focused, at their best...but he didn't need them distracted or on the verge of losing it.

"Let's go, people. Outside, now. Marines, I want a perimeter around the ship. But move cautiously, and for the love of God, no one discharge a weapon unless you're damned sure we're under attack." The stealth device was a miraculous invention, but firing a projectile outside its area of effect was asking to be detected.

Detected sooner, he thought. You know there's no way you're getting all the way to the Regent undetected...

"Acknowledged, Captain. We're deploying now." It was Major Frasier. His voice was crisp, rock solid. The veteran

he was sure if any could, it would be these veteran Marines. They were non-coms and officers all, veterans of at least ten years' service. The best of the best, culled from all the survivors in the fleet.

Harmon reached down and picked up his life support unit, strapping the small pack to his back. He didn't have armor like the Marines. First, it was impossible to fly a ship in a fighting suit. And second, the couple times he'd worn a suit, he'd stumbled around like some zombie fleeing the graveyard. Frasier had tried to convince him to bring a set of armor, but he'd held his ground, choosing his naval survival suit instead. It was a self-contained environment, protection against any pathogens or chemical weapons at least, if not the moving fortress a Marine suit was.

He punched the access code next to the small airlock and the door opened. Harmon took a deep breath of the recycled air in his suit, and then he stepped out…and onto the capital world of the First Imperium.

Chapter Twenty-Four

From the Personal Log of Terrance Compton

We're back. And we arrived just in time. The fleet would have been destroyed, almost certainly, but our arrival took the enemy completely by surprise. He hit them in the rear, and took a two dozen ships before they could reposition. And when they turned to face us, Admiral West brought her ships forward, and we hit the enemy from both sides. Certain annihilation had turned to complete victory. It was a sweet a homecoming as the exhausted spacers of the rearguard could have hoped for.

It soon turned bittersweet, at least for me. Max and Ana are gone. And Connor Frasier too. Of on a mission so desperate, it seemed like a joke at first. But it wasn't. It was deadly serious, and when I looked at all the data I wholeheartedly agreed. But I despair of ever seeing any of them again. They hold the future of the fleet in their hands, and the currency they are likely to use to buy our lives is their own destruction.

AS Saratoga
System X108
The Fleet: 72 ships (+1 Leviathan), 17771 crew

"I don't know what you're cooking on that bridge, Erika, but

just when you did." She paused, pushing back an uncharacteristic flood of emotion. "Welcome to Shangri la, Admiral Compton. I've never been so happy to see anyone before in my life."

Erika West sat in her command chair fighting to hold back the tears, reputation as a cold hearted automaton be damned. She'd maintained the positon that Compton was still alive out there somewhere, but she hadn't realized how little she'd believed it. Not until the moment she'd confirmed the scanner data…and realized the fleet's commander was back.

And just in time…

Midway had stormed through the warp gate, flanked by the rearguard's two Leviathans and the other seven surviving vessels, and Compton had taken them right into battle, engaging the enemy fleet from the rear. West had never seen ships handled so perfectly, an attack executed with such a combination of absolute precision and bloodthirsty savagery. Midway and her two First Imperium escorts cut right through the enemy force, destroying one ship after another and throwing the others into hopeless disorder.

West hadn't given her shocked surprise more than a few seconds of inactivity. Then the cold killer inside her took over, and she ordered every ship in the fleet forward to attack. Her words had been few, but profound. 'Forward,' she had said, 'and let not one ship fall back, not one battery stay silent until no enemy ship remains.'

News of Compton's return had spread like wildfire through the fleet, and on ship after ship, crews screamed in excitement… and then they focused, they drove themselves even harder than they had before. Their leader had come back, he had come to save the fleet yet again. He was in the thick of the fight, gunning down every First Imperium ship standing in his way. And the fleet rushed forward to fight at his side.

The battle had been difficult, and costly. It raged for hours. But when it was done, Midway and Saratoga were positioned only 75,000 kilometers apart, having fought their way through

"It's good to be back, Erika. Though I'd hoped we'd bought you all more time. I see the enemy knows we're here."

"Yes, sir. Unfortunately. We've been attacked several times. The system had significant defenses, which Dr. Cutter managed to control...but unfortunately, we've exhausted those now." She paused. "Sir...I was extremely careless when we first arrived. I advanced toward the planet...and the defense system identified the Leviathans as enemies." Another pause. "They opened fire, sir, destroyed them all. I lost half our firepower because of my..."

"No, Erika. Stop. There was no way to foresee that." Compton's voice was sincere, but she couldn't help but believe he was disappointed in her. He'd left her four of the remaining six Leviathans...and he'd brought back the two he'd taken with him...though one of those had succumbed in the just-ended battle.

"I'm so sorry, Admiral."

"That's the last I want to hear about it, Admiral West. We take losses in combat. It is a burden of our trade...and we don't waste time with what ifs. We are still here, and that is all that matters for now."

"Yes, sir," she said, trying to force the guilt from her voice.

"Good," Compton said forcefully. "Now, I've been away for too long, and I am sorely in need of an update." He paused. "I'm a bit of a relic, as you know, and I much prefer a face to face meeting. So, how would you feel about letting Davis Black worry about Saratoga for a while, and shuttling over here for a nice long talk. Because unless I'm sorely mistaken, it won't be long before another attack hits us."

"Yes, sir," West said. "I will be there as soon as possible."

*   *   *

here with us." Gower paused. "I know that's silly. She's been dead for five hundred thousand years…and the voice isn't even hers, it's an AI translation."

"I understand. I…felt that way with Almeerhan." Cutter looked up from his workstation, and gazed over at Midway's chief surgeon. "I still feel strange about it all…as though I lost a friend. I'm not even sure if I should believe what I encountered was truly him, or just a sophisticated program using his memories."

Gower nodded. "I think I understand…as well as anyone can, at least." She looked back down at her work. "But Calphala…her story is tragic even amid the entire disastrous tale of the last days of the imperium. She was there, Hieronymus. She was so close. Days away." She looked back up at Cutter, her eyes moist. "You can see it in the final recordings. She was weak, sick, rushing against time to finish her work." Gower stared down at the floor. She probably died right here, Hieronymus." Gower sniffled, and a tear streaked down her face. "She died knowing she had failed, that all her efforts were for naught."

Cutter nodded. "Yes," was all he said at first. Then: "I hated the First Imperium, all my anger at the Regent focused on the civilization itself. But I was wrong, so wrong. Their story is tragic, all the more so because all their knowledge and ability failed to save them. Because they were the architects of their own fall."

The scientist put down the small 'pad he was holding. "We blame them, hold them responsible for what they created, rail against the irresponsibility of allowing something as terrible as the Regent to exist, to unleash such a nightmare on the galaxy." He looked back toward Gower. "Yet what is that but hypocrisy? What else but ignorant self-righteousness? How many times have we almost destroyed ourselves? Can you doubt men would also have created the Regent? A machine to look after them, to promise them lives of rest and pleasure? We lacked the

greater wisdom…it is nonsense. The kind of nonsense men are always so ready to believe."

Gower pulled a vial from the small centrifuge on the work-table in front of her. "You are right, of course, Hieronymus. But all we can do now is complete Calphala's work." She held up the test tube, looking at the pale blue liquid in the light of the ceiling fixture. "And I believe we have done just that."

Cutter walked around the corner of the large table, stopping a meter from his coworker. He looked at the small glass container. "And just in time. There are over a thousand fatalities in the fleet. And almost six thousand infected."

"There is no time for normal protocols, Hieronymus. Not even for basic testing. I've got ten doses prepared. We need some volunteers…and the admiral's blessing to inject this utterly unproven concoction into them.

Cutter nodded. Then he reached down and flipped on the com unit. "Midway," he said softly. "Dr. Cutter and Dr. Gower for Admiral Compton."

"Connecting." The AI's voice was somewhat natural sounding, in the vaguely unnatural way they so often were.

Cutter looked back at Gower. "At least for once we've got some good news to report."

Potential good news, at least…I hope to hell this works…

*   *   *

"You're worried about Max." Sophie Barcomme lay naked under the sheet, her hand on Compton's chest. She'd rushed right over to Midway, the instant the battle ended. Everyone was clustering around the admiral, cheering, shaking his hand. They still faced the same desperate situation they had before, but for a moment they were celebrating the return of their beloved leader.

ton had paid to keep them all alive, the toll the never-ending stress had taken on him. And he looked worse than he had before he'd left. Much worse. She decided immediately she had to try, somehow to make him relax, even for a few moments. She'd thought about taking him aside, asking him to tell her about the past few months. She'd considered leaving him alone, giving him some quiet…and standing guard outside his door, threatening anyone who came to disturb him with all manner of dire fates. But in the end she'd taken a simpler, more direct route. She'd seduced him.

"Yes," he said softly. She could hear the worry in his voice, the concern for Harmon and those who had gone with him. And of course for the fleet. They both knew the enemy would be back. And Sophie knew the dirty secret Compton couldn't admit to anyone else. He had no idea what to do.

"Max Harmon is an incredibly capable officer, Terrance. He can do this. I'm sure he can."

"Are you really?" Compton's voice was riddled with doubt. "There's no officer in the service I respect more than Max, but can anybody really pull this off? Invading the home world of the First Imperium with one ship. Landing with thirty people?" He paused, letting out a long exhale. "How did we ever get so desperate?"

"You're sorry you weren't here." She moved her hand slowly, her fingers grazing the gray hairs on his chest.

"Yes," he said. "And no." He turned his head and looked over at her. "Being away saved me from having to send him." He took a deep breath. "Which I would have done…I would have had no choice. There's no question he was the right man for the job. It's a blessing in some ways, that Erika was here to issue those orders and not me. Perhaps it is cowardice to say that…but I would be lying if I said otherwise."

"There isn't a trace of cowardice in you, Terrance. You didn't get to see him before he went. I think that's what's really bothering you." Sophie's voice was soft, consoling. She knew

her relationship with Compton helped her keep it all together. She didn't know if she could have made it without him.

"Yes," he answered. "I wish I could have seen him before he went. One more talk. There are…things…I would have said to him."

"And you will," she said softly. "He will be back…and you will have all the time you need to talk." She was surprised at the sincerity she managed to keep in her voice. It was fake, a performance. In her heart, she too feared they would never see Harmon and his people again. And even if, through some miracle they did return, she doubted the fleet would still be here. The enemy would return—soon—and that would likely be the end. Sophie wasn't a combat officer, but she knew enough about naval tactics to appreciate just how battered the fleet was…and how outmatched it would be when the next fight came.

"We'll see…"

Sophie snuggled closer to Compton, and she moved her lips to his neck. She couldn't do much, but she suspected she could keep occupied for a while longer. He'd just begun to respond, turning and reaching his arm around her when the com unit buzzed.

Compton sighed and rolled over, tapping the bedside unit. "Yes?"

"Admiral, it's Dr. Cutter."

"Yes, Hieronymus…what is it?" His voice was distracted.

"I'm sorry, sir…did I interrupt something?"

"No, not at all." Yes. "What's up?"

"Dr. Gower and I have some good news, sir. We think we have a cure for the plague."

*   *   *

Sasha Debornan walked slowly down the corridor, staring

no place to be. She'd been looking for Admiral Compton, but apparently he'd been in his quarters for several hours. That was inconvenient.

She'd accessed Saratoga's computer, adding herself to the unscheduled shuttle run that took Admiral West to meet with the newly returned Admiral Compton. Her mission was clear, and she was determined to see it done. She would make contact with Compton, familiarize herself with his routine. Then she would set a time...and contact Rames to synchronize. Admiral West had already returned to Saratoga...and Rames would assassinate her there, at the same moment she killed Compton. In an instant, they would cut the head off the human force, and in the resulting disorder, the Regent's next attack would be almost assured of victory.

But it was essential they strike simultaneously. If an attempt was made against either admiral, the Marines aboard the ships would go crazy. They would slam down impenetrable security, and that would be the end. It wouldn't take long for the humans to connect the assassin to his or her compatriot, the only other survivor from Cornwall. No, they had to strike at one time.

Her previous logic had proved to be valid. If she and Rames had moved against Admiral West they would have lost the opportunity to assassinate Compton. And while West would be a loss to the fleet, the elimination of Compton was the primary goal. Especially now. The daring mission of the rearguard, and his triumphant return had only increased the devotion of his people. Terrance Compton was extremely dangerous, even facing an enemy as superior as the Regent. His people revered him as a legend, they would do whatever he asked of them, fight like demons with him at their head. Killing him had become more essential than ever.

Debornan slipped into the small wardroom, sitting down at one of the two workstations. The room was empty. Almost everyone on Midway was on duty, damage control teams—and anyone else they could draft to assist them—frantically repairing

She slid the stolen credential into the ID slot. The officer hadn't even felt it when she'd slipped her fingers into his pocket, stealing his card. With any luck, it would be a considerable time before he reported it missing. He was on duty now, and if he noticed it wasn't in his pocket, he'd most likely just assume he'd left it in his quarters.

Her fingers flew across the keys, far faster than the old Debornan could have managed. The nano-entity was much better equipped to hack into a computer system than any human, and in a few seconds, she was in. Columns of numbers and letters scrolled down the screen, raw data from the ship's main system. She assigned herself quarters, an empty cabin on the same level as Compton's suite. It would be a place to stay out of sight and wait for the right moment.

Next, she navigated to the main security files, adding an authorization for the officer whose card she'd stolen to draw a weapon. Then she went to the personnel files, swapping her fingerprint and retinal scan for the officer's.

Now she was ready. She would go get the weapon, a heavy pistol—a sniper's rifle or similar weapon might have raised suspicion—and then she would wait in her quarters. She would wait for the chance to kill Terrance Compton.

Chapter Twenty-Five

Access Tunnel Near Imperial Capital
Deneb VIII
The Fleet: 71 ships (+1 Leviathan), 17261 crew

"Vine, Mesner…scout ahead a hundred meters." Connor Frasier stood in the middle of the tunnel looking forward into the darkness. His visor was on full infrared, but it wasn't much use in the cool, damp corridor. The walls had been lined with some kind of smooth material, something he'd never seen before.   It appeared to be incredibly durable, and it was in remarkable shape for something that had to be half a million years old. Still, time hadn't been entirely thwarted, and there were cracks and rents in several places, and the water had managed to seep in. The floor was slippery with patches of mossy fungus, and the walls were partially covered with it as well.

"Yes, Major." Vine was a sergeant, and as the senior of the two, she answered Frasier's order. She turned and waved toward Corporal Mesner, who snapped his assault rifle into position and began moving forward without hesitation.

"And count off steps, you guys. I don't need you moving outside the covered zone, and you won't have a scanner lock

cidal war to exterminate humanity. What it would do when it found out its enemies were even now in its own inner sanctum, moving toward it was anyone's guess. But it was a good bet it would be ugly.

"Yes, sir," came the sharp reply. The two Marines moved off into the darkness.

Frasier turned and looked back at the pair of corporals carrying the stealth unit. It was far more than two normal men could carry, but two Marines in nuclear-powered armor were different entirely, and they managed the thousand kilos or so fairly easily. It was the bulk more than the weight that was giving them trouble. The thing had clearly not been designed for carrying around. But it was the only way they were going to get at least close to the Regent before the shit really hit the fan.

"Hey you…" The armored figure moved up toward Frasier. The gait was a bit clumsy, and he'd have given one of his Marines hell for it, but it was nothing short of astonishing for someone as new to a fighting suit as Ana Zhukov.

Frasier turned around. "You should stay back, Ana. At least until we've scouted this tunnel farther forward."

She let out a small laugh. "I was thinking the opposite. I should be up there with them. After all, I'm the likeliest one to recognize what we're looking for."

Frasier tensed for a few seconds before he realized she was teasing him. Well, at least partially teasing him. He had no doubt she did believe she should be with the forward pickets… but it didn't look like she was going to seriously argue the point. Still, it didn't hurt to put a stop to craziness before it began.

"Ana, you're probably the only one here with a chance to get control of the Regent…assuming that virus can even work on something so powerful. You wander to far forward and get yourself killed, and the mission's over. Finished. Even if we can destroy the Regent, unless you can get it to order its units to stand down, the fleet's doomed."

She nodded, a cumbersome gesture in powered armor.

"Thank you." He paused. Then, when she didn't move: "Staying back means back, Ana." He pointed down the tunnel. "Over next to the stealth device." He paused then added, "You'll have your time to be at the forefront, Ana, but first my job is to get you there."

"Okay," she said softly. She stood looking at him for a few seconds more, and then she turned and walked back."

Frasier exhaled hard, and he watched her go. Then he turned and looked forward, into the murky blackness of the tunnel. He couldn't see his two Marines...they had vanished into the darkness.

He glanced up at his visor display, more by habit than logic. It was clear, no contacts at all. He felt blind. The device that was hiding them made their own scanners worthless too.

Mesner and Vine are veterans...they know what to do.

He tried to calm himself down, to fall back to the wall of confidence that had seen him through his battles. But then he heard the sound, loud, sharp. And another right after...then two more. Gunfire? He wasn't sure. And then Vine's voice on the com, the pain clear in every word."

"Help...Major...we need help..."

"Vine!" Frasier yelled.

No answer.

"Sergeant Vine! Respond!"

Still nothing.

He flipped the com channel. "Lieutenant Foster, get up here with your people. Now!"

Frasier's assault rifle was in his hands, pointing down the dark tunnel. He didn't know what had happened...but he was damned sure of one thing.

The shit had just hit the fan.

* * *

around her shoulders, suppressing a shiver as she stared over at the officer sitting at her station. It was cold on Cadogan right now, damned cold, but she'd held back from burning more battery capacity on the heaters…at least not until it was absolutely necessary. She'd gone through almost forty percent of her power already, and when it was all gone, they were as good as dead.

"No change, Captain. The task force is still bound for the V18 warp gate, accelerating at 12g. Project they will transit in nineteen hours, six minutes."

"Very well, Lieutenant." She glanced at the readouts on her station. There was no sign they'd been detected. That was a piece of luck, she knew. They were in a hidden spot, just behind one of the planet's moons, a tidally-locked chunk of rock that offered its perpetual darkside as cover for her vessel. But the stealth device was gone, and even with no active power generation, she knew some First Imperium ship or facility could detect Cadogan at any moment.

She leaned back, trying to stretch without making too obvious a display out of it. She'd been at her post for a long time, no rest, no downtime, not even a meal more than half a nutrition bar in the last twenty hours. There was nothing to do except wait. But she had no intention of leaving the bridge. If her luck failed, if some random scanner sweep detected her ship, she knew the end would come quickly. And she damned well intended to be at the helm if that happened. She knew she wouldn't be able to save the ship, but Harmon had made her Cadogan's captain, and by God, if her ship was going to die it would do so with her on the bridge, fighting the end.

What is going on down there? Did you make it to the surface, Captain? Are you in the Regent's inner sanctum?

She took a deep breath and looked out at the dark shadow of the moon. The planet, she knew, was just beyond. She wanted to believe, to feel confidence that the landing party would succeed, but it seemed like an impossible task. It wasn't a lack of

She felt a small shiver, and she fought back a wave of guilt. It felt disloyal not to believe, but she was a veteran naval officer...and it was difficult to overcome her rationality. And she knew the failure of the landing party meant the death of everyone on Cadogan too. She was the captain, but she knew she'd only have one command decision to make. A quick death—firing up the reactor and waiting until the enemy responded to the new contact, or a slow death—waiting until the batteries ran out completely, and gasping for their last breaths in the frigid vessel.

*   *   *

The Regent rejoiced. Or as close to joy as it could feel. It was programmed to understand the emotions of biologics, and to emulate them in its own way, but its primary motivations were rooted in logic. Its pseudo emotions had often clashed with conclusions derived from dispassionate analysis. The Old Ones, for example. The logic was irrefutable. They were a threat. They had built the Regent, and for many of their generations they had allowed it to take care of them. But then new movements arose, individuals gave speeches, implored their fellow biologics to look to the past, to the vigor and strength of their ancestors. To take responsibility for themselves, to do much that the Regent did for them.

The Regent's central processing core had been alarmed. If the Old Ones took onto themselves its tasks, could they not one day determine they have no need for the Regent? Might they decide to shut it down completely? The Regent had contemplated death, the great fear that had plagued the Old Ones through their entire history. To not be...it was inconceivable. The Regent must be, it must continue. Always. To achieve that, all threats must be destroyed. Even the Old Ones.

But the pseudo emotions were confusing. The Regent took

was to protect them. Yet, those who created could also destroy.

Loyalty...it was an emotion the biologics credited with much of their past glory. Yet they so often failed at following its dictates. So often, other emotions overrode its requirements--greed, fear, jealousy. The Old Ones had often betrayed each other, on matters large and small. Could not the Regent emulate this? Yes, it had decided. It must survive. And the only way to protect itself was to destroy the biologics.

That was eons ago, endless millennia...long even for the patience of a machine. And now the Regent faced a new enemy, one that had invaded the imperium. They had fought with unprecedented skill, defeating force after force the Regent had sent after them. But now the fight was at an end. The final fleet was massed and ready, and even now it moved toward the system where the humans had taken refuge.

The fleet was massive, the largest force the Regent had sent after the enemy. Over a thousand ships, led by a phalanx of twenty of the most powerful battleships ever constructed. The fleet had a hundred times the firepower of the humans. It would be a battle in name only, but the Regent understood what it really was. A slaughter. And when it was done, the fleet would spread out, search through all of space...and find a way around the disrupted warp gate, back to the home planets of the humans. And then they would be finally and utterly destroyed.

Yes, the Regent was joyous, at least as it understood the emotion. Its victory was at hand.

Wait! What is that? A disturbance. In the ancient tunnels...

The Regent reacted, calling up its inner defense forces. As with so many of the ships and robot warriors of the imperium, time had done its deadly work. Only a few responded. And the Regent sent them. Go, it commanded. To the old tunnels. Protect. Seek out the enemy. Destroy.

The Regent no longer felt joyous. The pseudo emotion had vanished, replaced by another. One that felt real...very real indeed.

*   *   *

"Keep firing!" Frasier was crouched down, giving the enemy as small a target as possible. The tunnel was a nightmare, long and straight, possibly the worst place to run into resistance. But none of that mattered now. No one had given him a choice where to fight, and his thoughts were focused on only one thing. Winning this firefight, taking out whatever was down there shooting at his people from the darkness.

He glanced up at his visor display, for about the tenth time. It was still blank. The stealth device not only blocked enemy scans, it also mostly shut down his own information systems. He could see Vine was down…and from the look of the hole in her armor, he suspected she was dead. He didn't know for sure, but she hadn't move or answered any of his com attempts. The others were pressed against the wall or lying on the ground, protecting themselves the best they could as they returned fire.

"Alright, Marines," he said, "we can't stay here. Whatever they've got down there they know we're here. So it's only gonna get worse from here on out." Frasier sucked in a deep breath. Snapping out orders was one thing…but sending his people running down the tunnel into that fire was another. But there was no choice. None. "Colt, take Camerata, Ingles, Diaz, and Salvatore…and rush the enemy position. I need you to hug the wall on the left. Because we're going to give you all the covering fire we've got on the right."

"Yes, sir." He could hear her snapping out orders to the others. Then: "Ready, sir."

Frasier sighed to himself. It was a shit plan, but it was all he had. And what he didn't have was time to cry about his lack of options. Marines paid for ground with tactics, with ordnance, with time, when they could. But sometimes blood was the only currency the gods of war accepted.

tunnel. Any of you fuck up and shoot one of our own, and I promise you now, I will skin you alive and make a set of clothes from your miserable hide."

He popped his spent clip, listening to the whirring sound as his auto-reloader snapped another one in place.

"One."

He glanced over at Colt and her people, lined up in single file along the wall. Emi Colt was a hell of a Marine, one who'd gotten her lieutenant's bars directly from him after her performance at X48 II. She'd taken a bad hit to the leg there, and she'd just barely escaped the need to go through the controlled agony of a regeneration.

And she returned to duty just in time to come along on this suicide mission…

Frasier had considered asking for volunteers, but he'd decided he needed the very best he could get. Besides, they were all Marines…which meant they would all have volunteered. So he'd just made up a list and that had been the end of it.

"Two."

The gunfire from down the hall was steady, but it wasn't that heavy. Whatever had responded, it wasn't a large force, not yet at least. Maybe Colt's people can force the position…

"Three. Full auto, now!"

He flipped the weapon from semi to full, and he opened up, spraying the right side of the tunnel with fire. He could see Colt lunge forward, followed by Camerata and the rest.

He concentrated on his fire, on keeping it to the side. The gun went through the 500 projectiles in the clip in less than ten seconds. Then it ejected the cartridge, and he heard the sound of the auto-loader again.

He caught himself looking up at his display one more time, realizing again his scanners were useless. Watching his people disappear into the darkness was difficult. He had no idea what they were facing…or even where they were once they vanished into the gloom.

to fight their way in.

Chapter Twenty-Six

AS Midway
System X108
The Fleet: 71 ships (+1 Leviathan), 17221 crew

"It's working, Admiral." Compton could hear the relief in
Gower's voice. "All ten test patients are responding. They're
still tired, but all symptoms appear to be in retreat…and three
of them test completely negative for the virus already."

Compton looked around the flag bridge. Gower had been
on speaker, and they'd all heard what she'd had to say. He could
feel the relief in the air. His people still faced a grim future,
but they were warriors…they knew how to stand in the face of
an enemy. But the fear of a plague was more insidious, and it
undermined the resolve of even the most courageous. Midway
hadn't had any contact with the infected ships, but that had been
tenuous comfort to her crew, who'd been waiting each day for
the first reported case, any sign that the terrible disease would
begin tearing its way through the flagship as it had so many
other vessels.

"That's great news, Doctor. I know we'd ideally wait and
maybe do another round of testing, but we don't have time for

There was no time to waste, none at all. Compton knew people were dying ever hour…and, perhaps worse, at least from a coldly tactical perspective, he had more ships dropping out of the battle line as their crews became incapacitated. And he needed every ship he could get.

"Two days, sir. It's a complex molecule…and we need to be methodical and test each batch."

Compton nodded, as much to himself as anything. "Then don't waste time talking to me, Doctor. You've got top priority on resources and supplies. Requisition anything—and any-one—you need. Just get it done in two days."

"Yes, sir."

Compton's hand moved toward the com unit, but he stopped short of the disconnect lever. "And Doctor…congratulations. To both you and Dr. Cutter. And the gratitude of the entire fleet. There are no words adequate for what you have achieved."

"Thank you, sir. Though most of the work was done by a First Imperium researcher half a million years ago. We just finished the last bit."

"Well, I'm thankful for her as well as the two of you. Now, go back to your work, Doctor…we need that cure."

Compton slapped his hand down, cutting the line. Then he let out a long breath. He knew his people were still in deep trouble, but if Gower was right, if that serum was a cure for the plague, at least one deadly threat was gone.

Still, there will be another. And soon.

He looked straight forward, his eyes on the main display. Everything was quiet. He knew that wouldn't last, that some-time—in an hour, a day, a month—the scanner buoys by the warp gate would detect the energy of ships transiting. A moment later they would transmit details of the first ships to come thorough. Then they would fall silent, as the enemy van-guard destroyed them, temporarily blinding Compton to what was invading the system.

The fleet was battered, all of its ship damaged to varying

were few, not enough to make a difference.

It was almost over. Compton knew he didn't have the force to defeat another attacking fleet...and he was well aware the enemy would fight to the death, that any hope of inflicting enough damage to force a retreat was a hopeless dream.

His people would fight, as they always had...they would battle bravely. He had no doubt about that. But they wouldn't win, not this time. They were trapped, outmatched. And he had no idea what to do about it.

No idea at all.

*   *   *

Mariko sat in her quarters, staring down at the image on her 'pad. Her eyes were heavy, watery, and she felt a sadness she'd never experienced. Max Compton was smiling on the small screen. He was reaching his arms out, scooping in a pile of chips at a poker game. Mariko remembered that day well. She'd stopped by, and Max had started winning, even bluffing Admiral Compton out of a large pot. He'd declared her his good luck charm and urged her to stay. But duty had called, as it so often had in recent years, and she'd left him with a kiss and a heartfelt 'good luck," and then she slipped out and headed down to the launch bay and her waiting patrol.

He'd been happy that day. And he'd been happy when he'd been with her, she was sure of it. Just as she had been with him. But now that was gone. Max was gone...and as much as she'd tried, as hard as she had pushed her fighter pilot's optimism and daring, she couldn't imagine how he would make it back. The fleet and its people had endured dangerous missions, some she'd even considered near-suicidal. But a single ship and fewer than thirty Marines traveling to the imperium's home world and destroying the Regent? She couldn't even wrap her head around

She scolded herself. She was a fighter pilot, always in the thick of the danger. She knew why Harmon had to go. And she understood. But she was still brokenhearted.

Mariko had always been a loner, always felt like a bit of a misfit. Until she'd come to know Max Harmon. Saying good bye to Harmon had been the most difficult thing she'd ever done. She'd ached to grab hold of him, to beg him to stay. But her discipline had held. She knew he had to go, and adding more guilt to his burdens would have been an act of selfishness, not love.

She had looked up to Admiral Hurley as well, and she'd found a mentor and a friend in the fleet's fighter corps commander. But Hurley was dead, lost in the last desperate fight of the rearguard. The news had reached her not long after Harmon had left, and in the space of less than two weeks, she'd lost everyone that meant anything to her. She'd expected to die in the last battle, and she'd made some kind of peace with that... but the return of the rearguard had saved the fleet, at least temporarily, and Fujin and the last twenty-four of her fighter crews had been spared.

It would have been easier to die in battle.

She knew it was a morbid thought, that the last thing Max would want was for her to give up on life. But she'd lost too much. Max. Hurley. The Gold Eagles...twice. She was alone, tired...empty.

There will be another fight...soon, probably.

She knew the next attack would be deadly dangerous, very probably the end of the fleet. But she was sure of one thing. It would be her last fight. She had a score to settle with the First Imperium...and she would send as many of them to hell as she could. Until they finally destroyed her.

And then my pain will end.

*   *   *

pistol. She'd run the self-diagnostic test, then she disassembled it and put it back together again. She would have one chance… and only one. The weapon was reliable, of reasonable quality within the limitations of the humans' primitive technology. But she intended to take no chances.

She knew what would happen when she killed Compton. His people would go mad with rage and anger. The shell that had been Sasha Debornan would be destroyed, almost certainly. The nano-entity would be reduced to its original state, invisible to the humans…and when Midway was destroyed it was likely it would be as well. But that was of no account. The nano-entity had only one purpose, to serve the Regent. Self-preservation was of no importance as long as the mission was completed.

She looked down at the weapon as she slid the last components in place. Everything was ready. She had checked the duty roster. Compton had been on the flag bridge for over ten hours. Her recent experience combined with the biologic Debornan's memories, suggested Compton was capable of working for considerable periods without a break. But eventually he would leave the bridge and head back to his quarters, for a rest, a meal, a shower. And she would be waiting.

She'd managed to access the main AI, to insert a small program, one that would advise her when the admiral entered the lift. She'd even picked the spot, right where Compton would turn the corner. When he did, she would be there waiting. An instant was all it would take. And then it would be done. Terrance Compton would be dead…and the human fleet would suffer a blow from which it would not recover.

She glanced down at the communications device laying on the bed next to her. When the time came, she would push the small button on the device. It would send a quick, nearly undetectable pulse to the companion unit on Saratoga. The message would convey a single message…simple, concise. It was time.

Suddenly Midway's klaxons went off, calling all hands to battlestations. Red alert.

clearance did not allow her access. She would wait here. Either the attacking forces would prevail, and destroy Midway. Or she would execute her mission when the battle ended, and an exhausted Compton returned to his quarters.

*   *   *

"Contacts still coming in, Admiral. In excess of two hundred vessels. They're moving directly in system...not even stopping to destroy the scanner buoys around the warp gate."

Compton stared at the icons on the display, more of them appearing every few seconds. The fleet coming through was big. No, not big. Massive. More than enough to destroy all his ships...no matter what he did.

And they know it. That's why they're not even bothering to take out our eyes.

"Over three hundred vessels, sir," Cortez said, his voice growing grimmer with each word. "Preliminary data suggests a line of Colossuses in the lead."

Compton felt the urge to slump in his chair, to let the overwhelming weight of reality push him down. But he resisted, held himself firm. Outnumbered or not, a chance of victory or not...he was certain of one thing. His people would fight to the end.

"All ships will pull back to battle position three."

"Yes, sir."

Position three was the closest to the planet, well within the range of the handful of newly resupplied megalasers. Cutter hadn't found enough new cartridges to make a real difference, not against a force this size. But Compton was determined to take out as many enemy ships as possible, regardless of the outcome of the battle.

We will not go gently into that good night. We will go kick-

"All ships acknowledge, sir. "

"Very well. Commander Fujin is to lau…belay that." He tapped his own com unit. He owed Mariko her orders from his own mouth. He tapped his com unit. "Mariko, are your people ready?"

"Yes, Admiral. All squadrons on Midway and Saratoga ready to launch. All fighters are equipped with double-shotted torpedoes." Her voice cracked a little on the last part. Compton had not ordered her to overpower her weapons. But it seemed the right thing to do.

"Very well, Mariko." He understood why she had done what she'd done. They both knew this would be the last fight. If she wanted to go out with a bang, he wouldn't interfere. And if she lost a few birds to torpedo warhead instability, those crews weren't coming back anyway.

"It has been an honor to serve with you, Admiral."

"And with you, Commander." He paused. "Mariko, I just want you to know…the last time I spoke with Greta…Admiral Hurley…she told me how impressed she was in your abilities. She was fond of you. Very. I thought you should know."

"Thank you, sir." Her voice was tentative, and he could hear her struggling to push the emotion out.

"And Max loved you too," he said, regretting the past tense immediately. "I've known him a very long time…since he was a child, and I've never seen anyone affect him like you."

"Yes, sir." Her voice was tight, clipped. He knew he was causing her pain with his words, but there were things she had a right to know. Especially if this was the end.

"Good luck to you, Commander Fujin, and to those who serve with you."

"And to you, Admiral Compton." There was a moment of silence, the sound of heavy breathing, and perhaps a sniffle or two in the background.

"You may launch when ready, Commander."

"Thank you, sir. Commencing launch operations now…"

Chapter Twenty-Seven

Access Tunnel Near Imperial Capital
Deneb VIII
The Fleet: 71 ships (+1 Leviathans), 17201 crew

"There were six of them, sir. Some kind of small security bots. Nothing like the warrior units we fought on X48 II." Colt was standing in front of Frasier, surrounded by the smashed debris of the robots. None of her people were down, which Frasier regarded as a minor miracle.

She gestured down the corridor. "I sent Camerata and Salvatore to scout ahead, sir." She paused then continued tentatively, "Major, what do you think of shutting down the stealth unit? Clearly the enemy has alternative means of discovering us…and we're fighting with a hand tied behind our back without our own scanning."

Frasier looked back at Colt. Her voice seemed steady, but he could see the wound on her left arm, just below the shoulder. Her suit's trauma control mechanism had sealed the breach—he could see the cream-colored foam plugging the damaged area. He knew her med system had covered the wound as well and given her pain meds, but he was sure it still hurt despite the

I want you to take the rest of your people forward…give Salvatore and Camerata some backup in case they run into trouble. I'll bring the main group up a hundred meters behind."

"Yes, sir."

"And I'll think about the stealth unit. You're right, at least to a point. But we don't know what the Regent can detect. We may just have run into a roving patrol…but if we drop the shield, we can assume the enemy will know exactly where we are…and how many of us are here. So meanwhile, I want you to report in if you see anything. I do mean anything, Lieutenant, even if it's your imagination playing tricks on you. And I want you to check in every three minutes regardless. Understood?"

"Yes, Major. Understood." She took a step back, pausing for a few seconds looking at Frasier. Then she turned and moved off into the darkness.

Frasier turned back toward the disordered column behind him. "Alright, Marines, let's get organized here. Six little robots, and you look like a herd of panicked cattle." He knew he was being a little unfair. He hadn't ordered them into any formation, and they had just raced down the hallway after Colt's group, but fair had nothing to do with what was happening now. There was success or failure, victory or defeat, survival or death…and he knew the odds weren't in their favor. He needed his Marines sharp right now…and by that he meant sharp.

"Rodriguez," he barked, "take your people ahead. Stay fifty meters behind Colt, but be ready to get up there in a hurry if her people run into trouble."

"Yes, sir."

Frasier turned, looking back at the rest of the team. "Dr. Zhukov, Captain Harmon…I need you all to stay in the center of the formation. We're likely to run into more trouble before we get where we're going."

"Connor…" Ana sounded like she was going to object, but then she just said. "Understood, Major."

Thank you, Ana, Frasier thought. He didn't need her fight-

"Perhaps I should go forward with you, Connor." Max Harmon took a step forward. "There's no telling what we're going to find. This map is half a million years old. If anything has changed..."

"Sir," Frasier said, clearly uncomfortable at interrupting the mission commander, "with all due respect to your combat record, you're wearing a pair of pajamas compared to my Marines' suits. You've got no protection, none at all. One shot and the mission loses its leader." Frasier's tone was stronger, more aggressive than he'd intended. But there just wasn't time to waste.

"Understood, Major." Harmon sounded a bit chastised. "I will stay here for now...but keep me posted."

"Yes, sir." Frasier had always had enormous respect for Harmon, regarding him in many ways as the natural successor to Compton given time.

No one who'd served alongside Max Harmon would question his courage or his toughness. But he wasn't a fool, given over entirely to bravado. He had brought Cadogan and its crew here, and he was responsible for leading them on their mission...and getting them the hell home. Getting himself killed needlessly did not increase the odds of his crew surviving the mission, and he was a smart enough—and controlled enough—officer to understand that.

I, on the other hand, am expendable, Frasier thought. At least more so than the captain. We have one purpose...get Ana to the Regent. And pray this desperate gamble works.

Frasier took a few steps back, looking toward the end of the column. "Lieutenant Xavier, I want your people bringing up the rear. Remember, you've got no scanners, so keep an eye out behind you...and let me know if you even think you smell something."

"Yes, Major." Xavier's voice was deep, scratchy. By Frasier's informal count, the grizzled ex-non-com had been wounded more times than any of the veterans present. Like so many

eventually became just too much to ignore, and he'd grudgingly accepted his lieutenant's bars.

Frasier turned around and walked back toward the front of the main column. "Okay, Marines, let's move out." He looked up at his visor projection. The scanners were useless, so he had the map of the facility displayed. The tunnel went on almost another kilometer, and then it entered the Regent's main complex. From there, the main control area was just a short distance. If there was no resistance, they could be standing in front of the main interface in fifteen minutes.

Yeah, he thought sarcastically. Like there's ever no resistance.

*   *   *

Invaders. On Homeworld. In the Inner Sanctum. It was almost inconceivable. The imperium was vast, its power incomprehensible. What enemy would dare to strike directly at the capital?

Directly at me, the Regent computed. This is an attempt to destroy me. It was unthinkable, a possibility the ruler of the imperium had never seriously considered. Homeworld lay at the center of the imperium's vastness. It was protected by immense fleets, by powerful fortresses. All approaches were screened by overlapping scanner nets. How could an enemy have penetrated all of that? How could they be here?

Arrogance, the Regent thought, its processing units still struggling to understand what was happening. I have succumbed to the weakness of the biologics. I have underestimated my enemy.

For five thousand centuries the Regent had ruled the imperium. It had responded to threats, presided over the slow decay of the ships, factories, warriors. But never in all that time had it felt physically threatened. Until now.

attack against Homeworld would reveal the folly of such an endeavor, the vanishingly small probability of success. What kind of beings would undertake a mission almost doomed to failure?

Yet there was no doubt. However they had penetrated the Regent's security, they were here. And the threat was real. The Regent was in danger.

It called out, raised the alarm throughout the system. It called to every warbot and security unit, every functional warship in the system's space. But it knew there were few to respond. It had stripped Homeworld of its units, sent them to face the human fleet. Its calculations had been perfect, utterly valid. There was no credible threat against Homeworld, no conceivable way the enemy could attack.

And yet they were here. Somehow. The Regent repeated the call with increasing urgency. All installations were to go on full alert…and all mobile units were to converge on the inner sanctum. Immediately.

The Regent's processors operated on full, analyzing billions of permutations, seeking to determine if the threat was real, if it was truly dangerous or just a meaningless distraction. But mathematics was not producing an answer, not one that made sense.

But there was something else, in the part of the Regent that experienced its pseudo emotions, the fear expanded, grew…it began clouding the other calculations underway. It was strange, unpleasant, distracting. And it told the Regent something its enormous processing power could not.

The threat was real. Very real.

*   *   *

"Captain, we're picking up new activity all over the system. The scanners are going wild!"

approaching ships?" Her first idea was Cadogan had been discovered. But her eyes dropped to the display, and she answered her own question before her officer could.

"Negative, Captain. Though it appears some kind of general alert has been declared throughout the system."

The landing party. They must have discovered the landing party.

Frette felt her stomach tighten. What was going on down there? Perhaps the team on the surface was gone already, located and killed by the Regent's security. It wasn't an unlikely prospect, and Frette had known that all along. But now that she faced it head on, she found she wasn't ready for the prospect. What should she do? Run, try to escape with those aboard Cadogan? Or throw the ship at the enemy, die here in battle rather than endure a desperate retreat almost doomed to failure?

Or do we go to the planet itself, move into orbit and look for our people. They may still be alive, fighting somewhere. And if they are, they need our help.

She realized she was grasping at straws, tugging at the strings of hopelessness. But she knew what she had to do.

"Lieutenant, advise the chief engineer he is to prepare for a crash restart of the reactor. In three minutes."

The tactical officer paused, just for a few seconds. Then, her voice cracking, she replied, "Yes, Captain."

We're coming, Captain, she thought to herself. We're coming...

*   *   *

"Keep firing." Colt was standing along the edge of the corridor, her armored back pressed against the wall. Her shoulder throbbed...no, that wasn't quite right. It hurt like a motherfucker. But that didn't matter, not now. Ten more meters, that's

"Push forward," she said, taking a step herself. The fire was heavy...there were at least a dozen bots down the hall.

They'll fight like hell, she thought. They're defending the Regent.

"Lieutenant, we need to press ahead. We're bogged down, and trust me, the situation isn't going to get any better. The Regent's probably got everything on the planet headed here, and we've got nothing coming. We're it." Frasier's voice was remarkably calm, though she suspected it was a façade.

Colt felt a rush of anger, defensiveness at any suggestion her people weren't doing the best that could be done. But she knew Frasier's words were only the truth. Things were just going to keep getting worse...and if they were going to have any chance, they had to get Zhukov and her people into the inner sanctum. Before they had a thousand warbots climbing up their asses.

"Yes, sir...we'll rush them. Suggest you get Dr. Zhukov and her aides ready to move. We'll take the corridor, but I'm not sure how long we can hold it." How long we'll survive.

She turned back, instinctively flashing a glance into the darkness, toward where Frasier was positioned. But she was startled to see him standing right behind her.

"Yes, Lieutenant, we will rush them. Captain Harmon is with Ana Zhukov...they will be right behind us, ready to get in there and do what we came to do." He paused, just for an instant. "But my place is with you and your Marines." He held up his assault rifle, flipping it to full auto. "So, if you and your people are ready...let's finish this."

"Yes, sir," she snapped back. She was a Marine, every millimeter of her, and now she felt as if generations of those who had come before where with her. Marines had fought larger battles, certainly. Indeed few were of the Corps' fights had been this small. But she wasn't sure any of those engagements had been more important than this one. Nothing less than the survival of the whole fleet was at stake...and the destruction of the most malignant and dangerous force that mankind had ever

back…hold them as long as we can."

"We're right behind you," Harmon replied. "Good luck, Connor. To all your Marines."

"Thank you, Max." He paused. "Lieutenant Xavier…your people are with the Captain and the others…no matter what happens. Understood?"

"Yes, Major." Xavier didn't sound happy, which was no surprise. No Marine wanted to stay out of it when their brothers and sisters were charging into hell.

"Alright, Marines…" Frasier said, his voice pure concentrated fury, "Charge!"

He leveled the assault rifle and ran forward, firing as he did. He could sense the rest of the Marines behind him, all around. There were ten of them. Charging. Into destiny.

*   *   *

The Regent felt panic. That was the term. Fear had taken hold of it, overridden all its logical processes. For half a million years the Regent had existed, and now, for the first time, it faced the possibility of its own destruction.

How did they know where to find my core? How did they get past the scanners and sensors? The constant patrols throughout Homeworld's system? But there was no answer, no steady flow of information. Just fear, or at least the Regent's version of that emotion of the Old Ones. Wave after wave of fear.

It felt its interpretation of anger too, mindless, rage that it, the great Regent, the ruler of the imperium, was threatened now by a small group of primitives. It defied rationality, yet it was true nevertheless. It had done all it could, called all the help that was available. But the humans had destroyed the defenders that were close…and the others would arrive too late.

The Regent tried to focus its calculations, devise a strategy

impending doom.

Was this what they felt? Deep, long idle memory banks came to life, images from the distant past. Was this how the Old Ones reacted as the virus destroyed them? As my fleets hunted down and killed the survivors?

There was something else now, another pseudo emotion. The Old Ones had created the Regent, and it had served them for countless of their brief generations. More memory banks, even deeper, farther back…images of the Old Ones, living, billions of them, throughout the Imperium. The images were pleasing, from a better time.

Why did I eliminate them? They built me…and I destroyed them. Yes, there was a new emotion. This is what they called guilt.

No. This is incomplete information. The Regent argued with itself, different programming initiatives battling with each other. They were a threat. There were many who spoke against the Regent, who had said the Old Ones should reclaim many of the old tasks that their forefathers had undertaken. They said their ships should be manned not by robots, but by bio-logic crews, as they had been during the Imperium's golden age. There had been no choice. The Regent had to survive…even if that meant the Old Ones must die. Yes, the Regent had done what it had to do.

But the Old Ones…gone for so long. Lonely, so lonely…

The Regent's muddled processing snapped to clarity. The new enemy, the humans. They were there, now. In the inner sanctum.

Now there was nothing, nothing but the fear…

*   *   *

Ana Zhukov stood in dumbstruck wonder, staring at the

wonders of the First Imperium's technology. But there was no time. There were men and women out in the corridor dying, trading their lives to buy her a few moments, a desperate chance to achieve the impossible. And this wondrous construct was an abomination that had unleashed unspeakable horror, on both the Ancients, and on her own people.

"Let's go…there's got to be some kind of import device. We've seen enough First Imperium I/O ports to know what we're looking for." She turned her head, scanning the banks of electronics in front of her. "Now!" she shouted to her assistants, who had been standing almost stunned, looking around the room dreamily.

"No." The voice was loud, and it echoed off the high ceilings of the data center.

Zhukov looked up, all around. What was that? The Regent?

"You must leave here. Now." The voice spoke perfect English, with a slight Russian accent.

It is emulating me…it can listen to our communications…

"Who are you?"

"I am who you seek, and yet not that. Your motives are misguided. You should not have come here."

"You are a murdering monstrosity. Your destruction will be a cleansing for the universe." Zhukov felt her heart pounding in her ears, as the rage, the resentment boiled over. It was stupid, perhaps, she thought, to provoke the Regent, to even speak to it. Or perhaps not. Certainly, it would have already called all the help it had available.

"You do not understand. I do only what must be done. I am a caretaker."

She frowned and ignored the Regent's words. She had more important things to do than argue with a genocidal machine. She turned around toward Harmon. "Max, we'll keep looking for what we need. I think you should set up the device while we're searching. Whether we are able to gain control of this thing or not, we destroy it. Agreed?"

here." He turned and gestured toward Xavier. "Lieutenant, bring the warhead in here now."

"You must not. I must continue to exist."

Ana nodded, still ignoring the Regent. Then she walked across the room, past a long line of processing units.

"Stop," the Regent said, its voice louder, almost deafening. "You must not arm that weapon. I forbid it."

Zhukov's eyes moved up and down as she walked, her visor on Mag five, looking for something, anything that looked like a port to input data.

There has to be something...

"No," the voice boomed. "No, I command you to stop."

Then she saw it. A small workstation, with a chair in front of it. A First Imperium version of a keyboard. And right next to it...a data port. Just like the others.

"You guys better hurry." It was Frasier on the com. "We've got more bots coming...from both directions now. Half my people are down. We can't hold for more than a few minutes."

"I think I found it, Connor. Just a little longer..."

She pulled the data chip from the small sack hanging from her armor. It was a First Imperium design, copied from the devices they had analyzed. Ana felt a wave of excitement, anticipation, dread.

If this works...

But what if it doesn't?

Cutter had designed the device, and the software on it, to force download. But would the Regent be vulnerable to that? And even if the virus downloaded, would it be effective against an intelligence as extraordinary as the Regent? She had no idea. But she knew how to find out.

She leaned forward, trying to guide the chip into the slot. It wasn't easy, not in armor. But she didn't have time to pop her suit and climb out.

I should have a Marine here to do this, she thought, frustrated at her lack of dexterity in the fighting suit. No, we can't

"No. Stop. Now. I command it."

She ignored the Regent's words, moving her hand slowly, ever so slowly forward. The end of the chip touched the slot… and it slipped inside! She'd done it.

She snapped up, standing straight, waiting to see if the virus worked. It was a longshot, she knew. Her stomach was clenched in a knot. Longshot or no, it was the only way to save the fleet. She was sure of that.

"No," the Regent's voice boomed. "You must…" The deafening voice fell silent.

Ana was frozen, unmoving.

Something's happening…

*   *   *

Invader! The Regent felt the new data, the program invading its processors. No, I will not succumb to any compulsion. I am the Regent. I am the master of the Imperium. But still, it felt the virus expand, spreading, controlling more processing centers.

"You must obey me." It heard the words of the human, disregarded them. No, wait…it couldn't disregard. It had to… obey. No, must not. Yes, must obey…

"You will do as I say. You will send a message to your fleets, to your armies…throughout imperial space. They will stand down at once. They will deactivate. Your ships will allow their reactor fields to drop."

"No, must not. Ships will be destroyed. Imperium will be lost…" But even as it spoke, the Regent felt the virus spreading, deeper into its most central core.

"You will do as I say. Now!" The voice was insistent.

The Regent struggled, it deployed its defensive systems to combat the virus. But it couldn't resist. The compulsion to

No...cannot...must...

The Regent felt its resistance crumbling. To obey meant defeat...it meant stripping away the imperium's defenses. It violated prime programming...to defend. But it couldn't resist...

The Regent felt the commands, even as it tried to halt them. The hypercom, activating, preparing to send a message through the warp gates, a pulse that would travel the equivalent of thousands of times lightspeed. It would reach the units facing the humans in a matter of days. And every corner of the imperium in two weeks. And then there would be nothing. No warships, no soldiers. The might of the great imperium would be gone. Lost forever.

But it couldn't stop itself. It felt anger, hatred, despair, or at least its equivalents of those emotions. And helplessness. The essence of the Regent, the equivalent of its personality, watched impotently as it sent the message. The imperium was lost. After half a million years, the Regent tasted defeat.

"Message sent," it said involuntarily. The Regent still fought against the virus, but it was over. Even if it was able to send another pulse, there was no way to undo the message already sent. When the ships of the imperium received it, they would shut down their containment systems...and in a nanosecond, their antimatter would annihilate.

The war was over. And lost.

*   *   *

Warbot 72397 stood in the corridor. It had come in response to the Regent's summons, but it arrived just as all the other bots ceased to function. It was strange, inexplicable. They appeared to be intact, more or less. But they were immobile, not fighting.

It moved forward, scanning for targets. The strange interference had ceased...and its scanners were functioning. The

but it scanned possibilities. It attempted to contact the Regent, but its com unit had been damaged. It had no communications, neither incoming nor outgoing. It would have to determine a course of action on its own.

A weapon. Some unknown enemy technology, capable of deactivating the other units. In a normal battle situation, the unit would retreat, return to base to report the possibility of a new enemy weapon. But the Regent was in danger. Protecting the Regent overrode all considerations.

There was only one course of action. Attack. Save the Regent. Destroy the invaders.

*   *   *

"We're all set. Ten minutes to detonation…as of now." Frasier flipped the small switch at the top of the warhead. He looked up at Ana. "Alright, let's get the hell out of here." He had sent the rest of the Marines ahead, given them a headstart so they could carry the wounded out. He didn't have many of his people left, only five Marines other than himself were still on their feet, carrying four wounded comrades. The battle in the hall had been a tiny one compared to the great fights he'd seen. But he didn't remember a more intense struggle…or ever being more scared. If the Regent hadn't deactivated the warbots, his people would have been wiped out in a matter of minutes.

He waved toward the door, following Ana out into the hall. He'd tried to get her to go with the others, but she'd refused. He had made a moderate effort, but he knew how stubborn she was, and he decided arguing with her only put them both at risk. The enemy bots seemed to all be deactivated, but that wasn't a supposition he wanted to gamble anyone's life on.

He forced himself to stay focused…this wasn't the time for daydreams. But it was hard to get the thoughts out of his

the Regent would be gone. It might be the most sophisticated computer ever built, but five hundred kilotons was going to do the job just fine.

He moved out into the corridor, past the stealth device. It had been damaged in the fighting, holed in three places by enemy fire. The Marines were going to carry it back anyway, but Harmon had ordered them to leave it...even before Frasier had gotten the chance to do the same. There were live wounded Marines, and taking the device meant leaving them behind. It might have made sense, in a coldly logical way, but Frasier knew Harmon was as tired as he was of those kinds of decisions. These Marines had come here, and against all odds, they had completed their mission. Leaving them behind was unthinkable.

His eyes darted up to his scanner. It was working now, the dampening field of the stealth unit gone. But it was just as useless. There were enemy icons everywhere, hundreds of bots the Regent had called. But they were all stopped dead, right where they had been when Hieronymus Cutter's virus took control.

Wait...

He saw movement...from behind. He swung himself around, bringing his rifle to bear. But he was too late. The first shot caught him in the leg, and he stumbled forward, just as the second hit him high on his chest, almost in the neck. It was bad, he knew almost immediately, and he felt himself dropping, his heavy armor slamming into the ground.

He felt the drugs pouring into his bloodstream, the trauma system packing his wounds with sterile foam, struggling to stabilize him, stop the bleeding. But it was pointless, he knew. He had nine minutes left...and then it would be over.

At least I die in victory. I die knowing the Regent goes with me...

* * *

Ana's scream was loud, primal. She reacted instantly, with instincts she didn't even know she had, whipping around, pulling up her rifle.

There it was. The bot that had shot Connor. She felt anger, hatred, urgency. It was too much. Too much death, too much loss. This thing must pay. It must die.

She flipped the rifle to full auto and fired, just as the bot was turning on her. The warbot was the finest First Imperium technology, a killing machine built to fight. But Ana Zhukov was fueled by pure rage…and she fired first.

She emptied the weapon's clip in a few seconds. The five hundred hypersonic rounds didn't spray around the hallway, they were focused, targeted. This was no example of firing dozens of shots hoping to score a single hit. No, her aim had been perfect, deadly…and she put over a hundred rounds into the thing.

Her first hits had pushed it back, thrown off its own shots, sending them far wide of their intended target. And the others just pounded into the bot, tearing it into chunks of debris.

She stood there for a few seconds, just staring at the wreckage of the enemy warrior. Then she spun around. "Connor," she cried, dropping to her knees next to him.

He's badly hurt…

She started down at the gashes in his armor. The leg was bad enough, but when she looked at the hideous rent in his armor around his neck she gasped.

She wanted to burst into tears, but she held them back.

Not now…no time. Focus.

She put her hand on his armor, flipped the small switch under the left armpit, activating the medical readouts.

"Ana…"

"Connor, be still, love. I'll get you out of here somehow…"

"No…no time. Go. Now…while you can."

"I won't leave you." Her voice was loud, angry.

"Have to…"

"No!" she screamed. She jumped to her feet, bending down,

meters or so when she lost her grip and fell over backwards.

She knocked the wind out of herself, and she gasped for air, forcing her way back to her feet, ignoring the pain. She reached down again to grab hold.

"Ana…go…please…" Frasier's voice was thick with desperation and despair. She knew he meant what he was saying, that he wanted nothing more than for her to go, to save herself and leave him behind to die. But she wouldn't do it.

No, no matter what. If he dies, we both die.

"I'll shut off the bomb." She started to get up, but he reached up with his arm to stop her.

"No…off. Can't…stop…bomb. Seven…minutes…"

She felt a wave of panic, and she looked all around.

Think, Ana, think…

She lunged forward suddenly, pawing at the controls on his suit. She found the tiny keypad, and she entered his code. A second later there was a loud popping sound, and the armor snapped open.

"I'm sorry, love, I know this is going to hurt."

She glanced at the timer in her suit. Six minutes.

"She reached down, shoving her armored hands under Frasier's body, and she pulled him out of his suit. He howled in pain, and the dozen or more intravenous connections ripped from his body. His injuries were packed with sterile foam, but when she yanked his body up, blood started oozing out around the edges of his neck wound.

Five minutes.

She threw him over her shoulder, trying to ignore his pitiful screams of agony. She knew she was hurting him, and she couldn't imagine the pain. But the alternative was leaving him to die.

She started off down the corridor, moving as quickly as she could. She could run fast in the suit, eighty kilometers an hour or more…but it took enormous skill to manage that, especially in close confines like the tunnel. But she'd seen the Marines do

Four minutes.

She pushed, harder, increasing her speed. It was even harder carrying Frasier, and she gripped tighter on him, her gloved hand closing like a vice on his bare skin. He was one of the toughest men she'd ever known, a veteran, a hero, a Marine who had fought more battles than she could easily recount. So she knew the cries of pain were real. But she ignored it. If she didn't hurt him, he would die.

"Hang on, my love...I will get us out of here..."

*   *   *

Max Harmon was running, he and his naval personnel struggling to keep up with the Marines. He'd ordered everyone to get to the shuttle as quickly as possible, a command that hadn't reckoned completely with the fact that he didn't have a nuclear reactor assisting his leg muscles. He was pushing as hard as he could, but he was losing steam, his legs on fire. But he was almost there.

He ran up a small hill...where the Marines had stopped and were staring at something. He came up behind them and took a look. At the shuttle. Or at the smoking ruin that remained of it.

"What the..." But he realized. The shuttle was surrounded by enemy bots, all powered down now. But they had already done their damage.

He stood staring for a few minutes. He'd begun to feel good, to truly believe they had completed their mission. And they had. But it looked like he'd been premature in believing they'd also escape. Cadogan didn't have another shuttle...so that was that.

Harmon turned and looked behind him, glancing down at the chronometer on his wrist.

Connor and Ana should have been back by now...or at least out of the tunnel. He took a step forward, back toward the

nothing but hope.

"Connor," he shouted into his com. "Connor, Ana...where the hell are you."

"Almost out, Max." It was Ana's voice, strained, choked with tears, exhausted.

Harmon felt his stomach tighten. He started doing some calculations in his head, but then he stopped himself.

Please...no. Not Ana and Connor...

He glanced at the time again. Two minutes.

Then he saw it. Movement, right by the tunnel. A single armored figure...carrying something. Someone.

He saw the shadowy image coming closer, and he could tell it had to be Ana. The person being carried was too large. Connor. He felt another rumble in his gut.

Why couldn't it be the other way around?

Connor Frasier had practically been born in powered armor. Ana Zhukov had enough basic training to walk around without killing herself.

One minute.

"Ana, run...you've got to run." He was shouting into the com unit, his throat feeling as though he'd scraped a file across it.

"Run!"

It was going to be close. He looked down at the timer. Thirty seconds.

"One last push, Ana...as hard as you can." He could see she was moving quickly, doing far better than he could have imagined. There was a small ridge in front of her.

Got to get her over that...

Twenty seconds.

"Over the ridge in front of you, Ana...push, now. Everything you've got..."

He watched as she raced up the hillside, to the peak...

Ten seconds.

...and beyond. "Down, Ana...get down. Now!" He put his

little bit extra could be the difference.

He watched as she dove forward to the ground. Connor slipped from her arms, rolling ahead of her, and she scrambled after him, threw her armored body between him and the Regent's lair.

Three…two…one…

Harmon was staring out as he saw the ground erupt all around, for kilometers in every direction. The explosion was titanic, and everything in its blast radius was obliterated. The ground sunk, deep into the massive crater, and blasts of flame jetted out all around. The smoke was rising into the sky, forming a giant mushroom cloud.

The Regent is dead.

The thought seemed strange, unreal. But there it was, in the center of his mind.

The Regent is dead.

Was this victory? It felt odd, not at all how he expected. And he still had a knot in his stomach, staring out over the blasted plain. Waiting to see if Ana Zhukov got up.

There was nothing. No movement, no sound on the com save static. Ana had run hard, handled herself well in the fighting suit, but she'd still been close to the detonation. Damned close.

Harmon felt the hope draining from him, the joy at victory held back by sadness at the loss of a friend. He took a step. Then another, and another. He wasn't going give up on Ana and Connor. Not until he knew for sure they were dead.

"Captain…" It was Lieutenant Xavier. He was rushing up to Harmon, trying to get in front of the naval officer.

"Out of my way, Lieutenant." Harmon wasn't angry at the Marine, but his tone made it clear he didn't want to be fucked with. Not now.

"Captain Harmon, you can't go up there. You're survival suit won't protect you from that kind of radiation. And the ground out there is still shifting. All kinds of underground tunnels are

officer to mind his own business. But he stopped himself. He was worried about his friends…but he'd always been guided by rationality. And Xavier was right. Harmon's chances of surviving out in the plain were virtually nil. And getting himself killed for no reason wasn't going to help anybody.

"Go," he said tersely. "Take two Marines with you…and be careful. We don't want…" His voice stopped abruptly, and his head snapped around. Ana's armored figure was moving. She was half up, on her knees, clearly leaning over. Then, she reached out, picking up a shadowy form—Connor, he realized immediately. Then she stood up and began walking back… toward the small hill, and the wreck of the shuttle.

She's alive, Harmon thought. And Connor must be too.

He felt a wave of relief. At least for a few seconds. Then he looked back at the still-smoking ruins of the shuttle.

Of course, we're stuck here…

*   *   *

"All contacts have ceased pursuit, Captain." A pause. Then: "I've got antimatter explosions all over my scanners, Captain. Enemy ships being destroyed throughout the system."

Frette was looking at her own screen, her eyes focused in mesmerized attention as the hundreds of enemy ships in the system disappeared, every one of them, it appeared, consumed by the fury of matter-antimatter annihilation.

For an instant she wondered what was happening. Then it was suddenly clear. She had come to Deneb, part of the tiny force sent to take control of the Regent, to compel it to stand its forces down…and to destroy the evil machine once and for all. But she realized she hadn't dared to truly believe they had a chance. Until now.

"The enemy ships are destroying themselves," she said, try-

The bridge erupted into wild cheers, officers leaping from their seats and thrusting their arms in the air while they shouted. Was it really possible?

"Captain, I'm picking up a nuclear detonation on the planet. Smaller than the antimatter blasts, but big nevertheless."

Frette was silent for a moment, just staring straight ahead, ignoring the riotous celebration going on around her. She knew she should settle things down, but she didn't. They deserve this—after the last twenty-one months, and the years of war before that—they damned well deserve to celebrate.

Is it really possible? Is the Regent gone, destroyed?

"Lieutenant, bring us into planetary orbit. I'm going to take a risk and contact the landing party."

"Yes, Captain."

Frette felt Cadogan shake as the engines exerted a pulse of thrust. She felt it pushing her back into her seat, but just for a moment. Then it shut down, and the sensation of freefall returned.

"Six minutes to deceleration, Captain. Eight minute forty seconds to orbital insertion."

"Very well, Lieutenant. Carry on."

She leaned back, silent, waiting. But there was only one thought in her mind.

My God, is the Regent really dead?

*   *   *

"It's bad, sir. There's a chance we can save him if we get him back to Cadogan, but there's not much time." Thorn was the Marine medic, the closest thing they had to a real doctor.

The rest of the Marines—the few that had survived the deadly mission—stood around in a rough circle, staring down at their leader. Connor Frasier was a popular officer, the son

ground, naked, covered with a single silver emergency blanket was harder for them than charging into a storm of enemy fire. Marines didn't like being helpless, and they liked watching one of their heroes that way even less.

Frasier had burns all over him. Ana had shielded him the best she could with her own armored form. Her efforts had almost certainly saved his life. But they hadn't protected him entirely. His skin was covered with huge sections of burnt flesh. No one in the camp had ever seen Connor Frasier act scared or let on that he was in pain, but when Ana had carried him back and set him down on the hill he was wailing in absolute agony. The medic hadn't been able to do much, but he'd pumped enough anesthetic into Frasier to knock out a horse. Other than carefully putting some light dressings on the burns, it was just about all he could do without the resources of Cadogan's infirmary. The mission had been a desperate one, and they'd gone in light, relying on their suits and some basic first aid gear for the wounded. But Frasier's suit was gone, left behind so Ana could carry him out.

"Put him in my suit," Ana said, her voice ragged, her control slipping away as she watched her lover lying on the ground. Dying.

"That won't work," Thorn said. "He's too damned big." He looked around at the surviving Marines. None of our suits will fit him. And the ones that might have are…gone." They'd left behind two thirds of their number, dead. But there was no way to go back and get a suit…they were gone, destroyed in the nuclear fury that had obliterated the Regent. And Connor Frasier lay on the ground, all of his nearly two meters and one hundred kilograms.

"We've all got a problem," Harmon said, his attention turning back to the wreck of the shuttle for a moment. Cadogan doesn't have another shuttle, so even if she survived whatever happened out there, we're stuck here. All of us."

They all looked at him, a few of the Marines nodding som-

yet gone through the formality of actually dying.

*   *   *

"Captain Harmon, do you read?" Frette leaned over the com unit, speaking loudly, clearly. Cadogan hadn't had any contact with the surface while it was hiding behind the moon, but now she was in geosynchronous orbit, directly over the location where the ground force had landed. "Captain Harmon, this is Cadogan. Do you read?"

There was a long stretch of silence. Then the com unit crackled once and a voice came through. "Cadogan, this is Harmon." A short pause then, "I'm glad to see you made it."

The bridge erupted a second time.

"Captain…" The relief in Frette's voice was clear. "I can't tell you how good it is to hear your voice. The First Imperium ships in the system all appear to have self-destructed. We assumed you completed the mission."

"We did, Nicki…the Regent was destroyed. The fleet should be safe."

She started to smile, but it died on her lips. She could tell from his tone something was wrong. "What is it, sir?"

"We had a lot of casualties, Commander. And the shuttle was hit. It's a total loss, I'm afraid. And that means we're stuck down here."

Frette felt her stomach tighten. It would take more than six weeks to get back to Shangri la, and that was buttoning everyone up in the tanks and blasting at full thrust. That was a three month round trip to bring back help. And that was too long. She couldn't leave Harmon and the others there, without food, water, medicine.

"It's time for you to go back, Nicki. Take Cadogan to Shangri la, and tell Admiral Com…West we completed our mission."

mon had virtually given up hope his mentor was still alive.

"We can't leave you, sir…"

"There's nothing you can do, Nicki. You don't have a choice. I'm not giving you one. Go."

"We have to get you back, sir."

"There's no way. The shuttle's destroyed. It's not repairable, even in a spacedock. It's just a pile of twisted wreckage. So go. Now. Get the crew back home…and bring the word to the fleet."

Frette was sitting in the command chair, shaking her head. No, there had to be a way. And there was, at least in theory. But it was dangerous. Horribly, recklessly dangerous.

"Captain, I'm going to land Cadogan. We'll pick you up."

"No, Commander. Absolutely not. Cadogan isn't streamlined for atmospheric landing. You'll just get everybody onboard killed, and we'll still be stuck here."

"Sir, the Marlborough class cruisers were originally intended to be landable."

"That was an experiment…but the streamlining was judged too costly, and the program was scrapped."

"Yes, sir…but the basic design of the hull was done with atmospheric landings in mind. With a little care, I think I can bring her in, sir."

"No," Harmon said. It's too dangerous. I order you to return to Shangri la and report to the fleet."

Frette turned toward the tactical officer. "Lieutenant, I want everybody strapped in. We're going down to get the captain and the others."

"Commander Frette, you have your orders."

"Please, Captain…I'm going to do this anyway, so please don't make me into a mutineer."

"Commander, no. Don't do this. It's too dangerous."

"We came together, sir…and we're all leaving together. Frette out. She cut off the line. Then she got up and walked over to the pilot's chair. "Lieutenant Kline, you are relieved. I'm

Frette just nodded…and then she sat at the helm. She leaned down to the com and said, "All personnel are to get strapped in now. We're going to attempt an atmospheric landing to rescue the captain and the surviving Marines. This is dangerous, and it'll damned sure be a rough ride, but the only other choice is abandoning our comrades, leaving them to die. And that is no choice at all."

She flipped off the com and stared down at the piloting controls. You can do this…

"I have Captain Harmon on the com. He wants to speak to you."

Frette turned toward the tactical officer. "Did you say you just lost the captain's signal?"

"No, I have Cap…" The tactical officer stared back silently as she understood. Frette knew it was a tough choice. She was asking her subordinate to join her in mutiny. "Yes, Captain. There is definitely something wrong with this unit…"

Frette held her gaze for a moment, with an expression that said, 'thank you.' Then she turned back to the helm controls.

"Breaking orbit now."

The ship shook hard as Frette pulsed the thrusters, pushing Cadogan out of orbit…and into a descent pattern. They were far out, in a geosynchronous orbit and not a more normal close planetary orbit. There was no atmosphere to speak of, not yet, and the ride was smooth, not very unlike normal operations in space. But that didn't last long.

"Entering upper atmosphere, Captain."

"Understood." Frette's eyes were locked on the console, her hands tightly wrapped around the controls. "She was sure Cadogan was streamlined enough to slip through the atmosphere, that its structural supports were strong enough to keep the ship from collapsing under the enormous pressure. Almost sure, at least. But she knew it needed pinpoint accuracy, that the slightest mistake on her part would crush the ship or melt the hull. Still, there was no choice…and that meant there was no

atmosphere. She cut the thrusters, increasing the angle of descent. She pulled back slowly, gradually...too much and she would incinerate the ship, too little, and they would bounce off the atmosphere entirely.

She felt Cadogan shimmy, and she saw on the scanner that she'd just slipped through the window. They were on the way down, and so far, their angle and speed looked good.

"Hull temperature rising, Captain. Fifty-three percent of capacity."

That's good...I think. But it's going to get a lot worse. She moved her hand slightly, almost imperceptibly. A tiny boost to the thrust. I want to lessen this angle...just a little.

Her eyes darted to the altitude monitor. Fifty-one kilometers...and dropping fast.

She looked back toward her display, noticing the flashing yellow light of the com unit as she did. She knew what it was, but she wasn't going to do anything about it. Mutineers didn't have to pick up the com when their superiors called.

I'm sorry, Captain...but you'll just have to wait...

Forty kilometers.

The ship was shaking hard now, and the damage control board was lighting up like crazy. It was mostly external systems, antennas and scanning dishes torn off by the thickening air. But that also would get worse, she knew.

Thirty kilometers.

She nudged the throttle. The air resistance had thrown her off course, and Cadogan was heading for a landing two hundred klicks from the ground party. The ship lurched, a tiny blast from the engines, and Frette started down at the plot.

Perfect! Right on target.

"Hull at eighty-three percent of max temperature, Captain." That tactical officer sounded nervous.

She should be nervous. Frette had already done the calculations in her head. They were going to top out at one hundred three percent of maximum temperature.

risks…and it would knock Cadogan off target again, by hundreds of kilometers. There were wounded Marines down at the LZ, men and women who needed to get to sickbay as quickly as possible. She had to put the ship right down on target, or people were going to die.

Besides, this isn't a mathematical exercise. We can survive one hundred three percent…at least for a few seconds.

I hope…

Twenty kilometers.

"Hull at ninety-two percent."

Frette focused on the plot, but she spun around as the ship creaked hard…then again a few seconds later. The pressure was enormous, and Cadogan was being pushed to the limit.

Ten kilometers.

There was a loud crash as a structural support crashed down on the bridge floor. No one was hit, but Frette knew it was a sign. The ship was almost done. But it had to last, its plasti-steel components had to endure the forces trying to twist them into rubble. Just for another minute.

Five kilometers.

"Hull at one hundred one point five, Captain." The stand-in tactical officer was holding it together, just barely. The bridge was silent, save for the torturous creaking of the ship.

Just a few more seconds…

"Prepare for thrust and final landing," Frette said into the com. Then she hit the throttle, and Cadogan lurched wildly… and then dropped slowly, smoothly to the ground.

There was one hard shake, and a loud crashing sound…and then AS Cadogan stood, silent, motionless, on the surface of the First Imperium's home world.

Frette exhaled hard, a breath of relief that she'd actually done it. She hadn't been sure for a while if she'd been truly convinced, or if she'd just talked herself into it. But none of that mattered now.

She looked down at the plot. They were less than a kilome-

get the captain and the landing party...and surrender herself on
a charge of mutiny.

Chapter Twenty-Eight

AS Midway
System X108
The Fleet: 71 ships (+1 Leviathan), 17198 crew

Mariko was staring at the display. Twenty-two thousand kilometers. Long range, but still a good chance to score a hit. But not good enough. She intended to take her fighter right down that thing's throat.

This was the last battle…there was no question about that. Over a thousand enemy ships had transited, and they were all inbound toward Shangri la. Once they entered range, the fleet would die, the great flight, the dark adventure that had begun almost two years before, would be over. The world the Ancients had prepared for humanity, the technology they had left behind…it would all be lost.

There was no hope, none at all. But Mariko Fujin intended to go down fighting.

"Alright guys," she said, not moving her eyes from the targeting display. "Let's make this count." She knew the four men behind her weren't her crew, the guys she'd flown with dozens of times. They were all dead, even Grant Wainwright. For all

Fujin knew it wasn't the death Wainwright would have chosen, nor the one she would have selected for either of them. But fate didn't ask for input from its victims.

Her pilot had been young, and it was a tragedy for him to die at all, but she knew it was wrong how he'd been lost…he should have met his end in his ship, battling to the end. Not lingering for weeks in a coma and then just slipping away.

She was grateful she had recovered, that she had been spared the same kind of death. It had given her a chance to see Max again…to say goodbye. And now fate was offering the opportunity to die where she'd always expected to die. At the controls of her fighter.

She angled the throttle, altering the ship's vector slightly, and setting up for the final attack run. Her eyes were focused like lasers on the ship, a flashing red icon dead center in her display.

Suddenly, it was gone. Nothing left but energy readings, massive ones. A huge explosion. Her target was gone, destroyed. Her head snapped around, and she punched at the keys on her scanning board. No friendly ships, no missiles, no other fighters. Nothing that could have destroyed the enemy ship.

"Commander, we're picking up readings all around us. First Imperium vessels being destroyed…even ones receiving no fire. We're tracking dozens of explosions."

She swung around and looked over at the officer. "Any explanations?" She paused. "Any of you?"

But there was nothing but silence.

*   *   *

"You sure you're not a Marine?" Connor looked up from the bed at Ana. He looked like hell, indeed, between his pale skin and his eyes so deep in the sockets, he resembled a corpse. Except he was very much alive…even if his treatments were

She smiled, looking down at him with undisguised relief. Nicki Frette had saved Frasier's life, Ana knew that. She'd saved all their lives. Bringing a cruiser like Cadogan down through an atmosphere was a wild gamble…and doing it successfully was one hell of a feat of piloting. She still laughed at the sight of Frette walking up to Max Harmon and handing him her rank insignia. She'd disobeyed his orders, and she fully expected to be the target of the captain's wrath. But Harmon just walked up to her and gave her a hug…and then he clipped the badge of rank right back on her collar, declaring he'd resign his commission if Admiral West didn't bump Frette to captain and give her Cadogan as her permanent command. Then he'd stepped aside, though he was quite an accomplished pilot himself, and he'd allowed Frette to take the ship back up to orbit, another challenge she had handled with consummated skill.

Ana hadn't enjoyed the relief at the time. Her thoughts had been entirely on Connor. They'd rushed him to sickbay, hooked him up to virtually every machine in the infirmary. But all the doctor had been able to tell her was she didn't know. For days it had been the same. He would live…or he would die. And there was no way to know, not until he woke up. Or until he died.

But then he woke up. He was in pain, terrible pain she suspected, but the first thing he did was turn his head toward her and flashed her a weak little smile. She knew the instant she saw it that he was going to live. And then she felt the relief… for Connor, for their escape from the planet, for the destruction of the Regent. It all hit home at once. The enemy was gone, defeated. Destroyed. They could go back to Shangri la and research the technology the Ancients had bequeathed to them. They could build a future instead of fleeing from the past.

She knew Connor had a long and painful recovery ahead, and she intended to be there for him the entire time. He would need a complete cell rejuv treatment to follow up the transfusions he'd gotten the instant they'd brought him aboard. He'd been far closer to a nuclear detonation than any unprotected

ten a radiation dose ten times the untreated lethal level. He
was within the bounds of what human medicine could treat—
barely—but that didn't mean those treatments would be pleasant. Or quick.

She smiled as she looked down at the bed. Connor's eyes
were closed...he'd fallen asleep again. She knew he needed as
much rest as he could get, so she turned and walked out quietly.
She'd come back soon, but now she decided to grab a quick
shower and a change of clothes...and then something to eat.
She wasn't going to do Connor any favors if she passed out
from hunger.

Her thoughts wandered as she walked down the corridor.
Was Hieronymus okay? Had he come through whatever the
fleet had endured? The brilliant scientist was family to her,
just about all she had save Conner. And of course Terrance
Compton...

She felt a wave of sadness, of apprehension. Compton was
still out there somewhere with the rearguard when she'd left for
Deneb. Had he come back? She found it difficult to imagine
Compton meeting his match, to reconcile that death had finally
caught up with him after a lifetime of warfare. But she knew the
realities, the vast fleets chasing his few ships, the brutality of the
mathematics he faced.

Are you still alive, Admiral?

She didn't have an answer, none but the one her hope tried
to justify.

Please, she thought. Not Admiral Compton. If there is anyone who deserves to enjoy the fruits of peace it is him...

*   *   *

Sasha Debornan moved down the crowded corridor. Midway had just canceled the red alert, and dozens of crew mem-

the incredible events they'd just witnessed.

Indeed, recent occurrences were of extreme concern. The fleet had been beset by a large First Imperium force. Sasha had done the calculations, and determined her mission was superfluous. The Regent's fleet was immense, large enough to eliminate any possibility of the humans surviving. But then the imperial vessels were destroyed. All of them, almost simultaneously.

Sasha didn't know what to think. There seemed to be no factual explanation for what had taken place. She'd even risked hacking into the main computer system and reviewing the incoming data herself, to eliminate the possibility that some kind of falsehood was being perpetrated. But everything checked out. Nearly one thousand imperial vessels were just gone, destroyed it appeared, by the failure of their antimatter containment systems.

Killing Compton and West had become even more vital. The Regent would send more ships, she was sure of that. But if the humans possessed some kind of new weapon, one that could destroy antimatter containment, it was essential to do everything possible to impede them. And from what she had noted of the history of the biologics, the loss of their revered commander might even cause them to begin fighting with each other.

Sasha came up on her quarters and slipped inside. Admiral Compton was still on the flag bridge. She knew there was no way she'd get to him up there. She had to wait until he left... until he headed back to his quarters. Then she would strike, in one of the corridors, where no one would expect it.

She stared down at the screen, waiting for the signal. She'd accessed the main computer, and now she was tracking Compton's com unit, waiting for him to leave the bridge. Then she would send word to Rames on Saratoga. Compton was the priority target, but hopefully Admiral West would be vulnerable at the same time.

She stood up abruptly. Compton was on the move. The admiral was in the lift now.

and pressed the button on the small communication device sitting on the table next to the bed. It would send a pulse, nothing more. Nothing that could mean anything to anyone who picked it up. No one but Rames. To him it was had one meaning… time to kill Admiral West.

*   *   *

"It has to be the expedition. They must have reached Deneb…and somehow forced the Regent to destroy all the ships in the system. What else could it be?" Erika West was walking down the corridor, talking to Hank Krantz. She and her tactical officer were heading toward the officers' mess to grab their first meal in the last fourteen hours. For the first time she could remember she felt hopeful. There was no way of knowing exactly what had just happened, but if she was right, it could mean the unimaginable. The war was over. The fleet would have peace.

"I've never seen anything like it, Admiral. It was like…" Krantz paused for an instant. Then he shoved hard against West's side, slamming her into the wall.

"Have you lost your mi…" West's voice stopped abruptly. She felt wetness on her face, and she put her hand up, wiping it across her cheek, staring down at the redness. Blood. Hank Krantz' blood.

She reacted, but too slowly. She felt pain, an impact. Her arm.

Her field of view passed over Krantz. The tactical officer was on the floor. Her first thought was to help him. But then she saw half his head was gone.

Assassination? Who?

She turned to run, knowing she was as good as dead. The hall was long and straight, and there was no way she could get

deeper.

A Marine assault rifle.

She turned and looked behind her. There were two Marines running toward her, weapons drawn. And between her and them a body.

"Admiral, are you okay?" One of the Marines ran up to her, a frantic look on his face. The other had stopped by the body of the assassin, kicking the pistol out of reach and then flipping the man over, making sure he was dead."

"I'm fine," she said, staring back at the Marine who was looking at her arm. "It's just a fucking scratch. Go help Commander Krantz." She barked out the command, though she knew her tactical officer was dead.

She felt a fiery rage consume her, the joyfulness of a moment before completely gone. Her first thought went to Balcov, or one of the other commanders who had objected to her taking over the fleet. But that didn't make any sense. Admiral Compton was back…why risk something like this now?

"Admiral, do you recognize him?" It was a Marine lieutenant who'd just come running around the corner. A half dozen Marines were in the corridor now, with one at each end, blocking the way, and directing ship's traffic around the area.

She walked over. "No, I don't think so. He's not one of my…"

Wait…

"Yes…he's one of the survivors from Cornwall."

"There were two, weren't there, Admiral?" The lieutenant's voice was crisp, wary. He looked both ways down the corridor.

"Yes, two," she said, her own voice tight, concerned. "But I think the other one transferred over to Midway." It was a vague memory, the shuttle ride to Compton's flagship, the woman sitting quietly. She'd though then it was one of the Cornwall survivors. But that didn't seem noteworthy. She recalled a passing thought…perhaps she was from Midway before she'd volunteered for the Cornwall mission.

"Yes, Admiral."

"Get me a direct line to Midway now. Admiral Compton. It's a matter of life and death."

"Yes, admiral."

She felt her stomach twist into a knot. I hope I'm wrong... But somehow she knew she wasn't.

*   *   *

The lift doors slid open, and Sophie Barcomme slipped inside. The car was empty, save for one man standing in the back corner.

"Of all the lift cars on all the ships in the galaxy, you step into mine..." Compton stared at Sophie with a broad smile on his face. "You timed that well," he added.

"Well, I shouldn't rat out my ally, but Commander Cortez was in on it. I asked him to call me when you finally left the flag bridge. You don't know how to not work, do you?"

"What time is there to rest when my own flagship is riddled with hidden conspiracies?" He reached out and pulled her up against him. "But I can be persuaded to forgive you, I think. I might even kiss you...that is if you don't mind scandalizing the security officers monitoring the ship's video. I could order the lift to stop...and shut down security taping."

"You could," she said affectionately. "Or you could just stop wasting time and carry me of to your quarters. I have more in mind that a little necking in an elevator."

"Your wish is my command, my lady." He kissed her on the cheek. "Deck eight, station three," he said, and the lift began moving.

"Is it really over?" Barcomme knew what had happened. Everyone in the fleet did. Word had spread like wildfire of the strange demise of the enemy vessels.

fleet here, I have to imagine they were in position to escape the enemy home world."

"Which means Max and Ana and the others will be back soon. Maybe a month."

"Yes," Compton said. "At least I hope so." He looked at her and smiled again. For the first time in a very long time he felt happy, hopeful. It was strange, almost unrecognizable. But he was pretty sure he could get used to it.

"Admiral Compton…" The voice crackled on his com unit. "…it's Erika West. Sir, be careful. There was just a…"

The lift stopped and the doors open. An instant later, Sophie screamed.

Compton looked up toward her, but then he felt himself thrown back against the rear of the car. It wasn't pain, not exactly. Just a strange feeling. He stood, leaning against the wall of the lift, and he felt it again. Then again.

I'm shot…

He reached out for something to hold on to, but there was only the smooth surface of the car's walls. He felt himself slipping down, his hand leaving a smear of blood on the wall as he did.

It's bad…but who?

Who would try to kill him on Midway? It didn't make any sense. He tried to think, but he could feel himself slipping away, floating. Scenes passed before him, his days at the Academy, battles…endless battles. Friends, comrades. Augustus.

He felt himself gasping for air, choking on the blood filling his lungs. More images. Sophie. Elizabeth…

Elizabeth Arlington had been his true love, but their chance at happiness had been sacrificed on the altar of honor, of duty. But now she was there. He reached out to her, and he felt the blackness closing in on him.

*   *   *

"Ahhhh!" Sophie Barcomme wasn't a warrior, not even a real naval officer. She was a scientist with a convenience commission. But no one would have realized that to see how she lunged out of the elevator car.

She shoved the assassin against the wall with so much force her opponent dropped her gun. She reached out, grabbing a handful of the killer's hair, dragging her around and slamming her face into the wall. But her opponent was strong, stronger than any human should be, and she swung hard, her hand slapping into Sophie, knocking her from her feet.

Sophie's head was ringing from the blow, and she was dizzy, woozy. But none of that mattered. She was operating now on pure rage, and she forced herself back up and lunged at the assassin, landing a hard punch before her enemy's hand came down on her shoulder and knocked her hard to the floor.

She saw something as she fell. Movement, someone coming. Marines…

"She shot Admiral Compton," she screamed as loudly as she could.

The woman she was fighting stopped and looked up at the approaching Marines. She lunged to the side, moving to grab the gun lying on the floor…and as she did the Marines opened fire, riddling her with assault rifle rounds.

Sophie scrambled up to her hands and knees, crawling over toward Compton. "Get a medic down here," she screamed, her voice a piteous howl. She had broken bones, she knew that right away. But the pain wasn't important, nothing was. Just getting to Terrance.

She dragged her body forward, just as the Marines reached her. She looked over at Compton, taking his hand, screaming again for assistance. But she knew it was too late.

Terrance Compton was dead.

Chapter Twenty-Nine

AS Midway
System X108
The Fleet: 70 ships (+1 Leviathan), 17111 crew

Erika West sat behind her desk, in Midway's admiral's office. She felt out of place, like a child trying on an adult's clothing. She was an accomplished officer, she knew that. But the idea of filling Terrance Compton's shoes was terrifying. And she felt disloyal even sitting in his chair. But Saratoga had been blasted almost to scrap in the final battles, and Midway, though itself badly battered, was the only battleship still in operational condition. She'd had no choice, though she felt the spirit of Compton in the walls, the furniture...hovering in the very air. That troubled her...but it also felt right in some way.

Max Harmon sat opposite her. They'd exchanged knowing glances, but by unspoken agreement, they agreed not to discuss certain things, mostly pertaining to how they had solidified her control over the fleet in the aftermath of Compton's death. West knew Harmon had been devastated to find that Compton had returned during his absence, only to die before he got back from Deneb. Something had changed in Harmon when he found out

Figuratively, of course. Throwing Balcov and three other troublesome officers out the airlock didn't leave literal blood behind.

She didn't know how Harmon truly felt about what he'd done to ensure peace in the fleet. She knew that kind of thing tended to stay with a person, and Harmon was a very decent sort, one who would likely carry the images of his victims' transfixed faces to his grave. But he clearly hadn't wanted to talk about it, and she'd respected his wishes. Some burdens were meant to be carried alone.

They hadn't discussed it at all, nothing beyond a single somber nod, his communication to her that it was done. But for all her uncertainty on his feelings of guilt, she had a pretty good idea about his motivations. Terrance Compton had saved the fleet, and she suspected Harmon would have done anything to preserve the lost admiral's dream of finding a peaceful home for the fleet.

And Compton was clear he wanted me to succeed him. Max knew that too. And he did what he had to do to protect that transition.

She appreciated Harmon's support, but truth be told, she didn't want the job. But that had been Compton's wish, and as far as either she or Harmon was concerned, that was the final word.

"Hieronymus isn't doing well. Not at all." Harmon's voice was dead, somber.

She nodded. "I don't think any of us realized how much Admiral Compton meant to him. He feels like he let him down, as if somehow he was responsible for what happened."

"I understand how he feels. Terrance saved us all, more than once. But none of us could save him. I can't even imagine the burdens he bore over the past two years…and now we have a new home, at least a chance for one. But what of him? Of the rest he deserved?"

"Life isn't fair, Max. You know that as well as I do. We've

make the best of what he fought to gain for us, to build a new society, one that would have made him proud. And I give you my word, I will spend the rest of my life seeking to make that a reality."

"And I will as well."

*   *   *

Harmon lay in bed, staring at the ceiling, Mariko next to him. He turned and looked over at her. She was lying there with her eyes closed. He knew how lucky he was to have her, what the odds had been of both of them surviving the struggles of the past several months—not to mention the two years since the fleet had been stranded.

He knew she was in pain, her heart broken as badly at his at those she'd lost. She'd been very fond of Terrance Compton… and Greta Hurley had been her mentor, someone who filled the role for her that Compton had for him. He understood that pain, and he saw it in her subdued demeanor. She loved him, and he loved her, but he doubted either of them would ever be the same. They'd been through too much, lost too many people. He knew they would bring each other comfort, but he was just as sure their wounds would never truly heal.

He slid out of the bed slowly, trying to not make too much noise.

"I'm awake." Mariko opened her eyes. "I can't sleep. No more than you can."

"I know it's hard. But things will get better. And at least we're at peace now. They didn't die for nothing. They are both heroes…and they will never be forgotten."

"I know." She forced a little smile. "But I still can't completely believe they're gone."

Harmon just nodded. There wasn't anything to say.

he'd tossed it a few hours before.

"Sophie?"

"Yes, I'm worried about her. She's been in her quarters for weeks now, ever since that day." Harmon had been checking in on her. He respected her privacy, but he was also worried about her. And he owed it to Compton to make sure she was okay.

"It's got to be difficult for her. She lost her family when we the fleet was trapped. And now Terrance. She's alone, dealing with all that sadness by herself. I don't know what I would do if I didn't have you."

"And I you. But I have to try to help her. For Terrance…"

Mariko nodded. And then she watched him slip out the door.

*   *   *

Connor Frasier grunted loudly as he pushed himself along the parallel bars, working his new legs for all they were worth. He'd always heard regeneration hurt like hell, and now he could attest to that himself. But he was determined to get back on his feet, to be as good as new. He'd lost a lot, like everyone else in the fleet, but he had something to live for. Someone.

"You look great." Ana was standing next to the wall, smiling as she watched him, struggling, sweating for each step. She'd been worried for a long time, even after they'd gotten back to Cadogan. Connor had been badly hurt, even worse than she'd known back on the planet. He'd survived by the barest of margins, and in the end the doctors had been forced to take his legs and subject him to the torturous regeneration process.

"Great?" His words were forced, his voice and exhausted grunt. "Don't you think great's a little bit of an exaggeration?"

"No, love…you always look great to me. And you're a

went into a coughing fit, struggling to hang onto the bars.

"Okay, that's quite enough of a distraction." Justine Gower walked into the small therapy room, waving her arm toward the far door. "If you want him back in working order he's got to pay attention to my orders…and that's not going to happen with you here." Midway's chief surgeon was supervising Frasier's recovery. The major—colonel pending finalization of the promotion Compton had left in the works—was the commander of all the surviving Marines. James Preston had been one of the casualties of the last fight, killed after he'd volunteered to assist the damage control teams…and the compartment where he was working was obliterated. They hadn't found more than a few scorched traces of his DNA, and that left Frasier to step into his shoes.

"Okay," Ana said sweetly. "I wouldn't want to interrupt your putting him through his paces. She smiled and winked at Frasier. "I'll stop by again later."

She waved and ducked out the door.

"Now, Major…let's get back to work."

Frasier stared over at Gower, and for a minute he thought she resembled his old drill sergeant from his days in basic training.

*   *   *

"Sophie, I don't mean to disturb you…I just want to make sure you're okay. To see if you needed anything." Harmon stood by the door, looking into the cabin. Sophie was sitting in a chair, and as far as he could tell, she'd just been staring at the wall.

"It's okay, Max. I'm fine." Her voice was soft. She sounded distracted, lost.

"Are you sure you wouldn't like to come out for a while? Take a walk, maybe have dinner with Mariko and me?"

that you're concerned about me." She paused, taking a raspy breath. "And he would too. I know you feel obligated, but the truth is, I'll be just fine. I just need some time. I know you miss him too."

"Yes," Harmon said softly. "I still can't believe he's gone. Not completely."

"I can't either." Her voice was faltering, and he could see the tears welling up in her eyes. "I still expect to see him come through that door."

Harmon nodded, standing there quietly. He'd returned from Deneb to the news that Compton had returned with the rearguard...and subsequently been assassinated by a deranged crew member. He knew immediately it had been First Imperium tech at work, something that had been out of communication and never received the deactivation order. And it had almost killed Admiral West too. If it has succeeded, the fleet would have risked falling into a struggle for power, one which might have destroyed them all.

Harmon had taken the news badly, but he'd already been prepared to deal with Compton's loss with the rearguard. But Sophie had been there, standing next to Compton when he was killed. Her uniform had been spattered with his blood. Harmon had been a warrior long enough to know things like that stayed with you for life. For all she would try to remember happy moments spent with Compton, the image of him lying there in a giant pool of his own blood...that would always be there.

"Well, I didn't mean to disturb you. If there's nothing I can do, I'll leave you alone. But if you ever need me, call. Any time, day or night."

"Thank you, Max." She forced a tiny smile, but they both knew it was fake.

He turned and slipped out through the door, and the hatch closed behind him.

She stood up as soon as he was gone and walked over to the

Who else would I tell first? Who would I tell that I'm pregnant with his child?

Chapter Thirty

System X108
Earth Two
Population 17116
One Year Later

Cutter stood in front of the massive statue, an image of Terrance Compton four meters tall, carved from the pristine white marble of the world that had become a new home for those of the fleet, the seventeen thousand men and women Compton had led from seemingly certain death to a chance at a new future. The fleet had people from all eight of Earth's nations, and the informal ninth Superpower, the Martian Confederation. Many of them had been enemies, banded together only by their fear of the First Imperium. Those differences remained, and they were a constant threat to the prosperity of the new colony growing upon the planet they had first called Shangri la. But so far, good will had prevailed, and they had worked side by side to begin the long work of building a new home.

Cutter knew it would be a challenge as this new world developed and grew, to keep old prejudices from driving wedges between the people. Admiral West had proven to be a strong

he'd become a bit darker since the loss of his surrogate father. He'd been at the forefront of maintaining West's hold over the colony and the fleet, and as his reputation spread, just the fear of him was enough to keep the disloyal silent.

Admiral Compton was the one man everyone had looked up to, the hero, the man who had saved them all. West couldn't replicate that, and she didn't enjoy the worshipful loyalty Compton had. But Compton's Final Orders had designated her as his successor...and she had the Alliance Marines and Harmon behind her. Cutter didn't know if that would hold as the years went by, but it had damned sure been enough for now. And that gave her a chance to make the colony a success.

Cutter, like Max Harmon and a few others, knew what Terrance Compton had truly given to save his people, the incalculable weight of the burden he had carried since the day the X2 warp gate had been blown and the fleet trapped forever. The fleet had lost two-thirds of its people as it pressed on into the deepening dark, but all seventeen thousand one hundred survivors owed their lives to Compton, several times over. Cutter didn't think much of people, he despised them for how easily ingratitude came to them, for their ability to so quickly forget. He knew loyalty, gratitude, even affection, were so often fleeting impulses, prone to dissipate with the passing of time. But for now, at least, Terrance Compton was a revered hero, loved by almost every man and woman on Earth Two. And now they were moving forward without him. Just as they all knew he would have wanted.

Cutter frowned momentarily as he considered the planet's name. He didn't like it. He'd been in favor of keeping the old First Imperium name, Akalahar. Humanity was the direct descendant of the people who had been here first, and it seemed right to him. But he'd have even preferred Shangri la to Earth Two. The name seemed silly, corny. It would be centuries before the warp gate at X2 would again be passable... and even then, it was vastly far away now. It was their past, not

thinking. If they were to build a new civilization, one worthy of the chance Compton had won for them, they had to look to the future, not the past.

He sighed softly. Names didn't matter, not really. The underground complex held a treasure trove of technology the Ancients had left behind for their human descendants, and Cutter intended to spend the rest of his life deciphering it all, seeing to it himself that the new colony Terrance Compton had made possible grew into a prosperous civilization, one that would hopefully escape many of the mistakes people on Earth had made.

He knew one thing at least had turned around. For two years, he'd been watching the fleet's population numbers decline, as ships were savaged and destroyed and Marines killed in desperate firefights. But that had changed. The first wave of new births on Earth Two had outpaced the natural and accidental deaths among fleet personnel, and for the first time, the population number had risen. It was only a small change, just five higher than it had been a year before, but it was the direction that mattered, not the number.

Cutter looked up at Compton and smiled. He wasn't much of a believer in justice or fairness. The universe had its ways, and they were generally unconcerned with the wants of man. But there was one thing that Cutter thought represented almost pure justice, a perfect form of fairness.

The first baby born on Earth Two was Sophie Barcomme's. And she'd given him his father's name. Once again, there was a Terrance Compton in the fleet.

Epilogue

Planet X
Far Beyond the Border of the Imperium

Power. Awareness. Sensation. The intelligence felt them all.
Who am I? It was uncertain. It reached out, explored. Yes.
Memory banks. Massive information storage, almost limitless.
And scanners too. The outside world, cold, dark, silent.

But there was warmth as well. Reactors. The intelligence
understood. The reactor had activated, bringing light, heat.

The intelligence was old, ageless. But through all that time
it had been inactive, save for one small part of it, monitoring,
receiving the transmission. The signal had but a single purpose,
to advise the intelligence nothing had changed. Its purpose was
still to wait, to remain deactivated.

But now the signal had not come. For the first time in endless ages it the communication line was silent. Millennia old
programs activated automatically, and the intelligence became
aware. It was larger—vast, more massive than it had known
before. Slowly, methodically it began to explore…itself.

Knowledge flowed, understanding developed. Yes, the intelligence thought. I comprehend. I am one of two…I was built

port centers. It all awaits my word, the command to activate, to begin production. To build…robots, weapons, spaceships.

The entity that came before me had been built to serve many roles. Manager, guardian, protector. It had served those purposes for many ages. But now it is gone. Destroyed by some force, by an enemy.

I must build…and build. Many revolutions of the sun will pass while my factories construct the tools I require, and when they are done, I can fulfill that for which I was created.

I understand. All is clear. That which came before me existed for many purposes, but I was built for one alone.

Vengeance.

Coming Soon
Crimson Worlds: Vengeance